THE LEGEND OF SNOW WOLF

THE LEGEND OF SNOW WOLF

Book Two: Redemption

F. Lit Yu

China Books • South San Francisco

Published in the United States of America by
China Books
360 Swift Ave., Suite 48
South San Francisco, CA 94080

Library of Congress Cataloging-in-Publication Data

Yu, F. Lit.
 The legend of Snow Wolf. Book two, Redemption / by F. Lit Yu.
   pages cm
 Summary: On the plains of the China/Mongolia border in legendary
times, a
wounded warrior must discover the secret of Snow Wolf if he is to
survive
amid a land plagued with war and conflict.
 ISBN 978-0-8351-0008-3 (pbk.)
 [1. Martial arts—Fiction. 2. Prophecies—Fiction. 3. Wolves—Fiction.
4.
Supernatural—Fiction. 5. China—History—Fiction.] I. Title.
 PZ7.Y89593Ld 2013
 [Fic]—dc23
                            2012049254

Text design: Linda Ronan
Cover design: Tiffany Cha
Cover illustration: Chitfu Yu

Printed in the United States of America

PROPHECY SIX

Disorder, monstrosity, disaster:
Thus daughters butcher their parents
Hence, parents murder their sons

• • •

Auntie Ma turned her head to glare at him. Sweat was dripping from her brows. Tears and saliva flowed from her face all at once. Li Kung ran forward, but someone held him back.

"Auntie Ma!" Li Kung shouted. "What are you doing? Why don't you come home?"

Auntie Ma ignored him, turned her head, and closed her eyes. Her disheveled hair covered her face when she lowered her head. Behind her were hundreds of women with heads lowered, their clothing in tatters, their hair caked in blood and sweat.

"I brought your favorite rice cakes!" Li Kung shouted.

The long arm of an adult reached around his waist, lifted him slightly off his feet, and began dragging him away. He tried to kick the person behind him, tried to hammer the arm with his little fists, but it was useless.

From a distance, he thought he saw Auntie Ma smile.

Then, a huge man with a hairy chest stepped behind Auntie Ma's prostrate body. Li Kung barely saw his face, or did he have a face at all? There was a heavy saber in his hand.

Li Kung's eyes bulged in alarm. He had seen this before, though he wasn't sure when.

"Auntie Ma!" he shouted.

The big man swung his heavy saber across Auntie Ma's neck. Her head struck the floor tiles and rolled away.

"Auntie Ma!" Li Kung screamed.

• • •

Li Kung's eyes opened. He squinted against the morning sun; then gradually, as the sting left his eyes, he began to see the valley below him. His heart was racing, his head throbbing in dull pulses, and a cold sweat drenched his back even as the image of his dream faded. He quickly remembered where he was. He had fallen asleep on the ledge of a shallow cliff, on the southern side of Phoenix Eye Peak, where he had spent the past month training in the Flame Cutter.

He pushed himself up on one elbow and leaned into a seated position facing the deep valley. His head rested against the coarse stone behind him, and slowly, he closed his eyes again. Who was Auntie Ma? He'd been having the same dream, repeated over and over again, for almost a month now. Why couldn't he remember who she was?

But Li Kung did remember why he was on the edge of a cliff, high up on the side of a mountain no one could climb— no one except a master of the Flame Cutter. Snow Wolf had left three books, buried behind her tombstone for her chosen warrior, and in the three volumes that she handwrote fifty years ago; she left behind only this one Martial Arts skill. The Flame Cutter, an art of dynamic agility, channeled lightning-fast reflexes and sensitivity to changing surfaces to enable the user to move with such speed that he could extinguish the flames beneath his feet.

Li Kung took a deep breath and opened his eyes. His headache was fading, and he felt calmer, in control again. He had never felt powerful before, not once throughout his childhood, not during the years he followed the Three Saints of Yunnan around the country training to become a doctor, not until he chanced upon Snow Wolf's tomb, where he passed the tests she designed and became her chosen warrior. Every night he studied her book of strategy, her battle formations, her use of deception and psychological warfare, and in a short month, he suddenly felt that the world was a toy in his hands for him to shape and bend at will. Human beings were weak. With all that he had learned from Snow Wolf's books, was there anybody he wouldn't be able to manipulate?

He was wealthier than any man he ever knew. Slowly, each day, he submerged the toxic treasures that Snow Wolf left behind in the alchemic solution she buried beside her tombstone. The gold, the precious stones, the jewelry, were there for him to use for his mission.

"She chose me," he whispered under his breath. "She chose me to eliminate the evil of the land."

The Red Dragon House and the Green Dragon House, two groups in the Martial Society equal in power and cunning, were like warlords in the northern provinces. They controlled the land, the businesses, the arms, and the wealth. With the black paste, the Red Dragons were plotting to control the people too.

Li Kung thought of how his three crazy mentors, the Three Saints of Yunnan, came to the north to learn about this black paste. It was a powerful alchemy that took away a man's mind, leaving him soaring in the air, riding through clouds and sweeping through the heavens while his body withered away. Wei Bin, the leader of the Red Dragon House,

in all his cowardice, was about to cripple Chinese civilization with this black paste. Being supreme leader of the Red
Dragons was not enough—there was always more power to
be had.

But why would his hated twin stand by and watch Wei
Bin's empire grow?

That was the key. Wei Bin and Wei Xu, the evil twins of
the two Dragon Houses, must be enticed to kill each other off.

But first, before embarking on any mission, before ex-
ecuting the enormous task Snow Wolf left him, Li Kung
needed to find Suthachai.

• • •

The rugged farmhouse, hidden in the depths of the forest,
loomed mysteriously before him. Li Kung breathed in excitement, in anticipation. His crazy mentors, the Three Saints of
Yunnan, would be inside, asleep perhaps, but waiting eagerly
for his return. He had been gone for weeks—the longest he
had ever been away from them. Nevertheless, he was home.

Li Kung had traveled the entire day on foot, running
mostly, and never once did he stop to sniff the air. His face
was hot with excitement, his mind bent on vengeance.

Pun's laughter echoed in his mind every time he
thought of Suthachai. All she wanted to do was save the hideous Mongolian. Yet, in cold blood, he nearly slashed her in
half and walked away while she died.

If Suthachai was still alive, Li Kung would have his revenge by nightfall. He was superior in speed and cunning,
and he would have the element of surprise. But most importantly, Li Kung would be well prepared, even if his foe was the
greatest warrior of the Mongolian plains. Suthachai may be
poisoned, weak, dying, but Li Kung took nothing for granted.

He had a simple plan and it was almost certain to work.

Li Kung had never been to Mongolia. From childhood stories, he envisioned endless grasslands and desert, filled with scattered tents and herds of sheep. He reasoned that a Mongolian warrior, used to open space, would not know what to do when surrounded by fire.

He needed more of Shifu Two's green powder—a lot more—and he would raise a powerful inferno so brilliantly hot that Suthachai would have no chance of escape.

Deceit and preparation. He had come home to prepare for battle.

Li Kung stood in front of the farmhouse and hesitated. He wanted to run in shouting at the top of his voice and tell his mentors all that had happened to him. He wanted to tell them about Snow Wolf, the skills he had acquired, the treasures now in his possession, the book of strategy . . .

But he couldn't move. He stared at the front door that all of a sudden didn't seem to welcome him. What if they wouldn't stand behind his mission? What if Shifu Two and Three, in their childish madness, would tell the world about his mission before he had time to master Snow Wolf's arts? What if he couldn't trust his three mentors?

A cold feeling gathered in his chest. Faced with the impossible task of destroying both Dragon Houses, he suddenly felt lonelier than ever. He was destined to become the hero the world had been waiting for. Why would anyone be his friend?

Slowly, he turned and headed for the back door.

• • •

Master Wei Bin, the supreme leader of the Red Dragon House, stood in front of the Grand Stairway and glared. He had fallen for Fei Fei's ruse, and he couldn't decide whether he was angry or proud. She had come into his training hall without her disguise and taunted him into believing that she would reveal his secret to the world, just so he would send all his men to the Grand Stairway to stop her. Then, staring down the narrow, winding stairs—the only path from Redwood Cliff—he realized his daughter had come with a plan to deceive him, and she had executed it perfectly. By then, most of his elite warriors, including the Gentle Swordsmen and the Red Headbands, suspected the alarm on Redwood Cliff was false and began to grow impatient.

Master Bin thought of how she threatened to expose his secret when she had sealed the door behind her and disappeared, and he understood. She wanted him to intercept her while she pretended to flee. Fei Fei was after the sheepskin. She was after the formula for the black paste.

With a roar of anger, Master Bin redirected his men to the back of Redwood Cliff.

The Gentle Swordsmen were the first to break through the silver pine forest. They closed in on the dead oak tree, the secret entrance to Master Bin's underground facilities, and then stopped. One by one, they dropped to their knees.

The Butcher was kneeling in front of them, his back to the tree, his head bowed and awaiting punishment. The Gentle Swordsmen touched their heads to the ground. They couldn't remain standing while their instructor knelt.

Master Bin slowed to a walk, and, eyeing the Butcher, stormed into the underground room. His fists were clenched, his lips drawn back into a snarl. He knew then, without a doubt, that Fei Fei had possession of the sheepskin. He had to retrieve it.

But this was the day. Master Bin drew a deep breath to calm himself. This was the day his twin called for a meeting at the Chestnut Pavilion. Lord Xu wanted a truce—after the massacre at their mother's funeral—Lord Xu had taken it upon himself to unite the Martial Society and call for peace.

But Master Bin's old strategist Tao Hing knew better. Why would his twin form a coalition with other Houses in the Martial Society only to negotiate peace? Lord Xu was planning an invasion of Redwood Cliff.

In a moment, the Red Dragon master resurfaced from the underground room, his face pale, his eyes red with rage.

"Was it Fei Fei?" Master Bin asked the Butcher.

"Yes."

Master Bin whipped his hand across the Butcher's face and sent him sprawling. "It was coal residue!"

The Butcher acknowledged with a slight nod.

"You idiot!" Master Bin screamed. "If the whole world knows you're afraid of Old Snake, then the whole world will pretend to use Old Snake's poison! How could you fall for it?"

The Red Headbands arrived, and they dropped to their knees behind the Gentle Swordsmen.

Master Bin's face flushed to a crimson red. "Fools! All of you are such fools! I want her back alive! I want everything she stole from me either brought back to me or completely destroyed!"

The elite warriors were silent, huddling back. There were broken footsteps of a man running through the forest. In a moment, Tao Hing emerged, his breathing heavy and uneasy.

"Master Bin," the old strategist said between gasps for air. "I heard that . . . that . . ."

"You heard that Fei Fei, laughing like the Flute Demon, broke through the worthless guards by the Grand Stairway. She should already be at the bottom of the cliff by now, right?"

Tao Hing stared. His breathing calmed, but deep lines of stress wove into his face. "Master Bin. All these warriors here . . . You don't intend to hurt Fei Fei, do you?"

"I hurt whomever I please!" Master Bin spun around and smacked the Butcher across the head. The Butcher recovered, resuming his prostrated position again. Master Bin's eyes blazed fire. "Yes, the Flute Demon is my daughter in disguise, and if I could whip her in public, I can kill her as I please. Today, I want every one of you to go down there and look for her. I want her alive, and I want everything that she stole from me returned. I will personally execute her!"

Tao Hing asked, "You won't really kill her, would you, Master Bin?"

Master Bin glared at him once, then turned to his men. He lifted his hand and pointed to the Gentle Swordsmen. "I want all of you, with your idiot instructor here, to ambush the small crossroads leaving He Ku to the north. If she leaves, she will go north to Mongolia. Someone will convince her that we don't have enough men to catch her up there. She's not to get to Mongolia, understand?"

"Yes, Master Bin," they said in unison. Master Bin frowned at the lack of enthusiasm. He glanced at the Butcher with disdain, then pointed at the Red Headbands.

"I want every single one of you to march into He Ku tonight to find her. Start with the Blue Lantern Inn." He paused, as if about to change his mind, then mumbled, "You useless bunch of fools. She'll outwit you at every step."

Master Bin turned to Tao Hing. "I want you to lead these Red Headband morons and chase Fei Fei out of He Ku. If you're as smart as I think you are, you'll walk her into the Butcher's ambush in the north, and you'll have limited casualties capturing her."

Master Bin stopped and waited for Tao Hing to acknowledge his orders. The old man remained silent, staring at him wide eyed, as if in shock. "Do you understand me?" Master Bin shouted.

Tao Hing bowed quickly. "Yes, Master Bin."

"Good!"

"Master Bin, I don't believe it's wise for all of us to pursue her today."

"And why is that?"

"Lord Xu is waiting for us at the Chestnut Pavilion this evening—"

"Ignore my idiot brother!"

"We suspect an ambush," Tao Hing said, quickly. "We need to keep our best warriors on Redwood Cliff. If our elite fighters walk around He Ku tonight, we could easily stroll into the very ambush that we fear. Redwood Cliff will be unprotected."

Master Bin's face became redder. "Are you afraid, Tao Hing?"

"I'm afraid for the well being of the Dragon House, Master Bin. And I'm afraid for the safety of our men."

"Then find a way to defend the cliff without them! These are my orders! I want Fei Fei back on Redwood Cliff by tomorrow morning! Prepare your weapons and set out at once!" He flung his sleeve and turned to leave.

Tao Hing hurried after him. "We're facing a formidable enemy today."

Master Bin paused and looked at him; the anger flushed through his veins unchecked. It was uncharacteristic of him. "You have my orders," he said. "The Flute Demon is not easy to capture."

"I have no weapons to prepare," Tao Hing said. "I'm an old man. I can barely keep up with you."

Master Bin ignored him, and his left hand unconsciously gripped the handle of his sword.

"Master Bin," Tao Hing said, almost out of breath. "I understand Fei Fei deceived you. But overlooking the offense is not such a shameful thing. She's your daughter. For her to carry out a brilliant strategy would only mean that you taught her well. You should be proud."

"I should be," Master Bin said, sarcastically. He walked even faster.

"What did Fei Fei steal? Why is it so important that we retrieve it right away?"

Master Bin gritted his teeth and didn't respond.

"The Butcher knelt in front of the underground room," Tao Hing said, struggling to catch up. "So I reckon Fei Fei stole the sheepskin. But you've already memorized the formula. Our ancestors left behind this medicine to cure the illnesses of mankind. Why would it be a bad idea for her to have the original? She's your daughter. Eventually, she will come home. If the family treasures are not passed onto your sons, they will go to her. If she tries to create the formula, mankind would only have more medicine to fight disease with. Why is it a bad thing?"

Master Bin spun around and bellowed at him. "I've given you a direct order, Tao Hing! I did not ask for your advice!"

"You're taking a tremendous risk, Master Bin. You do believe Lord Xu has been preparing for this—for at least a month now. We don't know where they are, how many people they have, or what they intend to do. We only know that he's been secretly meeting with other leaders of the Martial Society. Don't let this happen, Master Bin. Fei Fei was only playing, at best. Please don't take it as an insult."

Master Bin took a menacing step forward. Tao Hing

bowed his head but held his ground. The old strategist appeared weak, fragile, his wrinkled face dripping with cold sweat, while Master Bin towered over him like a predator.

The younger man lifted his hand, and gently placed it on Tao Hing's shoulder. "I've always depended on you, Tao Hing. I'll explain everything to you when you return."

He turned around to walk away. Tao Hing remained frozen, a disturbed look settling across his knitted brows.

• • •

"Lord Xu," the messenger said with a bow.

Lord Xu waved his hand. "The good news?"

"The Red Dragons have reached the base of Redwood Cliff."

"All of them?"

"We recognize the Butcher and Tao Hing from a distance."

"And the Gentle Swordsmen and Red Headbands?"

"They're all there."

Lord Xu smiled. "Good. Wei Bin's coming to our truce meeting with his very best, as planned. And what about my brother?"

"We haven't spotted Master Bin yet."

"Any news on our coalition?"

"Master Liang has taken position in the south of White Clay Village, and Master Chen is hidden west of Redwood Cliff. The rest are assembled by Southern Pass and awaiting your instruction."

"Good," Lord Xu said. "Tell them that by sunset the Red Dragons will be at the Chestnut Pavilion. They can attack at sunset."

"Yes, master."

. . .

Suthachai stood between two fresh horses, waiting for the woman he loved. He was in a desolate forest just west of He Ku, not far from Lake Eternal. Fei Fei chose this location because it was close to her uncle, and Red Dragons avoided the area. Fresh snow covered the road enclosed by forest—a road not traveled upon since the last snowstorm.

Suthachai's massive frame was wrapped in a brand new coat, which he had bought for the special occasion—this occasion. He had bathed in the morning, perhaps for the fifth time this year, and had begun preparations for the journey. With the gold that Fei Fei gave him, he had bought two horses, plus enough feed for the animals to comfortably cross the desert. He had bought dried meat and grain, additional water flasks, and with the remaining money, acquired a war bow and a full quiver of arrows. Fei Fei warned him that her people might give chase. He gripped the bow firmly and waited. They would make it across the desert and only death would separate them again.

Perhaps he had another month to live. Li Kung's mentor had told him that when blood flowed from his ears, the poison in his body was nearing its final stage. He would die, for sure. But to die in Fei Fei's arms, an entire month from now, was more than he could hope for. Life was good to him.

In a moment, he saw her. Her lithe figure, so agile and alert, awash in the reddish twilight, approached him. His heart pounded with excitement.

. . .

From a short distance, crouched in a nearby tree, Li Kung stared at the Mongolian like a vulture. He had left the Three

Saints of Yunnan without showing his face, and taking only the green powder, he ran straight to the Blue Lantern Inn. His intention was to lure Suthachai out into the open and surround him with layer upon layer of flaming walls until the Mongolian's poison depleted his strength, then cover him with the powder and burn him alive. Suthachai was strong but could not run far. There could be no escape.

But the two horses outside the inn responded to the Mongolian's commands, and Li Kung hesitated. Somehow, Suthachai had acquired two tall stallions, and he appeared strong and alert. It would be impossible to surround both horses with fire, especially with a Mongolian warrior riding them.

Suddenly without a viable strategy, Li Kung could do nothing but follow Suthachai into the woods.

Suthachai stopped in the middle of the road and patiently checked the provisions he carried. The Mongolian didn't choose a higher vantage point on the road, and Li Kung knew then that he was waiting for a friend.

But Suthachai had no friends in the mainland. He and Pun were his only friends.

There were two horses, both prepared for an extensive journey. Who would travel with the Mongolian?

The sun began to set. Li Kung noticed Fei Fei approaching and thought at first that she was a wealthy merchant's daughter. Perhaps she was lost in the forest and was about to stumble upon the barbarian. His heart throbbed with anxiety. Suthachai was a monster, and he was sure to kill her with one swipe of his heavy saber, like how he had killed Pun. If he attacked now, Suthachai would have the use of both horses for escape, plus a full quiver of arrows to defend himself. But if he waited any longer, the poor girl might lose her life.

Li Kung moved undetected around the Mongolian, running silently across the barren treetops. He was almost next to her before he could see her face. Her beauty and her majestic presence overwhelmed him with both awe and curiosity. This must be the daughter of Wei Bin, he told himself, because no one else in the world could live up to her stunning beauty.

What did this mean? Was Suthachai somehow involved with the Red Dragons?

Fei Fei traveled down the snowy path, and Li Kung followed in the trees. He watched Suthachai secure his bow against the saddle of one horse, quickly mount it, then gently slap the other horse forward. Both animals trotted up the path with a snort.

Then, like lightning, Fei Fei ran down the side of the road, brushing so close to Li Kung that for a second, he thought she was attacking him. She was instantly on the second horse.

How could Master Bin's dainty daughter move with such speed?

Both horses began to gallop down the trail, their backs toward the setting sun. Li Kung was left with no choice but to follow.

He ran as hard as he could, no longer silent, but the pounding horse hooves completely masked the sound of his chase. For a while, he managed to keep up with the horses. He saw Fei Fei pass something to Suthachai, some type of fabric, or skin, which the Mongolian promptly tucked into his coat.

Far into the outskirts of He Ku, Li Kung began to feel the fatigue. Even with the Flame Cutter, his stamina could not last as long as two speeding horses. He slowed to a walk. Suthachai and Fei Fei became smaller and smaller, only to disappear around a bend in the road, and Li Kung cursed himself for not attacking sooner. Now how would he ever catch them?

He drew his breath and picked up his pace again, wondering whether the woman with Suthachai really was Master Bin's daughter. Snow Wolf had warned that if Master Bin's secret alchemy was not destroyed, his successors not stopped, then Chinese civilization would come to an end. If Master Bin's daughter had to be eliminated, then so be it. It didn't really matter why she was with him.

With a dark glint in his eyes, Li Kung picked up speed and continued to chase.

• • •

Suthachai rode with his head low, barely seated on the saddle, feeling alive for the first time. Fei Fei rode beside him like he had always dreamed. The cold wind gently brushed the horse's mane into his face, and he breathed in its familiar scent. In two nights, they would be at the mouth of the desert. Afterward, it would only be another two weeks of hard riding to reach the steppe.

He looked over to her. Her eyes were on him all along, a light smile illuminating her face. She reached out to touch him, and he took her hand in his; he rode closer and drew her palm to his face. They looked into each other's eyes, mesmerized, locked in a dream, suspended in another world.

There was a subtle movement to Suthachai's right. He broke free, bow and arrow instantly in his hands. Like lightning, he turned around and fired point blank into the barren woods. A scream of agony emerged where the arrow struck, and men poured into the road out of nowhere. Lost in each other's smiles, both Suthachai and Fei Fei had failed to see the new footprints in the snow.

Their horses struggled to pull back. Suthachai released another arrow at short range. Fei Fei drew her sword, reined in her horse, and signaled her intention to charge. Men continued to pile up in front of them.

Suthachai tucked in his bow and drew his saber. It was not the first time he had to break free from armies of men. He recognized the Red Headbands, the heavy cudgels raised above their chests.

"Hit-and-run tactics," he said, under his breath. He knew Fei Fei heard him. "I will butt heads with them while you break their formation from the side."

Fei Fei nodded. The Red Headbands locked into position, their mass movement sweeping up the snow, hindering their visibility. "We'll surround them two to two hundred," she said with a smile.

Suthachai drew three arrows at once and fired them blindly. One struck a warrior's arm, the other two were deflected by heavy cudgels. But the sudden attack was enough to break their focus. With a roar, Suthachai squeezed his horse's belly and charged. He rushed down at them, saber raised, eyes pinned on his target and yearning for blood.

In response, the front line of warriors separated, and an old man rode forth on a horse.

"No!" Fei Fei bolted forward, sword in hand. She lurched in front of Suthachai and barely intercepted his heavy saber. Sparks flew. All three horses backed away. Suthachai looked at her—her pleading eyes—and withdrew.

• • •

Fei Fei held her blade in front of her, warning the Red Headbands not to advance. So her father had sent Tao Hing. It was smart of him to assume that she would outwit the Butcher.

Tao Hing came forward again. "So you really are the Flute Demon. Little Fei Fei with double braids. Even I was fooled."

"Weren't you supposed to ambush me on Northern Pass? That's how I would get to Mongolia."

"That's why I don't need to look for you there. You wouldn't go where you're most expected."

Fei Fei sneered. "Where's the Butcher?"

"Somewhere preparing an ambush, of course."

Fei Fei relaxed and lowered her sword. "How do you expect to stop me with cudgel users on foot?"

"I don't," the old man said, "especially since you personally trained them. They all know who you are now, and they still have undying respect for you. The question is, how many of your own students are you willing to kill for the sheepskin?"

"You can do better than that, Uncle Tao Hing. I'll kill every man who attacks me. The question is, how many men are you willing to send to their deaths for the sheepskin?"

Tao Hing smiled lightly and began to walk his horse forward. Fei Fei understood and began to withdraw, increasing the distance between her and the Red Headbands. In a moment, they were out of earshot. Suthachai stayed behind, glaring at the Red Headbands, warning them not to advance.

Tao Hing rode closer to Fei Fei. "What is really on the sheepskin, my child?"

"Are you going to take my life for this sheepskin?"

"How could I ever take your life, Fei Fei? I waited outside when you were born. I was the first to hold you when your father brought you out." Tao Hing chuckled. "I even beat Old Snake to it."

"Then why all this?"

"To bring you home. Your family needs you."

"No, Uncle Tao Hing. You're here because you're afraid of my father, because you were taught to obey orders all your life, and you don't have the courage to take a stand for yourself—"

"Stop. You know that won't work on me." Tao Hing's voice became more urgent. "Now, tell me about the sheepskin before I take you home."

"What makes you think you can?"

"The sheepskin! Your father looks like he's ready to sacrifice anything—even sacrifice you for it. What is it? What's happened to him?"

"Power," Fei Fei said. "The prospect of absolute power. He no longer needs any of us."

"The sheepskin could give him absolute power? I've read the writings on it. It's nothing but herbal formulas, medicine that our ancestors left behind to cure mankind's diseases. What are you telling me, Fei Fei?"

Fei Fei's eyes sparkled. "Do you really mean you don't know? Or are you testing me?"

"When have I ever lied to you?" Tao Hing asked. "I've just told you everything I know."

Fei Fei took a deep breath. "Fine. And if you don't leave the instant after I tell you what you want to know, then . . ."

"Then you're at war with me," Tao Hing finished for her. "An old man without an inch of steel, nor the strength to slaughter a chicken."

Fei Fei smiled sarcastically, suspended in thought for a moment, then said, "The herbal composite on the sheepskin is a strange alchemy, complicated and unusual. The herbs are ordinary, but each element is combined and processed in a manner that only a genius could have devised."

She went on to tell him about Pan Tong Village, about the paste Black Shadow gave her, which she tried. She told him about the confrontation with her father, the hidden training hall where the sheepskin was found, and how Old Snake discovered the underground laboratory and read the formula.

"So Old Snake memorized and recreated the formula in his own laboratory," Tao Hing said, "and he hid this from me all along."

"He didn't know the implications of it," Fei Fei said quickly. "What would happen if word got out that my father intends to poison the Martial Society?"

"And this threat of making an antidote can stop your father?"

"What other solution is there?"

Tao Hing sighed. "He'll kill anyone who could endanger his plan. I've known him all my life. Meanwhile, the Red and Green Dragons will be killing each other for a long time. Wei Xu will go to war to stop this alchemy from scorching his men. There won't be another moment of peace."

A long pause. Fei Fei gazed at him, a tear in her eye. "Would you betray me, Uncle Tao Hing?"

Tao Hing looked away. "I want you to be safe."

She sighed, stared at the two hundred men standing in formation, and asked, "Would you give me safe passage from this land—with Suthachai?"

Tao Hing turned to the Mongolian. "So he's the lucky man. The mark of a true warrior in his eyes. I've heard of him before. He's been poisoned by the Soaring Dragon Candles?"

Fei Fei nodded.

"Silly child," Tao Hing said, shaking his head. "What would your future be like if you go off with a dying man?"

"What would my future be like if I leave him?"

Tao Hing reached out and patted her hand. "You'll be

safe on Redwood Cliff. The Flute Demon is dead, leaving behind a beautiful princess who needs to be protected. I'll talk your father into forgiving you—it won't be difficult—he only needs a reminder that you're his favorite child, and your life will be simple and peaceful."

"And Suthachai," Fei Fei's voice trembled. She already knew the answer to her question.

Tao Hing sighed.

Fei Fei's eyes flashed fire. "He would be so heartbroken, and so disappointed with me, and with the world . . . "

"But he would be dead, and it wouldn't matter."

"It's not the length of life that matters," Fei Fei said, "but what happens when we're still alive." She turned her horse around. "Will you or will you not let me leave with the man I love?"

A deep smile crept onto Tao Hing's face. "I'm happy for you, my child. But I still have to take you home today."

"Why?"

"So I won't have to watch someone else bring your body home tomorrow."

Fei Fei gritted her teeth. "So we're at war then, Uncle Tao Hing?"

"War with many casualties."

"I'm sorry."

"I'm sorry too, my child."

There was a flash of light. Suthachai bellowed a war cry. A figure leaped out of the woods and, both swords drawn, slashed at him with lightning speed. Men with double-edged swords appeared out of nowhere, completely blocking the distance between Fei Fei and Suthachai. They swarmed the road like flies.

The Butcher! Fei Fei squeezed her horse's belly to charge, but one hundred men, skilled in the double-edged sword, jabbed at her horse's legs and sent it rearing back. Meanwhile, a wave of men closed in and slaughtered Suthachai's horse. The Mongolian leaped onto the ground and was immediately locked with the Butcher in a critical exchange of blows. The Red Headbands surrounded them, but none dared to venture close.

The Butcher, with both swords in hand, attacked with such vehemence that Suthachai could do nothing but retreat. In seconds, there were multiple cuts on his body.

Fei Fei extended her sword and held its tip against Tao Hing's throat.

"So you'll kill Suthachai? Is that the tactic of the great strategist Tao Hing?"

Tao Hing moved gently away from her blade. "The Mongolian cannot be touched. At least not until his poison overwhelms him."

"And when it does?"

"By then, my child, you would've cut a path through your men, and you would be locked in a close battle with the Butcher and his Gentle Swordsmen. They won't be able to capture you right away, at least not until the Mongolian escapes."

Fei Fei sneered. "Suthachai would never leave me in battle."

"He would if you render him unconscious on a speeding horse."

She glared at him, unsure of whether to show her admiration or disgust. "You would hand the sheepskin back to my father, and endanger every soul in the Martial Society? You would do that, Uncle Tao Hing?"

"I would be highly disappointed if the sheepskin is still with you by now," Tao Hing said with a smile.

Fei Fei wanted to spit at him, but there was no time.

She sent her horse flying forward and managed to send the Gentle Swordsmen into temporary retreat.

Meanwhile, Suthachai noticed the Butcher's recent injuries and began to capitalize on them. He realized that the Butcher was cut across the chest, and, when striking upwards, could only deliver limited force. He leaped into the air and began to rain his heavy blows from above.

The Butcher crumbled under the incredible weight.

In a moment, the number one warrior of the steppe, who found no competition in wrestling beyond three beats of the drum, lifted his assailant high above his head and threw him horizontally through the air.

The Butcher slammed helplessly against a tree trunk. The Red Headbands closed in. Suthachai was completely surrounded.

His heart was beating faster, his chest was heavy, and the nausea that he had come to know so well began to flood through his body. He would not last long. Fei Fei was in her own heated battle—she was too far away to help him. He didn't understand why she refused to fight the Red Headbands when their chances were better, and he didn't know why she waited for the Butcher to appear. But none of that mattered. He had to stand by her decisions.

Suthachai hammered through a row of swinging cudgels, attacking in every direction.

No one knew how to defend against the Mongolian's heavy saber. A weapon of such immense weight would be considered too cumbersome even as a bashing weapon. Yet Suthachai used it with the agility of a dagger. Quickly, the entire group of Red Headbands began to fall back.

Meanwhile, Fei Fei continued to fight on horseback but couldn't press through the Gentle Swordsmen. She was not on a warhorse—the stallion wouldn't move forward in the face of so many men. She realized that Suthachai had already lost his horse, and she knew his poison was weakening him.

The Gentle Swordsmen were in perfect order, their formation as a hundred-man unit in solid lines more than five layers deep. The Butcher had trained them specifically to fight as one, with each attack and retreat executed in unison. Fei Fei had no chance of striking them one at a time.

Then, noticeably, she saw the Mongolian's face turn ashen white, and a slight trail of dark blood emerged from his lips. She watched his slow movements, his feet increasingly unstable, his attacks more brutal but less continuous. It wouldn't be long for him. Her own hit-and-run attacks became routine against the swordsmen, and nothing she did seemed to shake their positions. They would bury her. If she didn't break their lines decisively, they would find her weakness and outflank her from both sides—one hundred to one.

She glanced at Tao Hing a short distance behind her. The old man tilted his head back, exposing his neck with a smile. Fei Fei understood. She jerked her horse back and reached the old man with two steps. She stretched across the gap between her moving horse and his, riding around him at incredible speed, and with a silent word of thanks, yanked him off his mount and hauled his bony figure onto her horse.

"I have your commander!" she shouted, kicking her horse's belly. Her left arm wrapped around his waist to protect him from falling, her blade pressed dangerously close to his throat. She drove her horse down the front line of Gentle Swordsmen. "I have your commander!" she shouted again. "Stand aside or he dies!"

"Stand back!" Tao Hing screamed. "Stand back!"

She kicked the horse harder. Every warrior from Redwood Cliff hesitated, uncertain of what to do, unable to react. Fei Fei screamed a war cry that resonated the howl of the Flute Demon, and rushing down on the retreating swordsmen, she leaned forward to kill.

"She took Master Tao Hing hostage!" someone shouted. No further excuse was needed. Fei Fei slashed left and right from her horse, pelting them with a volley of deadly blows that easily broke through the men retreating in front of her. In a moment, the Gentle Swordsmen scattered.

Fei Fei broke through the surrounding Red Headbands and lunged at the Butcher from the side. The famed swordsman of Redwood Cliff struggled to retreat, barely deflecting her sword from his face. As he stumbled back, Suthachai dove across the snow and slashed him heavily across the thigh.

The Butcher collapsed. Blood immediately seeped through his trousers. His men moved in quickly to shield him. Suthachai also crumbled, a new stream of blood trickling from his mouth.

"You win," Fei Fei said to Tao Hing, her expression calm all of a sudden. "I go home with you, so Suthachai can live."

They were completely surrounded. Her single horse could not carry three people and still run from three hundred warriors. She leaped off her horse, still dragging the old man. Then she suddenly broke free from him and struck Suthachai heavily on the side of his neck. The Mongolian fell, unconscious. She lifted his huge frame over her shoulders, her knees buckling under the weight, and, stumbling toward the jittery horse, threw him horizontally across the saddle.

The Gentle Swordsmen stormed forward. Somewhere in the background, the Butcher shouted, "Attack! Surround her and attack!" Fei Fei screamed at them, a war cry so shrill and hideous that for a moment, every man hesitated. They could never forget. The Flute Demon in full rage was virtually unstoppable.

Fei Fei slapped the horse's rear with a stinging backhand and sent the animal running with a snort. She dragged Tao Hing by a bony arm and ran alongside the stallion. The old man could not keep up, but she needed him, or they would surround her and Suthachai would never escape. She ran next to the speeding horse, her sword slashing left and right, and, using all her energy, scattering the men until Suthachai completely broke free.

Then she stopped, burnt with exhaustion, and pointed her weapon against Tao Hing's throat. The old man's eyes were closed, his clothing in tatters. He lay across the snow, having been dragged at the speed of a running horse, and he breathed heavily, painfully. Fei Fei turned her face and watched. The man she loved remained unconscious on the disappearing horse. A small murmur escaped her lips.

The men quickly gathered behind her, next to her, all around her, weapons poised to strike. She released Tao Hing's arms, hoping that she had not hurt him, and with a sigh, dropped her sword and waited.

•   •   •

By the time Suthachai regained consciousness, his frightened mount had already slowed to a trot. The Mongolian's gloved hand floundered for the reins while nausea overwhelmed him. The world darkened before his eyes.

The dying man slid helplessly from the saddle. With a muffled thud, he landed face first into the snow, the lurid taste of blood still in his mouth. He tried to remember where he was and why he was there.

Fei Fei . . .

His hands pawed the snow, and somehow, he climbed to his knees. He was shaking and his lips were trembling. He turned around and around, pivoting from one weak knee to another, searching for her. But she was nowhere in sight. His horse returned, snorting restlessly, and then it dawned on him. It was her horse. His was slain. The only way he could have escaped on her horse was if she had placed him there and stayed behind to cover him while he fled.

He shook in heaving spasms then. Tears welled in his eyes. The agony, the helplessness, all blurred before him. He gnashed his teeth and fought for control. She told him the night before that if her father caught her, she would be executed without a second thought. Wei Bin would sacrifice her to secure the opportunity for complete power.

But she was alive. The old strategist seemed kind to her. He wouldn't allow his men to murder her. At least not yet.

He tasted blood in his mouth and felt a new pain in his skull. Warm blood trickled from his ears. He felt the poison steadily creeping into his bones. In horror, he wiped the blood from the side of his face and stared at his stained gloves. It was his time. When blood seeped from his ears, the poison had reached its final stage, and he might be dead by nightfall.

"Cannot die . . . " he whispered, his voice hoarse. "Fei Fei . . . "

The world became dimmer, more obscure; the shapes of trees around him became distorted. The ground in front of him began to bend. Sucking in the cold air with his head in painful spasms, Suthachai shrieked with fear and suffering. It was time to die. How could this happen now, when the fate of the woman he loved hung by a meager thread, when she would meet certain death if she returned to Redwood Cliff? He felt fear for the first time, a fear beyond anything he was trained to endure. He knew she was not afraid to die, and neither was he. But it was fear for his waning life that led her to sacrifice herself so that he could escape. And it was fear of her death that he suddenly found himself confronting.

Suthachai, my boy. Seeking life is hardly a worthy quest.

Faintly, in the murky near-distance, he thought he saw a familiar face. It was a thin figure, armed with a massive cudgel that seemed too heavy for the figure's slender arms.

Fei Fei.

Suthachai felt his head swell. He could barely see the familiar face, and he didn't care. He had to find her, had to hold down her enemies so she could escape. The world around him was barren except for the thin man with the hawk-like gaze who stood motionless before him. For a moment, Suthachai thought he recognized him.

He stumbled forward, almost touched the man that blocked his path, and lifting a trembling finger, pointed.

"Li Kung . . . " he whispered, suddenly able to see the face so close to his. A ghastly smile briefly surfaced beneath the trickling blood.

"They will kill her, Li Kung," he said. But the excitement of seeing an old friend instantly faded when he heard his own words: *They will kill her, Li Kung.* The face disappeared. Somehow, his childish friend moved quicker than he could see. Suthachai shook his head clear. He could only think of Fei Fei, slowly trudging to her death on Redwood Cliff, surrounded by the warriors she had trained, tied down by the old man she looked up to. Lifting a weak hand to his swelling brain, Suthachai uttered a muffled grunt, unaware of the thin man taking position directly behind him.

• • •

Li Kung had pursued Suthachai and Fei Fei since they left the forest near He Ku. Unable to follow their speeding horses, he had watched them disappear, cursed himself for not attacking earlier, and eventually resumed his chase.

He found them locked in a battle against hundreds of men. He watched in awe as Fei Fei tore apart the Gentle Swordsmen with Tao Hing's throat against her blade, and, in the desperate struggle, managed to render Suthachai unconscious.

Li Kung had then stripped a cudgel from the corpse of a Red Headband and pursued the fleeing horse. This time, he managed to stay close to his foe. He did turn around once and caught a glimpse of Fei Fei dropping her sword in surrender. But the image of her sacrifice, however intense, quickly left his mind. The horse he pursued eventually slowed to a steady walk, and the man he had dreamed of killing remained unconscious on the rigid saddle. Li Kung slowed to a walk and eyed the saber in Suthachai's hand.

When Suthachai fell from his horse, Li Kung had circled behind him faster than Suthachai could see. Li Kung stood with the single cudgel held high above his head, his eyes so inflamed with hate and disgust that he could barely keep them open. The bashing weapon suddenly didn't feel so heavy.

Suthachai stood so pathetically in front of him, so helpless and distraught. Li Kung wanted to grab the saber and slice his enemy through the liver, the same way Pun was slashed, or to amputate him one limb at a time. He envisioned himself killing the Mongolian a little at a time, so that he would suffer like Pun had suffered.

The gods were on his side. Certainly they were. They must have heard his weeping and recognized his suffering. Never had he been stronger, and never had he seen the

Mongolian in worse condition. He could do anything now; blessed with the superhuman speed that Snow Wolf had endowed him with, the plan of attack that he so quickly devised, the desolate location, the handicap of his enemy . . . all guaranteed his vengeance at its fullest. The man was in front of him, vaguely conscious, the rear of his skull in a direct line with the raised cudgel. All he had to do was strike with all his strength and weight, and it would be over—the hate, the rage, the self-pity.

Suthachai stumbled forward, his hazy eyes neither focused, nor closed in submission.

Li Kung could not attack. Nothing could stop him now, yet it seemed simple, too simple. He hesitated. Did he want it to be over so easily?

"Why?" he heard himself asking. The cudgel held high above his head became increasingly heavier, but he didn't care. Something was missing. "Why?" he repeated, taking two giant steps forward. Once again, the cudgel was directly above the Mongolian's head.

Suthachai slowed. He evidently heard, but he didn't understand. He trudged forward, fresh blood trickling from his ear. He mustered a deep breath, as if there were sand in his lungs, and shouted, "Fei Fei!"

A blinding film of rage swelled into Li Kung's eyes. He twisted his body with a shout and swung the cudgel low, aiming for his enemy's legs. The bashing weapon landed with poor accuracy on the Mongolian's shin, but the strike was heavy. Suthachai crumbled. But the new pain in his leg seemed poor competition to the nauseous agony in his head. He lay sprawled, face down on the snow, shaking in sporadic pulses.

"Why?" Li Kung shouted. "What did Pun ever do to you? Why her? Why me?" His strained voice became hoarse, but the wind lifted and he could barely hear himself. Angrily, he kicked the Mongolian's broken leg. Suthachai merely twitched in response. Unsatisfied, Li Kung lifted a foot and stepped on the damaged shin.

His face hauntingly pale, his eyes dulled to a dim gray, the Mongolian disregarded the broken leg and struggled to stand.

"Where are you going, Suthachai?" Li Kung held the cudgel over his enemy's head again, this time aimed above the bloody ear. "Are you going to run from me?"

Suddenly, the giant Mongolian lurched upwards and stood firmly on his feet. His body was hunched over, but the heavy saber, planted deep in the snow, supported him. Li Kung released his hold. He watched Suthachai take a step forward, then another, dragging the broken right leg behind him like a useless log.

"Fei Fei," he whispered. "Can't let them kill her. She needs me. I have to get to her. Let them kill me . . . "

"Who? Wei Bin's daughter? She's as evil as you are! You two fit perfectly together!"

Li Kung swung again, this time on the other leg. He crushed it with a devastating blow. The Mongolian's entire lower body collapsed, his two useless legs stretched out behind him.

Planting his saber deep into the snow, Suthachai lifted his upper torso, raised his face, and screamed. Dark blood streamed from his mouth. Li Kung smiled. His enemy screamed in pain—perhaps for mercy—and victory was nearly his. If the Mongolian remained defiant, he would break his two remaining limbs and watch him twitch on the ground. If he begged for mercy, Li Kung would grant him instant death.

He had never killed anyone before. The anticipation, the

excitement pumped blood into his veins and flame into his eyes. He lifted the cudgel high above his head. He shouted: "You want to die with her? Do you think you can? *I* didn't even get to. You think you can?"

Suthachai dropped the saber and withered like a falling leaf. He reached out, his rigid fingers extended, and securing a firm grip on the ground, he began to pull himself forward.

"My legs are broken. I think . . . I still have my hands. Fei Fei needs me." His voice was even weaker than before. His head nodded incessantly, beyond his control, as the pain that attacked him gradually took over his remaining limbs. With a growl, Suthachai continued to crawl, dragging the two broken legs behind him.

The world was becoming darker. The huge figure on the ground became just a shadow in the dense gray of dusk. Li Kung walked next to the two broken legs, the bashing weapon now lowered to his side. He watched his enemy inch forward. A puzzled look grew on the young man's brows. Suthachai wouldn't beg for a quick death, didn't struggle to escape or fight back, he didn't even faint from pain. He continued to move forward, regardless of what was done to him.

What if I was severely injured, Li Kung asked himself out of nowhere. He shook the thought from his mind, disgusted with himself for allowing his attention to wander. He raised his weapon again. He didn't need to show mercy.

What if I was in such pain, at the brink of death? Li Kung gritted his teeth, his skin crawling from the thought. A cold sweat broke on his neck, and again he reprimanded himself for hesitating.

Would I lay still and wait for the moment to come?

The Mongolian inched forward with such difficulty, with such passion. Li Kung stared. The strange thoughts enveloping him, out of nowhere, could not be resisted. He closed his eyes. He imagined himself with both legs broken, beaten and defeated in a desolate land where he had no friends and no help. He envisioned Pun in trouble, were she alive, but she would be far away and beyond his reach. He would no longer have the use of his legs, and death would be imminent, though destined to be slow and painful. What if he knew where Pun was, but he was mortally wounded? Would he have the courage to persist, just so he could die beside her?

The vision ate into him. The final ecstasy of revenge took over his mind and he lost sight of where he was, and what he was doing. Once again Pun was slashed across the torso by the Mongolian saber. Once again, he saw himself holding her, helpless, while she bled. He thought of the loneliness that swept through him when he sat alone with her cold body, while he wept bitterly, pitifully. He thought of how he tried to kill Suthachai that very night with a stick of wood, only to have his life spared so he could return to bury the woman he loved.

But what if Suthachai had completely destroyed him that night, but he didn't immediately die?

Then he saw it, as if suddenly faced with an unknown horror, and he threw his eyes open to fight off the image. He saw himself curled in a tight ball on the snow, clutching his injuries, crying and whimpering with self-pity. He saw himself lying pathetically on the ground, waiting, hoping to die, his face dripping with tears, his sobs hollow with helplessness. He saw himself going to sleep, praying that the sleep would be permanent, while Pun's body was left to the wolves.

And Suthachai, at this moment, with both legs shattered and the poison in its final stages, continued to crawl forward, the words "Fei Fei" lingering on his lips.

Li Kung spat on the crawling body, his heart twisted in a new anguish that he had never felt before. Was it guilt? Was it contempt for himself?

Did he love Pun enough to endure such torment, just so he could die next to her?

"How far can you go, Suthachai?" he shouted. "How many more inches can you crawl so you can die with her?"

Suthachai froze. This time, he realized that someone was speaking to him.

"I must not die with her . . . " he said with difficulty. He choked on a surge of blood.

Li Kung thought he was going to laugh. But Suthachai found his words.

"I must die, so that she may live . . . "

Suthachai's arms shook so drastically he could barely control them.

"There is not enough time," Li Kung heard the Mongolian whisper. "They will kill her. I do not have enough time . . . But they may come back this way, and I can . . . I can . . . "

Suthachai spat up more blood. Li Kung couldn't believe he was still alive. Yet some people hang on to their existence with one breath of air, and one bit of hope.

Tears flowed from the young doctor's eyes. He watched Suthachai drag himself forward, one arm length at a time, with nothing to drive him through the intense pain—nothing other than the faint hope of reaching the woman he loved. With both legs shattered and the poison eating into his bones, Suthachai continued to believe.

Li Kung's lips trembled. Would Pun want him to kill Suthachai at this moment? He lifted his face to the darkening heavens, a slow murmur escaping his tortured soul. Pun was a much better person than he. How did he ever deserve her?

"Why did you have to kill Pun . . . " he said quietly, and lowered his face.

The Mongolian paused, as if he recognized what was said. For a moment, he remained motionless. Then, shaking his head, he continued forward.

Li Kung watched Suthachai move farther and farther away from him. Maybe today, for the first time, Li Kung had seen what love is. Perhaps his feelings for Pun were not true love, but just dependency. Perhaps, if he had really loved her, he would have done what she would have done.

"Wait here," he said. "I'll bring her to you. Then I will kill you. You will die, and maybe, so that Wei Bin's daughter may live . . . "

In a flash, he was gone, the intensity of the Flame Cutter propelled by the fire in his heart. His decision was so abrupt, yet so certain that he barely had time to think. This is what Pun would have wanted him to do. Above and beyond vengeance, Pun would have wanted to see two people, deeply in love, finally be together.

He ran so quickly that the rising wind whipped through his hair and sent it streaking behind him like the mane of a horse. He felt strangely confident.

His mind raced through his options. Rescuing Fei Fei from the hands of the old strategist would not be easy. He thought of what he had seen that morning when he stood at a high elevation surveying the terrain. He recalled seeing hundreds of men from different schools of the Martial Society. He thought of the scouts who toured the hilltops, many of whom carried the flag of the Green Dragons. Something was brewing. So many armed men, so well organized and communicating across great distances, could not be a sign of peace. They all seemed to move in the direction of Redwood Cliff. Perhaps the Red Dragons were under attack.

But Tao Hing seemed oblivious to it all. How could that be, Li Kung wondered. It was unlike the old strategist to be unaware. Why would Tao Hing bring hundreds of men to capture Wei Bin's daughter? What was he afraid of? Perhaps he could take advantage of the uncertainty behind the old man's mission.

Li Kung shook his head, gathering his energy to ascend a steep incline. He might never know, nor did it really matter to him. Eventually, he would find himself exterminating the Red and Green Dragons so there would be peace in this cruel land. But this day, just for this one moment, he must focus on a separate mission.

Li Kung stood high above a mountaintop and surveyed the land. After a long time, he noticed them. Along a small trail, rapid and silent, was a long line of armed men. He could vaguely differentiate the Red Headbands from the Gentle Swordsmen, all marching in perfect formation. Apparently Tao Hing was aware of the Green Dragons, and he had chosen a hidden trail, the Cicada Trail, to bring his men back to Redwood Cliff.

Li Kung couldn't see Fei Fei, but he knew she was there. He decided on a plan of action. On such a narrow trail, over half the Red Dragons could not see their commander, who rode in front. They would instinctively respond to verbal signals and warnings from anyone next to them. The trail, embedded deep within the forest, was vulnerable to ambush, and Li Kung was certain the Red Dragons knew this. He smiled to himself. Paranoia would be running high. They would be afraid of anything they didn't recognize.

He needed to move quickly so he could have ample time for preparations. Preparation was vital. Preparation and deceit.

• • •

Master Liang of the White Tiger House glared at three old women standing at the base of Redwood Cliff. They were sweeping the snow with little straw brooms and humming a song like nothing in the world could harm them. Occasionally, they would turn to each other and smile. Every stroke of the broom increased the tension in Master Liang's face.

Where could the ambush be? Liang leaned against a small tree, watching every movement at the mouth of the Grand Stairway. He was waiting for darkness to settle. His men had already lit their torches by early evening. The clusters of light would certainly be noticed on Redwood Cliff. Why was there no movement from the Red Dragons? Surely they would know that thousands of armed men had gathered around the base of their *zhuang*.

Master Chen and Master Gao were hidden along the rear end of White Clay Village. Between all fourteen Houses participating in the invasion, every possible road to the Grand Stairway was effectively occupied. A double drumbeat from the hills would send the warriors charging in for the kill.

A small group, consisting of a few men from each House, formed a new team under the flag of the Iron Palm School. Wei Xu had insisted on it. The flag of Liu Yun's late father would be in the forefront, so the cause of the operation would be clear for all. To protect Liu Yun from being harmed, each House assigned a few able men to help.

Master Liang eyed the old women with increasing frustration. They didn't appear to be the baits of an ambush. Untrained warriors would be nervous, fidgety, their eyes darting back and forth in fearful anticipation. These old women were too cheerful, almost as if they had accepted their fates and come prepared to die. Perhaps no ambush existed, and it was a mere ruse.

Tao Hing . . . It was typical of the old strategist. Maybe they were buying time for the formidable Gentle Swordsmen to return.

Liang raised his hand so his scouts could see. There was no more time to lose. He would signal for a full-fledged attack. The old women would be slaughtered for their insolence, and the Grand Stairway would be burned and Redwood Cliff would be stormed.

A scout approached him, moving with so much noise that Liang wanted to smack him for his incompetence. The scout bowed and said, "Master Gao would like you to reconsider the attack for fear of an ambush."

"Master Gao is a fool," Liang said with a hoarse whisper. "Where would the Red Dragons hide? There's open space in front of us. We're prepared to shield ourselves from anything, even if they drop from above. Tell Master Gao not to worry."

"Yes, sir."

The scout ran off clumsily and Liang prepared for action. He lifted his hand to signal a charge.

Another scout ran forward. Liang cursed himself for hesitating. This one came from Master Chen, who was his equal in rank in the Martial Society.

"Master Liang," the scout said with a bow.

"Go ahead."

"Master Chen would like to test the situation with a few men before calling a full-fledged attack."

Liang scowled. "Does Master Chen also suspect an ambush?"

"He believes you suspect an ambush yourself," was the reply.

Turning slightly red, Liang nodded and turned to his men. "Hold your charge," he said. "Allow Master Chen to show his talents."

The scout bowed again and ran off. Liang leaned back and watched the forest, where, hardly hidden from view, Master Chen prepared a small group of five warriors.

"Fool," Liang whispered. "He'll kill the old women with stealth and surprise, using his best warriors, and the whole world will laugh at his cowardice."

Slowly, the unit of five proceeded into the open, a small lantern hanging in front of them. Their swords were sheathed. The old women looked up, smiled, then hunched over and lowered their brooms. They produced small bundles of twigs, which they ignited.

"What are they doing?" Liang asked.

One by one, the old women knelt in front of the snow and lit a row of candles. No one saw the candles earlier.

"Soaring Dragon Candles!" Liang whispered in alarm.

The small unit of five froze. They looked at each other for a second, before turning to Master Chen. Slowly, they began to withdraw.

The old women finished lighting the candles, five in all, and gently lowered them into red lanterns. They smiled to each other and picked up their brooms again.

● ● ●

Li Kung closed his eyes to meditate on the moment. He was crouched like a coiled animal prepared to spring on its prey; his arched figure hovered over a steep drop, where below, the Cicada Trail twisted like a dying eel. Timing was everything. Moments ago, he detected the approach of the Red Dragons, and he waited patiently for them to move closer. He was high up enough to see great distances, despite the darkness, and the road below him was narrow enough for the Red Dragons to be wary, even paranoid.

Li Kung had gone far ahead to the foot of Redwood Cliff to watch the hundreds of torches surrounding the Red Dragon *zhuang*. It was apparent: a complex attack was being formed against Master Bin, involving a multiple ambush of Tao Hing's returning warriors and perhaps even an invasion of Redwood Cliff itself.

There was no time for him to investigate further. Satisfied that no one else was on the Cicada Trail, Li Kung returned to his position.

Heavy snow blanketed the world in a strange, silver gray. The mountainside on which he crouched yielded a complete view of several important roads in the region. He had deduced this area was most vulnerable to suspicion and confusion. Wrapping around the mountain was Northern Pass, where Green Dragon scouts roamed freely. Northern Pass was higher up, along a desolate plateau yielding clean views of Middle Pass. The small forest separating Northern Pass and the Cicada Trail was incredibly sparse. He had planted dried twigs on both sides of the trail, firewood that he had sprinkled with green powder, which would generate the confusion he needed.

Li Kung stared at the Green Dragon scouts a short distance away, calculated the speed of their movements, then calculated the rapid pace of the Red Dragons. It was time to act.

With a short jerk of his body, Li Kung descended the steep mountainside in silence, his feet picking up speed so naturally that he seemed to be floating. The forest at the foot of the mountain loomed before him. He turned sideways, ran diagonally against the slope, and gradually approached the base without losing speed. He watched the Green Dragon scouts from the corner of his eye, still counting the rhythm of Tao Hing's approach. Time was tight, but too much time would be equally disastrous. He bolted through the sparse forest separating the two trails, heading straight for Northern Pass where he would collide with the scouts.

There were about twelve of them. Young and fleet of foot, scouts were normally trained to move in silence, communicating with visual signals and transmitting silent orders across hostile terrain. When Li Kung ran past them earlier, he noticed that one of them carried the flag of the Green Dragons. They were pacing back and forth on Northern Pass, perhaps waiting for signals to transmit. Li Kung smiled. He closed in on them, still undetected. How far would they go to keep the flag in their hands?

In a flash, Li Kung was on Northern Pass. He was upon them then, running so quickly that he swept past them before they could react. He stirred so much wind into their torches that the group was instantly thrown into confusion. While they scrambled for answers, Li Kung disappeared into the dark forest, shooting out a second time from behind them and heading straight for the flag bearer. He knocked the scout off his feet and took the flag from him.

Li Kung held the flag high above his head, making sure they could all see. Then, he darted to the side and smacked one man on the nose, letting out a cold, mocking laugh before standing back.

"Who are you?" one of the scouts shouted.

"How do you call yourself a warrior of the Martial Society if you lose the symbol of your House so easily?" Li Kung laughed again, sheer contempt in his voice. "You can't take this flag from me, so why don't you go home to your mothers and weep in front of the family altars."

Fuming with rage, the twelve scouts drew their weapons and charged. Li Kung waited for them to come dangerously close, then turned tail and fled. He maintained a slow enough pace for them to stay behind him, but quick enough so that no matter how they tried, they could not touch him. He had been counting the footsteps of the Red Dragons in his heart, and he knew exactly where they were. He skipped into the forest; the scouts immediately behind him, unknowingly headed for the line of Red Headbands. The Cicada Trail was only wide enough for two men to travel abreast on, and the hundreds of warriors following Tao Hing's horse would form a very long train—so long that the front could not see the back.

Li Kung laughed and waited a heated second for most of them to close in before unleashing an ear-piercing scream and bursting forward again. The scouts had come so close to slicing him in half, and, forgetting their orders to maintain stealth, roared back their own cry of war. Li Kung smiled between screams. They were close to the Cicada Trail. The Red Dragons must have heard the commotion and their weapons would be drawn and ready.

The Cicada Trail was but twenty steps away. Li Kung drew in his energy to prepare for a mad burst. He could not see the Red Headbands in front of him, but he knew they were there, and he knew the Gentle Swordsmen were far in front. Ten steps. The Red Dragons intentionally traveled in the dark, and the sudden torches in the night brought every single one of them to high alert.

Five steps. The skin on the back of his neck tingled with excitement—or was it delight? He sensed the Red Headbands, startled by the screaming, preparing to bash down whatever came out of the forest. He knew that far in front, Tao Hing must also have heard. The most powerful warriors from Redwood Cliff were focusing their attentions on the anticipated ambush.

Two steps in front of the Cicada Trail, Li Kung suddenly came face to face with the Red Headbands. He smiled at them. With a harsh kick against the snow, he shot into a nearby tree, using his enormous momentum to launch up the trunk and into the bare branches above. The scouts behind him ran straight into the armed warriors. In a mad confusion, they slashed out at the Red Headbands.

Li Kung threw the flag deep into the forest and leaped across the tree branches, over the Cicada Trail, and onto the other side. Shouts of the Green Dragon scouts emerged from far within the extensive line of Red Dragons as the scouts fought. Their meager numbers and inadequate skills were completely overwhelmed. The confusion was complete. Shouts of a Green Dragon attack brought the Gentle Swordsmen spinning back, and hundreds of warriors rushed toward the center of the line.

Meanwhile, Li Kung dropped onto the other side of the trail and quietly ignited a fire. Heaps of stolen firewood, prepared just moments ago, lined the side of the road, hidden behind thin foliage; each sprinkled with the flammable green powder that burned with a roar. He flew past the wood.

A brilliant light perfectly parallel to the road emerged.

More panic was drawn.

The twelve scouts were completely outnumbered and inevitably killed. Then, a new chaos erupted in the forest. The warriors of Redwood Cliff watched a line of flames grow behind the trees, along the Cicada Trail. They shuffled into defensive positions to face the new threat.

Li Kung continued to light the firewood. He moved in a silent blur behind the dark foliage, raced to the very front of the line, and glanced at his target. Tao Hing and Fei Fei were riding the same horse, Fei Fei sitting quietly behind Tao Hing, her hands bound by thick rope, her eyes closed. She was completely motionless, her head bowed, and nothing—not even her own fate—seemed to matter. Tao Hing sat as tall as he could, quietly surveying the confusion behind him. He occasionally glanced at Fei Fei with a strange smile on his face.

He knew, Li Kung thought to himself. The old man knew that the attacks were meant for her. But he must be expecting Suthachai, because there could be no one else. The Mongolian's poison would topple him shortly, and that's why the old man was confident. He was waiting for his enemy to fall.

Li Kung broke out of the forest behind the Red Headbands and crossed the Cicada Trail completely undetected. He appeared amongst them, in the middle of their line, and screamed, "Archers! Archers behind the forest!"

The Red Headbands reacted, and more screams echoed his. "Close the distance!" Li Kung shouted. "Close the distance!"

No one really knew who shouted the orders, and no one bothered to question. With a roar, the Red Headbands bolted into the forest, their heavy cudgels shielding their faces against anticipated arrows.

"Wait!" a muffled voice called from afar. Li Kung recognized Tao Hing's voice. He didn't have much time. The old man would see through his simple plot. With a quick glance, he saw that Fei Fei was still in the same position as before. Li Kung leaped into the forest, away from the Red Headbands charging into the elusive enemy. In a moment, a new row of flames emerged behind them, on the other side of the Cicada Trail.

"Archers behind you!" Li Kung stood in the middle of

the road shouting. "Kill them before they fire! Archers on both sides!"

This exacerbated the confusion. The Gentle Swordsmen rushed diagonally into the growing flames, hoping to protect the Red Headbands from a side ambush. Li Kung again disappeared into the forest.

In seconds, the Red Dragons reached the fire. Uncertain whether to charge deeper into the forest, their paranoia enhanced by unyielding darkness, every warrior shouted his own set of warnings. Li Kung circled behind them, silently, moving to the very front of the line where Fei Fei quietly waited.

He suddenly appeared in front of the horse Fei Fei and Tao Hing were riding.

Tao Hing's back was turned. Li Kung took the opportune split second to fling green powder onto the horse's head, blasting the frightened animal into flames.

The horse reared, screaming in pain, its face temporarily on fire. It plunged into the snow to smite the flames, instantly throwing Tao Hing and Fei Fei from their mount. Li Kung drew a small knife from his belt and leaped to Fei Fei's side.

"Suthachai is waiting for you," he whispered into her ear. Her eyes widened. He slashed the ropes around her wrists, and with a harsh tug, yanked her into the forest.

• • •

Tao Hing twitched in the snow, his old bones bruised from being thrown off the horse, and for a long time, he couldn't recover. He knew that Fei Fei had escaped. A deep fear pierced his heart; he was certain now that Wei Bin would personally go after her, and the confrontation between father and daughter would be inevitable. Fei Fei would never survive.

A group of Red Headbands, their weapons drawn, their eyes wildly searching for invisible attackers, began to wrap themselves around the old man. Tao Hing's vision recovered, the initial shock having ebbed away, and he stared deep into the forest with hopes that Fei Fei would return. The rows of flame flickered without further threat, then died against the snow. Once again, they were in total darkness.

The Butcher limped forward, his injured thigh no longer seeping blood.

"Who?" he asked Tao Hing.

Tao Hing shook his head.

"The Mongolian?" the Butcher asked. "Green Dragons?"

"The men who jumped out of the forest were Green Dragon scouts," someone stepped forward to report. Angry murmurs spilled forth like rushing water.

"Green Dragons!" the Butcher growled under his breath. Cold rage welled into his eyes. He lifted his hand and made a gesture. The Gentle Swordsmen responded, falling into formation with their double-edged swords brandished by their sides.

"It was one man," Tao Hing said. "He was so incredibly fast." It could not have been the Mongolian, nor the Green Dragons. Neither possessed such speed and stealth. But whoever it was didn't carry a helpless Flute Demon away. She followed him willingly.

Tao Hing shook his head. There was no time to ponder. He had to recover Fei Fei tonight or Master Bin would believe she duplicated the sheepskin. The Red Dragon lord, afraid that the formula would fall into many hands, would start killing people to seal his secret.

"Formations!" Tao Hing shouted. "They could not have gone far. We'll pursue!"

"Where do we start?" the Butcher asked. "Back toward He Ku?"

Tao Hing thought for a second. If the person who snatched Fei Fei was not the Mongolian, she would do everything in her power to go and look for him. Maybe the road back toward He Ku would not be a bad idea.

"We'll cut across the forest to Northern Pass and go toward He Ku again."

· · ·

Li Kung breezed through the cold air with Fei Fei closely behind. They were on a smaller path, hardly ever used in the winter, which extended from Cicada Trail into Middle Pass. Sharp twigs jutted into the twisting road, and the uneven surface under the snow made the journey difficult.

Strange thoughts floated through his head. He was given a mission by the greatest legend of all time, a heroine the common people worshipped as a goddess. His mission was to annihilate the Dragon Houses and preserve Chinese civilization. Why was he protecting Wei Bin's daughter—perhaps the future successor to the evil Red Dragons—and leading her to Pun's murderer?

Stranger things have happened.

He suddenly halted without warning and spun around to face her. Barely stopping, she quickly veered to the side to avoid a collision and stepped past him.

"You're really Wei Bin's daughter?" Li Kung asked.

"I was once Wei Bin's daughter, not long ago," she replied, then quickly added, "Where is Suthachai? How much farther?"

Li Kung smiled. The first thing on her mind was Suthachai. Maybe he hadn't made a mistake after all.

"We'll find him where you fought the Red Headbands earlier." Under the moonlight, he noticed a brilliant ray of hope in her eyes, a sparkle of eagerness, despite everything.

"You move like a cat," she said. "Somehow, the shifting angles on the ground don't seem to affect you. Who are you?"

Li Kung walked closer. "If you're really the Flute Demon, you've seen me before."

Fei Fei stared. "Li Kung," she said, in wonder. "The young doctor Li Kung. You're Suthachai's friend."

"I was once Suthachai's friend, not long ago," Li Kung said, mimicking the phrase she had just used. "He's waiting for you. But before we go any further, I need to know what the old man spoke to you about when he had you and Suthachai surrounded in the forest."

"Why do you need to know that?"

"Because it's fair exchange for what I'm doing for you."

Fei Fei stalled, and gave a bitter smile. "Tao Hing was asking about a family heirloom that I stole."

"The sheepskin you gave to Suthachai today?"

Fei Fei took a step back. She bit her lip, then admitted, "Yes, a sheepskin. How did you know?"

"I saw you," Li Kung said. "Hundreds of men were sent down here to capture you. You must have stolen something important."

"It's a family heirloom," she said again. "My father wants it back."

"But the old man didn't really want this heirloom," Li Kung said. "Everyone knows Tao Hing is a wise, honorable man. Does that mean he didn't want Wei Bin to recover the sheepskin?"

Fei Fei stuttered. "Where's Suthachai?" she asked. "You told me that we will be . . . "

"I will tell you when you explain to me how lotus crystal

and sheep sorrel can be fused together with alcohol!" Li Kung took a step forward. "Is it black magic? How did your father devise a way of manipulating those herbs, which even *I* have never heard of? Explain!"

"I . . . I don't think my father devised it. He inherited the formula."

Li Kung shook his head. "Don't lie to me. You're his daughter. You're all the same. Does it please you to know that this alchemy could destroy the lives of tens of thousands? Are you proud to see your father and your uncle destroy the Martial Society and wipe out entire civilian populations just for power? Are you pleased to participate in these murders?"

His voice grew in anger, and he moved forward, menacingly, before realizing what he was doing. He had forgotten. The beautiful face in front of him belonged to the Flute Demon. He was toying with fate.

Fei Fei stared into his eyes, and strangely, a smile emerged on her face.

"Do you have the sheepskin?" she asked. "You're a doctor. If you study it, maybe you can find an antidote for the alchemy. Maybe the tens of thousands of civilian lives would not be destroyed after all."

"So the formula is on the sheepskin," Li Kung said. "Just as I suspected. But your father must have memorized the formula by now. Which means that you stole the sheepskin to create your own alchemy."

"I don't need to be judged by you!" Fei Fei shouted. "I have no intention of murdering innocent civilians. Listen, Li Kung. I believe you're a good man. After I die, there's no one else who will stop my father. Tao Hing is loyal to the Red Dragons—he has been all his life. He won't stand against his master. There's no one else."

She reached into her hair and pulled out a jade hairpin. "Take this," she said. "Take this to Old Snake and he'll know I've left my final instructions with you. Take this to him, and tell him he must help you find the antidote for the black paste. He's come close already. If he works together with you, the alchemy can be neutralized. You must believe me, because you're the only friend Suthachai has in China, and I trust you because Suthachai trusts you. You must believe me, and find an antidote for the sake of so many innocent people."

Li Kung stared. He was the only friend Suthachai had in China? A thick knot formed in his throat, and he felt the heat rise to his face. The man who murdered Pun considered him his only friend in China?

Stranger things have happened. He took the hairpin from her and turned his back to move on. He was satisfied with her answers. The path in front of him was clear. If, before he could destroy the Dragon Houses, the alchemy became widespread, he would still have the backup strategy of using an antidote to prevent drastic loss of life. He tucked the jade hairpin into his pocket.

"I'll keep my promise," he said. "We'll go to Suthachai now."

He took off, and Fei Fei ran as hard as she could to keep up. He moved even quicker than before, excited with the progress he had made, and somehow more confident with the mission that Snow Wolf had left for him. Once he reached Suthachai, he would take the sheepskin from him. He would have brought Wei Bin's daughter to the dying Mongolian, something that Pun would have wanted, and then, he would be free to leave them to their fates. Suthachai would be dead before the night was over. Li Kung smiled. The sheepskin would help him formulate the antidote, perhaps even with Old Snake's help, and he would have ample time to destroy the evil Dragon Houses.

But something continued to bother him. Fei Fei said that Suthachai considered him his only friend in China. How could that be? How could he murder Pun in cold blood and still consider him a friend?

Li Kung shook his head and glanced quickly behind him before veering into a thinner area of the forest. He heard Fei Fei's rhythmic strides, the only audible footsteps in the night, and wondered how long it would take for Tao Hing to find her again. The old man was shrewd, his foresight and sense of deceit polished by years of experience. Though armed with Snow Wolf's book of strategy, Li Kung felt inadequate.

They strode across Middle Pass at an opening free from Green Dragon scouts. They picked up their pace again and took an even smaller trail that twisted and turned against a downhill slope.

"We'll find him where Tao Hing first surrounded you," Li Kung said in a loud whisper. "Move quickly. Your father's old strategist will also think of going there."

In a moment, they broke into the wide road where, just before sunset, Tao Hing had cornered Fei Fei with the entire army of Red Dragons. The hardened snow, trampled by hundreds of footsteps, was stained by trails of blood. The remains of a few Red Headbands lay strewn in the middle of the road.

Li Kung halted abruptly, held up a hand to indicate silence. A gentle breeze lured the trees to sway calmly from side to side. Deep in the distance, Li Kung saw a figure on the snow, slowly shifting and crawling with only his hands. He was slow, barely moving at times, but not for a split second did he lay still. Suthachai had not given up yet.

He lifted his finger and pointed. Fei Fei took off, running as fast as he had ever seen her run.

"Suthachai!" he heard her call. The Flute Demon should know better than to shout in hostile terrain. Li Kung turned his head slightly, watched her fly toward the slow figure in the snow, and he swallowed hard. This was the right thing to do. This was what Pun would have wanted.

Suthachai would be dead soon, and it wouldn't matter whether he was killed, or whether he died of his own accord. The man who murdered Pun would be dead, and yet Li Kung granted the reunion of two people in love. He turned away and stared at the horrid face of a Red Headband corpse. With a sigh, he stooped down to strip the body.

"I'm good at this," he said aloud, tearing the clothing of the Red Dragon warrior. Fei Fei had already reached Suthachai, and they were locked in a deep embrace. Li Kung muttered something to himself. Strange, how the scavengers hadn't located the feast of Red Dragon carcasses yet. He moved to the next corpse, and one after the other, tore through the clothing until he had an armful of thick cloth.

It was the end of winter. The cold air and freezing winds were no longer brutal. He glanced back, noticed Fei Fei shredding a piece of her own robe to bind Suthachai's legs. If only he had the chance to bound Pun's wounds the same way. If only he had more time to halt the bleeding. Li Kung shook his head. He couldn't have saved her even if he had all the time in the world. Suthachai nearly sliced her in half. There was no chance. He moved on to the next corpse to tear the clothing.

Li Kung stood up suddenly, his body shaking. Flute Demon or not, there was time to personally slay Pun's murderer. The Mongolian was so vulnerable, if he merely distracted the Flute Demon, he would have a firm chance of vengeance. Li Kung reached for the green powder that would burn both of them alive. He had united them, as Pun would have wanted to see, and now he was free to kill them.

The Mongolian and the evil Red Dragon princess. Snow Wolf trusted him to exterminate at will.

He took a step forward, then another. He watched Fei Fei strap Suthachai's second leg before she wrapped her arms around him and lifted him to his feet. The Mongolian couldn't stand with both legs broken, but she sufficiently supported his weight so he could be dragged forward in an upright position. Li Kung moved quickly, planning the savage assault that would strike them by surprise and quickly dispatch the Flute Demon. He opened the pouch in his coat and reached for the green powder, his eyes locked on their every movement.

Fei Fei saw him approach. Instantly, she slid a hand across Suthachai's chest and into the depths of his coat. Li Kung's eyes flashed in alarm. A weapon! There was another weapon in the big coat, one that was never revealed. While he foolishly stayed behind to strip the corpses, they had plotted together to kill him. Li Kung sucked the cold air between his teeth and shot forward.

In a flash, he was in front of them, just as Fei Fei drew her hand out. He slipped to the side, about to cover them with flammable powder, when he froze. She had the sheepskin in her hand, nothing more.

"This is the sheepskin," she said, while hoisting Suthachai's heavy frame with one arm, "with the formula, and detailed instructions on how to make the alchemy." Li Kung stared. The stark sincerity in her voice left him with a strange sensation of guilt.

"You can devise something to reverse this!" she continued. "You have the Three Saints of Yunnan on your side, and Old Snake will help you. Just show him the hairpin I gave you and he'll help you."

He was speechless, motionless. She stuffed the sheepskin in his hand, then closed his fingers around it. "Please," she said. "After my father kills me, there'll be no one who will step up to the task."

Li Kung looked at the sheepskin in his hand. He wanted to ask her why she was defying her father, why she would strip such power from the Red Dragons whom she had grown up with. And most importantly, he wanted to ask her why she didn't keep the formula for herself. Could it be that even the notorious Flute Demon cared about the innocent lives threatened by this alchemy?

Suthachai coughed, and slowly, the dying Mongolian opened his eyes. Fei Fei seated him on the snow, shifting his rigid legs one after the other. Suthachai looked around him. He looked into Fei Fei's eyes, and a painful smile emerged from his face.

"Fei Fei . . . " he said, lifting a bloody hand to touch her cheek. She clasped his hand to her lips.

"Who broke your legs?" she asked, wiping the blood on his face with her fingers.

Suthachai stopped for a moment, looked at his crippled shins, and tried to move them with disbelief. "I don't know," he said. He leaned into her arms and closed his eyes. "Someone behind me. I don't know."

Li Kung stepped forward. "I broke them."

Fei Fei's eyes widened. She looked into Li Kung's face, at the cold hate in his eyes, and suddenly grimaced. She climbed to her feet, trembling with disbelief.

"You? You broke Suthachai's legs?

The young doctor nodded.

"You're his only friend in China! Why did you break his legs?"

Li Kung took a deep breath, expecting her to attack. He lifted a finger and pointed it at Suthachai. "This man, this man killed—"

Suthachai suddenly gasped. His mouth opened in surprise, and in joy.

"Li Kung," he said weakly, and reached out a hand. "Is it you, Li Kung? Where have you been?" His arm collapsed to his side, too weak to hold up much longer. He panted in deep breaths, gazed at his friend, his brows knitted with confusion. "You don't recognize me?"

Fei Fei reached down and took Suthachai's hand, squeezing it. She stood protectively in front of him, her eyes on Li Kung, with a disturbed, yet firm expression on her face. "Why?"

Suthachai gripped her hand and pulled at her. "Your father's men. They are coming. I can sense them coming. Help me stand. We will bring Li Kung to a safe place."

Fei Fei's eyes flashed. "The great doctor Li Kung can take care of himself."

Suthachai breathed heavily, his energy no longer sustaining him. He swayed like he would fall into unconsciousness any moment. "No," he said, struggling. "Li Kung . . . Li Kung does not know how to fight. We need to help him. It is . . . it is because he is alone this time and . . . " He stopped and turned in the darkness to look for someone.

"Where is Pun?" he asked.

Li Kung's face turned hot at the mention of Pun. He stepped back, his trembling lips unable to express the hate re-emerging out of nowhere, and again, he reached for the green powder. Fei Fei moved closer to Suthachai.

"Where is Pun?" Suthachai asked again. Then, his

twisted mouth dropped in horror. "Oh, no. Did something happen to her?"

"Yes," Li Kung managed to say. "Something happened to her."

Suthachai gritted his teeth. Somewhere, somehow, he found the energy from the depths of his soul, and he lurched upwards to stand on his feet.

"Who?" he roared. "Who would hurt a girl like Pun?"

Fei Fei spun around to help him. Suthachai stood on a broken leg and a streak of pain flashed across his face. With a grunt, he collapsed into her arms again. Blood dripped from his ears. He struggled in her embrace. "We will get Li Kung to safety. We will get Li Kung to safety before something happens to him too . . . " He tried to stand again.

"Suthachai." Fei Fei tried to calm him, wrapping both arms around the Mongolian.

"I do not have much time left," Suthachai said, struggling to remain on his feet. "You are safe. Help me . . . Help me see to it that Li Kung is safe before I die . . . "

Li Kung stood dazed. He was lost, the haze of hatred in his eyes rapidly yielding to a look of emptiness and pity. For a long time, he stood there, his arms hanging loosely by his side, his dark brows bent into a deep frown. He took a silent step forward with his eyes searching the horizon, as if the answers were there. Fei Fei stood defensively in front of Suthachai, the same way Pun had stood in front of him in the face of danger.

"Quickly," Li Kung said, almost in a whisper. "Take me to a safe place. Tao Hing's men will be here soon."

Suthachai faded into unconsciousness again. With a deep sigh that seemed to expel the very essence of life from his lips, the Mongolian collapsed into Fei Fei's arms.

"Can you carry him?" he asked. "All the way to Mongolia?"

Fei Fei shook her head. "He won't make it to Mongolia," she said, touching his cheeks tenderly. "We lost both our horses. We'll find a quiet place, and he'll go in peace."

"And you?"

Fei Fei tilted her head back and laughed. "Me?" She shook her head again. "Can I trust you, Li Kung? Are you really a good person?"

A long silence.

"I guess I'm not."

"My father will find me," she whispered, "and I won't last long. Whatever reason you have for breaking his legs—whatever your differences—don't let that hinder what you're going to do about the black paste. Don't let this ruin thousands of lives. Just take the sheepskin and go. No one knows you have it."

"Why do you trust me?" Li Kung asked. "How do you know I won't use it for my own benefit?"

"I don't," she said, "especially since I won't live to find out. But you refused to treat my grandmother because you didn't think she was curable, even though you were offered so much money to merely try. Maybe that really was an act of honor, and not stupidity."

Li Kung swallowed hard and nodded.

"Black Shadow also knows about the alchemy," she continued. "But his intentions are unclear. He's so unpredictable, we have no way of knowing whether he will help, or whether he's hungry for power like my father. Be careful."

Li Kung whispered a word of thanks and turned to leave. But he had taken no more than two steps when his eyes caught sight of the pile of clothing he had shredded from the corpses. He had the means to try. He turned back to look at them. She sat in the snow with her arms around Suthachai, not a weapon in hand.

"How do you intend to escape?"

She looked up. "Escape to where?"

"You said you'll find a quiet place for him to go in peace."

"Snow is everywhere," she said. Suthachai stirred in her arms. "Our fresh footprints can be followed. But if we stay here, no one will notice your footprints, and you'll be safe."

Li Kung felt a lump in his throat. Tao Hing would surround her soon, and maybe this time, they would kill her. Hundreds of men with double-edged swords and heavy cudgels would bash her into an unrecognizable pulp, just so he would have time to run.

Suthachai opened his eyes. A smile emerged on his ashen face.

Fei Fei touched his lips with her finger. "It's a beautiful night, my love. The stars are out, and the snow is soft."

"So many stars," Suthachai whispered.

Li Kung stepped forward and pressed his fingers on Suthachai's wrist, reading his pulse. "He's still strong. Maybe he can last a few more nights."

Fei Fei looked up, her eyes sparkling. "Really?"

Suthachai sat up; his head suddenly cleared. He managed to support his weight on one arm.

"Fei Fei, take Li Kung and run. I have reached the last stage of my poison and I have run out of time. You are safe. That is all I have ever prayed for. Run!"

Fei Fei held a hand over his lips to silence him. "I'm not leaving you again. We can die together, and . . . " She turned to Li Kung. "He really has a few more days to live?"

"I think so. We still have time to run. You want him to

go peacefully in your arms. You don't want him to be stabbed to death by a hundred swordsmen."

"No!" Suthachai tried to stand, and Fei Fei held him down. "No! I will hold them off. Fei Fei, take Li Kung to a safe place, and go into hiding . . . "

Li Kung picked up the pile of clothing. "Let's go. We don't have much time. Lake Infinite is completely frozen, and they'll lose your footprints from there."

"They'll cross the lake and pick up on the footprints," Fei Fei said. "Lake Infinite is small."

"I'll hold them at the lake," Li Kung said. "There are a few caves on the other side, and you can hide there. He may have a few more days of life."

"Fei Fei," Suthachai interrupted. She covered his mouth with her hand again.

"We'll go together, Suthachai. We'll both be safe." She looked at Li Kung. "And Li Kung will be safe too. The great doctor Li Kung can take care of himself." She climbed to her feet.

Li Kung turned to Suthachai, reached out his hand. "I need your brick of salt."

"Salt?" Fei Fei asked.

"Mongolians carry their salt around with them. I need it."

Suthachai reached into his coat and produced a large brick of salt, a full year's supply for most Mongolians.

"How will you hold off two hundred men, Li Kung? You have never killed anyone in your life. You are not even armed."

Li Kung sneered. He took the salt, gripped the Red Headbands' cloth under his arms, and began to walk away. Fei Fei took a deep breath, supporting the Mongolian across her shoulders, and followed.

• • •

Cricket leaned back from the edge of Redwood Cliff and wrapped his coat tighter around him. He was the son of the great Master Bin, but he felt small, weak, and vulnerable in the chilly wind. When were they going to attack? The enemy should have realized by now that the candles were fake. The smoke from the candles would obviously rise and drift to the Red Dragon warriors on the Grand Stairway, so how could the candle smoke be poisoned?

"The catapults!" Master Chen shouted from the edge of the forest. "Get the shoulder-mounted catapults! We'll hurl balls of ice into their lanterns and extinguish them!"

"Excellent idea!" someone else shouted. Cricket closed his eyes. The Green Dragons never suspected the candles to be fake. Tao Hing overestimated their intelligence.

It took no more than a few minutes before chunks of ice were torn from the ground and secured in the catapult holders. Three men hoisted the wooden devices down the main road, toward the foot of Redwood Cliff.

Cricket stared. He clenched his fists with a slight shudder. So they did come equipped to launch fireballs. With swarms of invaders making preparations below him, he could not help but feel afraid. When would Tao Hing return?

He was originally ordered to hold the Grand Stairway with the help of the Butcher and the Gentle Swordsmen. They would kill as many as they could while retreating in feigned defeat. Tao Hing would be waiting above, with the Red Headbands hidden in ambush, and when the enemy reached the center of the cliff, the Red Headbands would seal off the mouth of the stairs behind them. His father would personally lead the remaining force of Red Dragons, with his brother Dong, and annihilate the enemy. The plan was so simple—almost flawless.

But events had taken a drastic turn when Tao Hing instructed him to hold the stairs alone. The Butcher, the Gentle Swordsmen, and the Red Headbands were all sent away to pursue his sister. Cricket was suddenly thrown into the worst situation he could imagine. He scrambled to prepare himself mentally. He had never been in a real battle before. But his father didn't seem to care. The Red Dragon leader had lost all sense of reason, stopped caring about the Red Dragon House, and become obsessed with bringing his sister home.

Cricket shook his head in confusion. To make things even worse, Tao Hing took away another three hundred men in addition to the Red Dragon elite, leaving Redwood Cliff virtually empty. Most of the three hundred were junior students. They were told to wear red headbands, though none of them possessed the skill or muscular stature for which the real Red Headbands were known. But Tao Hing needed them. They were hidden in nearby forests and used as decoys.

Far below him, slabs of snow and ice were propelled from a distance, slamming into a small area at the base of the cliff. The lanterns were crushed and the candles extinguished.

There was a moment of silence. Then, the pounding of drums shook the cold air. They were attacking.

Cricket felt beads of sweat roll down his face, only to dry instantly against the biting wind. He shuddered but managed to lift his hand and direct his men. Heavy caskets, already lined across the stairs, were pushed to the edge. The lids were taken off, and they waited.

Cricket searched for signs of Tao Hing and the Red Dragon elite in the distance. Part of him didn't want the old man to come home. For Tao Hing to return so quickly would only mean one thing. Fei Fei had already been captured.

The warriors of Wei Xu's coalition began to pour in like swarms of insects. With steel bared, banners held high, and a sea of torches illuminating the night, the first wave of men charged.

At their very forefront, strong men bearing the shoulder-mounted catapults began to ignite their first round of fireballs.

"Wait!" Cricket called to his men.

They closed in and met no resistance. More excited than ever, Master Liang barked for the catapults to launch. The primitive stone catapults, devices barely capable of propelling beyond twenty paces, fired a blazing volley of flames into the air. The fireballs pounded the stairs and for a short moment burned so heavily that Cricket thought the Grand Stairway had actually caught fire. Then the flames died. Master Liang shouted at his men to ascend the stairs.

"Hold!" Cricket shouted.

The Grand Stairway was narrow compared to the open road at the base of the cliff. Wei Xu's coalition all stormed in at once. As the first wave of men moved up the stairs, the hundreds behind them crowded each other into a standstill.

"Now!" Cricket shouted.

The caskets were tipped over. White powder, in tremendous quantities, dropped down the side of the cliff. The world below them turned white. Powder rose up in plumes from the ground.

"Poison!" someone shouted. "Retreat!"

Then, there was mass confusion. Blinded and fearful of Old Snake, the warriors of the coalition turned tail and fled.

"Flour!" someone shouted. "It's only flour!"

No one heeded the call. Every man scrambled for their

lives, torches were dropped and trampled, and catapults and heavy weapons were left behind. In a moment, the base of Redwood Cliff completely emptied.

"That was the signal," Cricket said to one of his men. "When we dropped the flour, our three hundred decoys were to start marching. That was the signal."

"What will the decoys do?" someone asked.

"Hopefully, Wei Xu will be fooled and turn back to defend his *zhuang*."

• • •

Tao Hing stared at the bodies. Strange. Why were their overcoats stripped? If some peasants had done it, the fabric would have been removed carefully. Yet pieces of torn cotton and silk were scattered everywhere.

"I knew we should've brought the bodies back with us," someone growled. "The damn Green Dragons were here, and they stooped so low as to humiliate the dead!"

"So where's the Flute Demon?" the Butcher asked, his voice as cold as the biting wind. "Maybe she was the one who came and tore the clothing off her own students."

Tao Hing slowly shook his head. "They only took the outer coat, and only from some of the bodies. It seems random. Definitely random, and there was no further desecration to the bodies. Whoever did this merely needed the fabric."

The Butcher sneered, turned to his men with a debasing smile and rolled his eyes. Tao Hing ignored him and held his torch closer to the ground.

"These footprints are fresh," he said. He turned to a group of Red Headbands waiting quietly for instructions. "Where do these footprints lead?"

After a moment, a warrior stepped forward and said, "Toward Lake Infinite, sir."

Tao Hing smiled. "Yes, yes. That makes sense. The lake is frozen and they could lose their footprints there. Whoever took her was alone, but she now has the Mongolian with her. Drops of dark blood everywhere—smells toxic."

The Butcher let out a laugh. "Lose footprints in the lake? Lake Infinite is small. They must walk off the lake at some point. We have so many men—we can comb the edge of the lake. How will they hide their footprints then?"

"Alone," Tao Hing muttered to himself. He raised his voice. "It was one man who snatched Fei Fei from us. One man."

"Yes, you've said that many times already," the Butcher said, a notable tone of contempt in his voice. "And we have many men, and we will surround him, and hack him into mincemeat. Now, do we need a strategist to propose that plan?"

Tao Hing ignored him and continued to mutter to himself. "Surely, he must know we'll pick up on the exiting footprints. He was smart enough to snatch her from our hands." He shook his head and dared to imagine the impossible. "Would he try to stop all of us at the lake, alone?"

"Red Headbands!" he called. Fei Fei's old followers stepped forward for their orders. "You are to follow me to the lake for a closer look. Butcher, I need you to take the Gentle Swordsmen, circle around the hills on the south side of Lake Infinite, and try looking for them near the caves to the west. That would be an ideal place for them to hide. If you find her, you are to surround her from a distance, but do not approach her. Wait for me to arrive. We need to bring the princess home safely."

The Butcher didn't respond. With a snicker, he motioned for his men to follow.

Tao Hing shook his head. "Impulsive and arrogant," he whispered. "You're no match for the Flute Demon."

• • •

Lord Xu stood at a high elevation, watching the assault on Redwood Cliff. His Chaos Spearmen stood by his side. He would wait for Redwood Cliff to fall, wait for Wei Bin and his Red Dragon elite to return, then suffocate the mouth of the stairs so his brother would be trapped. His new coalition, by then, would control the stairs on the top of the cliff, and the Red Dragons would be imprisoned, with no way up, and no way down.

Slowly, his coalition gathered themselves at the edge of White Clay Village. They finally realized that they were assaulted with flour. Lord Xu smiled, waiting patiently. Eventually, pride would take over their dim wits. The coalition would unleash their assault so furiously that the poorly trained warriors left behind on Redwood Cliff would have no choice but to retreat.

"Master . . ."

Lord Xu nodded, his eyes on the men regrouping below him. "You may speak," he said.

"We have word that our scouts were killed on Northern Pass. Also, a large group of Red Dragons appeared out of nowhere. They wore the Red Headbands."

Lord Xu stood up. "Red Headbands? Where are they going?"

"We don't know, sir. But they seem to be marching west."

A deep frown settled on Lord Xu's face. They must have

tortured one of our scouts, he thought. They could have discovered that the Garden of Eternal Light was not protected—perhaps they decided to attack our home.

He abruptly turned to order a retreat, then hesitated. That would be impossible. How would they cross the lake without losing half their men to our archers? Then there was Black Shadow to worry about.

But the cold feeling grew inside him, and he could not relax from the nagging suspicion. He thought of the battle at his mother's funeral, where his men were clearly caught by surprise. Wei Bin was capable of great deception, and there was the old fox Tao Hing who had an endless arsenal of strategies.

The Garden of Eternal Light had always been a fortress, much like Redwood Cliff, because the Green Dragons owned every vessel on the lake. The only means to the island was by rowboat, and the few used by fishermen could barely carry four people at a time. It was impossible for anyone to bring their own boats, much less row across without being spotted and shot down.

The boats. Their transports were left along the shore of Lake Eternal, the massive lake that never froze, each of the boats tied down and idle. He never ordered the boats back to the island. They would be waiting for him there, all six of them, guarded by poorly armed men who expected his quick return. Once captured, the only form of transportation that could penetrate his island would be available to Wei Bin.

There were enough vessels to carry three hundred men across. Wei Bin must have counted on this moment to counterattack. The archers wouldn't fire into their own ships, at least not until they saw the invaders' faces. Then it would be too late.

He reeled around to order a retreat. His best warriors

were with him, and they were all capable of covering great distances in a short time.

Yet if he abandoned his position now, the invasion would never take place. He could not possibly give up this crucial opportunity. How would the new coalition submit to his leadership if he deserted them now? He gritted his teeth, flung his hand, and harshly dismissed the messenger.

His eyes roamed across the men in front of him. His Chaos Spearmen were all there, one hundred strong and eager for battle. There were about forty Thunder Broadswords—that would be plenty of men to recover the boats.

He decided. He pointed to the Thunder Broadswords, and said, "There's a chance Wei Bin may counterattack our *zhuang*. I want you to take the shortest but least traveled route and return to Lake Eternal at once. There are two groups of Red Dragons in the vicinity. Follow the path along Lake Infinite, avoid both groups, and get to our boats as quickly as possible. Move the boats back into the Garden of Eternal Light, and they will have no means of attack."

"Yes, sir!" they shouted. Forty Thunder Broadswords quickly organized themselves, stepped forward, and bowed for permission to leave. Wei Xu waived their formalities and ordered them to depart at once.

• • •

Lake Infinite was indeed small. It was much greater in length than in width, and a man could walk horizontally across in two hundred steps. Li Kung was left with little room to maneuver. If a hundred people stood in line, three rows deep, and advanced down the length of the lake, he would never break through them. He knew full well that Tao Hing had at least three hundred men.

Yet there was nothing he could do but try. The ice was thin, as expected; it was barely strong enough to tread upon and dangerous in some places. This, perhaps, was the only advantage he had. Li Kung worked quickly and made the simple preparations. He then stood in the middle of the lake with a blazing torch in hand. The flame could be seen from a great distance, and Tao Hing would have no trouble finding him.

The wind was gentle, and he was thankful for that. The dark night seemed quieter than usual, though the bitter cold of recent weeks had eased and he felt a curious warm tingle on his face. For a long time, he listened to Fei Fei's heavy footsteps as she dragged the Mongolian toward the other side of the lake. Li Kung assured them that he would have no problem escaping if he failed. He told Suthachai that he would talk Tao Hing into turning around, that the flawless speech he prepared would persuade the old man of great health hazards before him on the thin ice. After all, he was a doctor. Suthachai didn't seem convinced.

Fei Fei's footsteps faded. Li Kung knew they had reached the inviting hills on the other side. For them to survive the night, he would have to force Tao Hing to turn back. Merely stalling the three hundred warriors would do little good. Without a horse, Fei Fei and Suthachai would be stormed from behind in no time.

He looked around him, a little anxious, yet beaming with excitement for what was to come. He focused his gaze on the distant torches that slowly began to appear.

Rhythm. The key was in the rhythm. If they advanced all at once, or in segments, or in a continuous stream, he would need to sense their movements like his own pulse, and time his own reactions.

He was the hero that Snow Wolf left behind. It was this path that decided his future. Either way, he had no choice.

There was longing in his face. He thought of Pun, of his powerful family now in ruins and disgrace, of the great doctor he was meant to be, and of the warrior he unwillingly became.

The Red Headbands were in full view by the time Li Kung snapped out of his thoughts. They approached cautiously, with heavy cudgels held in front to protect against flying weapons. There really was something eerie about a single man, in the dead of night, apparently unarmed, standing in the middle of a lake without cover.

The Red Headbands lined themselves along the shore and waited, uncertain of what it all meant.

Tao Hing emerged from the back of the road, took a good look at Li Kung, then lifted his hand to command silence. Li Kung waited. He knew what Tao Hing was listening to. Small winter birds chirped in the near distance. If many men were hiding beside the lake, the birds would have disappeared.

Tao Hing ordered the Red Headbands forward.

• • •

The Gentle Swordsmen ran through the back roads, driven at an unusual pace, each straining to keep up with their commander. Out of breath, yet fearful of the Butcher's explosive temper, every swordsman struggled to ascend the sweeping hills south of Lake Infinite.

The Butcher had been silent since they parted with Tao Hing. He kept a hand on one sword at all times, agitated, a murderous glint in his eyes. He flirted with the idea of bringing his men directly to the Garden of Eternal Light. How could the senile old fool truly believe that one woman would be running away alone? How would one woman have the nerve to defy the all-powerful Red Dragons? Someone was protecting her.

He wanted to scream at Tao Hing, but somehow, almost instinctively, he suppressed his boiling rage. Was the old fool blind? Green Dragon scouts had ambushed them on the Cicada Trail, and Fei Fei subsequently disappeared. Lord Xu had, for many years, made attempts beyond reason to re-cruit their best fighters. The little quarrels that the woman had with Master Bin must have sent her directly into the arms of her uncle. The Flute Demon had switched sides. She was leading them into a trap. There was no doubt about it.

There was a light rustle, and the Butcher sprinted for-ward, his bloodthirsty eyes seeking the hateful woman who dared to run from him. There, he caught a glimpse of slight movement in the bushes. He attacked, both swords tearing out of their sheathes, a cold grin on his lips.

There was a dreadful scream of agony, followed by a flash of steel, and the Butcher leaped away with dripping blood on his sword. He was disappointed to hear the cry of a man.

The Gentle Swordsmen caught up with him, and in a flash, drew their swords and moved into battle formation. Men began to appear out of nowhere. They were perfectly hidden before the Butcher detected them, and now, slowly and almost hesitantly, they began to shift into their own battle formations.

"Green Dragon Thunder Broadswords," the Butcher said under his breath, then shouted, "The pathetic likes of you intend to hide her? Are you good enough?"

The Thunder Broadswords, in a small group of forty men ordered to take the shortest route back to Lake Eter-nal, were told that the Red Dragons would never travel on this path. Yet, as they moved swiftly and silently through the hills, a train of moving torches had approached them at high speed. They had decided to hide and avoid contact. But they didn't hide well enough.

"Where is she?" the Butcher roared. The Green Dragons shifted uneasily, eyed the threat and noticed that all one hundred Gentle Swordsmen were there.

"We're dead," one of them whispered.

Another growled: "So we die killing them."

"Where is she?" the Butcher shouted again.

"They've come to invade our *zhuang*," one broadsword user shouted, loud enough for his brothers-at-arms to hear. "Protect our House! Protect our master!"

A man darted forward, his torso already dripping with blood. Wielding his heavy broadsword, he slashed out at the Butcher. It was the Green Dragon that he had stabbed earlier. With a glinting smile, the Butcher sidestepped the injured man and ran him through a second time.

Every Green Dragon suddenly broke out of their formation and slashed at the Butcher. The Gentle Swordsmen responded, pouring in from behind. All one hundred of them, in perfect formation, lightly, very gently, jabbed and twirled their long swords and pressed the Green Dragons back. They had always prided themselves on the swordplay of gentlemen, where every graceful move was almost courteous in manner, yet deadly with precision. Outnumbered one hundred to forty, the Green Dragons began to fall.

"Kill!" one of the Thunder Broadswords yelled. "Kill the Red Dragons! Die killing them! Die killing them!"

In a mad chorus of rage and terror, the Green Dragons charged forward and plunged their bodies into bare steel. Screaming in pain, choking as death tore through them, they wrapped their arms around the Gentle Swordsmen before the swords could be pulled out of their bodies. As the first line of Green Dragons ran themselves through so the hilt of enemy swords slammed into their chests, the second wave from behind, equally suicidal, vaulted forward and stabbed their brothers through the back. The Green Dragon broadswords, buried to the hilt in their brothers' bodies, punctured deeply into the Gentle Swordsmen tangled on the other side, none of whom were able to break free from the initial embrace.

The Butcher stared at his dying men in horror. He drew both swords and slashed into the second line of Green Dragons, but was forced back. They threw their bodies at him, throats extended, their chests widely exposed to receive his sword. Never had he seen such madness. They knew they were going to die, and it was clear, in the desperate maelstrom of murder, that they would die inflicting heavy casualties.

The Butcher gritted his teeth and screamed, "Formations!"

The Gentle Swordsmen drew back to form a jagged line with alternating fronts, so that the warrior in the back could always strike from the gaps between each man in the front. The front line made small circular motions with their swords, slicing and trimming against the opponents' wrists and elbows, attempting to disarm them and clear a straight path to the throat. The second line, shifting naturally between the gaps of men directly in front, faced the opponent with their sides and only used straight thrusting movements. The Green Dragons recognized the formation and withdrew to gather themselves. There were barely twenty-five men left, but they were determined, not just to kill, but to die protecting the Garden of Eternal Light.

• • •

Slowly, the Red Headbands formed a line on the ice. Their hands were on their cudgels. There was a blatant look of contempt on their faces. There was nothing before them except one puny man with a single torch in a wide-open space that couldn't possibly hold an ambush.

Li Kung glanced at his battle formations and told himself that he had already gone over the plan at least twice. Any failure would be in his execution. The Eight Gates Formation was meant to be used by legions of crack troops, trained to move together in sophisticated combinations—to attack, to withdraw, to enclose and suffocate—all done by highly mobile armies. Now, being completely alone, Li Kung had little choice but to use the Eight Gates Formation so that the enemy, and not himself, would remain in constant motion.

The Eight Gates: Delay, Survive, Injure, Desperation, Entice, Perish, Surprise, and Fortify. Each abstract position represented a trap with a different function—to manipulate the enemy's movements, to deceive and entice.

Li Kung reached into his pocket, pulled out balls of fabric, tightly rolled and no larger than his fist, and patiently waited.

The Red Headbands stood in a towering row by the bank. The gates of Entice, really two openings that appeared invitingly harmless, stood invisible in front of them. Li Kung glanced at the small pockets of Delay, positioned so close to them, but yet unseen.

Tao Hing walked to the front of his men. "I believe you're the young hero who effortlessly snatched Fei Fei from us. Are you, perchance, a friend of hers?"

Li Kung smiled and took a step forward. He lit a roll of fabric and threw it at them. The flaming ball landed ten steps in front of Tao Hing. A pile of fabric doused in green powder burst into flames. Tao Hing took a step back, clearly noticed another two piles of fabric before him, and recognized the stripped clothing of the Red Headbands. They were ignited in the same manner.

The gate of Delay, normally formed by an intimidating legion of warriors, was now reduced to piles of burning fabric on bare ice. But they would hesitate, Li Kung said to himself. Even trained warriors were wary of what they didn't understand. There would be delay.

He took another step forward with a smile. "I'm the Immortal of Phoenix Eye Peak, descendant of the nine deities. I was born from the constellations that forged these high mountains and placid lakes. I am the source of all life. I am your lord. Bow to me! Submit, or forever perish!"

The Red Headbands turned to each other, a knowing look on their faces. This boy was either mad or plainly looking to die.

"What rubbish are you blurting, young man," Tao Hing said, loud enough so all could hear. "Don't pester us with the supernatural—cheap tricks outdated even for children. We're here for a member of our family of the Red Dragon House. If you know where she may be, we would very much like to speak with her."

Li Kung laughed, mockingly. He stood motionless and waited, watching their every twitch.

In a moment, the men began to clench their weapons and lean forward, as if already committing their weight to an attack posture. Li Kung took a deep breath. Delay had changed to Entice, and the formation transformed. He knew too well that Tao Hing could not afford to lose more time. The old man would need to send his men forward.

With many rolls of fabric held tightly in his fists, Li Kung took a few steps back, shouting, "Bow to me! Submit, or you will all die here!"

"Insolent fool!" one warrior shouted, shaking his weapon.

He's waiting for me, Li Kung said to himself. The word "entice" was different for everyone. Tao Hing was looking for an indication of fear.

The three piles of fire began to flicker and die. Li Kung ignited a roll of fabric, tossed it at a dwindling flame, but missed. It fell short, and with a few helpless flickers, extinguished itself on the ice. Then, all three piles of flames died with a slow gush of smoke.

"Boy. Was that your magic?" one warrior laughed through his teeth. At that instant, Tao Hing stared into Li Kung's startled face, lifted his bony hand, and ordered his men to attack.

Bashing weapons raised, eyes flashing fire, the Red Headbands roared straight down the middle. Li Kung focused on their rhythm, the even pace of hundreds charging through the slippery ice, their menacing figures forming two clusters, one in front of the other. There was a long strip of cloth placed diagonally in front of them, still impossible to see, yet unmistakably glittering with green powder.

In a flash, Li Kung darted across the width of the lake.

As the Red Headbands charged, a wall of flame emerged diagonally across Lake Infinite. It almost reached the height of their faces. The fire roared with such intense heat that the men were forced into the southern side of the lake, crushing into each other. The flaming wall, a gate of Fortify, was meant to slow their advance. But they were well trained, as Li Kung expected. The Red Headbands maintained their cool and circled around the fire to continue their assault.

More tricks with fire, some of them mused, noticing that none of their brothers had been harmed. Then, Li Kung ran directly toward them, into them, and almost passed them before they could swing at him. A scatter of flaming balls dropped from the young man's hand, and a thundering row of flames blew across the ice. This was the gate of Surprise. It formed an arrowhead with the gate of Fortify. Li Kung retreated deeply into the middle of the lake.

The ice was thinner along the southern side of Lake Infinite. Li Kung had planted the gate of Surprise by cracking the surface ice with a handful of salt before coating it with green powder. The intense heat collapsed the face of the lake. Many Red Headbands were thrown into the freezing water. Men fell with shouts of astonishment, their arms flailing about them. Some scrambled instantly to the solid ice nearby. Others floundered in confusion.

The gate of Surprise became the gate of Perish, which, through the enemy's desperate struggle to survive, would force the men back toward the center of the lake. They would move deeper into the length of the long oval surface, along a wide-open space that was another gate of Entice, and inevitably toward another gate of Surprise.

Red Headbands scrambled around the first wall of flames, then, as expected, into the center of the lake. Many stayed behind to help their brothers from the freezing waters. Li Kung moved like lightning, slipping through their scattered positions to ignite another wall of fire—a gate of Desperation—and instantly sealed their path of retreat. They were separated into two groups.

In a second, more ice cracked under the roar of a huge, greenish flame. A narrow strip of ice plummeted into the waters; it was nothing his assailants couldn't leap over, yet the Red Headbands instinctively moved away. The new trench of broken ice became an instant gate of Fortify.

Less than a hundred warriors were in the center of the lake. Li Kung nimbly leaped backwards and hurled a ball of blazing fabric to trigger another burst of flames. The searing heat caused the ice to crack like a never-ending chain of firecrackers. The center of the lake began to shift and buckle. The Red Headbands turned back in frenzy, but it was too late. The surface of Lake Infinite opened up from underneath them, caving them in like so many ants being swallowed whole. They scrambled, some to the aid of their brothers drowning in the frigid water, some struggling for a surface that didn't threaten to collapse. The rift in the lake expanded dangerously, growing in width and quickly shrinking the area of solid ice. More men were thrown into the water.

Li Kung moved back farther, torch in hand, and waited. There was such a state of confusion that another gate of Perish wouldn't be necessary. The Red Headbands had lost their taste for battle. They were struggling to stay alive.

"Hold it!" a voice shouted from behind. "Stand where you are!"

It was Tao Hing, slowly emerging from behind. He walked carefully along a ridge of solid ice, quietly motioning his men to haul each other from the freezing waters. Clearly, the splits in the lake were broken ahead of time, and no more ice would cave in if Li Kung didn't cause them to. The short-lived fires disappeared, leaving behind an eerie black smoke hovering over the men.

"Positions!" Tao Hing called. His thin figure reached the center of the lake where Li Kung stood in wait. Most of the men had been fished out of the water. They shook with cold and suspicion, and reluctantly moved into a broken formation.

With his heart pounding, the cold sweat on the back of his neck now turned to frost, Li Kung stood in awe at what he just accomplished. It was his first taste of true battle, and his first attempt at what Snow Wolf called "the higher form of war." He had faced two hundred men alone in wide-open terrain, armed only with time to prepare, and he had clearly defeated them. Staring at the pathetic men climbing out of the water, their robust figures panting in frustration, their glaring eyes dark with shame, Li Kung couldn't help but smile. They didn't look so tough after all.

"Who are you?" Tao Hing asked.

Li Kung saw the fear in the old man's eyes. He would have liked to kill them, every one of them, including this devious old man. It was his responsibility to do so before their alchemy destroyed the country. Yet he could do no more than frighten and humiliate them tonight. He was not trained to fight, not even strong enough to strike them without hurting himself, and he had used all of his green powder. If they gathered their courage, regrouped, and attacked again, he would have no choice but to flee.

"You'll have to turn back," Li Kung said to Tao Hing, his head held high. A calm smile passed across his lips. "Your men are in no condition for battle. Your enemies are everywhere tonight, and you have a long way home."

"Who are you?" Tao Hing repeated. Li Kung didn't answer. Tao Hing glanced at his men and lifted a hand to call their attention. "Retreat slowly," he said. "Wait for me by the rear bank. I'll speak to this young master alone."

The men acknowledged their orders and trickled away. Once they were out of earshot, Tao Hing turned to face Li Kung.

"You know how to use the Eight Gates Formation," the old man said. "Snow Wolf had no disciples, and judging from your age, your father wouldn't have been born when she died. Who are you?"

Li Kung hesitated. So the old man recognized his formation. He would need to divert Tao Hing's attention. "Don't you know, old strategist Tao Hing, that your *zhuang* is under attack, and that your defenses are inadequate? All your men are chasing one woman, and there's no one left to defend Redwood Cliff. If you don't return soon, it'll be gone."

Tao Hing took a deep breath. "If the young master does not wish to disclose his true identity, then so be it. I have no choice but to withdraw in the face of Snow Wolf's Eight Gates Formation. Thank you for sparing the lives of my men."

Li Kung nodded, his heart pounding with excitement. He forced himself to maintain composure while waiting for the old man to go.

Tao Hing stepped toward the far bank, but halted and turned around to look at Li Kung one more time. "Interesting," he said. "The last person to use the Flame Cutter in this world was Snow Wolf. Perhaps a coincidence with the Eight Gates Formation."

The old man didn't wait for a reply. He lowered his head, muttered something to himself, and walked away. The defeated Red Headbands stood waiting for him a short distance away, their cudgels hanging limply by their sides.

Li Kung lowered his torch into the ice to extinguish it. Under the cover of complete darkness, he began to move toward the western shore.

• • •

The Butcher stood tall, his sword pressed against the throat of a fallen foe. It was the last Green Dragon Thunder Broadsword, kept barely alive for questioning.

Half the Gentle Swordsmen were wiped out. So unexpected was this sudden loss that the Butcher remained stunned, silenced. The suicidal tactics used by the Green

Dragons caught them completely by surprise. Being un-prepared for an absolute battle to the death, the Gentle Swordsmen were unable to protect themselves, despite their superior numbers. Every Green Dragon that died took at least one enemy with him.

The Butcher leaned forward and pierced the throat beneath his sword point. There was nothing left to question. Carnage had befallen his men, and the damage was irreversible. The Green Dragons, the Flute Demon—they would all pay for this.

The Butcher lifted his head and roared at his men. What was left of them would follow him to the ends of the world. He would find the Flute Demon with her Green Dragon accomplices, and he would execute her.

• • •

Li Kung stood high on the side of a mountain, from a short distance away, watching the Butcher systematically regroup his men. Beyond the hills to the east, on the small roads merging into Redwood Cliff, a thousand torches were approaching the Grand Stairway. It was an invasion. It could be nothing else. Judging from the numbers, Lord Xu could not be invading alone. Perhaps the Martial Society finally decided to seek vengeance for the men they lost at Lin Cha's funeral.

The old strategist, so famous for his flawless plots of deceit, couldn't possibly stand aside and permit Redwood Cliff to fall. Somehow, Tao Hing would have a plan.

The Butcher was leading his men west. They were heading for the caves behind Lake Infinite, where Fei Fei and Suthachai were concealing themselves.

But what if Tao Hing made a mistake? What if Wei

Bin's obsession with the black paste left the old man with no choice but to put the cliff in danger? Li Kung paused, and turned to stare at the distant lights. Redwood Cliff may fall. Was it likely?

Who would destroy the Green Dragons if the Red Dragons were eliminated? Who would demolish the Red Dragons if the Green Dragons fell?

The Red Dragons must survive for now, or Lord Xu and his new coalition could become too powerful to destroy. Similarly, if Tao Hing prepared a trap on Redwood Cliff, the Green Dragons would perish, and Wei Bin would dominate the Martial Society. The invasion must be stopped. Either outcome would neutralize his chance of eliminating the Dragon Houses.

The Green Dragon Thunder Broadswords had been secretly headed for Lake Eternal. They had hidden—it was evident—and they were discovered by accident, then subsequently slaughtered. Why would Lord Xu send his Thunder Broadswords back to their *zhuang*, when a full-fledged invasion was being carried out at Redwood Cliff?

There was no other explanation. Wei Xu was a deeply suspicious man. He must have feared a counterattack on the Garden of Eternal Light.

The Butcher and his men had all departed. Li Kung traveled briskly to the remains of the Thunder Broadswords. Once again, he looked into the horrid faces of death. Most of them had died with eyes staring and ghastly mouths gaping open.

He reached for the body least stained with blood and knelt down to strip it. A cold sneer parted his lips. Stripping a corpse seemed like a regular task for him now. How many did he strip in Snow Wolf's tunnels?

Shortly afterwards, disguised in the bloody clothing

of a Thunder Broadsword warrior, Li Kung pretended to be wounded and stumbled into a handful of Green Dragon scouts.

"Red Dragons!" he shouted. "They're invading! They're invading us! Warn Master Xu! Hurry! They've killed . . . They've killed most of us!"

• • •

At the foot of Redwood Cliff, the coalition warriors marched toward the Grand Stairway one final time. The shoulder-mounted catapults were lined in front of them, preparing to charge, when gongs of retreat were sounded.

Cricket had taken his men back to the surface of Redwood Cliff, hid them inside the pine forest, and waited. Once the invasion truly began, his father would have other plans to fight the enemy.

His brother Dong was ordered to wait in ambush with a small group of archers. Cricket began to worry for his quick-tempered brother, who, like himself, had limited talent in combat. Only their sister possessed unusual fighting ability. Their father had no choice but to train her as a warrior. If only she were there to command the men, and he to fight by her side . . .

Then, he too heard the gongs of retreat. He motioned for a scout to investigate. In a moment, the scout returned, his face flushed with excitement.

"Master Cricket! The invaders are retreating!"

"Really? Why?"

"I don't know, sir. But Lord Xu's men suddenly withdrew. They sounded their gongs."

Cricket didn't know what to say. His uncle abandoned the invasion? What had changed his mind?

• • •

"Go . . ." Suthachai said, trying to sit. He reached around Fei Fei's shoulder with great effort.

She held a finger to his lips.

He shook his head. "Go. Save yourself . . ."

She covered his mouth with her hand and glanced at the distant torches. There must be something in the cave she could use as a weapon.

After separating from Li Kung, they had hidden in a secluded cave west of Lake Infinite. It was small, barely deep enough to conceal them, but it was the closest one she could find. She leaned Suthachai against a boulder to rest, then left him to search for wood splints. She needed to strap his two broken legs.

Then, an incredible sight caught her eye. She stood on the side of a hill and her mouth opened in awe as she watched a single man fight back two hundred on a lake.

But the Butcher and the Gentle Swordsmen were nowhere in sight. The men Li Kung confronted were clearly the Red Headbands. When a number of torches approached along the southern hills, Fei Fei realized that the Butcher had been permitted to pursue separately. She should've known. Tao Hing would've taken nothing for granted.

She returned to Suthachai as quickly as she could. There was little time to bind the broken legs, but she couldn't carry him much longer. The thick wood strapped around his legs would enable him to remain on his feet. She would support most of his weight, and hopefully, they could evade the Butcher.

Fei Fei had no real plan of escape. If she continued to the top of the hill, she would have nowhere to go except down to the fields below. She would then be in wide-open space, and the Butcher would see her. The Gentle Swordsmen would surround her.

She could try hiding in a deeper cave, but the risk was high. Maybe none of the caves had more than one opening. If the Butcher was smart enough to use smoke at the mouth of every cave, they would be forced to crawl their way out.

She wrapped the thick wood around Suthachai's legs, her eyes focused on the approaching lights. They were moving quickly, as if in a full run. The Butcher was desperate to find her, in a frenzy even, and he would comb every cave to ensure her capture.

"We need to hide," she said. "The Butcher's impatient. He'll divide his men to search the caves. We're in a smaller cave, so fewer men will come here. We need to hide long enough to strike with surprise. That'll give us a little time to flee."

"Go," Suthachai said again. "I will die anyway. You can escape if you go alone. I will hold them off."

Fei Fei didn't respond. She hoisted him to his feet, picked up a large rock the size of her palm, slung an arm around his back, and drew him behind a boulder. His massive frame was barely hidden, his stiff legs unable to bend or hide from view. She knew they would soon be discovered.

She seated herself at an angle and maintained a close watch of the approaching lights. They waited, tensely at first, but as she thought of the moment when death would eventually take her, she closed her eyes and calmed. They would go together, Suthachai alongside her. Perhaps, in her lover's arms, she would feel the blade of the Butcher's sword shredding her belly open. But the pain would be drowned out by the warmth of the moment, and it would be all right.

She opened her eyes. The approach of lights was beginning to slow. The Gentle Swordsmen had reached the cluster of caves on their side of the hill, and the search had begun. She placed the heavy rock closer to herself, and waited.

"Fei Fei," Suthachai whispered, delirious.

She took his hand and held it to her face. "Yes, Suthachai?"

"They are coming for us?"

"Yes," she said, moving closer to him. "Are you ready?"

Suthachai smiled and shook his head. "How can I be ready? I am in no condition to fight. I do not have the strength to kill an ordinary man anymore."

She paused, a strange feeling of helplessness in her heart. She turned away. She really was alone in this world—alone to confront and betray her father, alone to face some of the greatest warriors of the land while armed with only a rock. A sneer emerged on her lips. "I never thought I would hear the number one warrior of the steppe say something like that," she said in one breath. There was a tone of anger in her voice, perhaps even disappointment.

Suthachai reached out with his other hand to touch her cheek.

"I'm not angry with you," she quickly said. "It's just that . . . "

"Just that our situation is desperate," he whispered, completing the thoughts she refused to admit.

She nodded, swallowing hard.

"Do you hate them?"

She opened her mouth, but for a second, couldn't respond. "Hate? Hate whom?"

Suthachai turned and glanced at the men in the distance. She understood.

"I—I don't know. I don't know."

"Maybe, if I truly hated them," he continued, "I would stand on these two broken legs and cut them down one by one. Maybe . . . " He gasped for air, his voice fading, but a strange look of comfort filled his face. "Maybe, if I was not poisoned, and I did not come to China, I would die, years from now. Years from now, I would lie in bed waiting to die of old age, peacefully, but I never would have met you. My life would have gone by in a short sixty or seventy years . . . but I would never have known . . . "

He paused and took several heaving breaths. He reached into the depths of his coat and drew out an old book. "My grandfather's diary," he said weakly. "I will read the last page to you." His hands shaking profusely, Suthachai flipped open the wrinkled pages and angled it toward the moonlight.

Outside, the torches of the Gentle Swordsmen moved closer, but Fei Fei disregarded them, and closed her eyes to listen. "So many years have passed," Suthachai began to read. "Yet, each day, I thought of her, and how she died at the peak of her youth and beauty. Each day, I pondered the same questions. What if I had died with her that day, so many decades ago? What if I knew then that my miserable life would drag on for so many more years, with only her memory to comfort me each night? Were these extra years of life worthwhile for me? These questions, I can no longer answer. When the gods above take me, I will search for her in the afterlife, and she may answer for me, if I find her. She will tell me why I bothered with these years of suffering."

Suthachai closed the book. The sounds of many footsteps drew closer. "I chose to come here," he said. "As the Elder said, I may not find life by coming here, but maybe I will find something better. I consider myself so fortunate. There is no one left for me to hate."

Fei Fei sighed. She looked at the shadowy figures of two men approaching their cave, and her fingers closed around the heavy rock. She paused.

"Go," Suthachai said. "I will die knowing that something so beautiful has happened to my life, and death will be good to me. Do not feel bad about leaving me behind. I have fulfilled my destiny. Go."

"But I can't," she said, her voice tightening, a tear rolling down her cheek. She firmly picked up the stone. "How can I continue to live on with my miserable life? I'll ask the same question each night. Will these extra years of life be worthwhile for me? These extra years without you?"

She leaped to her feet, springing with such force that she threw herself over the boulder. Desperately, she flung the rock at the Gentle Swordsman by the mouth of the cave. The heavy missile pummeled his face, snapped his head back, and instantly broke his neck. Fei Fei shot forward, reached his falling body and yanked the sword from his hip. The sound of vibrating metal resonated across the air. The other Gentle Swordsman opened his mouth to shout. His hand barely touched his sword before she sliced him across his mouth, almost splitting his face in two. A short gurgle escaped his lips before her returning blade decapitated him. But the damage was done. Shouts could be heard across the hill in response to the scream she couldn't prevent.

"Please," she said, rushing to Suthachai. "We need to run."

"We?"

"Both of us," she said, tears welling to her eyes. "As your friend, I would never leave you behind in battle. As your wife . . . I would rather die with you."

She didn't wait for him to respond, but felt no resistance when she grabbed his arm and pulled. She supported much of his weight across her shoulders and began to run. Suthachai gritted his teeth and flinched with every step. But he never made a sound.

The air was even colder outside the cave, and the slight hint of dawn announced itself on the horizon. It was a great distance to the top of the hill. The world around them was barren, covered with thick snow and empty of tall shadows to hide under. The shouts behind them came across in pockets of high-pitched sounds—like bad flute music, Fei Fei thought to herself. She struggled to focus her energy, picking up pace with each deep breath. The Gentle Swordsmen were driven to cut her down, and they might attack her from behind. She had to run harder.

With a crash, Suthachai collapsed. One of the wooden supports cracked underneath his weight, and the splintered bone in his leg gave way. Fei Fei heaved forward, supporting all his weight with a single arm, and reached around to prevent him from falling.

The sudden agony re-ignited the poison in his veins. He spat a mouthful of thick blood and struggled to stand.

Fei Fei watched the Gentle Swordsmen gathering from behind. Their swords were drawn, their courteous refinement cleanly forgotten. Vile slurs escaped their lips in a desperate display of courage. She leaned into Suthachai's body, received his entire weight across her back, and began to run. The top of the hill was well within view, but there was nowhere to go from there. Maybe it would then be time to die.

The Gentle Swordsmen began to catch up to her, closing the gap but never daring to move into striking distance. The edge of the hill loomed closer. The weapon in her hand felt alive, like in so many previous battles, yet nothing equaled the sensation that she felt now. She would die at the edge of this hill, without doubt, and she would die in the arms of the man she loved. But beyond that, she would face the Butcher and his Gentle Swordsmen, all feared across the land, all undefeated warriors.

The sound of bare steel whistled behind her. She was beyond pain or pleasure, comfort or anguish. She spun around, her blade locked into the sword handle of a swordsman, and, using a quick twisting motion, she flung his sword to the ground before tearing her own blade into his gut. The dying man shrieked in pain. She wrenched once, then twice with her sword, withdrawing just in time to evade a slew of attacks. Many more had caught up with her. She turned again and ran. The Gentle Swordsmen trailed closely at her heels.

The hill was not steep, but to descend with Suthachai on her shoulders would be impossible. It emerged before her, menacing, its gaping edge almost inviting her to jump. It warned her with a jeering smile that, rather than falling under the Butcher's sword, death would be more pleasant if they leaped to the bottom. Fei Fei eyed the edge, for a moment pondering whether to die falling in Suthachai's embrace. But she stopped. She would fight for the very last possible chance.

She halted before the edge of the hill, and turned to face her enemies. The Gentle Swordsmen gathered in a circle, their swords drawn. They eyed her suspiciously, cautiously, fearing that the Flute Demon really moved faster than a man could blink. Behind them, a slow moving figure, exceptionally tall but walking with a limp, pushed his way forward.

"The Butcher," Fei Fei whispered. No more than fifty men stood in front of her. Somehow, only half the Gentle Swordsmen were there.

She lowered Suthachai from her back and rested him in the snow. Her eyes were fixed on the tall warrior. This was the end. She had one more chance.

"Butcher," Fei Fei said, firmly but gently. "You won. You know I can't beat you."

The Butcher smiled, the fake canine protruding from his mouth. "I'm glad you know."

"I'm asking for mercy, Butcher." She took a deep breath. "Since we did fight side by side in so many battles, and since we both served the Red Dragons for so many years."

The Butcher's smile faded.

"Please," Fei Fei said, her voice heightened in pitch. "I give you my word. I'll come back to Redwood Cliff in three days. Three days is all I ask, so I can be by my husband's side during his final hours." Fei Fei felt her cheeks flush, but she lowered her eyes and continued to plead. "That's all I ask from you. Leave us in peace now, for three days, and I'll return to face my father on Redwood Cliff."

The Butcher stopped for a moment. The startled look on his face twisted in triumph and glee. Suddenly, he couldn't contain himself. He lifted his face to the heavens and broke into roaring laughter. Fei Fei looked up in despair, gripped Suthachai's trembling hands, and stared. The Gentle Swordsmen also began to laugh. The entire hill instantly resonated with hideous jeering.

"Drop your sword and kneel before me, woman," the Butcher shouted. "You and your pathetic husband. Kneel before me and beg for mercy, and I may consider your plea."

Suthachai clawed the snow, his nails digging into the frozen soil. He trembled, racking in spasms and oozing blood.

"This is your only chance, Flute Demon!" the Butcher shouted. "Kneel before me, and I'll let you live! Must I also demand that you spend the night with me?"

The Gentle Swordsmen roared. The Butcher clutched his belly and doubled over. A tear rolled down Fei Fei's cheeks—the rage, the humiliation—all her years of fame and glory passed before her eyes as the Butcher mocked her as a woman and not as an equal at arms. She felt Suthachai's heavy shaking by her knees, and she reached down and took his hand.

Suthachai calmed. A slight smile appeared on his lips. The blank gaze in his eyes grew weary, disinterested, as if the phenomenon of an approaching sunrise was more fascinating to him. Slowly, he reached out and pulled Fei Fei's hand away from his.

"Release me, Fei Fei. So that I may release you."

She turned to him. His gaze burned into her heart, touched her very soul, and told her, almost magically, that everything was at peace. She felt weak, tired, unwilling to break from the eyes that enclosed her with so much comfort. She fell to her knees, wrapped her arms around him and touched her forehead to his.

A blast of thundering laughter shook the air when her knees touched the ground.

"I love you," Suthachai whispered. He jerked away from her, planted his hands into the snow and threw himself back. Fei Fei's eyes widened with horror. She felt the urge to reach out and grab him, but somehow she knew it was too late. He flipped cleanly over the edge without a sound and plunged headfirst down the side of the hill.

She felt her heart stop, felt the air in her lungs sealed in by her constricted throat threatening to explode against her ribcage. She remained frozen, her eyes wide, burning, but she couldn't move, couldn't speak.

It was over, then. The long struggle, so treacherous at every step, toward a goal she was so certain of, had finally come to an end. The short-lived dream—the heavenly joy of being loved—at last came to its anticipated conclusion. She never realized that it would leave her so empty, so cold. He was gone. With the poison in his body, he couldn't have survived the fall. He was gone.

The men in front of her fell quiet, becoming deafly silent. A deep, murderous glint grew in her eyes. Her fingers were planted into the snow, her hair matted with sweat and tears, her lips parted, like a beast preparing to pounce on its prey.

Then, she broke into a slow, strange laugh. The Gentle Swordsmen stepped back, suddenly reminded that the beautiful woman kneeling on the snow was actually the Flute Demon. The venomous flash in her eyes pierced their courage. They took another step back.

Fei Fei rose to her feet. "Suthachai asked me earlier. He asked me whether I hated you or not. I told him that I didn't know. Why would I hate you? Would a lion hate the helpless animal it hunts?" Then she smiled. "But I'm not a lion. Lions kill for food. I kill for entertainment."

She lifted the double-edged sword and pointed at the Butcher. "And I will have fun tonight!"

She charged, her lips drawn back, her sword flashing. The line of swordsmen moved quickly to face her. She avoided the Butcher, veered diagonally along their lines to attack the edge of their formation. Sparks flew as steel collided. Fei Fei pummeled deep into their lines, through them and past them. The swordsmen rushed in to enclose her. She withdrew at an angle and forced them to lose their formation before moving in to kill.

Warriors fell. Blood flowed. The dull thud of damaged swords striking bodies and the hollow scream of dying men mingled into one draining rhythm.

In a moment, someone slashed her across the waist. She screamed and pounded her damaged blade into his gut. With a twist, she tore the sword across his abdomen. She wielded the sword with both hands, attacking in a hail of blows. Sparks flew in every direction. The carnage became increasingly savage, the slaughter increasingly hellish. No longer concerned with life or death, no longer aware of pain or pleasure, the Flute Demon slaughtered for the pure joy of sinking bare steel into human flesh.

He was gone. He didn't wait for her. He was gone.

Her blade was buried in someone's ribs when she was stabbed in the side. She shrieked in pain, wrenched the sword free. Blood spewed from her waist. The deep cuts covering her body had stained her robe into a blackened red. She was so drained and spent from murdering that she could barely catch her breath.

Fei Fei launched herself into the desperate warriors. Whirling her battered sword, lunging at every opening she could find, the Flute Demon tore through them again and again. The massacre was devastating. Across the hilltop, the dead and the dying lay strewn across the snow. The warriors who thought themselves invincible suddenly came face to face with extermination.

The Butcher appeared out of nowhere and ran his sword deep into her stomach. As each inch of blade tore through her flesh, she thought of Suthachai, of joining him at the bottom of the hill. She grabbed the naked blade embedded in her belly, and with a snap, broke the blade in half. She twisted around, bearing the pain with clenched teeth, and slashed him diagonally across his face.

The Butcher instantly lost one of his eyes. He clutched his face, shrieking in pain, and damned her with every obscene word he could find.

The world was spinning. She could barely see. The screams of dying men seemed faint, muffled by cries of pain inside her soul. Was it physical pain? Was the torment of watching Suthachai's death so impossible to endure that she could no longer feel the blade embedded in her body?

She felt the agony of approaching death in the marrow

of her bones, but something told her that death, like everything else, must appear when it chose to. Perhaps Suthachai
had told her so. Perhaps Suthachai wanted her to fulfill her
destiny before joining him, just as he fulfilled his.

With a roar, the Flute Demon pounded her sword into
the Butcher's approaching blade. She was suddenly able to
see clearly. She launched herself at his knees and tackled
him to the snow. The Butcher tried to stab her, but she embraced him firmly, like she had seen Suthachai embrace his
enemies in battle. His long sword was useless at close range.
With both arms pinned against his, the Flute Demon tore
into his neck with bared teeth. The Butcher howled.

Someone stabbed her from behind, bringing a new sensation of anguish into her body. Someone had survived. She
disregarded the pain and ripped at the Butcher's neck with
her teeth. Then, as he fumbled in agony and confusion, she
brought her sword around and stabbed him in the throat.

The Butcher gurgled like a child, choking in whatever
vile words he could muster before taking his final breath.
He dropped his arms and lay still with eyes wide and jaws
gaping open.

Her strength was gone, and so was the blood in her
body. She didn't know how she managed to slay her assailant. But somehow, she found herself lying on her side, staring at the dead men in front of her, her own wounds steadily
trickling with blood. Not a single body moved on the hilltop.
She had killed them all.

Suthachai would be waiting for her in the afterlife, she
thought. If she could only be with him, if she could hold
his body in her arms and pass her last breath by his side.
Fei Fei fought to maintain consciousness. She reached out
with both hands and began to crawl to the edge of the hill.
Suthachai would be waiting for her at the bottom. Perhaps

he hadn't gone yet, but remained conscious to wait for her, so they could go together.

The heat from her blood began to melt the snow around her. She would lose consciousness any second. The edge of the hill was close, but she would never make it. As the darkness settled over her eyes and the silence consumed her ears, Fei Fei made one last attempt to throw herself over the edge, but failed. Her limp body quietly gave in, and she lay motionless.

The sun began its rise into another bright, beautiful day.

PROPHECY SEVEN

Faceless heroes, pathetic kings,
Ignorant of collapsing mountains,
Weapons sharpened, shields positioned—
The fattened pigs await slaughter

• • •

The trickle of hot tea muffled the sound of approaching footsteps. Li Kung sat by himself at the pagoda, a fire in the old cauldron already blazing beside him. He didn't notice Old One ascending the steps to his morning chess game until the unkempt white hair came into view.

Old One smiled. Li Kung offered him a cup of overflowing tea.

"They say that a cup must be emptied in order for it to be filled," Old One said with a chuckle. "This one is already filled to the brim."

"But you also said that a cup must be filled before it can be emptied," Li Kung replied. "So now that it has already been filled, you need to drink it, so I can fill it for you again."

They laughed. Old One looked happily into the young man's eyes, as if nothing in the world troubled him. "You've been away for a long time, my boy. Have you found what you were looking for?"

"I . . . " Li Kung paused with uncertainty. "No," he said

with firm resolve, a tear almost welling in his eyes. "I didn't look for anything, but trouble came looking for me. And Pun . . ."

Old One lowered his cup of tea and patted his student's hand. "Sadness is a natural emotion. If you need to weep, there is no need to hold back. Weeping for someone you love is not a sign of cowardice."

Li Kung clenched his jaws. He couldn't permit his tears to flow. He had to be strong. So much depended on it. "Shifu One?"

"Yes, my boy."

"If there's something that I must do, something important . . ."

"You have my permission to leave. Go do what you think is right. And Shifu Two and Shifu Three will also approve. I'm sure of it."

"I . . . " Li Kung couldn't find the words. He always trusted his mentors, no matter how strange they seemed. But was it wise to tell his plans to Shifu One?

Old One stroked his long beard and reached for the teapot. "Too much on your mind, Li Kung. You're trying to save the world again."

Li Kung opened his mouth to say something, but Old One was not paying attention. He gulped down his tea, spilled half of it on his beard, then said with a laugh, "I haven't cleaned this beard in weeks. What do you know? A tea washing."

He looked at his student and almost playfully waved his bony hand in front of Li Kung's eyes.

"Interesting," he said. "You have a strange energy about you, almost like a type of presence. Haven't seen you in two months and you've developed a powerful inner strength. One would almost mistake you to be a martial arts master, if they didn't know you better. Tell me, did Shifu Two test a new energy booster on you, or have you just been sleeping better?"

He laughed to himself, as if he had trapped Li Kung with a bad joke, and rubbed his belly a couple of times. "I'm an old man. A very ordinary old man. When I was a not-so-ordinary young man, I had to sleep with a weapon beside my bed. Now I eat, I sleep, and I go use the toilet. When my belly's full, I'm happy. When I wake up to sunrise after a good night's sleep, I'm also happy. When I use the toilet, I relieve a lot of pressure from my body. There's so much satisfaction that each time I pull my pants back up, I wonder: why did I bother to be a not-so-ordinary man when I can have all this now?"

Then, without waiting for him to answer, Shifu One said with a laugh: "Speaking of Shifu Two, I heard he devised the antidote you were looking for. Your Shifu Two works very hard, as silly as he may be. He's never short of solutions. You should go and see him as soon as possible."

Li Kung nodded, somewhat relieved, and turned around to leave. Old Huang, Shifu One's chess companion, suddenly appeared out of nowhere and almost collided with him. Li Kung slipped around easily, bowed to his mentor's chess companion, and proceeded down the steps.

"Ah, the Flame Cutter," Old Huang said with a laugh. "I haven't seen that in about fifty years. It's a beautiful day for a little nostalgia."

Li Kung paused, spun around to stare, but Huang had already turned his back to set up the chess pieces. Old One was busy pouring hot water into the teapot, and neither of them paid attention to him. With a sigh, Li Kung ran down the steps.

● ● ●

On his way home, Li Kung thought back on what he had seen of that morning's sunrise. He thought of the golden rays that forked through the snowy hills; bringing warmth to all, perhaps even to the dead. When the first beams of light peeked over the horizon, he had paused to smell the foul stench in the air. They came from the dead bodies on a hilltop. He knew who they were, and he couldn't bear to look.

There had been over fifty bodies, with bloodstains seeping through the snow. They had all died violent deaths. One body, dressed in a feminine blue robe, lay face down at the edge of the hill. Her left arm extended over the ledge, dangling lifelessly in the air. She had been crawling to the steep drop to throw herself over.

Eventually, Li Kung couldn't contain himself, and he remembered turning to stare at the bodies. He couldn't decide what to feel, or what he was thinking. There was no sign of Suthachai's body at the bottom of the hill.

Shortly afterwards, he proceeded toward his three mentors' house. As he came closer to home, he began to feel better.

The door was closed. Li Kung easily scaled the cement wall, flipped over the tiled roof, and dropped into the little courtyard.

Shifu Two sat in a small room adjacent to the main chamber, his back hunched over a stone bowl, his arms rapidly stirring a pungent black mixture. He didn't notice Li Kung until a warm hand enclosed the stirring pole and playfully resisted his progress. Shifu Two looked up, his eyes wildly happy. But then, in the brief moment that his aging eyes focused behind Li Kung seeking another person, the cheerful look on the young man's face faded. Old Two leaped past Li Kung, bolted through the doorway with a dirty spoon in his hand, and resumed a fighting stance both awkward and hilarious. "Pun!" the old man called.

The room behind Li Kung was empty. Old Two's smile faded. He glanced about, but something in Li Kung's eyes brought a deep shadow to his brows. He walked up to his student, the dirty spoon pointed in front, and asked, "Where is she?"

Li Kung fell to his knees. "She . . . she's dead."

Old Two, his mouth gaping open, also fell to his knees. Tears flowed freely from his eyes. He held his face and wept. With loud, broken wails escaping his ancient lips, his old body huddled in a ball like a child, Old Two pounded his own head with his fists. It seemed endless.

Moments later, Shifu Three also emerged, quickly realized that Pun had died, and also fell to his knees to weep. For the longest time, two of the Three Saints of Yunnan mourned for the girl who played jokes on them, who sang to them when they were bored, who found humor in their ridiculous lives.

Li Kung crawled back to a wall, sulking in his own misery. He waited. They would demand a reason for her death and an answer to why she wasn't avenged.

Much later, Shifu Two and Shifu Three climbed to their feet, wiping their tears, and reached out to help him. Li Kung took their hands, his own eyes trembling with anxiety. They pulled him to an awkward standing position.

"Li Kung, my boy," said Shifu Three. "You must have sought vengeance for her death."

Li Kung's heart stopped. His lips trembled slightly, as if he wanted to say something, but only a light, incoherent whisper emerged.

"I've fought every great fighter I could possibly challenge," said Shifu Three. "But always just for fun. Never for revenge. Because if you hate a man for killing, why would you want to become like him? Why would you perform the same act that you hate him for?"

Old Two stepped forward and took his hand. "Li Kung, my boy. I've healed almost every illness I've ever encountered. But never once have I healed someone who was already dead. Every human being must die. If a man takes action to interfere, then another man will try to interfere with his actions, and there will never be peace in life."

"I—" Li Kung tried to find the words. Then, almost magically, he blurted out in a high-pitched voice, "I did what she would've wanted me to do. I did what I thought would be most respectful to her spirit. I . . . I did not . . . "

Shifu Two reached out and stroked the filthy hair on the side of his head. "Let's not think of this now. What's happened has already happened. Come, I have good news for you."

"You're not going to question me about how she died?"

"Of course not!" Shifu Three said with a grin, his red face still stained with dried tears. "Everyone must die. Soon, the two of us will die, and we forbid you to cut us open to find out how."

"Of course," Shifu Two said gently, "we need to first apologize for your troubles—and we need to apologize properly before we die."

"Troubles?"

"You *are* going to bury us, aren't you?"

Li Kung stood with his mouth open. "Of course I will. I don't mean to say . . . "

Shifu Three laughed. "So what don't you understand? You will need to dig through layers and layers of earth before throwing our bodies in, and it's extra work for you, so we apologize for the troubles."

"Oh."

Shifu Two chuckled. "You do know how to shovel the earth don't you? I really need to ask sometime before I die, just so I'd know."

"I've become very experienced with digging the earth lately," Li Kung stammered.

"Good. Good. Come, I have good news and bad news for you."

Old Two dragged him back into the little room where he was mixing his herbs. Old Three followed for a second, then, holding his nose, quickly retreated.

"Li Kung, remember the antidote that you asked me to find? The one for a poisoned Mongolian?"

"Yes?"

"I found the antidote to his poison. It was so simple! Mere scorpion poison—large quantities of it. The two poisons neutralized each other!"

A brief smile flashed across Li Kung's face. "Really? So you've created a pill for it?"

Old Two shook his head. "Of course not. Why bother?"

"Why bother?"

"My boy, how many times do I have to tell you? Dead people have no use for antidotes. You can't revive the dead."

"How . . . how did you know that he was dead?" Li Kung said, his voice trembling.

"I didn't know. Like most things in medicine, it was a matter of speculation. But the moment I thought that he had died, I felt such relief, as though I didn't have the responsibility of curing him anymore and every bit of research that I do would be just for fun. Just for fun! Now that is how research should be conducted."

He paused and watched Li Kung's face with amusement. "Don't—" Old Two said with hand raised, "don't tell me now that he's still alive. I released my entire collection of scorpions already."

"Huh?"

"Yes! Certainly, the scorpions have a right to their freedom. I went out early this morning and released them. They helped me solve a most interesting mystery. I know how to cure this poison now. So I thanked them properly for their help, and I released them."

Li Kung spun around and bolted out of the room. He disappeared in a flash.

"Silly boy," Old Two grumbled. "When did he learn to run that fast?"

• • •

Li Kung charged across the shoreline of Lake Infinite, picking up speed on a steady downhill. The frozen lake reminded him of the night before, where, with the precise placement of broken ice, he forced two hundred warriors to retreat. Just west of the lake, sweeping hills enclosed Middle Pass. Middle Pass was known to many as Bandit's Lane, but he crossed without bothering to watch for bandits. He would be visiting them soon.

He slowed to a walk and approached the hilltop where the Gentle Swordsmen were executed. The memory of so many corpses—once men of incredible skill, now mutilated and splattered across the snow—suddenly ran a chill down his back. He wanted to look away.

"Li Kung, you idiot!" he nearly said out loud. He forced his eyes toward the field of mangled bodies. He cursed himself again and repeated over and over in his mind that he needed to be strong, or he would never be able to destroy the Dragon Houses. There would be more moments like this. Many more. It was his responsibility to ensure that there would be many more.

A slight movement in the distance caught his eye. He quickly lowered himself on the side of the hill and ran across for a closer look. A strangely dressed old man, already a great distance away, was wheeling a hay cart through the snow. A harness was strapped across his shoulders, which was tied to a large, feathery surface being dragged behind him. It effectively smoothed the wheel tracks made by his cart. Li Kung ran, eager to catch up to him. He was certain who the old man was.

"Old Snake!" he shouted, closing in from behind. "We need to talk!"

In a flash, he was beside the old poison user. Old Snake reached into his robes, instinctively grabbed his only weapon—a small dagger. Li Kung leaped in front of the hay cart and planted his foot against the wheel.

"Wait!" Li Kung said. He held a jade hairpin in his hand.

There was a coffin on the hay cart. Li Kung noticed its lid was not nailed into place.

"Why a coffin?" Li Kung asked.

"Who are you?"

Li Kung handed him the hairpin. "She gave me this. She said you'll help me when you see this."

"Who?" Old Snake asked, his eyebrows knitted, his eyes narrowed. "Who gave you this?"

Li Kung gazed at the coffin, and for a moment, feeling Old Snake's pain, could not find his words. The poison user came well prepared to collect her body. She had planned on dying with Suthachai, and even Old Snake knew it.

"She did," Li Kung finally said.

Old Snake took a step back, looked once at the coffin,

then at him. "Are you," he asked nervously, "a friend of hers?"

Li Kung shook his head. "I'm not her friend. Nor am I her enemy. That's why she trusted me."

He reached into his pocket and drew out the sheepskin, held it out long enough for Old Snake's expression to change, then pushed it back into his own pocket.

"Where did you get that?"

"She gave it to me."

"She stole it," Old Snake said. His voice was still shaken. "Who are you, young hero?"

"She told me you'll help me when you see the hairpin. Is that true?"

Old Snake pondered for a second. Tears welled into his swollen eyes. "Yes. If it's her wish, then I'll carry out any task you wish. How would you like me to help?"

"Why the coffin?" Li Kung asked again.

Old Snake took a deep breath. "The coffin? Because it's bad luck to encounter a man pushing around a coffin. This way, people will leave me alone and I can take her body and bury her in peace, without anyone harassing me."

Li Kung nodded. "You didn't want her body to be found?"

"I was afraid . . . " he paused, and couldn't continue.

"You were afraid someone would find this sheepskin on her."

"Yes."

"Did you see the body of a Mongolian?"

Old Snake looked surprised. "No, I didn't. I was looking for him too. I thought that they would be together, but the coward . . . " He gritted his teeth. "The coward must've left her alone to face the Butcher while he ran for his life . . . "

"He can't run," Li Kung interrupted.

"I didn't see him," Old Snake muttered, then quickly added, "I recognize the sheepskin, and the hairpin. But before we talk further, I need to know who you are, and what you're trying to accomplish."

"Don't you recognize the Flame Cutter?" Li Kung responded, his voice equally firm. "Tao Hing did."

Old Snake's mouth dropped open. "Impossible . . . " he whispered, his voice trailing off, as if he couldn't find the strength to finish his words.

"Will you help me?" Li Kung asked, more gently.

Old Snake remained silent, his mouth still open, his startled eyes peering into Li Kung's young face.

"You're really a descendant of Snow Wolf's? Impossible! Snow Wolf's only child died over fifty years ago. I was there! She had no students, no one to pass her skills on to."

Li Kung inched forward, reached out to the frightened poison user, and placed a hand on his shoulder. "Will you help me? Like Fei Fei wanted you to?"

Old Snake shuddered. For a long time he merely stared. Finally, he gathered himself and nodded. "What would you like me to do?"

"I need you to do nothing. I need you to retire, and never use poison for the Red Dragons again."

Once again, Old Snake couldn't speak. He looked desperately at the coffin, then at Li Kung, and finally, as a tear flowed down his wrinkled cheek, he said, "Is that what Fei Fei wants for me?"

"I don't know. She asked me to decide."

Old Snake lowered his head and began to push the coffin, moving away. "You're very smart. Without someone using poison for him, Master Bin will always be in the light and you'll always be in the dark. Who do you really work for? Lord Xu?"

"Wouldn't it be easier if I stabbed you from behind? That would eliminate Master Bin's poison user."

Old Snake halted in his tracks and thought in silence. "Yes, that would be easier. You could've thrown my body in with the rest of the massacre, and no one would have known a thing."

There was no response. Old Snake turned around and Li Kung had already gone. There were strange footprints in the snow, impressions made by the tip of a man's toes, strides so wide that each step could have equaled three of an ordinary man's.

Old Snake stared at the jade hairpin, then at the footprints. "Flame Cutter."

• • •

The messenger scampered toward Silver Pine Forest. The sun was about to set. He had been riding back from the hills of Lake Infinite, charging with such speed that his horse collapsed, foaming. He was the last messenger to return to Master Bin.

Master Bin stood waiting for his messengers in front of the pine forest. He gave strict orders to admit only those bearing news for him.

The last messenger of the day found Master Bin with his back facing the road, head slightly tilted, and hands hanging limply by his side.

"Master Bin," the messenger said, bowing low. He lifted his eyes for a glimpse of the master, but Wei Bin didn't turn around.

The messenger waited, and finally, Wei Bin lifted his hand to wave away formalities. The man quickly began to speak.

"Master Bin, we haven't found the princess. We investigated everything carefully, and we believe her body was stolen before we got there."

The Red Dragon master breathed a strained sigh, his body heaving. A slight cough escaped his lips. After a long time he said softly, "How do you know?"

"Her footprints, sir. None of her footprints were found leaving the hilltop. All of her footprints were leading up the hill."

Again, Master Bin remained silent. The messenger shifted uneasily. "She was the only woman on the hill, sir. Her footprints are easy to identify, and it seems her body should have been by the edge of the cliff. A lot of blood was soaked into the snow where she lay. We found an old woodcutter by the hilltop, and he swore that a woman in a blue robe lay dead by the edge of the cliff—right around dawn. But her body wasn't there when we arrived. As if someone flew in from the heavens and took her. There weren't any footprints leading out of the hilltop."

"Then how do you know she's dead?" Master Bin asked suddenly, his voice weak and cold.

The messenger lowered his head. "We looked at the spot where the woodcutter said she lay, and there was so much blood lost on the snow that . . . No one could have survived injuries like that, sir. Not even the Flute Demon."

Master Bin took deep, grueling breaths, shivering. In a moment, he relaxed. "Will that be all?"

"Uh, no sir. We would like to report a strange set of footprints found by the hilltop."

Master Bin was silent again, and the messenger quickly added, "The footprints were along the side of the hill, and it ran horizontally across. The prints were tiny, like little wedges made by the tip of a shoe. At first, we thought some wild goat must've been there, but then we realized the prints were made by something with two legs."

"Someone came by with special shoes," Master Bin interrupted, his voice cold and broken. "Someone frightened you fools into believing that monsters carried my daughter away!"

"No sir," the messenger said. "We thought of that too. The special shoes, I mean. But, each step this man took equaled three of ours, as if he was able to take a running jump with every step, and as if he was able to maintain such speed that he wouldn't slide down the side of the hill."

Master Bin sighed as though he had witnessed the end of the world. There was nothing he could do but immerse himself in the sorrow of being alone.

"Dismissed."

The messenger took his leave.

Master Bin stood alone in the middle of Silver Pine Forest, his body trembling with sobs. He fell to his knees like a dying horse. With his face pressed into his hands and his elbows sunk into the ground, the lord of the Red Dragons swallowed the fear and the loss of all control. He lifted his face, his quivering lips in a spasm of prayers, slammed his fists into the earth, and screamed.

• • •

Li Kung fell to his knees and pressed his head against the floor. He came to bid his three mentors farewell.

The night was cold, eerie. The faint candlelight shimmered across the three old men. Old Two and Old Three seemed worried, but neither of them said a word. Li Kung knocked his forehead three times against the floor.

"What are you really going away to study, my boy?" Old Two asked.

Li Kung climbed to his feet. "A book of strategy. A book of strategy that I came across."

"You'll be safe?" Old Three asked. "Are you going to get into more trouble than you can handle?"

Li Kung didn't respond but slowly backed toward the door, tears rolling down his cheek.

"Oh, don't be silly," Old Two shouted. "You're only going to be gone for six months. Afterwards, you can come back and we'll make this new formula together. We'll make it into a white paste. It's going to be fun!"

Old Three turned on his chair and looked at his brother. "White paste?"

"I told you. You don't know a thing about your student. Li Kung found me a very special recipe for an *evil* alchemy."

Old One laughed when he stressed the word evil. "Nice! It's been so many years since we've played with an evil recipe. It should be fun."

"Yes, yes!" Old Two added, even more excited now. "So the antidote for this evil black paste will be a white paste."

"Why do you have to make it white?"

"Because it's for counteracting a black paste. So it has to be white."

"You're full of horse dung!" Old Three shouted, standing up like he wanted to fight. "You don't even know what herbs you'll use, and you already decided on a color. The extract from most herbs are black. How will you make it white? Add flour? Stir in rice?"

Old One roared with laughter, grabbing his belly and doubling over. Old Two stood up to argue, rolled up his sleeves, and bared his bony arms as if he, too, wanted to fight. He pointed a stiff finger. "What do you know? All you know how to do is fight! But to whom do you come for medicine when you're constipated? Huh? Who saved you when you ate too many red beans last month and had diarrhea?"

"Yes, all you can do is make people use the toilet, or stop people from using the toilet," Old Three retorted. "But you need hours to brew something for that. I can hit you in the stomach so hard, you'll soil your pants this instant. How about that, huh? My medicine is better. Instant results!"

Old One couldn't breathe over his laughter and almost choked. He took deep breaths to calm himself before leaving his comfortable chair and walking to Li Kung.

"Go and do what you need to do," Old One said, the deep wrinkles on his face curved into a smile. "But come back on time, I have a surprise for you."

"A surprise?"

"Not really. But at your age, you'll be surprised."

Old Three threatened to break his brother's limbs, while the latter vowed to poison his tea so Old Three would have diarrhea for a month.

"Go," Old One said. "They'll fight for the rest of the afternoon. You've already bidden them farewell, so it's not wrong to leave."

Li Kung nodded, bit his lip, and with a final bow to Shifu One, backed out the door.

• • •

Dong grabbed the guard's coat and slammed the trembling man against the door. "Even *I* can't go in?" Dong shouted. Spittle from his mouth showered the guard's face. "Who do you think you are? If you don't get out of my way now, I'll castrate you and feed you to the dogs!"

"I . . . I . . . "

"What?"

The man shook, his voice barely audible. "I have strict orders from Master Bin not to admit anyone—"

"I am not just anyone!" Dong again covered the man's face with spit. "I am his son!"

He jerked the man's coat and threw him to the ground. He kicked open the door, bellowing more profanities, and barged into his father's quarters.

Master Bin's physician barred his way.

"Get out!" Dong ordered.

The old doctor didn't move. "Sir, your father is gravely ill. It's important that he gets some rest."

Dong grabbed the doctor by the collar, lifted him off his feet, and tossed him aside. "I have no time for you, old man. Get out before I beat you to a pulp."

Dong walked angrily on. He threw open the main door, rattling its hinges, and marched loudly into the bedroom.

"Father!"

Dong stood by the bed, trying to peer through the silk mosquito screen, but he could only see a vague shape under thick covers.

A slight cough, and his father stirred. "Close the door, my son." Master Bin's voice was weak and lifeless, "and come closer."

Dong obeyed, turned and slammed the door shut before running back to kneel by his father's bedside.

"Is it true, father? Is it true Fei Fei killed the Butcher and all of the Gentle Swordsmen?"

There was a long pause before Master Bin could find the words to respond. "Yes, it's true. They're all dead." He heaved a painful breath and tried to sit. "Fei Fei stole the sheepskin, but someone stole her body."

"Stole her body?" Dong shouted.

"Lower your voice, you idiot."

"Yes, father. But . . . Is it Wei Xu? I'm sure it's Wei Xu! The Green Dragons. I'll go down there and take back what's ours."

Master Bin reached out and gripped his arm. "Don't be foolish. Fei Fei didn't kill all the Gentle Swordsmen. They encountered a group of Thunder Broadswords and half our men died fighting them. They're much stronger than we thought. Perhaps Black Shadow has been training them."

Dong fell back at the mention of Black Shadow, as if an immediate threat descended upon him.

"Black Shadow? I thought he comes and goes as he pleases."

"No, my son. He comes and goes, it's true, but everything he does is to benefit Wei Xu. That's why this brother of mine can afford to be so arrogant."

Master Bin sat up completely now and pushed himself back to lean against the wall. "That's why you're not going to make a move without my permission. You are to lay low and not start any trouble while I recover. While we recover."

Dong nodded.

Master Bin pulled open the mosquito screen to look at his son. "The Butcher is dead," he began, "and every Gentle Swordsman that he trained died with him. This is unexpected, but we need to move on and continue with our plan."

"What do we do?" Dong said, climbing to his feet and sitting himself by his father. "How do we retaliate?"

Master Bin held up his hand and shook his head. "What did I just tell you?" His voice trailed off, and he shook in a spasm. "We need to expedite the original plan. Since your sister destroyed our research facilities, we'll need to build a new one. A more hidden one. Deep past Silver Pine Forest are unexplored areas. It's quiet enough there."

"Quiet enough for what?"

"I want new laboratories there, Dong. Larger, better ones. We need to begin production at once. Enough wasting time testing the black paste on peasants. We can start using it. Before anyone understands the sheepskin, we'll have full control of the Green Dragons, and the rest of the Martial Society—if we're quick enough. Speed is everything. Can I trust you to get this done?"

"Of course. I'll build them. We'll begin production at once. You can count on me, father."

Master Bin eyed him, his own sunken eyes dull and tired. "I can count on you for everything, if you would only think before you act. Go ahead. No one's to know about it."

"I will, father."

"Shut the door when you leave."

"I have so many questions to ask, father."

Master Bin breathed heavily, annoyed but too weak to shout. "Speed is everything. You can ask one question."

"But there's so much I need to know!"

"One question." There was clear anger in Master Bin's voice this time. Dong opened his mouth and couldn't decide what to ask. But the hate and anger in his heart quickly decided for him.

"Why did Fei Fei turn against us? Was it Wei Xu? Did they offer her something?"

Master Bin slowly shook his head. "No, it's not your uncle. He's to blame for plenty of foul deeds, but he didn't change Fei Fei. I don't know what happened to her."

"But—"

Master Bin held up his hand. "If someone has the

sheepskin, then there's a chance someone will discover an antidote. We need to saturate the market before that happens. Go!"

Dong had no choice. He always obeyed his father. As he turned to leave, Master Bin called from behind, "Send for Tao Hing on your way out. He's been trying to see me."

"I will, father." Dong backed out of the bedroom and slammed the door shut.

. . .

Li Kung trampled through the snow, the little knapsack containing all his belongings bundled behind him. The air was thin and cool, with a light smell of burning firewood hovering around him. Someone was cooking nearby. He was almost there.

He wondered about his mission. Would his encounter with Snow Wolf's legacy be considered a stroke of luck or a decisive moment of misfortune? He had become stronger, had been blessed with incredible speed and cunning, such that his abilities rose to heights never before imaginable. But most importantly, the confidence, the quiet daring so characteristic of him had once again returned.

Yet, by embarking on a mission to destroy the two greatest Houses of the Martial Society, Li Kung would be placing himself in mortal danger. Would that not be considered ill fortune?

He shook his head. There was no time for cowardice. Innocent families needed him. Justice must be done. There was no one else.

The little cottage stood a short distance away. The familiar sight of freshly chopped wood evenly piled across the front door sparked a warm feeling in his heart. Li Kung picked up his pace for the first time that day and took off into a flying run, reaching the cottage in seconds.

"Old Gu!" Li Kung shouted. He struck his knuckles against the door. "Ying! Old Gu! It's Li Kung!"

In a moment, the door opened and a young girl emerged with a heavy ax in her hands. She recognized him, threw down her ax and leaped into his arms. She pressed her face against his shoulder and wept.

"Ying?" Li Kung asked, fearing the worst. "Where's your grandfather?"

For a long time, he held her while she wept. She gradually calmed herself, wiped lines of tears from her cheeks, took his hand and drew him away. Li Kung already knew. He squeezed her hand and followed.

They arrived at a small clearing in the forest, a short distance from the cottage. Old Gu's tombstone stood in the open space.

"How?" Li Kung asked.

Ying reached out, grabbed him, and angrily pointed a finger at the tombstone.

"I'm sorry," Li Kung said. "I was gone for so long. I . . . " He stared into Ying's eyes. "You went to look for me, didn't you? While he was ill?"

Ying nodded, her lips pressed firmly together.

"Did you at least find one of my mentors? Were they there?"

Ying shook her head. Li Kung sighed. "I'm sorry." He dragged himself to the tombstone and dropped to his knees, touched his head against the snow and whispered a prayer for his friend.

Li Kung looked up and pointed toward the distant hills.

"I need a living space on that hill. I need to live in seclusion for a while. Can you help me?"

Ying nodded. She pointed to her newly sharpened ax.

"A small shed would do," Li Kung said.

Ying reached for a piece of bark beside her. She carved a word on it and placed it in front of Li Kung.

It read, "Pun." Li Kung froze, and for a long time, couldn't respond.

"She's dead," he finally said, his throat constricted.

She looked at him, dazed, as if she heard incorrectly, or perhaps she wrote the wrong word. She grabbed the piece of bark and examined it before Li Kung interrupted her.

"Pun is dead!"

Her jaw dropped. Li Kung turned away and gazed into the distance, unsure of what to say next. Suthachai was dead. There was no one left to blame.

• • •

"Tao Hing would like to see you, Master Bin," the guard announced, stepping into the front room.

Master Bin nodded. The small kiln by his side offered little warmth. He wrapped the blankets tighter around his body, leaning back on his armchair and shivering with discomfort. But he had to speak with the old strategist. An immediate plan had to be prepared for the Red Dragons.

His illness had struck at a time when he was most fragile. Master Bin was devastated by the death of his precious daughter, and he vowed vengeance. His power deteriorated overnight and his flawless plan to control the Martial Society was instantly threatened with the theft of Fei Fei's body. Whoever took her body knew where she was, knew about the sheepskin, and possessed the skill and cunning to steal her without leaving a footprint in the snow.

Black Shadow came to mind. The strange warrior's identity was never revealed, his whereabouts never known to anyone. His abilities were unfathomable. He remained the key reason why Master Bin never invaded the Garden of Eternal Light, and why the Green Dragons were permitted to rise in power.

Tao Hing entered the room. Master Bin scattered his thoughts, and lifted a hand to welcome his strategist.

"You're ill, Master Bin," Tao Hing said, walking forward to take his hand. Master Bin nodded and motioned for him to sit.

"I've heard rumors, Tao Hing, but I want to hear it from you. How were you defeated with two hundred men under your command?"

Tao Hing took a seat and sighed. "By a single man."

Master Bin closed his eyes. "I feared as much . . . "

"It wasn't Black Shadow, Master Bin. It was a boy."

Master Bin's eyes flew open, looked inquisitively at the old man as if he didn't hear correctly.

"A mere boy," Tao Hing said. "He couldn't be older than nineteen."

"Are you sure? Maybe Black Shadow disguised as a younger man?"

Tao Hing shook his head. "No one could ever recognize what Black Shadow does. But I recognized everything this boy did."

"What did he do?"

"He used the Eight Gates Formation, supposed to be lost when Snow Wolf died. And he moved like the wind. His flying movements are known as the Flame Cutter, also a technique used by Snow Wolf."

Master Bin sat back. "How is that possible? If my aunt left behind her martial arts, why would it surface now, and not before? How would someone no older than nineteen have the strength to use the Flame Cutter? Are you mistaken, Tao Hing?"

Tao Hing shook his head again. "It can't be a mistake. He used the Eight Gates Formation on Lake Infinite. He left behind footprints so I could follow him, and he waited for me on the lake. He was bold, cunning, and somehow, very driven. I've never seen him before. I've never heard of such a person. One of the men said he looked like the doctor who came to treat the Old Grandmother last month. But of course it couldn't be the same person. That doctor was a frail boy who had trouble climbing the Grand Stairway."

Master Bin didn't respond, still attached to the notion that Black Shadow interfered. Perhaps the mysterious warrior had prevented Tao Hing from bringing Fei Fei home. Maybe Black Shadow killed the Gentle Swordsmen. It was possible—even likely. Black Shadow had re-emerged to help the Green Dragons.

Master Bin held up a hand, interrupting Tao Hing. "What I need is a plan. With the Butcher and the Flute Demon gone, our two hundred Red Headbands are no match against my brother's men. His are mostly intact. We have another thousand men on Redwood Cliff, but their fighting abilities are useless in comparison. Then there's the issue of Black Shadow. We need to buy time, Tao Hing."

"How much time do we need?"

"We need a year. Can you keep Wei Xu quiet for a year?"

Tao Hing's eyes dimmed, an awful look of horror across his face. "It takes many years to train our men," Tao Hing said, his voice weak. "Train them to the point where the Gentle Swordsmen can be replaced. It takes even more years to search the land far and wide for heroes willing to join us, so the Butcher and Fei Fei could be replaced."

"I understand," Master Bin said. "But I'd like to hear Master Tao Hing's plan on how to keep us protected for one year." Master Bin's voice was cold and sarcastic. "Your plans have always been . . . educational."

A wave of cold swept across Tao Hing's face, but he forced a smile and leaned forward to speak. "News has traveled of your illness and of our heavy losses. It's true we need to keep our heads down until we recover. But Redwood Cliff remains a formidable fortress, and the only way to invade is through the narrow stairway, which is almost impossible with the Red Headbands guarding it, or to circle the mountain chain behind the cliff, but that would mean a forced march across treacherous cliffs for a month, so that is also unlikely. Which means only our businesses across the country are vulnerable. They're protected by each branch master and his own men. They've always been strong, but they're certainly no match against Lord Xu if he were to bring large numbers into each province and roam the land destroying our branches."

"He would do something like that," Master Bin interrupted, his voice more gentle this time. "He'll certainly try to absorb our branches, now that he has the jade."

"We can't prevent it," Tao Hing said. "But I need to travel immediately to each branch before he gets there. I'll minimize our losses out there, and I'll start making friends with other Houses again. That way, when Wei Xu sends his very best to our branches, we'll delay them until we recover."

"How?"

"I'll have to assess each situation when I get there," Tao Hing said. "But in principle, our businesses are smaller repositories for salt and silk, usually with a central gathering point in each province. After the goods are sold, the branch master would empty his storage rooms and pass the winter months idle. There's not much to destroy in the winter."

"I see," Master Bin said.

"Which means Wei Xu will either murder our men or try to recruit them," Tao Hing continued. "Our men will switch allegiance when faced with death. So my first task will be to convince our men that they can win if they fight, and be rewarded for it, or executed as traitors if they switch."

"I'll trust you, Tao Hing," Master Bin said. "If there's anyone who can accomplish this, it is you. And you know you're free to kill anyone who disobeys you."

The guard outside had been waiting politely for some time. Master Bin lifted his hand and motioned for him to enter.

The guard bowed. "Sir, Old Snake is here to see you."

Master Bin paused, uncertain if he was prepared to answer Old Snake's questions. Questions about Fei Fei . . .

Tao Hing stood up. "I'll come back later."

"Don't leave," Master Bin held up his hand, as if holding back a collapsing door. "Old Snake is here to ask questions. Questions I'm surprised you didn't ask."

Tao Hing's face darkened, but he nodded politely.

"Help me come up with an explanation for what happened," Master Bin said.

Tao Hing sat back in his chair. "It's late," he said. "Old Snake should've heard about Fei Fei's death a day ago. I did. He's here for more than just questions."

Master Bin motioned to the guard. He leaned back, still pondering Tao Hing's words, when Old Snake strolled in.

"Master Bin, Tao Hing," Old Snake greeted them.

"Old Snake, my friend," Master Bin said. "I understand

your concerns and I know there's much you want to know. I'm here to answer your questions."

Old Snake shook his head. "I'm old. My health is deteriorating. It's not my position to know or influence what goes on around here."

"Why do you say that?"

"I'm not here to ask questions," Old Snake said. "I'm too old for that. I'm here to take my leave."

"Take your leave?" Master Bin's eyes bulged in surprise. He leaned forward in his chair, suddenly threatened. "What do you mean, take your leave?"

"I'd like to retire. And take no part in the Martial Society for the rest of my years."

• • •

It was a dark corridor, leading up to a metal door twice his height. Li Kung inched his way forward, holding his breath, hoping to hear the woman inside. She was emitting quiet whimpers. Perhaps she was dying. He couldn't see anything around him except for the metal door. All of a sudden, he was in front of it, close enough for him to touch the cold steel, to caress the rough surface before pressing his ear against it. The woman inside was wheezing for air.

"My baby . . . " he thought he heard her say.

Li Kung gasped for air and sat up in front of his newly built shed, his eyes wide open. The dream was not a horrible one, not compared to the repeating nightmare of Auntie Ma's execution. But there was something about this, something about the dark corridor, the familiar whimper behind the metal door, the voice of the dying woman inside. He had heard that voice before.

Li Kung wiped the sweat from his forehead. He lifted a

gourd beside him and drank its bitter contents with a heaving gulp. He had recreated the unusual formula that Snow Wolf left behind, and every day, he continued to build his strength. He had been frail all his life. For the first time, he felt strong and useful, even powerful at times.

"Come closer," he said out loud.

There was a brief rustle in front of him, and a man crept forward. He was large, rough looking, and armed with a small, curved sword.

"Master Li," the man said, glancing around

"Big Nose Han," Li Kung said with a smile. "You're here with information for me?"

"I . . . I am."

The hairs hanging from Han's massive nose were interesting. With a smile, Li Kung produced two coins from his pocket and Han's face lit up.

"I have news," Han said, reaching for the coins. "I heard the Green Dragons are mobilizing their Thunder Broadswords and marching south. They have the jade now, and people say they're going to absorb the Red Dragons' branches."

"Absorb?"

"Well, yes." Han seemed eager to leave, now that he had collected his money. "Everyone knows, the one who holds the jade will unite the Dragon Houses, and Lord Xu is the older brother, you know."

"He had the jade two months ago."

"But Master Bin is very ill now, and the Butcher and the Flute Demon have killed each other, and all the Gentle Swordsmen are gone." Big Nose Han wrinkled his nose. "What better time than now?"

"I see," Li Kung said. "Thanks for the information. Don't forget to come by when you learn more. And, I'm sure you'll remember not to tell anyone about me, or I'll no longer employ you."

"Sure," Han said, a big smile across his face at the word "employ." "Of course I won't."

. . .

Old Snake was alone on the road, creeping toward the Grand Stairway where he would descend for the last time. He touched his new robes, padded coats of fine silk that Master Bin had given him for his journey, and felt the heavy bag of gold in his hands, also a gift from Master Bin. Then, with a bitter smile, he dragged himself across the cliff. It came to this—after a lifetime of service—it came to this.

"Old Snake!" a light voice called from behind. The poison user's face lit up. He turned to see Cricket running toward him. "Old Snake! Wait for me!"

He looked so much like Fei Fei at that instant, but with boyish features. Old Snake wanted to jump up and hug him. At least someone had come to bid him farewell.

Cricket reached out and gripped the old hand. "You're really leaving, Old Snake?"

"Yes, I am. Are you . . . are you well, my boy?"

Cricket took a deep breath, "I . . . I understand what happened. I'm well."

Old Snake looked into his swollen eyes inquiringly and noticed that the young warrior had wept all night. "I heard you held the Grand Stairway until dawn," Old Snake said. "You left Dong completely idle protecting the Main Hall. That was some feat. I'm so proud of you."

"I wish I could take all the credit," Cricket said with a forced smile. "But I had no chance without Tao Hing."

"Speaking of Tao Hing. I thought he was my friend, but

the coward left when your father was questioning me. He didn't even stay to defend me."

"Questioning?" Cricket asked. "My father's sick. Even I'm not allowed to see him. How did—"

"I saw him," Old Snake interrupted, "and he gave me this new coat to wear, and enough gold to last me a lifetime."

"I told you my father's good to you. I wish you wouldn't leave. You're so well regarded here."

"Do you know why?" Old Snake asked.

"I don't."

"He ordered me to leave behind everything I have, especially the Soaring Dragon Candles. Without the crucial ingredient found only on Redwood Cliff, I can never make more. He took all my belongings, including the clothes on my back. Your father feels safe now. Only he, in the whole world, has the Soaring Dragon candles." Old Snake clenched his fists, his face suddenly a crimson red. "Did he truly believe I want to retire, only to sit in seclusion somewhere and make more poisonous weapons? Or does he think I'm going to work for Wei Xu?

"He gave me this money," Old Snake continued, "so I could replace all my belongings that I left behind. And he gave me the new robes and an expensive silk coat. I had to change into them, in front of him, to make sure I couldn't hide anything in my pockets. This is how much trust I've earned with a lifetime of loyalty."

Cricket suddenly placed a hand on Old Snake's shoulder, gripping his frail bones, and threw a quick glance behind him.

"Don't turn around," Cricket whispered. "People are following you."

"Following me?"

"They look like archers. Maybe I'll ask them why they're following you. Wait for me here."

"Wait!" A look of horror passed over the old face. "Your father sent them." Old Snake, powerless without a grain of poison powder on him, grabbed Cricket's sleeve and pulled. "It's the best way to ensure I'll never create the candles for anyone else. Stay with me. They can shoot from above on the Grand Stairway, I'll fall off, and no one will ever know a thing. They won't shoot if you stay next to me. Please! Walk with me!"

Cricket nodded, swallowing hard. He wrapped an arm around Old Snake's shoulders, shielding the frail body, and walked steadily toward the Grand Stairway.

Near the mouth of the stairs, Cricket muttered, "That's interesting."

"What is?"

"Tao Hing came to me earlier and told me to wait for you by the road. To bid you farewell. But he made me promise, on my honor, to stay with you until the bottom of Redwood Cliff. How interesting."

A wave of cold passed through Old Snake's spine. So that's why Tao Hing abruptly left the room earlier. His old friend had predicted Wei Bin's thoughts and was there for him all along.

"I'm not afraid to die, Cricket."

"I know." Cricket cringed at the increasing signs of archers by the road.

"I need you to stay with me. At least until I can disappear into the woods. I must live, Cricket. There's something I need to do, that only I can do. I must live."

"My sister called you uncle," Cricket said, a slight tremor in his voice at the mention of his sister. "I won't let anyone shoot you." He drew the old man nearer. "Stay close. They won't dare shoot at me."

• • •

The Garden of Eternal Light. A beautiful garden to some, a dangerous fortress to others. Lined along the shore of Lake Eternal were small rowboats not capable of transporting more than four people at a time. The boat operators were never there, being either asleep, or away from work. Only announced guests were promptly greeted at the shore, and everyone else was conveniently disregarded.

The dark veil, tied in front of Li Kung's face and exposing only his eyes, gave him a strange sense of protection. The strip of silk felt strong enough to serve as armor against thousands of Green Dragons. By hiding his face, by being able to do anything he chose to without being recognized, he felt charged with courage and resolve.

He kneaded the oar in the cold waters, propelling the stolen vessel at a constant speed, careful to avoid any noise that would alert the guards. It was dark enough, and the wind quiet enough for him to maintain stealth. The gentle breeze was no longer cold, and only small patches of snow remained on the island.

His boat drifted to a quiet side of the Garden of Eternal Light. Sharp stones tickled the surface of the waters, positioned in such a way that even a small rowboat could be damaged. This was the ideal place for Li Kung to disembark. He halted the boat, leaped out and darted across the surface of the water. He used the tip of each protruding stone as footing. In a moment, Li Kung stood quietly on a tree branch in the Green Dragon *zhuang*.

He roamed the island for most of the evening. One of

his paid informants—a small-time guard—told him about Lord Xu's habit of walking around the island at night. Though the Garden of Eternal Light was surrounded by a dense maze of trees and shrubbery, though guards monitored the only roads at night, Lord Xu insisted on personally patrolling his *zhuang*.

Finally, by the second watch, Li Kung spotted the man he was waiting for: the unmistakable gold dagger securing his topknot signalled the master of the Green Dragons. He followed Lord Xu into a desolate area, and, making sure that not a soul was in sight, gathered himself and prepared to act.

Li Kung launched forward, coming from behind Lord Xu, and right before slamming into the Green Dragon leader, he veered slightly to the side and dramatically passed him. Lord Xu jumped in shock. He slipped back, reaching for his sword, while the dark figure glided into the forest.

"Black Shadow!" Lord Xu called. "You're back! Our brothers have been waiting for you!"

But the figure standing in front of the forest didn't move or respond. A newcomer was on the island.

"Who are you?" Lord Xu asked. "How dare you venture into the Garden of Eternal Light!"

"I'm here to teach you."

Lord Xu drew his sword and pointed it at the stranger. "Teach me? Who are you?"

"I'm the Immortal of Phoenix Eye Peak," Li Kung said, his voice deeper and lower than usual. "I came to show you the way, so the world will remain balanced, and the myriad beings will continue to exist. You will listen to me. Carefully."

Li Kung's heart pounded as he waited, perhaps for Lord Xu to attack with the famous Dancing Dragon sword technique, or worse, for a response that would challenge his identity. He felt Lord Xu staring at him, felt him turn the narrow corner of his eye with utter distrust, and Li Kung shuddered. He had seen Lord Xu's fighting ability and knew that, if the Green Dragon leader attacked, he would have no choice but to flee.

He was showing weakness by permitting silence. Li Kung took a quick step forward, directly into the pointed sword. "Put the sword down. You have no chance against me."

Lord Xu sneered, then suddenly bolted forward, his sword piercing the air with a high-pitched vibration. He stabbed at Li Kung's throat with a deadly technique, a familiar one, always lethal against someone motionless and unprotected. But his sword struck air. In a flash, Li Kung darted backwards, standing too far away for a follow-up move.

Li Kung's heart throbbed against his ribcage. He thought the excitement alone would kill him. He had just avoided a powerful sword thrust from Lord Xu himself, and he had done it with so little effort that he could not suppress his shock. He understood the incredible speed of the Flame Cutter, but until this moment, never believed it could be used in close combat. He took a deep breath, his hands casually behind his back, and walked forward again. There was not a moment to lose.

"Pointless to attack an immortal," he said. Lord Xu's face darkened, and he lowered his sword.

Li Kung pulled out a scroll. He came prepared with a speech, a long sermon, meant to make Lord Xu believe. But with one sword thrust so effortlessly avoided, Li Kung felt he no longer needed it. He tossed the scroll into Lord Xu's arms and stepped forward to speak.

"You're aware of an herbal composition that your twin brother devised?"

Lord Xu's eyes widened. "Of course I am." He sheathed

his sword and leaned forward. "What can you tell me? What does it do?"

Li Kung shook his head. "Pure evil. The alchemy can destroy a man—and not only his health, but also his soul. It will place its victims under complete control." He paused and, very slowly, with keen emphasis, said, "Absolute control."

He thought he saw Lord Xu shudder. He had tapped into the Green Dragon leader's worst fears. Why did the Red Dragons suddenly reduce their intimidating presence from the Martial Society? What really was the twin brother plotting on Redwood Cliff?

Lord Xu composed himself. "I'm certainly aware of that." He opened the scroll.

"That," Li Kung said, indicating the scroll, "is crucial for balance in the Martial Society. It contains the counteragent against Wei Bin's alchemy. An antidote, in other words."

"This? This really is the antidote to—"

Li Kung pointed his finger, aware that Lord Xu was also afraid, threw his head back and laughed. "Wei Xu. I'm an immortal. I see the past like it was yesterday. But history rewrites itself for the victor. In ten years, you'll be remembered as the one man who stood against evil. You created a counteragent against this alchemy with your vast wealth and influence. This alchemy was meant for controlling the Martial Society, then the common peasants, then the imperial palace, until we were so weak that the barbarians up north could invade us. Our entire civilization would have been wiped out. But you were the man who saved us. This is the name that you'll bear—the name of a hero. You'll take this formula tonight and produce the antidote in large quantities, then distribute it across the land with the same channels that you use for wheat and silk. No one will ever know that you're doing this for your twin's downfall."

Lord Xu eyed him, speechless. Li Kung interrupted the silence again. "Tonight is a rare half moon, a strong time for the Red Dragons. Yet Wei Bin's personal constellations are quivering. In no more than five months, he'll be at his weakest. I've been watching the heavens, and the immediate future is clear as water. If you can produce enough antidote in five months, the threat of the black paste, Wei Bin's last great weapon, will be controlled. He'll be reduced to a hermit on Redwood Cliff."

Li Kung began to walk away, calmly, like a true sage. "Thus, the Martial Society maintains its crucial balance." He smiled underneath his veil.

In a moment, he retreated into the trees. He glanced once at Lord Xu, who remained standing in the middle of the road, his hands gripping the scroll. Li Kung sighed. He wished there really was an antidote for the black paste. Perhaps Old Two would be able to devise one soon.

There was a sudden sound behind him—slight, subtle, unmistakable. It was the sound of something moving toward him at incredible speed. He jerked to the side, throwing himself out of balance. Something brushed by him in a blur, faster than he could possibly see, and disappeared into the shadows. Li Kung drew his breath in panic, horrified at the danger he was in. He braced himself, listened for the sounds of soft footsteps, the rustle of clothing, and sensing movement to his left, surged forward with all his energy. The figure shot through empty air behind him, then reversed its footing without a pause. It flew at him. Much like himself, the shadow was completely clothed in black, masked by a thick veil so only the eyes showed.

Li Kung ran with all his energy, mustering all his power, and moved toward the shoreline like an arrow. But his pursuer, who fell behind while changing directions earlier, quickly closed the distance. His pursuer advanced with such velocity that Li Kung felt like he was standing still and waiting for a raging bull to slam him from behind.

Li Kung took a deep breath, darted to a slightly tilted tree, and, using the immense momentum, scaled the slender trunk directly into the upper branches. He glanced back and saw the black figure smash into the tree. Li Kung felt his footing waver, and in that moment, he knew who pursued him. There was only one Black Shadow.

The slender trunk blew apart when Black Shadow struck it with a flying kick, and the entire tree began to topple. Li Kung kicked off the branch. He nimbly dropped onto the limbs of an adjacent tree, regained his footing, and leaped to the ground. Black Shadow was upon him in an instant.

Li Kung's heart pounded; his face was drenched in sweat from fear and confusion. He knew that the only chance he had was to beg for mercy. No one ever confronted Black Shadow and lived to tell the tale. No one ever had the chance to run.

He knew then that he was going to die here, in the Garden of Eternal Light, his mission barely begun. But somehow, even in the face of death, a burst of pride surged in his heart. He wondered, almost out loud, whether he could be the first one ever to escape Black Shadow.

With a scream, Li Kung shot out with all his energy, veering to the right to escape his dark pursuer. Then, he suddenly changed direction with such agility that even he was shocked. He charged directly into Black Shadow.

He saw the eyes behind the mask grow wide with surprise. Black Shadow's forward momentum couldn't possibly be reversed. In the split second when he was completely thrown off by Li Kung's unexpected advance, Black Shadow reached out with one hand to intercept. Li Kung pivoted off a foot and spun his body to the side. In the final moment before collision, he slipped around Black Shadow and passed him. He continued to run, picking up speed with every stride, leaving Black Shadow far behind.

Why didn't he grab with his left arm? Li Kung came so close to Black Shadow—almost face to face—before passing him. He was easily within reach. But there was no time. He stopped completely, turned around and faced his assailant.

"Do you believe I couldn't have harmed Wei Xu if I wanted to?"

Black Shadow eyed him for a second, and moved closer. A wave of cold passed Li Kung's forehead. Black Shadow was testing him. Testing to see if he would hold his ground.

Li Kung was motionless with both arms hanging by his hips. He stood upright and laughed. "We're both masked."

"Who are you?" Black Shadow asked, his voice low and hollow.

"If I wanted you to know, I wouldn't have covered my face. If you wanted me to recognize you, your face wouldn't be covered either."

Black Shadow paused. There seemed to be a smile underneath his veil. "Fair enough. Why are you on this island?"

"That is how we're different," Li Kung said. "You're here to protect one man from harm. I'm here to protect all men from disaster."

"Disaster from whom?"

"From Wei Bin."

Black Shadow laughed, an ugly, mocking laughter. "Very good. You're young and quick in wit. You came prepared with generic answers. How dare you speak to me like you're my equal!"

Li Kung shuddered. He composed himself quickly and also broke out laughing, his voice equally demeaning. "You have not been able to catch me, Black Shadow, despite your fame and the mysterious fear that you command. You've been hailed as a great hero, yet you hide in cowardice while disaster is upon us. You've found the black paste that would destroy mankind, but you threw the responsibility to Wei Bin's daughter and freed yourself of the burden. Meanwhile, *I* have found the antidote to this poison, and *I* have taken action to prevent further suffering in this world. So how dare *you* speak to *me* as an equal!"

Black Shadow hesitated, and Li Kung knew that he found his target. Black Shadow was proud. The deep anger in his eyes was tinted with remorse.

"I've given Lord Xu a copy of the formula," Li Kung continued, as if Black Shadow was not good enough for him to address, "and Lord Xu will use his unlimited resources to help produce this antidote. Even he shows better character than you."

Black Shadow was glaring at him. Li Kung turned around, as if ready to leave, then stopped and looked back. "I already know I'm a better man," Li Kung said, with deeper mockery. "But I want to know who's the better fighter. I request a formal duel."

"The challenge is accepted."

"Maybe I'll kill you," Li Kung said. "Then you'll never help fight this evil. Maybe you'll kill me. Then no one will act against Wei Bin. If he succeeds, innocents will die. So this duel is to take place after the black paste is gone from this world, and after Wei Bin loses his ability to harm the world."

"The time is accepted."

"There's a giant fir tree on the south bank of Lake Eternal. When the time is right, I'll leave a note under that tree and specify the location of the duel."

Black Shadow nodded. Li Kung lifted his hands in a gesture of respect, and bowed. "Until then, we'll be on neutral terms."

Black Shadow bowed back, and Li Kung turned to go. In a moment, he reached his boat. He tore off the veil and covered his face with both hands. He hunched over, rolled into a tight ball, and shook in heavy convulsions.

• • •

A dense cloud passed across the surface of Redwood Cliff. It was a wet, stinging cloud that created a white blindness well known to the Red Dragon *zhuang*.

Master Bin was wrapped in a heavy coat that morning. He stood with his back to the pine forest, mindful of the man bowed before him. The sun had barely risen, but already, the fifth messenger of the day had come to report.

The first three, one after the other, came to inform him of skirmishes in nearby cities. Small businesses normally loyal to the Red Dragons were harassed and some destroyed. "Green Dragons," each messenger reported, their own voices shaking. Lord Xu's men used the jade to justify their actions, claiming that the Red Dragon businesses now belonged to them, under a united Dragon House, led by the man with the jade. Even Master Bin himself conceded the jade to his older brother, they claimed.

Further reports told of a new coalition in the Martial Society being formed, one in which Lord Xu would become supreme leader. Smaller houses would unite against the evil Red Dragons. Rumors racing across the land told of how Wei Bin plotted to murder the masters of each house. He would absorb them under his wing after their leaders were destroyed. Additional rumors portrayed Redwood Cliff as a monstrous community of human torture, where the Red Dragons took pleasure in the disemboweling of virgins. It was said that Wei Bin took on the form of a serpent when he tasted virgin blood.

Wei Bin listened patiently. He refused all suggestions to retaliate. The fourth messenger came from Tao Hing. The old strategist had visited Master Gao of the Northern Mantis House. He assured Wei Bin that any misunderstanding between their houses had been clarified.

The fifth messenger who bowed before him brought devastating news. Lord Xu was creating an antidote for an unknown poison, and he was doing so in secret.

"Master Bin, that is what I heard," the messenger said, surprised that Master Bin would be agitated by this insignificant report. "Sometimes, we pay for information."

Master Bin nodded, his face pale and sickly, his eyes swollen but alert. The messenger in front of him looked up. "And Lord Xu is expecting a major epidemic in the Martial Society. He ordered extensive facilities to be built. Many men are to work day and night for this special antidote."

"And who did you buy this information from?" Master Bin asked.

"From a member of the Green Dragons named Big Nose Han. He's a friend of some high-ranking guards in the Garden of Eternal Light. He collects this information when he drinks with them."

"And why would such an important secret escape the lips of a senior guard to this—Big Nose Han?"

The messenger appeared disturbed by his reaction, but answered promptly. "We're not certain, but he claimed to have gotten one of them drunk before learning this."

Master Bin breathed in the biting air, waved his hand to dismiss the messenger, and stood with fists clenched. Black

Shadow. Who else could have taken Fei Fei's body with the sheepskin? How else would Wei Xu know of the black paste, and begin seeking an antidote for it?

He bit his lip, cursing himself for telling Fei Fei about the sheepskin. She was his favorite child.

• • •

Li Kung was standing in front of the metal door again. Somehow, he knew he was in a dream, and he must have had this dream at least five times in the past two weeks. But the metal door appeared more familiar than that. He must have stood in front of that door, in the same position with his ear against the cold metal, more times than he could remember.

The woman inside was moaning. He could hear the sounds of her twisting in pain, and then the clang of chains brushing against other metal surfaces. He thought he wanted to cry. She was in pain, and he could do nothing to help.

She just wants to see me one last time.

The thought flashed through his head, and he felt like he wanted to vomit. The woman in the room screamed.

"My baby!" she shouted. "Kung! My baby!"

"Mother!" Li Kung shouted back. His little fists started to hammer the door. "Mother! Let me in! Let me in!"

Li Kung emerged from his dream in violent spasms, fists clenched, cold sweat dripping from his face. "Let me in!" he continued to shout. "Mother! Mother!"

Li Kung recognized his familiar surroundings and stopped. He was in his cottage, on his own bed. Slowly, he lowered his face into his hands and wept. "I haven't seen her. I can't remember what she looks like. I can't remember . . . "

The door of his one-room cottage creaked open.

"Ying," he said, looking up and recognizing the round face. "It's barely dawn. What are you doing here?"

Ying stepped in, her arms around a bundle of branches. She dropped the wood by the stove, turning to smile at him, a sweet, lovely smile that stopped his heart for a moment.

"I don't need to eat this early, Ying."

She shook her head, pointed at the cold stove, closed her fingers and opened them again with an upward motion to indicate that he needed a fire.

"You heard me screaming?"

Ying nodded.

Li Kung lowered his face again. "Remember I told you about this dream? The one where I stand in front of a metal door, and there's a woman inside?"

She nodded again.

"I was there. I can't remember when, but I was there." His voice broke, and he covered his face in his hands, his body shaking in silent sobs. He felt a warm hand on his head, and he calmed.

"I was there," he said again. "My mother was behind the metal door. I can't remember why. I can't remember if I saw her again."

He reached around Ying's waist, wrapping his arms around her, and leaned his head against her body. He closed his eyes and began to sob again.

"I don't remember anything."

• • •

Pigeon's Head, the notorious mountain next to Middle Pass, actually resembled the head of a pigeon. Middle Pass was known as Bandit's Lane. Usually, only armed men from the

Martial Society would travel down Bandit's Lane, and sometimes, they would escort wealthy merchants with expensive goods for a fee. Even then, both merchant and bodyguards were often ambushed and robbed, sometimes slain.

At one point, the robberies became so frequent that the local merchants begged for help in front of the magistrate. But the government refused. There weren't enough resources to battle two hundred bandits in hiding.

The merchants then appealed to the Red Dragons. They asked Wei Bin to exterminate the bandits, but they also refused. Goods escorted by the Red Headbands were never lost, and there was no reason for Wei Bin to interfere. Wei Xu gave the same reasoning, and since then, only the Dragon Houses were employed as merchant escorts.

The first signs of sprouting weeds attested to the coming of spring. Soon, the heavy vegetation would make travel impossible. Li Kung sat in an isolated section of Middle Pass, known to many as the Curve of Blood. The Curve of Blood was locked in a valley where screams could not be heard, and ambush impossible to avoid. Most robberies occurred here.

He sat with his eyes closed, breathing in the mild air, pondering distant thoughts. There was a slight noise behind him, and he smiled. They were here.

A tall man wearing a single eye patch stood towering over him. A fat man stood next to the tall one, his beady eyes darting back and forth. He had a pouch of gold in his hands.

"You, there," the tall man said, shaking his bare saber. Li Kung opened his eyes, stretched his arms with a loud yawn, and reluctantly climbed to his feet.

"What's your name, boy?"

Li Kung dusted the dirt from his robes, looked at the two bandits in front of him, and began to walk away. The tall man rattled the saber high above his head. "Hold it! I'm talking to you! You want to die?"

Li Kung turned around, amused. "Where did you find that bag of gold?"

"None of your business."

"I dropped the coins along a trail so you would follow me here." Li Kung said. "And you came to see if I had more, so you can slit my throat and take it from me. Right?"

The tall man stepped forward, his eyes bulging. "That's right! Now tell me where you got this gold from!"

Li Kung crossed his arms in front of him. "But you didn't answer my question yet."

"What question?"

"Where did you find that bag of gold?"

"You dropped it, you fool! What game are you trying to play?"

Li Kung shook his head. "No, no. The correct answer is, you found the first gold coin by your pillow, the second one at the foot of your bed, then at the door, eventually leading you to me."

The tall man began to shake, and threatened with his weapon again. "So what?"

"So if I could walk into your room when you're asleep and place a coin by your pillow, what makes you think you can kill me?"

By then, the fat man also drew his weapon, a shorter and thicker sword, perhaps to match his shape. "W-what do you want?"

"Come," Li Kung said, waving for them to follow. "I only want to meet your leader. Not much to ask, for so many gold coins."

"Our leader will not meet just anyone!" the tall one stammered.

"But I'm not just anyone. I'm the Immortal of Phoenix Eye Peak."

"Phoenix Eye Peak?" the fat one said, trembling. "The . . . the haunted mountain? Are you . . . Are you a . . . "

Li Kung shook his head, his eyes piercing the fat man's, driving him back a step. "I'm an immortal. I can summon gold to fall from the sky, or I can beckon the demons from hell to bring death and disease."

Both bandits took another step back. Li Kung's face relaxed. "The gold is for you to keep. I just want to meet your chief."

They looked at each other, took turns weighing the bag of gold in their hands again, then sheathed their weapons. With big grins, they gestured for Li Kung to follow.

The road to the top of Pigeon's Head was small and hidden. Along the twisting turns, fierce-looking men of all sizes stepped forward to intercept. When Li Kung's guides told them that he was the chief's honored guest, they yielded.

"What's your name?" Li Kung asked the tall one.

"One Eyed Shu," was the response. He pointed to the fat man and said, "And this is my brother, Fat Shu."

"Brothers," Li Kung repeated with a smile.

They came upon a large row of houses, mostly built of coarse stone, with heavy steel doors and armed guards.

"I thought bandits lived in caves," Li Kung muttered, then pointed to the row of houses. "Where's the chief?"

"Our chief lives in the large house at the far end. Wait for me here while I ask him for permission . . . "

In a blur, Li Kung was gone. Two guards at the front door drew their weapons and barred his way, but he said something to them, placed a gold coin in their hands, and continued.

In a moment, Li Kung stepped through the doors again.

He held the chief's decapitated head in one hand, a heavy bag of gold in another.

One Eyed Shu screamed. "Help! Help! The chief's been murdered!"

A wave of panic screeched across Pigeon's Head. Every bandit responded.

Li Kung stood at the door and waited for everyone to arrive. Hundreds of menacing criminals surrounded him with drawn weapons and vile words. But no one dared to attack.

"I am the Immortal of Phoenix Eye Peak," Li Kung said, his voice loud. "It has been foretold that I will bring balance to the chaos in this world. I've been granted power by the gods above and the demons below. I am your new master. Under my guidance, you will defeat and conquer the enemies of the land, the hated Dragon Houses and the pathetic government troops. You will reap wealth and power beyond your dreams. If you disobey me, great catastrophes will fall upon you."

He opened the bag and shook its contents onto the ground. A stream of gold coins struck the ground with the music of a hundred wind chimes. The bandits stood, jaws wide at the sight of so much gold.

"You will not be treated poorly," Li Kung said. "All wealth will be shared. Follow my leadership, and you will see gold! Disobey me, and you will all die!" He threw the chief's head into the air and watched it land untouched as the crowd drew apart to avoid it.

"We are one family now," Li Kung shouted. "I will lead you to victory! I will lead you to wealth and luxury!"

• • •

In the small city of Bai Yun, two days south of He Ku, the

United Martial Society Coalition grew in size and vigor. Wei Xu's men, now more numerous than ever, toured the city in flashy carriages and an extravagant array of banners and colors. They traveled in large convoys, moving together in such numbers that many thought the emperor was passing.

Chu's Ironworks, a family business of many generations, was located in the southern corner of Bai Yun. They employed over sixty men, produced kitchen utensils, farming equipment, and other steel products. The family had a tradition of refusing orders for weapons and armor.

The heavy steel doors in front of Chu's were always closed but never bolted. That day, as they began work on new sickle blades for the spring, the main doors burst open and armed men marched in. The warriors that poured into the courtyard were magnificent in appearance, each displaying strength, wealth, and physical perfection. Most of them carried the banners of the Green Dragons. The men entering last, far in the rear, carried the new banner of the United Martial Society Coalition.

Chu Tian, the master of Chu's Ironworks, emerged from the back rooms to investigate. A tall warrior stepped forward to address him.

"Are you the master of Chu's Ironworks?"

Chu Tian stood meekly in the forefront, a confused look on his face, his small eyes darting back and forth across the courtyard. "What can I do for you?"

The tall warrior snapped his fingers, and someone brought a silver-plated box to his side. He reached in and produced the multicolored banner of the coalition. Chu Tian took a step back, fully aware of what was to come.

"You've been invited to join the United Martial Society Coalition. As a member of the coalition, you will be protected by the strongest group in the Martial Society, under the leadership of Lord Xu, where there will be justice, and honor for all."

"We . . . " Chu Tian stammered, unable to find his words.

"We understand that you've been under the care and protection of the Red Dragons." The tall warrior held out the banner, his piercing eyes pinned against Chu Tian's. "Lord Xu has promised to overlook past mistakes and to welcome everyone into the new family." He took a step forward, extending the banner closer to Chu Tian's face. "Lord Xu welcomes you to the coalition."

Chu Tian, stunned and uncertain of what to do, turned his eyes toward his men. Every man looked away, afraid to meet his gaze, afraid to express an opinion.

The warrior moved the banner closer. "Master Xu welcomes you to the coalition."

Chu Tian took a deep breath, bowed low, and received the banner with both hands. The warriors in the courtyard lifted their weapons in unison and shouted, "Long live the coalition! Protect the innocent! Long live the coalition! Protect the innocent!"

The employees of Chu's Ironworks looked at each other, then followed suit. They lifted their fists, pumped them into the air and joined the shouting. After a long time, the tall warrior held up a hand for silence.

"The United Martial Society Coalition is a much larger and more ambitious organization than the Red Dragons. It vows to unite and protect every member under a single, strong leader. The influence of this new coalition will span across the land. You'll all be a part of the largest and most powerful group in the Martial Society!" He snapped his fingers again, almost routinely, and someone stepped forward with a scroll in hand. Chu Tian bowed low again to accept.

"This scroll contains extensive instructions on your duty as a new member of the coalition. It will include details on your yearly payments, and how you are to respond when members of the coalition are attacked. Remember, the Red Dragons are weakened, but not dead. But don't worry. Under the leadership of Lord Xu, we will all be safe from such evil!"

He turned around to leave. The group of warriors began to line up systematically, marching out of the main door in silence. They disappeared as quickly as they came.

• • •

The mountain chain behind Redwood Cliff was known as the Hen Shao Mountains. Normally, well-equipped warriors blessed with an iron will would require a month to travel through Hen Shao. The last time anyone made an attempt was decades ago. More than half perished. Since then, no one ever tried to penetrate Redwood Cliff unnoticed. Anyone who visited had no choice but to ascend from the front—the Grand Stairway—and submit to the Red Dragon guards.

It took Li Kung four days to get through it. Dressed in light black, a straw hat slung behind him and a small dagger tucked into his belt, he ran through endless valleys and cliffs at night, stopping in the daytime for only a few short hours to rest. He took routes that no one would ever dream of, scaling mountains and treading on rugged cliff sides to shorten his path into a straight line.

His new subordinates, the bandits of Pigeon's Head, were to begin archery training that day. None of them understood why bare steel couldn't accomplish what robberies Li Kung needed of them. Though some did resort to bow and arrow for a large ambush, few had respect for the long distance weapons. Yet, with a hundred taels of gold, Li Kung managed to find the best archery instructor in He Ku, and in the face of even more gold, the bandits reluctantly began their training.

That afternoon, when Li Kung slept under the warmth of daylight, he dreamed of himself as a child, reaching out to grasp something. He clearly saw his own face, the childish features of a ten-year-old boy with hot tears dripping from his cheeks, his hair disheveled, his elegant silk robes ripped to tatters. There was a man pulling him away, though he couldn't see the face, and he was screaming.

"Auntie Ma!"

Li Kung no longer jolted from the nightmare. His eyes slowly opened to the distant twilight and a long, dreary sigh escaped his lips. The same nightmare had repeated itself so many times that he was no longer surprised.

By sunset of the fourth day, he sat quietly under Silver Pine Forest on Redwood Cliff. He took a moment to calm himself and mentally prepared his plans for the night.

Darkness settled. He lit a thick candle, walked to the entrance of Little Butterfly's cavern, and, remembering how slippery the cavern walls were, decided to lower himself in with a rope.

"Little Butterfly," he called as soon as his feet touched the ground. "I'm sure you remember me."

He saw her out of the corner of his eye. Her hand snapped open, and he sidestepped. A stone hissed past him and cracked against the cavern wall.

"Don't attack me," he shouted, certain that she heard. "You've been waiting for me."

He sensed her motion. He slipped to the side again and another stone flew by. He bolted forward, sliding behind her and pressed a dagger against her neck. She opened her mouth in shock.

"Don't do this," Li Kung said. "I'm here to ask for your advice. We're friends, remember?"

The old woman nodded, and Li Kung withdrew the dagger. "Yes, we're friends," she said.

Li Kung walked around to face her, taking her hand and pressing it to his face. "Here. Now you know it's me."

Little Butterfly smiled. "It's you! And you've acquired incredible speed! How did you do it? How?"

"I've learned from a great master," Li Kung said. "And now I'm ready to take on Wei Bin and Wei Xu."

Little Butterfly chuckled. "I knew it," she said. "I knew someone would step forward to kill them. I knew it."

Li Kung reached into his pouch and produced a stack of rice cakes, followed by a flask of wine. He placed them into her hand. "Eat this. Scallion rice cakes. And I brought good wine."

Little Butterfly lifted the food to her nose, sniffed them for a long time, and suddenly, as if the smell of the cakes liberated her soul, she stuffed them brutally into her mouth. Li Kung sat back and waited. She had lost all interest in his presence, had even forgotten that he evaded her missiles. Long tears dripped down her cheeks as she devoured the food and wine.

"I can't bring you to the surface tonight," Li Kung said when the last piece of rice cake disappeared. "Not yet."

She paused, a sour look quickly clenching her face. "Bring me to the surface? Why would you do that?"

"You don't want to stay down here for the rest of your life, do you?"

"Why not?"

"Think of all the rice cakes you can have outside. There will be meat, there will be fresh fruits and fresh vegetables."

She clenched her teeth and shook her head. "There's no way out of hell you know."

"I know, it's hard for you," Li Kung said. "Here are more rice cakes. It's all I could carry."

She touched the cakes that he placed in front of her. "There's no way out of hell."

"You're not in hell. I'll get you out soon, but I need your help."

"You need my help?"

"I need you to tell me a story," Li Kung said.

"A story?"

Li Kung patted her arm. "A story about Wei Bin and Wei Xu."

For a moment, she appeared as if she understood. Then she shook her head. "When I fell in here, they were merely seven years old. How would I know anything about them?"

"That's exactly what I need," Li Kung said, leaning forward. "Stories about their childhood. I'm sure you understand."

Little Butterfly thought for a moment. A smile crept across her face. "I understand. It's not how they think and what they know. A person's childhood reveals their basic nature. Wait. Let me think."

Li Kung sat back with a smile.

After a long silence, she finally said, "I remember one."

"Tell me."

"This . . . " she began with uncertainty in her voice. "This is a story that Snow Wolf told me. But I'm sure it's true."

"Snow Wolf's story is perfectly true," Li Kung said.

Her voice trembled. "Yes, Snow Wolf always told the truth. She was a great woman. She was a great, honorable woman." Little Butterfly was lost in thought. "So many years ago. It was the autumn before Snow Wolf died. The twins began their martial arts training when they were really young. They were already trained in aggressive empty hand tactics by age five, you know. That autumn, I think they were seven—they began their sword training.

"Normally, their father Fei Xing would personally supervise their training. It was the tradition of the Dragon House. Only direct blood could receive the best of the Red Dragon martial arts system. But one day, for some reason—I don't remember—Fei Xing was away, and Snow Wolf personally supervised the twins."

"Was Snow Wolf's martial arts system different from the Dragon House's?" Li Kung asked.

Little Butterfly lifted her face and laughed. "Smart boy! How did you know that? Snow Wolf was taught by her father, and by the time she married Fei Long, she was already a world-famous warrior. Who didn't know Snow Wolf at that time?"

"But she was supervising Wei Bin and Wei Xu's sword training."

"She's Snow Wolf," Little Butterfly said. "She could teach a system that was not her own." The old woman paused for a second, lost in deep thought. "They used wooden swords, those bastard twins," she finally continued. "They were only seven and weren't allowed to touch steel weapons. Too bad they didn't—they could've hacked each other's heads off nice and early and wouldn't be a nuisance now." Little Butterfly giggled to herself. "The wooden swords were beautiful, both of them gifts from Fei Long, the leader of the Dragon House. The twins were so proud of them.

"That day, Snow Wolf had the twins spar with each other for the first time. She told them to make light contact and not hurt each other. Of course they couldn't wait to hurt each other. At first, they fought like gentlemen, but then they became more and more aggressive. Snow Wolf watched with worry. They began to beat at each other with all their strength, using forbidden moves that they weren't supposed to know. But the swords were wooden, and there was no danger in letting them carry on. Eventually, Wei Bin won. He forced the weapon from his twin's hand and pinned him to the ground. Then he backed away, very proud of himself, and looked at Snow Wolf for approval.

"At that moment, Wei Xu distracted him by saying something, and charged into him. He grabbed Wei Bin's beloved sword and ran off. Snow Wolf ordered him to stop, but he ran to the edge of a small hill and threw the sword over. It was a small hill. Wei Bin raced to the edge to look for his sword, and his brother pushed him over from behind, and watched him tumble down the rocky hill. He was badly bruised. Snow Wolf told me that Wei Xu had a smile on his face.

"She couldn't punish them too harshly, of course, because they weren't her children. She brought them to their mother, the evil witch Lin Cha. But it was Wei Bin who was punished by his mother. She beat him for being careless and told him it was his fault he fell for the trick.

"That night, Wei Bin gathered a group of older boys and led them into Wei Xu's room. They tied him up while he was asleep, and they beat him until he fainted. The next morning, when Wei Xu was found bruised and badly injured, his mother came into the room without a doctor and admonished him. She yelled at him for not anticipating his brother's revenge and for sleeping without protecting himself. After a long lecture, she finally permitted the doctor to come in and treat her son."

Little Butterfly paused. Li Kung waited, in case she had

more to say, but she was at the end of her tale. He climbed to his feet.

"Thank you. But one more thing. Was Snow Wolf there when Lin Cha punished Wei Bin?"

"Of course," Little Butterfly said. "She brought them back to the witch."

"Did she warn Lin Cha that Wei Bin might take revenge against his brother?"

Little Butterfly thought for a second. "I don't remember. But she did warn Wei Bin not to take revenge. She warned him the moment she scooped him from the bottom of the hill. I remember she told me that. She told him to forgive his brother."

"I see. Did she threaten to punish him if he did try to get even with his brother?"

"Maybe," Little Butterfly said. "She was a stern teacher."

"Thank you," Li Kung said. "Thank you for the story."

He began to back toward the rope dangling into the cavern from the surface, his eyes wary of Little Butterfly's every movement, almost certain that she would attack him and prevent him from leaving. But something was different about her. The cold, harsh woman who threatened his life months ago now seemed to have lost her fire. She sat motionless, her bony hand touching the rice cakes. Then he saw her wave at him. A strange anguish welled behind his eyes. He thought of her being alone again, without fire for warmth or a human voice for company. With a sigh, he turned and moved quickly toward the rope, afraid to look back.

Once outside, his thoughts were occupied with what he needed to do next, and he felt better. The air was cooler than he thought. He wondered whether Wei Bin, weakened by prolonged illness, would come out into the open at sunrise. According to informers, Wei Bin would leave his sleeping quarters well before the crack of dawn, stroll toward the pine forest by himself each morning, and go to an undisclosed location for his breathing exercises.

Li Kung blew out his candle and breezed through the pine forest. He relied on a vague sense of direction and a crudely drawn map, which, some days ago, he managed to purchase from a young patrol guard. Once outside the pine forest, he would be able to recognize at least some of the building structures.

He thought of his little monkey, which he had left behind with Shifu Two, then involuntarily thought of Pun. He had left her behind too.

He found a comfortable tree at the edge of the pine forest, seated himself, and waited.

The night passed quickly. Li Kung's eyes were half closed and his mind wandered.

The sound of footsteps came to his ears. They were quick, light, well controlled. He lowered the straw hat, shadowing his eyes. With Fei Fei and the Butcher gone, there was only one man on Redwood Cliff who could move like that.

Wei Bin was supposed to be ill . . .

Li Kung followed but maintained his distance. Wei Bin moved considerably faster than his twin did. An aura of energy seemed to vibrate from the man's body. But ever since encountering Black Shadow in the Garden of Eternal Light, Li Kung had ceased to doubt himself. He had escaped the mysterious warrior, a feat that no one would ever dream of, and he had even convinced Black Shadow that he was an equal.

They came to a small clearing and Wei Bin stopped. He reached for his sword, drew it with a shrill resonance that echoed across the forest and swirled the naked blade above his head. A shower of pine needles was swept into the air. He changed his sword pattern and slashed at the falling pine needles. His arm, his blade, all became an obscure blur.

Li Kung froze. Wei Bin was cutting the pine needles in half before they could reach the ground.

Li Kung almost gasped out loud. He thought of slipping away to re-evaluate his plan. He imagined Wei Bin's sword plunging into his gut. How could he move faster than a sword he could barely see? Why had he been so foolish as to come here?

But Snow Wolf had chosen him. He would pray to her, and she would help him. The common people of China depended on him. Li Kung summoned his courage and slowly moved out into the open. Wei Bin was completely immersed in his training, lost in his own world, unaware of the young man standing so close to him. For a long time, Li Kung watched his sword play. The initial shock had left him, and he began to recognize a pattern in each technique. Wei Bin's sword was fast, but his footsteps were much slower than Li Kung's. The sword could only reach so far—then the body must follow to close the distance. If Li Kung stayed far enough away, he would be safe.

He had even survived Black Shadow.

That thought made him feel better instantly, and sensation came back to his cold fingers. Wei Bin began to slow, then stopped.

Li Kung clapped his hands in applause.

Wei Bin spun around at the first sound of clapping. His sword was readied, but he failed to attack. The look of surprise was clear in his eyes—but it was more than that. There was a subtle look of fear.

Li Kung took a step forward, the straw hat shadowing

most of his face. "Truly, a master of your time. Congratulations Wei Bin, son of Wei Fei Xing."

Wei Bin eyed him, lowering his sword. "Who are you? How did you get on Redwood Cliff?"

"I am the Immortal of Phoenix Eye Peak," Li Kung said, his voice calm, despite his heart racing with excitement. "I'm here to teach you."

Wei Bin broke out with a short, mocking laugh. "Immortal?" He spoke with a gentle, sarcastic tone—obviously buying time to devise a plan. "Then tell me about the meaning of life? I'm sure you know."

"Ah, the meaning of life," Li Kung said. "What a foolish question. What more is there to life, other than to eat, sleep, and use the toilet? When your belly is full, the night becomes beautiful. When you sleep in a warm bed, the air becomes sweet. And when the pressure has built in your belly, and you finally use the toilet, there's so much relief that suddenly, everything is just fine. Wouldn't you agree?"

Master Bin froze, hesitating. Li Kung took the moment to drive it home.

"You're certainly worried, Wei Bin." Li Kung spoke in a louder voice. "Worried about many things. For instance, worried about how you can acquire lotus crystals in large quantities."

Wei Bin's expression darkened. "Why would I be worried about acquiring lotus crystals?"

"To fuse them with sheep sorrel, of course. In strong alcohol."

Master Bin's eyes bulged. He clenched the handle of his sword until dark veins bulged from the back of his hand. "Who are you?" His voice was menacing, cold, yet somewhat reserved. "You have my daughter's body? Who are you?"

"Wei Bin, son of Fei Xing," Li Kung said with a controlled smile. "How interesting. To believe that only by stealing your daughter's body could anyone gain possession to the Heaven and Earth Elixir."

"Heaven and Earth Elixir?"

"Yes, the Dragon House must reunite for the heaven and earth to be at peace. The elixir you're trying to develop is the only way of doing it. But it's unfortunate." Li Kung shook his head as he spoke. "Handed down by other immortals, perfected and left behind by great men. Now," he sighed, "now you're hindered by the one man who also has equal right to uniting the Dragon House."

Wei Bin took a step forward, watching Li Kung's every movement. But the night was dark, and Li Kung's face was completely shadowed by the straw hat. "Young master," he began, more courteous this time. "Can you tell me who you are?"

"To my mother, I am a son; to the gods, I am a servant. To my enemies, I am a nightmare; but to you, I am hope. I've come to help you, because I've watched the constellations in the heavens, and I've seen the future."

"What's in the future?"

"The future," Li Kung repeated with a sigh. "Death, bloodshed, chaos. A storm will hover over the Martial Society while the Dragon Houses kill each other. Both sides will fall, and a new leader will emerge—but this leader is weak, worthless; he will spend his time drunk in some brothel, and soon, he too will fall. More battles, more bloodshed, then a new victor will inhabit Redwood Cliff, and he will shut his doors from the chaos, and . . ."

"Who?" Master Bin interrupted. "Who would dare occupy Redwood Cliff? Are you speaking the truth, young master?"

"I invite you to see for yourself." Li Kung pointed toward the heavens, speaking almost casually. "The constellation of the Eighteen Myriad Beings. It's bright tonight. But the head of the star cluster is dim, while the Dragon's Vitality in the south is becoming stronger. It can only bode ill. Can't you see?"

Master Bin stared at the heavens, then looked back at Li Kung with a frown on his face.

Li Kung's heart raced faster, but he bit his lip to maintain control. What if Wei Bin really did know how to read the stars, and only played along to buy time? His exotic names wouldn't hold water if he gave any more specifics. "I'm glad you see," he quickly said, turning. "I'm glad you see. But there's a chance, as you can tell from the Mermaid's Arrow." Once again he pointed quickly toward the heavens, then lowered his hand. "If a decisive battle can be won, then the Dragon House will be united, almost overnight, and the bloodshed of the future can be avoided."

"A decisive battle?"

"A decisive victory. But Wei Xu is creating the counteragent faster than you can create the Heaven and Earth Elixir. With most of your superior warriors gone, how do you expect to unite the Martial Society?"

Master Bin remained silent.

"You're in no condition to defeat Wei Xu," Li Kung said. "That's why I'm here. That's why you must listen carefully, for the good of thousands."

"I'm listening."

He's suspicious, Li Kung thought to himself. But the show couldn't be any more elaborate, or flaws would be revealed. The battle plan alone must convince Wei Bin.

Li Kung reached into his robes, pulled out a short scroll, and tossed it into Master Bin's arms.

Master Bin grabbed the scroll and opened it under the moonlight.

"Decisive battles are won through careful preparation," Li Kung said, his voice becoming more intense. "The scroll in your hands contains a sophisticated battle formation. An indestructible one. It's called the Formation of the Octagonal Cage."

"Indestructible," Master Bin repeated. He stared at the scroll, then at Li Kung.

"And this," Li Kung said, producing a strip of cloth. "You'll need this formula."

Li Kung reached out while sucking in his breath, his eyes fixated on Master Bin's sword, anxious, yet daring himself, and firmly placed the cloth in Master Bin's hand. "You'll need this," he said again.

Master Bin flashed a smile and whispered a gentle word of thanks, then turned to the scroll again.

"You are to make large wooden shields, shields taller than your tallest warrior, and twice the thickness of any shield." Li Kung took a subtle step back, using his voice to mask his retreating movements. "You will then find the most potent herbs, as written on the cloth, and you will soak the herbs in oil for forty-nine days. Afterwards you will soak the wooden shields for thirty-six days. The shields will become indestructible, impenetrable to sword or spear. In a battle line, the shields will become a moving wall."

He knew then that he commanded Master Bin's attention. "Meanwhile, you will forge a weapon that can smash through the defenses of any warrior. You will create spiked iron balls, very heavy, attached to long chains, and you will train your men to swing them over their own massive shields. They will use repeated overhand strikes, so that the iron balls will rain upon the enemy from above. Your men will advance behind a moving wall while dealing heavy destruction with their chained weapons." Li Kung smiled and opened his palms in front of him. "Follow the instructions on the scroll, and train a new generation of warriors in a short amount of time. Help them learn the battle formation so they can attack with proper coordination and unison. This is the only solution against Wei Xu."

Li Kung took another step back, meaning to leave. Master Bin stared at the scroll, amazement in his eyes. A subtle smile emerged on his face. "Why should I believe you? Why would I want to destroy my only brother?"

Li Kung emitted a broken laugh. "Don't you remember?" he began. "Age seven, the first time you sparred with your brother using wooden swords? You did beat him, didn't you? But he tricked you by taking your sword and throwing it down a hill, then pushed you when your back was turned. Do you remember that?"

Master Bin's face turned ashen white, and he bit his lip until blood stained his teeth. He lifted his sword. "Who the hell are you? How would you know about that?"

"I've lived for many years, son of Wei Fei Xing," Li Kung said with a laugh. "That's what it means to be an immortal."

Li Kung began to walk away. The effects of his words had not worn off yet, and Master Bin would not follow—at least not yet. Li Kung knew that no one had ever seen an immortal before, and he was certain that Master Bin, always cautious, would refrain from challenging a supernatural being. Even if it was a self-proclaimed one.

●　●　●

The innkeeper of the Smiling Fortune Inn always smiled to his customers. On this special occasion, when his inn was twice as crowded as usual, his smile was even wider.

The guests were all personally invited. Having recently

joined the United Martial Society Coalition, the little inn-keeper became friendlier than ever, and in a warm gesture of brotherhood, he was hosting a twenty-course dinner at his inn. His best wine, stored for decades in the cellar, was opened that evening.

"My toast!" he called, late into the night, amidst the racket of over seventy men drinking and laughing. "My toast to my new Green Dragon brothers. No, I mean, brothers of the coalition, under a united Dragon House! My toast!"

A round of cheers thundered across the room. Each man drank his fullest.

"More wine!" one man with a thin beard shouted, lift-ing his empty cup. He swayed a little, laughing at the dizzi-ness. "Where's the waiter? More wine!" He lifted his cup again.

No one responded. The man with the thin beard growled and slammed the cup into the table, shattering it. Everyone stopped talking and turned to watch. "Where's the waiter? Innkeeper, is this the service you intend to provide?"

The innkeeper smiled. "Please sir, please calm down. Don't break anything. The waiter has gone home for the night."

"Gone home!" the man roared. Giggles floated across the room. "Why did he go home?"

"Because, sir, he didn't want to die tonight."

Then, out of nowhere, the man with the thin beard col-lapsed. His eyes rolled back, revealing only white, and he clutched his stomach in a choked attempt to scream.

Every man drew their weapons, jumping to their feet in silence. No one understood what had just happened. The cold voice of the innkeeper swept through the room. "I didn't ask him to die here with us tonight. It wouldn't be fair. But it's certainly due justice for all of you to die."

Suddenly, three more men collapsed. One warrior ran forward and held his sword against the innkeeper's throat. "What did you do to us? Poison? You poisoned us?"

The innkeeper broke into a deep, hollow laugh. "I've been loyal to Master Bin for as long as I can remember. Master Bin is a great man. He built his wealth with an honest salt business and never demanded money from me in exchange for protection. Now, you insects come along, tarnish his good name with filthy rumors, threaten the common citizens, and dare to force me into submission? How dare you! You'll all burn in hell!"

More men collapsed, one after the other. Another warrior leaped forward and pinned his sword against the innkeeper's forehead. "Antidote! Give us the antidote, or I'll kill you this minute!"

The innkeeper laughed again. "I'm already dead. And I'll die loyal to the Red Dragons. And you'll all die with me!"

Men twisted across the floor and screamed in agony. The innkeeper's laughter overwhelmed the dying screams. One by one, the men in the room began to fall. A dying warrior found the strength to barge forward. With a shout, he stabbed the innkeeper, instantly stopping the laughter. More screams, more cries of pain. In a moment, the Smiling Fortune Inn became silent. The last groans of dying men, emitted more in hate and anger than in pain, faded into the night.

• • •

"The rats were taunting me, laughing at me," Li Kung said, staring out the window of Ying's little cottage. "They knew. I'm sure they knew." He laughed. "I was there because I deserved it. I was dinner to them, as soon as my torches ran out, I'd be eaten alive, and there would be nothing I could do about it." He lifted the jug of wine, had trouble bringing the spout to his lips, and, impatient with the heavy jug, poured the alcohol directly into his throat. He choked, and wine was everywhere.

Ying grabbed a piece of cloth and reached over to wipe his neck and chin.

Li Kung smiled. "It's your birthday. You're seventeen today."

Ying shook her head sadly. She poured wine into her bowl and gulped it down. She motioned for him to continue talking.

Li Kung laughed, reaching over to touch the silk ribbons in Ying's hair. "I've told you the story many times. You're the only person I've ever told. And it's not just because you'll never be able to tell anyone. Even if you could speak, I know my secrets would be safe." He shivered, and he half closed his eyes. "I don't know whom to trust anymore. I don't know what I would become if, every day, I need to do this alone."

Ying shook her head as if she didn't understand. Li Kung felt a tear well in his eyes and roll down his face, but he made no effort to brush it off. "I don't know what I've become," he said. He grabbed the jug and poured more wine into his mouth, choked again, disregarded the sputter of alcohol streaming down his chin, closed his eyes and gulped the wine like it was water.

Ying reached out and touched his arm.

Li Kung lowered the jug, his head swimming, his vision hazy, and his eyes narrowed. "I—I'm happy. More happy than I've been for so long." His forehead dropped onto the old wooden table, and he sighed a long, painful sigh. He covered his face with his hands and began to shake. "Last night, I had another bad dream. I was so frightened . . . "

Ying took his hands and gripped them.

"Oh, it was just a dream," he whispered, as if only to convince himself. "I've been having the same two dreams over and over again. My mother's voice behind the metal door, and then the one with the woman being executed. Who is she? Do I know her?"

Ying leaned forward, her brows knitted.

"It was so real. I almost thought I'd seen Auntie Ma before."

Ying stared, and she bit her lip as if she too, wanted to cry.

Li Kung tilted the jug against his lips and drank abusively, and when the wine was depleted, he threw the jug across the room. It smashed with a violent explosion.

Li Kung lowered his head, swaying, and smiled. "I had something to show you. How did I miss this? At the end of Snow Wolf's third book, you know, the book where she wrote down her prophecies of the future?"

Ying nodded, tapping down once on the table.

"Yes, the present—not really the future." Li Kung reached into his pocket and drew out the crumbling book. "This book. The last page was stuck from the moisture. I didn't notice it until last night. It's about a journal she kept."

Ying looked up.

"Yes, Snow Wolf kept a journal. Here it is, the last page."

Li Kung began to read: "For all matters in the world, a balance and counterbalance must be enabled for peace to exist. Experiences in my life have left me crucial elements in this lesson. Throughout my life, I've maintained a daily journal of my existence, which I hereby bury in a safe location near my tomb. My lifelong experiences have taught me ample countermeasures to my own strategies, and in these journals, where I describe my life and work, reside the key to foiling the timeless knowledge that my destined warrior holds. It is possible that events could go horribly wrong. My chosen successor should use this secret to his discretion. Perhaps these books of strategy will be stolen, and the sacred knowledge used for evil purposes. Perhaps my chosen warrior will employ tactics that could spin out of control, and countermeasures will need to be utilized. Endless possibilities arise in warfare. Thus, if my chosen warrior completes his task, and the evil threat against mankind is eliminated, then the journals can be retrieved and studied. If the chosen warrior finds that he has lost control of his task, then the journals should be unearthed and utilized, so that countermeasures can be discovered, and perhaps properly deployed."

Ying frowned, shaking her head. She didn't understand.

"This . . . " Li Kung began. He was becoming more and more intoxicated. "She kept journals of all of her great accomplishments, and this means that I'm to unearth them and study them after I complete my mission. The great lessons in life are in these journals." He took a deep breath. "And I'm to unearth them if I become lost in my mission. If I make a mess, that is. I can learn from her past through these journals. It'll teach me new strategies."

The oil lamp next to them began to diminish in rhythmic flickers. He could read no more. "She wrote something else here, I don't remember," he said slowly, "about why it's essential that her journals not be unearthed before my task is completed, because they could fall into the wrong hands. I could be facing new enemies capable of defying everything I've learned . . . Then underneath is a small map of the area in which she buried the journals."

He sighed, and stared out the little round window, lost in thought. He placed Snow Wolf's book back into his pocket and wondered, for a brief moment, what he would learn in her journals. Her life, her soul, the work of a heroine who became a goddess. Then his thoughts roamed elsewhere. He thought of something, and a smile emerged on his lips.

Ying lightly tapped the back of his hand.

"I was thinking," Li Kung said. "About the training I've been putting those bandits through. Archery training. I myself can't shoot an arrow straight." He laughed, noticed that Ying was troubled, and paused. He watched her closely. "I'm sorry," he finally said. "I know you hate them."

She shook her head.

"We need them, Ying," Li Kung's face became solemn. "I'm sorry."

Ying drew a piece of bark from a box beside her, and with a little knife, carved four words for Li Kung. It said, "Be careful, fierce bandits."

Li Kung laughed. "They're not fierce bandits. They just look big and mean. I bet you when they rob someone, they're more scared than the victims. But don't worry, Ying. They're not robbing anyone anymore. They're being paid plenty of money to work for me."

• • •

Li Kung walked into the little inn and quickly surveyed the few people inside: two peasants drinking and chatting, a drunk with his head against the table and armed with a spear, and his informer, a small man with a hefty beard. The innkeeper and the waiter sat in a corner, half asleep. The gong for third watch could be heard on the streets of He Ku.

Li Kung seated himself in front of the small man with the beard. He placed ten taels of gold on the table, and said, leaning forward, "This place is empty. Tell me."

His informer glanced around. The only person perhaps close enough to hear him would be the drunk. "It's no secret. Violence is everywhere," the bearded man began. "The Chaos Spearmen marched into the western districts this month and burned the Red Dragon branches. They said the Red Dragons didn't submit to the authority of the jade and wouldn't fall under their command. Meanwhile, one Red Dragon warrior whose brother was killed last month doused himself with oil and set himself on fire, then charged into a Green Dragon silk storage. Everything burned down, including three other Green Dragons. Also, an old woman loyal to Master Bin realized that her sister was a Green Dragon, and after a small quarrel, the old woman stabbed her sister, and . . . "

"Anything else?" Li Kung interrupted him. "Other than news of the Dragon Houses killing each other?"

"Well," the bearded man said with a sly smile, "Master Liang is sick. His son was seen in the brothels again."

"Anything else?"

"One more thing."

Li Kung folded his hands. The bearded man scratched himself, trying to remember. "I know what I forgot to tell you," he said. "The Six Guardians came back to Lord Xu and asked for employment, but he said no."

"Six Guardians?"

"Mercenaries. They call themselves the Six Guardians. I'm sure you've heard of them. They used to work for Lord Xu. Great fighters."

Li Kung nodded. "But they left?"

The drunk behind him stirred, but remained unconscious.

"Lord Xu employed them to guard his *zhuang* because Black Shadow's so unpredictable. There were rumors that Lord Xu wanted them to assassinate his twin after the Old

Grandmother's funeral. But they refused, because they weren't paid enough for such a dangerous job. There was an argument and Lord Xu got rid of them."

"Unemployed mercenaries," Li Kung said with a smile. "What happened to them?"

"Well, Lord Xu was so angry that he made it a point to ruin their reputation, and now, they've come back to ask for work."

"And Lord Xu rejected?"

"Of course!" The informer laughed again. "These men are fools, and—"

"And where did they go afterwards?"

"Well, I wouldn't know. This was recent, I'm sure they're still in He Ku somewhere." The man leaned forward and whispered with a crafty smile. "Why? You don't intend to assassinate Master Bin, do you?"

Li Kung smiled back. "Of course I do. I have so much money, I wouldn't know what else to do."

They both laughed, and Li Kung poured wine for his informer. He tossed another three taels of gold on the table as a bonus and took his leave.

Outside, heavy rain pounded the roads of He Ku. Li Kung counted the days and realized it was the end of spring. He wondered if Wei Bin's men, with the invincible shields, would be ready for battle. Tao Hing would not return for at least another month. The hate between the Dragon Houses were at its peak and pushing them over the edge wouldn't be difficult. It was time to complete his mission.

There were uneven footsteps behind him, and his thoughts were brought to a halt. "Sir!" someone shouted. "Wait, I need to—"

Li Kung turned. The man behind him stumbled and nearly fell into a puddle. It was the drunk who had sat behind his informer. He babbled something, wiping the rain from his face with a tearing motion and said, "I need to talk to you."

A clash of thunder pounded the distant sky, and the drunk took a step back and shielded his face. In a moment, he shook his head as hard as he could to clear the alcohol. He stumbled up to Li Kung, nearly falling into him.

"You—you're looking for the Six Guardians?"

"How can I help you?" Li Kung asked.

"Help me?" the drunk seemed puzzled. He did not have a straw raincoat, nor a hat. The rain drenched him to the point where his robes pressed into his skin and water trickled from the tip of his nose. But he seemed excited, eager in some way. Li Kung waited for him to gather his thoughts. "Help me kill Wei Bin!" the drunk shouted, laughing out loud. There was no one else on the street, and Li Kung made no effort to silence him. He moved closer, took off his own bamboo hat, and placed it on the drunk's head.

"What's your name?"

"Liu Yun. From the Iron Palm School. Liu Yun."

"Liu Yun of the Iron Palm School. You need to go home and sleep off the hangover."

"The Six Guardians are great fighters, all of them. They could kill Wei Bin! If I had the money to hire them . . . " Liu Yun suddenly broke down sobbing, his face in his hands. He began to scream. "You have money, young master. You can pay the Six Guardians!"

The drunk paused to catch his breath. "You can't tell me to go home," he continued, between gasps. "I have no home to go back to! Wei Bin killed my entire family. Why? Because I found his dirty little secret! I found it but I wasn't able to kill him! They promised to help me, they said they would help me, but they retreated from battle, those cowards. I never got the chance to . . . "

174

Li Kung moved closer. "What secret did you find?"

Liu Yun wiped his eyes. "The secret." He was panting. His body swayed as he stared, lost in thought. Li Kung grabbed him with both hands and shook him, bringing him back to his senses.

"Wake up," Li Kung said.

"The secret," Liu Yun said. "A medicine of some sort. I paid for it, just out of curiosity, from a man in Pan Tong Village. When I tried it and realized what it did to me, my father and I tried to speak to Wei Xu about it. But Black Shadow intercepted us, and he took it. Something about Wei Xu starting a war if he finds out about this medicine. A few days after that, the Flute Demon came to exterminate our school. I want revenge!" His eyes suddenly bulged, his teeth chattering. "I want revenge!"

Li Kung placed a hand on his shoulder. "You can die in a war like this."

Liu Yun stared and swayed for a moment before throwing his head back to laugh. "Today is a great day to die! And why shouldn't I? Why should I live another day, knowing I'm powerless to kill the man who wiped out my family? Why live in shame?"

Li Kung frowned, his arms dropping to his side. He needed someone like Liu Yun, someone who could not be bought, who would never run in the face of danger. Would it be so bad to ruin just one more life, if it meant the destruction of the black paste?

"What I'm about to do is horrible," Li Kung said with a sigh. "Are you sure you want to be part of it?"

Liu Yun fell to his knees and planted his forehead on Li Kung's boots. "Master! If you'll kill Wei Bin, I'll do anything. I'll give my life! I will . . . "

Li Kung stooped down to help him to his feet.

Liu Yun's lips began to quiver. "Use me, master. Make it a good day for me to die."

• • •

None of the Six Guardians had individual names. They preferred being called First Guardian, Second Guardian, and so on. They were dressed completely in black, with pale, expressionless faces covered by scars of battle, with age in their eyes and indifference in their speech.

Li Kung sat before them, cross-legged on the floor. They were inside one of many abandoned temples in the region. "Six thousand taels of gold," Li Kung said. "Money is not a problem."

"Six thousand is fine," Third Guardian said. "But we're not clear what the mission is."

"There'll be many missions. You'll need to be available for three months." Li Kung folded his hands together. "Some of the missions are dangerous, but most are simple. With your skills—"

"Too much unknown," First Guardian said. "At least we need to know who we're going to target. Or are you hiring us to protect you?"

"I don't need protection," Li Kung said with a smile. "I need support, and as I promised you, very few of the missions will be dangerous. But I need absolute secrecy from you, and I need true loyalty in battle."

"We have a reputation to uphold. Once paid, there'll be no question of loyalty. But again, we can't agree to anything without knowing who we are to kill, when, where, and how many people."

"How about ten thousand taels?" Li Kung said. "For

three months. It should be enough for full-scale war on a daily basis."

They looked at each other then, their expressions as cold as ever, but after they each made eye contact, they nodded.

"We don't kill women and children."

"Good," Li Kung replied. "Because I'm going to have to burn you alive if you did."

• • •

The wind whispered, harshly at first, then steadied against the first warm day of the year. Li Kung had been meditating for the entire afternoon, and he felt strong, ready.

All around him, on every wall, were writings that he carved for himself. Every day when he opened his eyes he would read the writings at least once.

"Never forget the threat to the innocent," he read in a whisper. He focused his eyes on the second line. "Never forget the suffering of the people. Never forget the growing evil."

He clenched his fists and calmed himself. Circling the entire room, every line began with "Never forget." He had come this far. How could he ever forget?

That morning, One Eyed Shu came to tell him that the bandits were restless and eager for action. He claimed that all of them could shoot straight, hardly a believable feat, and that they had learned to fire on signal and in unison.

Li Kung had visited Wei Bin the day before. He was told that the new group of Red Dragons was strong and well prepared. More than half the men were capable of swinging their weapons with accuracy, and all were able to advance and retreat as one. They were responding well to the horn and drum signals.

There was a light knock. "Come in," Li Kung ordered.

Liu Yun peered in. "Master, the Red Dragon workers were caught sneaking south, as you predicted," he said. "We've captured them and we're awaiting your orders."

Li Kung watched his expression and didn't respond, but motioned for him to sit.

"Do we proceed as planned, sir?"

"Someone once told me the difference between chicken and man," Li Kung began.

"The difference between chicken and man?" Liu Yun asked. "I don't understand."

Li Kung was lost in thought. "Chickens are slaughtered to be eaten, to ensure the survival of man. Men are also slaughtered to ensure the survival of other men—the only difference is they're not eaten."

"I still don't understand."

"The difference is, since we don't eat men but we do eat chicken, and since the chicken poses no threat to man if not promptly slaughtered, then chickens are more useful, and therefore superior to man."

Liu Yun couldn't contain himself and broke out laughing. "I've never heard of anything so ridiculous. Who would say something so strange? A friend of yours?"

"He was no friend of mine. Though I've spent many painful days trying to save his life."

"Why?"

"I don't really know. Maybe because he understood the difference between chicken and man, and I didn't."

There was silence. "I'll think about what to do with the Red Dragon workers," Li Kung finally said. "Wait for my orders."

"Yes, master," Liu Yun stood up quickly with a bow. He turned and hurried out the room.

. . .

The following day, at the break of dawn when fog choked the streets of He Ku, Li Kung wandered the lonely marketplace by himself. He was lost in thought. In a short time, he had secured the might of the six mercenaries, the loyalty of forty-four impious bandits, and his plans, meticulous and subtle, had fully ripened over the months. What then? When would the hostilities between the Dragon Houses be sufficient for a devastating battle? They each had over a thousand men. The Green Dragons were much more numerous now that Wei Xu commanded the coalition. But Wei Bin had the Formation of the Octagonal Cage, so both sides would be pretty evenly matched in a full-blown battle. Both sides would face numerous casualties. How numerous would depend on how much they hated each other and how eager they were to fight to the death.

Shops were beginning to open. Li Kung stood silently by the side of the road, unsure of where he was going, or why he was there. Tao Hing would return from the south in a week. It would be a triumphant return, he heard, and the world would be harder to manipulate with the old strategist back on Redwood Cliff. Tao Hing had traveled through the land, stopping the endless depletion of the Red Dragon empire, and the Red Dragons had protected most of their branches as a result. They could be strong again. The Dragon Houses must not grow any further.

A large group of men, mostly on horseback, with flags and banners of the coalition fluttering behind them, approached the main road of the marketplace. Li Kung watched their slow, flamboyant canter, their mirror-polished weapons, the finicky details of each man's garment in a gaudy display of wealth and power. One warrior in the front struck a gong—once, twice—to announce their presence before falling into an even slower march.

Citizens of the marketplace rushed forward, as if it were a routine, and planted the flags of the coalition in front of their shops. The warriors passed through the street, leering back and forth at the storefronts, their cold faces nodding with approval at every flag they passed. In a moment, they disappeared down the road. Shopkeepers continued to open their businesses for the morning.

Li Kung stared. It was time. The Green Dragons' arrogance was at a new peak, and Wei Bin's men, repressed for months, were ready to explode.

· · ·

The scorching summer heat seared the man's bare flesh and burned his skin into an opaque crimson. He hung by his wrists, his body dangling, stretched to the point where his rib cage protruded from his skin. The weight of his body pulling against the rope left deep cuts in his wrists. Beads of sweat trickled from his forehead and left streaks across his tortured face. "I've sworn my loyalty! I won't tell! Why don't you just kill me?"

"Scum!" Liu Yun barged forward to kick him. Another man, bound head to toe with wet rope, lay naked on the hot earth, his gagged mouth twisted horribly.

"What are you doing, Yun?" Li Kung asked from a distance. In a flash, he stood before the naked man.

Liu Yun turned and quickly bowed. "Master, these are the Red Dragon workers we captured."

"Did you get them to talk?"

"Not yet. But I know how to."

Li Kung seated himself on a small tree stump and noticed the Six Guardians standing a short distance away, watching with indifference. They were on a desolate hill south of Middle Pass, in a rocky area free of trees and protection from the blazing sun.

One dead tree stood alone on the rocks, and the man had been hanging from it all morning. He had deep bruises across his ribs and was spitting blood, but despite the torture, he refused to talk. He glanced at his companion on the ground, bleeding from the coarse ropes, and tried to say something to him. But Liu Yun's fist found his lips before he could utter a sound.

"Wait," Li Kung said. "If you hit him anymore, you'll kill him."

"Yes, master," Liu Yun replied with a smile. "Can't kill him like that. I have other plans for him."

"Other plans?"

Liu Yun pointed to the sky. Li Kung lifted his face to the blazing heavens and noticed the vultures floating above them as if in a frozen standstill, watching, waiting. A cold feeling haunted him then, bringing a bead of sweat to his forehead, and the thought made him want to vomit.

"He's been dangling all afternoon," Liu Yun said. "His body is completely stretched out. If I cut around his waist, I'll be able to lift his skin and make his guts fall out."

Li Kung looked at Liu Yun, at the glee on his face, and felt his eyes burning. The man dangling from the tree started to moan, while the one squirming on the coarse sand began to scream through his gag.

"And then," Liu Yun said, pointing to the sky again, "we'll walk away so the vultures can come and eat his innards, and he'll be alive and he'll get to watch."

"And how are you going to question him if the vultures ate all his organs?"

Liu Yun laughed. "We have another prisoner, master! We'll string him up, stretch out his torso, and wait for more vultures to come. Then we'll give him a chance to talk, or we'll cut him the same way."

"I see," Li Kung said in a whisper. The Red Dragon worker twisted in horror, opened his mouth to scream but couldn't find the strength.

Liu Yun drew his knife and walked to his prisoner.

The vultures began to circle lower, as if they understood and sensed the meal before them.

"Wait," Li Kung said. The Six Guardians suddenly looked up, surprised. Li Kung shook his head. "Let me talk to him."

Liu Yun tapped the side of his blade against the man's belly, and with a laugh, withdrew his weapon.

"I can offer you gold," Li Kung began, walking up to the prisoner. "More than you'll ever see. If you'll tell me where it is, you won't die a horrible death."

A crude smile escaped from the man's lips. "Kill me. Make it quick. I'm not afraid to die. Master Bin is a great man. I'll never talk."

"You're but a pawn," Li Kung said. "A mere worker in Wei Bin's factory, whom he would slaughter without a second thought to protect his dirty little secrets. You're expendable to him."

Somehow, the man found the energy to laugh.

"Why should I believe you?" the man shouted, his voice suddenly strong. He glanced at his comrade on the ground again. "Master Bin is the true leader of the Martial Society. Master Bin's medicine will cure the diseases of mankind, and you—you're evil! You wish to destroy it, so people will suffer! Damn you! Damn you to hell!"

Li Kung shook his head with a frown. "You have no idea

what you're making in those laboratories. Can there be one medicine that can cure all diseases? If it's really for the good of mankind, would Wei Bin make so much effort to hide it from the world?"

The man spat at him, and Li Kung leaned away to avoid it.

Liu Yun drew his knife again, his eyes bulging. "You dare!"

Li Kung took a step back. Nothing worked. Wei Bin had taken great measures to protect the location of his black paste laboratories, and every worker was sworn to silence. Somewhere in the rugged mountain chain behind Redwood Cliff, the black paste was being created in alarming quantities, and this pathetic Red Dragon scum wouldn't tell where.

Li Kung knew that one essential ingredient for the black paste could not be gathered or created in a short time. It had to be purchased. He had paid the herb merchants of the six regions some months ago, whether they eventually joined the coalition or not, and they all agreed to notify him if anyone sought large quantities of the ingredient. A few days ago, as predicted, Wei Bin began to run out of many herbs, and someone was sent to negotiate with the merchants. The Red Dragons were followed and captured.

Liu Yun's blade was pressed against the screaming man's flank when Li Kung snapped out of his thoughts. "Wait!" he said. Liu Yun froze.

Li Kung lowered his head and looked away with a deep sigh. He needed to know where Wei Bin's laboratories were hidden, and Liu Yun's tactics would certainly yield results. But could he let a man watch himself being eaten alive, and then declare that it was for the good of mankind?

"Cut their ropes," he said.

Liu Yun hesitated. Li Kung turned and flashed a stinging glare, and Liu Yun quickly lowered his head. "Yes, master."

The Six Guardians, some of them shaking their heads, began to walk away.

Liu Yun severed the ropes of both men and quietly stepped back, eyeing Li Kung with disappointment, but not saying a word.

The prisoner who was on the ground scampered to his companion, who, for a moment, could not find the strength to stand. They embraced, trembling, weeping, their eyes wide with fear. What would happen to them next?

Li Kung crouched down and handed them some coins. "Go home," he said. "Don't go back to Redwood Cliff."

"Why?" one of them asked between gasps.

"Dong will notice that you've been missing and beaten up. He'll suspect that you've talked. He'll kill you. Go home, collect your family and belongings, and leave this province." Li Kung placed a flask of water in front of them, stood up, and turned to leave.

"Wait," the man originally on the ground called from behind him.

Li Kung paused, shaking his head. "Just go. Liu Yun's not going to hurt you anymore."

"Wait," the man said again. "There's no medicine that can cure any disease in the world. I believe you. I know where the laboratories are."

• • •

Two days later, Li Kung and the Six Guardians scaled the impossible cliffs of the Hen Shao Mountains. Deep within a narrow gorge, hidden against a slender pass and embedded between a complex disposition of natural rock protrusions, the laboratory for Wei Bin's black paste stood completely concealed. It was a large, simple

184

structure, built of solid stone with tiny windows scattered along the walls.

Li Kung pointed to a little trail behind a cluster of boulders. "Another half day's walk to the back of Redwood Cliff from here. We have no chance of returning the way we came—it'll take too long. We'll descend down the front, on the Grand Stairway."

The Six Guardians made no response, but Li Kung knew that they heard. He had taken them on a treacherous journey, along cliffs and peaks where no one dared to venture. On previous trips, Li Kung had mapped out a shorter route through these mountains, and had planted spikes and footholds along otherwise impossible routes. They arrived at the backyard of Redwood Cliff in only two days.

The Six Guardians were ready. Li Kung drew a deep breath. They had been ready since the moment they were paid. When would he be ready?

He began to move forward. The hated alchemy, destined to destroy the world, was created to place absolute power in the hands of one man. Wei Bin already had more power than anyone would ever dream of, yet, there was always more.

In three steps, Li Kung shot himself up the side of the rocky incline, his movements so quick and fluid that he seemed to be levitating. The Six Guardians followed, their speed substantially inferior.

Li Kung stood at the top, hidden from view, and began to untie the large sack he carried. It was full of the green powder that had become his preferred weapon. All he needed was a well-timed attack. He must ensure that no one escaped to warn the rest of Redwood Cliff.

When the Six Guardians closed in, Li Kung lifted his hand to stop them, then held up four fingers and pointed to the poorly guarded door.

First Guardian nodded and drew his sword. They proceeded forward, quiet and slow, then suddenly pounced into the open like a pack of hungry animals ambushing their prey. The laboratories were so well hidden that Wei Bin never saw the need for extensive security. In a moment, before a single groan or whimper could be emitted, all four guards outside the doors were dead.

Li Kung shot to the side of the door, without a word, and stood by the entrance. Second Guardian leaped forward and smashed the door. Li Kung took a deep breath and drew open his sack. The shocked, vacant faces of the laboratory workers were all he remembered seeing.

Without a sound, he bolted through the opening. He flew past a group of workers hovering by the door, flinging the green powder across the room. He ran harder. The powder swarmed through the air like so many hungry locusts seeking a place to land. The workers stared at him. For a moment, they couldn't decide what was happening. Then, the fire reached out like a gust of wind and engulfed everything in a searing inferno. The flame first swept the center of the room, igniting everything, even the workers that stood in its way. Then it licked through the wooden shelves lining the wall. The familiar sound of chaos, of agony, of fear, all reached Li Kung's ears at once. He didn't stop. The workers finally began to run. Each man pushed and slammed against each other in a battle to reach the door. Those who fell were trampled upon. Some couldn't run in time. They were burned alive. Some flailed around in panic and charged through the laboratory without any sense of direction. Some lost their eyes when the initial burst of flames burned their faces. They ran back and forth, never finding their way out.

Li Kung's sack was almost emptied. The fire couldn't

touch him—he moved too quickly to be vulnerable. Yet the dense smoke began to blind him. He could hardly breathe. He threw the rest of his powder into a storage compartment, almost choking, then bolted for the door.

The sack of green powder caught fire and exploded. More screams filled the air, each moment more dreadful than before. Li Kung leaped out of the laboratory as every man behind him caught fire. Then, the cries of dying men began to fade. He ran into free air to find bloody corpses all around him. The mercenaries had done as they were told. Every worker who ran out of the laboratory was slaughtered, without exception, without hesitation.

The heat clawed his back with a painful tingle. He stared at the horrid faces of death, breathed in the stench of burnt flesh, and shuddered. Did these men know that they were creating the black paste? Did they deserve to be victims?

The Six Guardians wasted no time. They threw a rope over the cliff behind the laboratory, and four of them began to descend. In a moment, they returned with large bamboo stretchers.

The stretchers were rolled open and bodies were piled on top of them. Only four bodies could fit on each bamboo sheet, and with two men carrying a stretcher, only twelve bodies could be transported at once.

First Guardian looked at him, inquiring. Li Kung glanced at the sun, knowing that they must take advantage of the pending darkness. He noted the small number of bodies and nodded his head. The Six Guardians picked up the bodies and moved into the forest at once. They would scale one more peak, a short journey that could be completed before nightfall, before descending onto the back of Redwood Cliff. They would be able to cross Silver Pine Forest immediately after sunset.

By the time they approached Silver Pine Forest, following familiar routes that Li Kung had drawn on a map, the moon was already high in the sky. The bodies they carried were heavier than Li Kung anticipated, and the Six Guardians moved slowly. They reached the center of Redwood Cliff by the second watch, almost in pitch-black darkness, and paused. Li Kung glanced at the guards strolling casually along the main road, then, in the distance, at the large group of men posted by the Grand Stairway.

"Speed is everything," he said.

First Guardian smiled. Second Guardian lifted his weapon. Both mercenaries ran onto the main road and attacked the guards. The remaining four Guardians grabbed two bamboo stretchers and ran toward Wei Bin's personal training hall.

Li Kung drew a strip of white fabric from his pocket and followed. He overtook the mercenaries in a second, reached the empty training halls and scaled the walls in one breath. He dropped into the courtyard and opened the front gates. The burnt corpses were dumped into the open space so the insult would be clear.

Meanwhile, the First and Second Guardians attacked the guards and prevented them from sounding alarms.

The other four Guardians returned for the remaining stretcher. Li Kung stood by himself and stared into the empty training hall.

The last four bodies arrived, and Li Kung draped the white cloth over the pile. He bolted the door shut before scaling the walls to exit.

The crude writings on the cloth read:

The Red Dragons are subordinates of the Green Dragons, and henceforth, all virgins loyal to Redwood Cliff below age sixteen must first sleep with a Green Dragon guard before being

permitted to marry. Violators will be burned alive and piled to-
gether for exhibition.

Li Kung joined the Six Guardians by the mouth of the Grand Stairway and began to descend. The guards posted at key points along the stairs were only trained to battle invaders from below, never against enemies from above. The Six Guardians slew them quickly and silently, always striking from behind, never permitting them a chance to sound an alarm.

The bottom of the Grand Stairway loomed before them. Timing was essential, and Li Kung felt that already too much time had been wasted. Liu Yun would be waiting at the base of the cliff with fresh horses. The Red Dragon guards at the entrance of the Grand Stairway should already have been slaughtered.

Li Kung and the Six Guardians ran up to Liu Yun, leaped onto the restless animals with one fluid motion, and without a word, headed down Middle Pass. They whipped their horses repeatedly, riding them to near death before stopping. Always, the bandits of Pigeon's Head waited at critical points on the road with fresh horses. They changed horses four times before arriving at the Night Hawk Inn in He Ku.

The flag of the coalition fluttered in front. Housed inside were the men who patrolled the streets of He Ku each morning, their coalition banners held high and mighty. Every morning, they toured the city, approving each storefront, sometimes harassing a civilian shop for not properly displaying the banners of the coalition.

It was no secret. They ate and slept in luxury inside the Night Hawk Inn.

Li Kung pointed at the door of the inn, a sick feeling overwhelming him. He barely found the strength to speak. "You're free to do your work. No one will interfere."

First Guardian nodded, dismounted quickly and moved toward the door. He opened it just a crack and slipped in. The remaining five followed, quietly closing the door behind them.

Liu Yun also leaped off his mount. "What do I do, Master?"

Li Kung watched the inn and didn't respond.

Liu Yun drew his weapon. "I'm ready! I'll kill anyone who comes out of those doors."

"The message," Li Kung finally said.

"I have it." Liu Yun pulled out the banner of the coalition. Written in blood, in his own handwriting, were three lines:

The United Martial Society Coalition was created for the crippled and useless. Men of true worth loyal to the Red Dragons will survive and prosper. Men loyal to the Green Dragons will die squealing like pigs.

All was silent, motionless. Li Kung seemed to hear the sounds of murder inside. He took a deep breath and waited, remaining on his horse, staring.

Much later, the Guardians emerged with blood-covered clothing. Li Kung spun his horse around and rode away.

• • •

At the crack of dawn, the warriors of the Red Dragon House gathered in front of the training hall to read the message. News had spread, faster than a raging flood.

Dong's face darkened when he arrived at the scene. He recognized the dead. The existence of these men was supposed to be secret. Yet, all of them, without a doubt, were workers from the hidden laboratory behind Redwood Cliff. His heart pounded in horror. These men ate and slept in the laboratory. How could they be singled out and slaughtered, then dumped in the training hall?

Dong charged out and grabbed the nearest man by the collar. "What happened? What happened at the Grand Stairway?"

"I- I don't know sir," the man said, trembling. "But I heard the guards on the Grand Stairway were also killed. I don't know."

Dong shoved him aside and bolted for the pine forest. The laboratories! Mixed thoughts churned in his mind, swollen with deep rage and hate. The Green Dragons. They were able to walk up the Grand Stairway as if his guards didn't exist? How? Could Black Shadow really be so powerful that no one had the opportunity to sound an alarm? He clenched his fists. None of this made sense to him. How could anyone penetrate the defenses of Redwood Cliff?

In a moment, he passed the dense silver pines. The smell of burnt flesh began to approach him in waves. He ran harder. The laboratory loomed before him: the charred corpses scattered on the rocks, the smoking interior. Heat swelled in his eyes. He clenched his teeth in helpless fury. They had discovered the laboratory and destroyed months of work on the black paste. They had once again depleted the Red Dragon's ability to recover its might.

A figure stood before him, motionless, out of nowhere.

"Father . . . "

Wei Bin's voice was quiet. "They found our secret. They infiltrated our *zhuang* while we slept. This is an experiment for them. Now that they've succeeded, they'll gather their forces and attack Redwood Cliff."

"We must strike at once, father!"

Wei Bin didn't respond. Dong shifted impatiently before repeating, "We must strike, father!"

Wei Bin suddenly turned around, his eyes blazing. "I'll have a personal duel with my twin."

"You can't possibly—"

"I'll arrange for a duel in wide-open terrain," Wei Bin said, a cold smile on his face. "My brother will suspect the worst, and he'll bring his very best men to accompany him. He'll bring the Chaos Spearmen, if not most of the Thunder Broadswords, or maybe even some of the fragile coalition he created. I'll fight him, then all hell will break loose. Our men will arrive in the middle of the duel to surround him, and we'll kill them all!"

"Yes, father! Yes!"

"I need you to set the stage for my duel. I need you to make it impossible for Wei Xu to reject the challenge. Go out there now, my son! Go out there and kill some Green Dragons. Kill as many as you can. Wei Xu will retaliate and kill some of our men. The entire Martial Society will be in chaos. Then, I will call a truce. I'll propose a personal duel to resolve this conflict, and Wei Xu will have no choice but to accept."

Dong nodded, a huge, crooked grin on his face. The anger of being victimized was suddenly alleviated by the prospect of revenge. Without a word, Dong turned around and charged across the pine forest. He found the Red Headbands gathered by the Grand Stairway, organized, their cudgels polished, their headbands neatly tied and ready for battle.

Dong lifted a hand to command their attention. Tao Hing was away. The Butcher and his pathetic sister were dead. Old Snake had deserted. His father entrusted him with a war. There was no one to stop him. He was all-powerful now.

"The city of He Ku is loyal to the Green Dragons!" he shouted. "The families of the Green Dragon men mostly live in He Ku. We'll avenge this insult today! We'll capture their women, we'll slay their fathers and their sons. They'll answer for this crime! They'll learn who's inferior!"

The Red Headbands lifted their cudgels and roared.

• • •

Lord Xu's adopted son gathered his men. Retaliation was not approved yet, but Stump knew that it was only a matter of time before the Green Dragons took revenge. The newly formed coalition could not permit such humiliation without a war. The Red Dragons had to pay.

Lined up before him, with blades newly sharpened and cleaned, were all two hundred Thunder Broadswords, a new generation of elite warriors trained to replace the ones killed by the Butcher. Black Shadow hadn't appeared in weeks, and the coalition couldn't wait for him. Stump snarled, his red face trembling with heat and excitement.

"We'll storm the village of White Clay, and we'll gut and hang every man, woman, and child loyal to the Red Dragons. They will pay for this! They will pay for this!"

• • •

Dong and the Red Headbands poured into He Ku like packs of mad wolves, hungry for blood, insane with hatred.

The streets were empty, but Dong saw them. At the crack of every window were peering eyes and whispering lips.

His own eyes wide and burning, Dong pointed his sword at the civilian houses. "Green Dragon accomplices," he croaked, his voice hoarse from shouting. "Kill them! Take the women! Kill the men!"

The Red Headbands screamed, lifting their cudgels and shaking them in the air. Blood! With a massive roar, the Red

Headbands charged into the civilian houses. Doors were smashed under their heavy weights. Horrid cries emerged from the houses.

Laughter, high-pitched and hardly human, flooded the streets. Dong stared with red eyes, a trembling smile across his face. He lifted his sword. "Kill them! Kill them all! Kill them all!"

"Animals!" someone screamed.

Dong turned. There was a flash of steel before his eyes. He drew back, avoiding the strike, before lashing out with his own sword. Sparks flew. Dong was thrown off balance.

It was the adopted son of Wei Xu. His face was red, his eyes narrowed and glaring, his sword held high. "Stump," Dong growled under his breath. The sight of his hated foe burned him with renewed fury. With a shout, he charged forward, entangling Stump in a barrage of short-range blows.

Men poured out of nowhere and attacked the Red Headbands.

"Thunder Broadswords!" someone shouted. Wei Xu's broadsword users were set for carnage, and the first taste of Red Dragon blood drove them mad.

At the end of the road, Dong pressed his assailant farther and farther away. He felt himself winning. It was only a matter of time before his sword tore into Stump's belly, and the thought brought a smile to his face.

Then it happened, as he had predicted. Stump began to retreat. Dong lifted his face to the heavens and laughed. The laughter made the Thunder Broadswords and his own Red Headbands turn to look at him, and the energy of the battle changed. The Green Dragons watched their leader retreat in cowardice. The Red Dragons watched their enemies become disheartened. With renewed vigor, the Red Headbands stormed their assailants; their bashing weapons swiping blindly with murderous strokes.

Dong laughed again. He rushed at his enemy. They rammed into the ground together, with Stump pinned underneath. There was a high-pitched scream.

The Thunder Broadswords turned to see what happened.

Dong drew a knife and brought it down with a shout. Stump grabbed Dong's wrist, just in time to prevent the steel from entering his chest.

For a moment, they were locked in a desperate position. Dong put his entire weight into the knife. Stump held on with both hands, trembling, fighting with all his strength. The blade pressed lower and lower.

"No," Stump gasped. "Don't kill me!"

Dong's face twisted into a perverse grin.

"No!" Stump pleaded. "Please don't!"

Dong shifted his weight and slammed his knee into his enemy's groin. Stump screamed and lost control of his arms. The knife sunk into his chest with a sick thud. His body arched in agony. He sucked in his breath once, in a long, winded gasp for air. Then he fell limp.

Dong rose to his feet and stared at the man he had just killed. The blank eyes were wide open, staring at him, cursing him.

The Thunder Broadswords witnessed Stump's death, and, with a surge of fury driven by a crazed instinct to survive, charged forward and smashed into the Red Headbands.

Every man told himself over and over again that he would die this day in defense of his home.

• • •

Master Bin's formal challenge letter read:

My dear brother, the conflict between our people can no longer be resolved with words. Hundreds on both sides have taken arms to seek vengeance, and blood has flowed like rivers. In two short days, countless men were slaughtered, our civilian town of White Clay attacked and burned, and the common folk in He Ku beaten and humiliated.

Yet, through all this, there were rumors throughout the Martial Society that you, my dear brother, are inferior in actual combat. This gossip came about because my son Dong, whom I've personally trained, defeated and slaughtered your adopted son Stump, whom you personally trained. It's natural for the uneducated to make such crude assumptions, yet, I extend my concerns to you about your reputation and the reputation of the coalition you worked so dearly to assemble.

It is, therefore, in my most humble opinion, now necessary for us to resolve this matter on a more personal level. I hereby issue a formal challenge for a sword duel to be held on Yellow Sand Plateau in three days. This duel will resolve all conflicts between the two Dragon Houses. It will be held in front of the great heroes of the Martial Society, so that they may bear witness to your true martial arts abilities, which, I am afraid, have been tarnished by the slain Stump.

Lord Xu slowly lifted his eyes from the letter, his face numb, burning. He was standing beside a wooden coffin—Stump's coffin. The body was brought back to him yesterday, and he had stood beside it ever since.

Master Bin's messenger was dressed in red, as if celebrating a joyful event. He stood with arms crossed and head held high. Was he mocking the death of his son? Lord Xu lowered his eyes and read the letter a second time.

Then, without warning, he shot forward and closed his fingers around the messenger's throat. He stared into the bulging eyes, smiled at his frantic attempt to escape and asked gently, "What did the oracle say, Uncle Tan?"

Uncle Tan, his only hand holding a cup of tea, stepped forward with his head bowed. "Master, the oracle wanted to know whether we prefer to sacrifice the head of an oxen, a sheep, or a horse."

The messenger began to spasm.

Lord Xu gazed gently at his servant. "And have you replied?"

"I haven't."

"Good. Tell him we'll use a human head. The head of a Red Dragon messenger."

Uncle Tan bowed. "Yes, Lord."

Lord Xu snapped the neck of his victim, and with one fluid movement drew the sword of a nearby guard and lopped the messenger's head off. Before the body could fall, he tore off his clothing.

On the naked back of the messenger, Lord Xu carved the words "invitation accepted." He ordered the body returned to Redwood Cliff.

• • •

Cricket stared at the letter in his hands. It was handed to him by a mute girl with an oversized axe and a little mule bell hanging from her waist. She came to him in front of White Clay Village where he was supervising the salt production in place of his older brother.

Cricket read the letter over and over again. He shook

his head each time and thought of burning the letter, but couldn't resist the temptation. Tao Hing was too far away, and Old Snake was gone. He had no one to consult.

With a deep sigh, he read the letter one last time.

Your sister is buried among my ancestors in Mongolia. She left behind a sheepskin that she wanted you to have. Come to the steppe and ask for the number one warrior. I will be waiting for you, and if you don't arrive by the end of summer, I will destroy the sheepskin.
Suthachai

Cricket folded the letter and buried it in his pockets. The end of summer was not far away. If his sister's lover had survived and kept the one article she left behind for him, he would have to leave right away.

. . .

Master Bin stood under the Triangle of Reform, where all corporal punishment on Redwood Cliff was carried out. He envisioned the Flute Demon dangling over him, her clothes soaked in her own blood, her lifeless body whipped again and again. It was on this platform that he truly lost his daughter.

A deep sigh escaped his lips. What if he hadn't enforced his authority that day? What if she hadn't died?

Then Old Snake would be here, and so would the Butcher. All one hundred Gentle Swordsmen would be guarding Redwood Cliff, and tomorrow's duel would be a fleeting thought.

He noticed Dong beside him. His hotheaded son had been quiet the past few days, even timid at times. Perhaps his temper had been drained by all the bloodshed.

"Is Tao Hing coming home?" Master Bin asked.

"I heard in less than a week."

Master Bin sighed. "I don't know if I've made the right decision—doing this without Tao Hing."

"We'll win, father. We'll destroy them."

"I hope so."

"We have the battle formation of an immortal. Our men are well trained and they have indestructible shields. We won't lose." Dong clenched his fists. "Even Black Shadow can't get past the moving wall."

"The immortal . . . " Master Bin said with a sigh. "Who is he, really? What does he want?"

"He's an enemy of Uncle Xu's for sure. Maybe Uncle Xu did something to him and he wants revenge. He needs to use us to kill off the Green Dragons. So we help each other. What's wrong with that?"

A long pause. Master Bin placed a hand on his son's shoulder. "I hope you're right. I did receive word that many Houses will attend. They're part of Wei Xu's coalition."

Dong let out a laugh. "The more the merrier. We can avenge our men with a single battle."

Master Bin said nothing. He remained transfixed on the Triangle of Reform, lost in thought. Dong began to pace back and forth.

"Where's her flute?" Master Bin suddenly asked.

"I don't know. It was lost." Dong paused and looked into his father's eyes, a hint of jealousy on his face. Master Bin muttered something and turned away.

"I believe the Immortal knows where your sister's body is."

Dong froze. "He does? Then where is she? Where's the sheepskin?"

"The sheepskin's no longer important," Master Bin said

with a sigh. "My brother already has a counteragent. Tomorrow, we'll eliminate the coalition, and the battle will be so bloody even the emperor will hear of it. He'll thank us. The imperial kingdom is always afraid of armed coalitions. If we win, we'll rule the Martial Society. I just wish . . . " His face darkened.

"Fei Fei's gone, father," Dong said. "She betrayed us. She killed the Butcher and our best men. She's the one who brought this upon us."

Master Bin closed his eyes and took a deep, trembling breath. He changed the subject. "How many of the Red Headbands survived?"

"Only sixty." Dong lowered his head. "But we killed more than we lost—much more. Almost all of the Thunder Broadswords are wiped out. Uncle Xu trained a new generation of broadsword users and we've killed so many of them that—"

"Wei Xu has many more capable fighters," Master Bin interrupted him. "And there's always Black Shadow. We need to win tomorrow, no matter what."

• • •

The bandits of Pigeon's Head, all forty-four of them, sat together in a large storage room lit by numerous torches and candles. Some of them were counting their arrows, some cleaning their weapons, while others were tying together small bundles of hay. A few of them were asleep on the floor, and another group sat together tearing apart large chunks of roast pork. Caskets of rice wine were being passed around the room, each bandit taking a sip and handing the alcohol to the man next to him.

Li Kung sat in the far end of the room, watching them,

a smaller bottle of wine in his hand. Ying was tying hay bundles next to him.

Liu Yun approached them and bowed once at Ying before turning to Li Kung. "Master, are you going to give me some of that green powder? For tomorrow?"

Li Kung reached for a large canvas sack beside him and tossed it to Liu Yun. "Be very careful. If it catches fire anywhere near you, your entire body will look like that roast pig they're eating."

"Yes, master," Liu Yun said with a smile. He took the powder and turned away.

A large bandit with sideburns came forward. "Master Li, I haven't received my coins yet."

Li Kung turned to Ying. She reached for a cloth bag next to her, produced a small scroll containing a long list of names, and combed through it. After awhile, she turned to the bandit with a nod and handed him a heavy pouch. The bandit grinned and reached out with both hands to accept his coins.

"What are you going to do with all that money, Big Tong?" Li Kung asked, sitting up.

"I don't understand, Master Li."

"It's a lot of gold. What do you plan to do after tomorrow?"

"Well, I haven't thought about it, Master Li," the large bandit said. "I know we can't come back here. You want us never to set foot here again . . . "

"I don't want any one of you being a bandit again. And you don't need to. You have enough money now. The people's lives are hard enough—they don't need to worry about being robbed or kidnapped."

The room was quiet then. Everyone stopped what they were doing to listen.

Li Kung turned to Fat Shu. "What are you going to do after tomorrow?"

Fat Shu smiled and turned to look at his companions with a wink before placing his shiny saber in front of him. "I'm going to get a wife."

The room roared with laughter. The caskets were passed around again as a few men drank to his bold plans, while a few started to unleash vulgar remarks at him.

"Wait!" Fat Shu shouted over their jeering. "What are you laughing at?"

"Who are you going to kidnap this time?"

"Who said anything about kidnap? I'm getting a real wife. A virgin."

The laughter in the room suddenly became so loud that no one could shout over each other. Finally, after a long time, someone stood up and shouted, "You can't get a virgin! They don't sell them at brothels!"

"Maybe you can get an old widow if you're lucky!" someone else shouted.

Fat Shu picked up his shiny saber and pretended to threaten the men around him. A few drew their own weapons and stood up to fight.

"That's enough," Li Kung said. The noise quickly faded, and Fat Shu resumed his seat. Li Kung turned to another bandit. "And Skinny Lin, what are you going to do with your money after tomorrow?"

"I'm going to He Ku to open a dumpling shop," Skinny Lin replied.

"Dumpling shop?" Fat Shu asked, leaning forward, his mouth opened.

"I'm going to have a shop and I'm going to make dumplings."

"Do you know how?"

"Of course I do!" Skinny Lin shouted, his face beaming with excitement. "My mother used to have a dumpling shop in the city. She taught me all about pork dumplings before she died."

"How did she die?" Li Kung asked.

Skinny Lin paused. "Well, I don't really know."

"Of course he doesn't know," Fat Shu said. "Because she didn't. She ran off with another man."

Skinny Lin jumped to his feet, grabbed his own saber, and launched at Fat Shu. Two men slipped in front of him, holding him back and pulling him away. The room exploded into laughter again.

Li Kung frowned. Skinny Lin looked like he was about to cry.

"Horseface Mi!" Li Kung said, as loud as he could. The bantering men in front of him quickly retreated.

"Yes, Master Li!" Horseface Mi responded. A tall man, his ridiculously long face enhanced by a curly moustache, came forward.

"Have you thought of what you're going to do with your money?"

"I certainly have, Master Li. After tomorrow, I'm going to pack my bags and go to a distant province."

"What are you going to do in a distant province?"

"I'm going to buy myself a government post. I'll have enough money to become a judge."

"A judge?" someone asked from the back of the room. "How? You can't read or write."

Horseface Mi grinned. "Judges don't need to know how to read or write."

"Then how would you know how to judge?"

"Judging is easy. I'll just favor the side who gives me the best bribe."

Everyone, even Li Kung this time, burst into laughter. Men were slapping their knees, rolling over on haystacks, some choking on their rice wine.

"What's so funny?" Horseface Mi asked. "Everyone takes bribes. It's not robbery, so Master Li doesn't have a problem with it."

Li Kung shook his head and turned away. He noticed Liu Yun standing by himself in a corner, his face frozen, his eyes locked on the floor tiles, his hands clutching the pouch of green powder that Li Kung had just given him.

"Liu Yun," Li Kung called.

Liu Yun slowly lifted his head. "Yes, master."

"What are you going to do with your money after tomorrow?"

"I've already spent my money, master."

"You have? How?"

"I've paid for three hundred people to come and cry at my funeral."

A wave of eerie silence swept across the room. Every man turned to stare.

"My funeral is next week," Liu Yun continued in a low, monotonous voice. "I won't make it out alive tomorrow. I don't have any family to cry next to my coffin, but it's going to be a glorious funeral. You can count on it."

Liu Yun turned back to the pouch of green powder in his hands and again seemed oblivious to the men around him. The bandits looked at each other, then at Li Kung.

"I'm going out west after tomorrow," Li Kung said quickly. The bandits relaxed.

"What's out west, master?"

"I don't know yet. There are some mountains and waterfalls out there that I heard can reach the heavens. And then maybe I'll go south to see the country of Dali."

"Are you going alone?" Fat Shu asked with a mischievous grin.

Li Kung turned and glanced at Ying, who kept her head down and her eyes lowered.

"I'm taking Ying with me," he said.

Every bandit stood on his feet to cheer, and the room shook with applause. Ying turned away, her face blushing to a crimson red.

. . .

"The duel's tomorrow, Tan," Lord Xu said, leaning against the trunk of a tree beside Lake Eternal. His servant was the only one with him.

The Green Dragon master sipped from a gourd of wine, chuckling. "Wei Bin has no one left. His Red Headbands are nearly gone, and even Old Snake is gone. He's really going to have to face me alone—that's why he wanted a duel. Too bad Stump is not here to see this."

Uncle Tan shook his head. "My lord, maybe it would be safer if you don't go tomorrow."

"Why?"

"It seems too easy. Wei Bin never does anything without a plan, and right now, we don't know what his plan is."

"I've thought of that too. But Tan, we'll be in a wide-open valley, with so many men beside us. Maybe the only move left would be to catch me by surprise in this duel—to try to kill me with a single death blow."

"Then it's dangerous," Uncle Tan said in alarm.

Lord Xu pulled open his robe, revealing a thin, chain armor underneath. "This iron shirt is a rare item, left behind by my father. Wei Bin's sword can't pierce this. I'll win the duel. I'll avenge Stump."

"Can it be that easy?"

Lord Xu leaned back again and casually sipped his wine. "New swords will be issued for the duel, just in case he poisons the blades. Our men will comb the area to detect poison. We have him outnumbered. Don't worry. He's not so smart without Tao Hing."

. . .

Deep into the night, at the home of the Three Saints of Yunnan, Old Two rummaged through jar after jar of dried herbs. "Stupid boy," he mumbled. "I'll make sure I punish him for this. Makes a mess out of my herbs and leaves for six months. Stupid boy. I'll breed some fire ants and slip them in his pants so he will scratch all day in public."

He opened a jar, one that he didn't recognize, and paused. He sniffed it, then touched the ingredients. "What do you know?" he said with a smile. "The stupid boy likes to light fires so much he changed the green powder into an oil. How wonderful!"

He closed the jar and scratched his head, still mumbling to himself. "Oil makes big fires—bigger than powder. It might even explode. That should be fun."

. . .

By the time Li Kung arrived, Yellow Sand Plateau was already packed. Warriors from across the land, representing their respective Houses in the Martial Society, stood quietly in small clusters. Most of them were members of Lord Xu's coalition, and they were invited, or rather, compelled to gather in the center of the plateau. They formed a tight circle with row upon row of armed men.

Yellow Sand Plateau was virtually hidden behind the mountains above Northern Pass, just east of Phoenix Eye Peak. It was so far north, yet low enough in elevation, that the dry sands of the Mongolian desert would drift into the arid plateau during every dry season—hence the name, Yellow Sand Plateau. The terrain was in a bowl-like shape, with the lowest point, the bottom of the bowl, designated for Master Bin and Lord Xu's face-off. All spectators would then be on a slightly higher elevation.

Over three thousand people surrounded one small area—a strip of bare sand the length of two hundred steps—and three thousand pairs of eyes peered into the horizon, waiting for Master Bin to arrive with an army of men.

Li Kung edged closer, silent, artful, his eyes surveying the people around him. The most elite of the Green Dragons, the Chaos Spearmen, stood directly in front of him, all of them facing the center of the circle, their long spears planted by their sides. At the very forefront, Lord Xu stood tall like a great general, the shiny dagger horizontally planted in his topknot glistening against the sunlight.

Further around the circle were the primary members of Lord Xu's coalition, including Master Liang of the White Tigers, Master Chen of the Tuo Shan House, and Master Gao of the Northern Mantis. Their men, each numbering well over a hundred, stood behind them with weapons clasped to their sides.

Li Kung smiled. This was Lord Xu's reward for those loyal to him during the failed invasion of Redwood Cliff. He granted them some leadership in his coalition.

Behind each coalition unit were more groups of the Martial Society, each personally invited to bear witness to the duel. Once again, schools from across the land were compelled to send representatives in yet another showdown of the Dragon Houses. They gathered an armed mass of such numbers that even the emperor would have been alarmed.

Whispers began to float across the plateau. Someone was casually approaching on horseback. He was alone, dressed completely in white, and unarmed.

"Master Bin," the crowd whispered all at once. "He came alone . . ."

Li Kung smiled. This truly was an ingenious way to use the Formation of the Octagonal Cage. Master Bin would need time to set his new warriors into position. This could only be done with a long, drawn-out duel, where every pair of eyes would be focused on the twins. No one would notice a thing. Li Kung also needed time for his own men to assume positions. At the sight of the Red Dragon leader strolling in on horseback, as if nothing in the world bothered him, Li Kung uttered a sigh of relief. Master Bin would set an ambush in wide-open terrain, and Li Kung would take advantage of the ensuing chaos. It could only be perfect.

Everyone noticed the smile in Master Bin's eyes. He seemed to be passing by for afternoon tea, or to recite poetry on a beautiful spring day. He greeted each school of men with a light nod and a pleasant smile, folding his hands together like a true gentleman. The remarkable ability to be calm and carefree had always been Master Bin's most admired characteristic—and no one expected less of him.

He brought his horse to a halt in the middle of the circle, dismounted and bowed to his brother. He slapped the horse, sending it away, and walked forward. Every man on Yellow Sand Plateau held his breath.

A young man stepped forward, his head bowed, an embroidered box in his hands.

"My younger brother first," Lord Xu said with contempt. The box was brought to Master Bin, then opened. There were two identical swords inside, both newly sharpened and polished. Master Bin lifted one, held the naked blade in front of his eyes, and smiled.

"These are beautiful," he exclaimed. The sword bearer delivered the second weapon to Lord Xu.

Master Chen came forward and held up both hands, indicating that he wished to speak. Wei Bin moved to the side and waited.

"We're gathered here today," Master Chen of the Tuo Shan House began, reciting the formalities from memory, "to witness a call of truce between the Red Dragons of Redwood Cliff, and the Green Dragons of the Garden of Eternal Light. Decades of misunderstanding have brought about much bloodshed between these two prominent Houses, and it's through the wisdom and sacrifice of both leaders that a final resolution will be reached today."

Li Kung leaned forward for a better view of Master Bin's face. Impossible . . . Master Bin would be trapped inside his own Octagonal Cage during the duel. He needed to break out of the encirclement before revealing the formation.

Then, Li Kung noticed a subtle smile. A confident smile. The Red Dragon leader did have a plan to elude three thousand men. Somehow, despite being enclosed by an armed audience loyal to his brother, he seemed certain of his escape.

"The friendly duel today may result in injury or death," Master Chen was saying. "It has been agreed upon between both parties that no further retaliation, and no additional grievances, will be sought between the Red and Green Dragons after this duel. This contest will be the conclusion to all past and present conflicts of the Dragon Houses."

A match between two leaders would only fuel the hate between their men, Li Kung mused. It was clear that Master

Bin needed this opportunity to use his Octagonal Cage formation. But why did Lord Xu agree to it?

Master Chen quickly departed from the enclosed arena, glad to be away from the center of attention. Slowly, Lord Xu stepped forward, his lips quivering, his glaring eyes narrowed, his fingers gripping the sword so that veins protruded from the back of his hand.

Li Kung understood. Sheer hate caused the Green Dragon master to blunder. The desire to avenge Stump had shadowed his logic, and the eagerness to eliminate his brother had weakened his use of deceit. His men, though numerous and strong, were already in the open, while Master Bin came alone with his main weapon still hidden. The victor was already decided.

Wei Bin lifted his sword, held it vertically in front of him with both hands, and bowed. Lord Xu sneered, took a bold step forward, his weapon chambered by his side. He moved within striking distance.

Every man on Yellow Sand Plateau held his breath. No one blinked, no one twitched a muscle, and no one made a sound. A subtle breeze floated across the air, accompanied by fine particles of yellow sand, blurring the atmosphere. Li Kung peered far into the edge of the plateau and watched for signs of the Octagonal Cage Formation. But not a trace of sand was being disturbed in the distance.

He looked at his own men: the tall bandit dressed as a swordsman in the thick of the crowd, the bearded bandit with the straw hat at the rear, and a smaller bandit hidden behind the rocks in the distance. Beyond the shallow drop at the edge of the plateau, completely out of sight, Li Kung knew that the Six Guardians and over a hundred men from Pigeon's Head were making preparations.

Lord Xu suddenly moved so decisively that the audience didn't even have time to gasp. A stinging flash of steel preceded a barrage of blows, all sidearm strikes, attacking Master Bin like so many arrows approaching from every direction.

The swords crossed. Dust flew around them in an expanding whirlwind.

Li Kung glanced toward the edge of the plateau in eager anticipation. Master Bin could not be fighting his hardest. He was waiting for the Octagonal Cage to form, so that most of the coalition, with the elite warriors of the Green Dragons, could be eliminated together.

The swords moved with blinding speed. In a moment, the blades were too badly damaged to cut silk, but the twins continued to pound at each other.

Then, both swords broke in a massive collision, and new swords were immediately presented to them.

Finally, Li Kung saw it. A glimpse of rising sand arose from the edge of the plateau, hardly in view, but unmistakably there. It was about to begin. He turned to signal the bandit buried in the middle of the crowd but found the tall ruffian staring at the duel with his jaw hanging open. Li Kung clenched his fists. He knew the wretches were unreliable. He stared at the bandit, hoping to catch his attention, but all eyes were focused on the frenetic battle.

The dust of coarse sand, stirred by tremendous movement, became larger and denser. Li Kung blinked. There was too much sand, and all coming from the same direction. It could not be Master Bin's newly trained warriors. He glared at the bandit, his heart pounding. Look at me, he almost shouted out loud. Look at me!

At the rear of the crowd, the bearded bandit was standing on tiptoes, also watching the duel with absolute fascination. Li Kung shifted, wanting to seize their attention, but a warrior in the crowd glanced at him. He hesitated. It was no time to bring notice to himself. He had to wait.

The speed of the battle accelerated, taking on a new dimension of murderous resolve. Lord Xu wielded his sword with both hands, attacking only at close range, slashing with massive swipes. He struck with intent to kill. In a moment, both swords blew apart again.

New swords were brought forth at once. Lord Xu gasped for air, and, grabbing the new sword, charged forward again.

Li Kung heard a heavy rumbling in the distance, as if thousands of men were advancing. He braced himself. Yes, the noise! It would bring confusion, and he would have time to signal his men. But Master Bin wouldn't send a thousand men, all of his men, into the plateau for a final showdown. Something else was approaching.

No one heard the rumbling yet. The sound of metal colliding at incredible velocities dominated the plateau. No one paid attention to anything else.

The Green Dragon leader received a vicious cut to his forearm, and grimacing with frustration, began to strike with random blows. He's making mistakes, Li Kung thought. His movements were beginning to show fatigue and inconsistencies. His stamina was falling. But Master Bin couldn't possibly be so stupid as to kill his twin now.

Then, the deep rumbling from the edge of the plateau became unmistakable. Many in the crowd finally turned, only to see an onslaught of horses—hundreds of them, all charging at incredible speed. Their backs were bare, their snouts free of harnesses.

Master Bin suddenly leaped backwards, turned, and struck at the front of the audience.

No one expected a murderous move toward the spectators. No one expected an act so cruel. Again and again,

Master Bin slashed the men of the coalition. They fell back in chaos, in frantic retreat, struggling to draw their weapons. Shouts of anger and frustration emerged across the plateau. More fell to Master Bin's lightning-fast sword. Lord Xu stood motionless, hesitating, staring wide-eyed with shock.

The horses were storming directly at them, their flowing manes and whipping tails blurred against the sunlight. Sand was beaten into the air by a thousand horse hooves, forming a cloud, masking the number of approaching animals.

Master Bin uttered a shout, jerked his body in a twisting spin and flung his sword at his brother's face. Lord Xu blocked, and in a flash, the younger twin was upon him. They crashed together into the coarse sand, Master Bin on top, both weapons dislodged. He began to pound his older brother's face with bare fists.

Then, the horses were upon them. The crowd fell into absolute chaos. Every man bolted into each other to avoid being run over. Weapons were drawn in panic. Men swung at the animals to protect themselves. The ground shook. The thunder of running horses implied that war was already upon them.

Amidst blankets of flying sand, Li Kung moved straight into the storming horses. He ran between the charging beasts, moving through them in the thick of the sand clouds, his lean figure virtually invisible. He reached the bearded bandit in the back of the chaos, grabbed him, drew his face close and shouted, "Run! Give the signal!"

The bearded bandit nodded once and took off toward the other end of the plateau. Li Kung spun around and ran in an opposite direction.

The horses tore through the crowd of three thousand men like a sharp knife slicing through paper. The charging animals only injured a few. Most of the men evaded the onrush, but the agitation and disorder intensified. Leaders of each school screamed for order. Lord Xu's spearmen tried to form lines and slay the animals, but they couldn't find each other in the chaos.

In a moment, the horses swept past them. Like a gust of violent wind, the animals left them behind.

"Wei Bin!" someone shouted. More shouts. The warriors of the coalition stared at the fading horses, at the one charger with a single rider quickly disappearing into the horizon. Finally, they realized what had just happened. Wei Bin had mounted one of the horses and escaped their thick encirclement with no effort. All they could do was watch.

The men stared at each other, muttering amongst themselves, each eyeing Lord Xu with a subtle look of ridicule.

Then, the sound of rushing feet drew their attention back to the far ends of the plateau. Out of nowhere, as if born from under the sand, four solid walls of dark brown wood began to move toward them—one from each direction—each wall taller than the tallest man on the plateau. The dust had not yet settled. No one knew what approached them, but instantly, panic took over.

Half blinded by the haze of sand, distrustful of each other and fearful of the new threat, the men of the United Martial Society Coalition began to back into a tight circle. The walls closed in. The leaders of each House shouted their orders as loud as they could, but for a moment, no one responded.

"Chaos Spearmen!" Lord Xu roared. "Formations!"

The elite spearmen of the Green Dragons fell into position, moving quickly to the very front of the circle, forming a battle line three layers deep. They clenched their heavy spears in front, arced slightly upwards, and the men in back positioned themselves between the shoulders of the men in front.

. . .

The enemy came closer, and Lord Xu realized it was not a wall, but a long line of massive shields held closely together. There were about sixty shields approaching from each direction, creating the eight sides of an octagon, boxing them in.

"Coalition!" Lord Xu shouted. "Draw your weapons! Prepare to fight the Red Dragons!"

Every man's weapon was already drawn. A beat of drums sounded out of nowhere, and the wall accelerated.

"Attack!" someone shouted. "Kill them!"

Over three thousand men simultaneously responded. They roared their own desperate war cries and charged with weapons held high. No one bothered to verify who ordered them forward—it didn't matter anymore. The only thing they could do was fight and kill.

"No!" Lord Xu screamed. But the bellow of three thousand men muffled his voice. A sudden wave of fear struck him, and he screamed again. "No!"

No one knew how these walls attacked. The men of the coalition were poorly organized, uncoordinated, running into walls with false courage while mentally unprepared. A cold sweat broke on Lord Xu's head. He should have known. His brother wouldn't challenge him to a duel with such innocence.

The walls closed in rapidly, to the point where the adjacent lines prepared to merge. Then, the southeast wall began to bend away to form a straight line against the southern wall. The other three corner walls also began to shift, pivoting from one end while moving forward, forming new corners while changing the octagon into a square. In a moment, four long walls, hardly a gap between them, began to enclose the coalition. The Octagonal Cage Formation became the Square Cage Formation.

Li Kung understood. The enemy was too few for the formation he copied from Snow Wolf's manuals. Master Bin had modified the Octagonal Cage to transform at will.

Then, the shields began to spread apart—just a crack, but enough to see the muscular men wielding them. The shields were mounted on each man's left shoulder, their right arms dragging a chain behind them.

Master Chen raised his sword and charged. His men were close behind.

"No!" Lord Xu extended his hand, as if he could get to them in time and pull them back from instant death, as if the muted shout would ever reach their ears.

The Red Dragons, almost completely hidden behind their shields, twisted their bodies and swung the chain they had been dragging.

Lord Xu's eyes widened with horror. Huge, spiked balls of solid iron, attached to the chains, heaved into the air like a tidal wave and collapsed downward with the force of falling boulders.

Master Chen's head exploded. The men directly behind him shrieked in horror and tried to flee. But the entire wall moved forward one leaping step. The spiked iron balls rained upon them with a second volley, then a third, crushing the unfortunate ones who could not run in time. Men dropped, their bodies so badly mangled that they instantly became indistinguishable from each other.

The ground shook. Lord Xu spun around. All four sides of the plateau began to thunder in violent tremors. The walls were closing in rapidly. The warriors of the coalition floundered back from all four directions, lost in terror, fumbling for footing. They screamed to renew their nerves, crying to the gods for mercy, shouting vile insults and profanity to boost each other's morale.

The proud warriors of the Martial Society screamed like cornered animals and swarmed directly into the murder.

"No!" Lord Xu shouted. "Attack the ends! Attack the far ends of the walls!"

No one heard him. A thousand men, no longer under control, charged headlong into the enemy.

The Red Dragon formation was there to receive them. Hundreds of spiked globes rained upon them from the sky. The first wave of men crumbled under the heavy steel. Behind them, the coalition warriors continued to charge, taking hold of the instant when the chain was being retracted, in between swings, when the murderous ball had not yet come around. They attempted to narrow the distance.

The Red Dragon wall instantly closed together and formed a seamless barrier. Now, using the shields as weapons, they propelled themselves forward and slammed their charging foes.

The coalition vanguard flew back and collided into the next wave of men behind them; their weapons lodged into the wooden shields and were instantly rendered useless. They became entangled. As they packed into a maelstrom of scrambling bodies, the Red Dragon walls opened again. The iron balls launched into the air once more.

The men had nowhere to run. The steel globes smashed everything in its descending path, killing instantly. Some were merely grazed by the steel globes, but the long spikes tore through skin and muscle. There were screams, and more screams. Wave after wave, the chained balls of spiked steel pummeled the helpless men.

Lord Xu ordered his spearmen to attack the ends of the eastern wall. But all they could do was retreat. The rain of death descended at incredible speeds, pounding a thick cloud of sand into the air every time it struck. It completely blinded the spearmen, offering them little chance to slip forward between the chains. A few managed to attack the shields—they knew they had one chance—but their spears could do nothing against the treated wood. The Red Dragon shields were impenetrable. The warhead of a spear always pierced halfway into the wood and became impossible to withdraw.

Meanwhile, the rest of the coalition gathered for another desperate charge, this time with courage that was never there. Death was certain, imminent, not the glorious death so romanticized in the Martial Society, but a cowardly one. In the face of extermination, the warriors of the coalition rushed forward, the sheer mass of their numbers capable of toppling the wall supported by a single line of men. But they were disorganized. Their attack was poorly timed, such that a gap was left between the coalition warriors colliding with the dark wooden shields and their comrades who supported them from behind.

The Red Dragons were trained for this in a manner clearly outlined in Li Kung's scroll. With a shout, the warriors behind the shields suddenly drew back, foiling the momentum of the onrushing men. As the first wave of coalition warriors struck empty air, the shields closed together into a perfect wall and slammed forward once more.

The warriors of the coalition were trained to fight single opponents all their lives, and had never seen such large-scale coordination. They were hit so hard that they caved into those behind them, like layers of tiles being swept away by a hammer, so that every man was thrown backward into someone else. They struggled for footing, for some sort of direction or sense, when the heavy iron globes roared into the air. Murder rained upon them again, tightening its choke on three thousand men.

· · ·

At the other end of the plateau, Li Kung hid completely unnoticed behind a row of boulders. He clenched his fists as the horror unfolded before him, his eyes wide, in shock, his lips quivering.

Far in the distance, standing on a higher elevation, Master Bin stood with a group of men to watch the slaughter. Li Kung had noticed them there for some time. Originally, Green Dragon scouts had occupied the area. But Dong had slipped in from behind when the horses were released and quietly slaughtered them. Now, with war drums readied, Dong stood beside his father with a cold smile on his face.

"We need to wait," Li Kung said, almost to himself. "We need to wait for the Red Dragons to win . . . "

Out of the corner of his eye, he saw a figure tear across the surface of the plateau. For a moment, he thought it was a black horse that had somehow returned. Then, it dawned upon him that it was a man, a masked man dressed completely in black. He moved with such speed that a cloud of sand, as tall as a horse, trailed behind him. Li Kung's heart skipped a beat. Black Shadow!

Meanwhile, almost a third of the coalition had perished. Those still alive were completely enclosed, with nowhere to retreat, and no chance of escape.

But the Octagonal Cage couldn't advance quickly. The carpet of corpses beneath their feet, now on its third layer, was so bloody that the warriors behind the shields couldn't gain proper footing. More than once, the Red Dragons slipped or stumbled, slowing the entire formation. But gradually, almost inevitably, the formation progressed forward.

The morale of the coalition had completely collapsed. Men were belting each other, struggling to escape the advancing enemy, scrambling as close as possible to the center of the circle they were imprisoned in. Some shoved each other forward, to their deaths, so the pile of bodies could be stacked higher, and, perhaps into a barrier that would temporarily block the onslaught.

Lord Xu fought his way into the dense circle of struggling men, his elite Chaos Spearmen closely around him. The men of the Martial Society were being hacked down and demolished. "This is it," he said out loud, though no one heard him. "I lost."

Then, amidst the thundering of the iron globes, despite the screams of the butchered men, a distinct shriek of pain could be heard. It came from behind the shields, from a Red Dragon. Lord Xu looked up with hope. A shadow flew past the back line of Red Dragon men and more cries were heard, followed by a break in the middle of the northern wall. Three men fell forward on top of their shields, their backs shredded to ribbons.

"Black Shadow!" Lord Xu shouted. "Break the north! Break the north!"

Black Shadow darted forward with the speed of an arrow, cleanly decapitating a Red Dragon with his sword. Then, as he reached the edge of the western wall, he drilled a devastating kick into the side of the line. Five more shields went down. A gaping hole was instantly opened in the formation.

Lord Xu turned to his men, grabbed two swords from nearby warriors and struck them together. The distinct sound of colliding metal instantly drew the attention of hundreds. The coalition heard, and responded.

"Attack in unison!" Lord Xu shouted. "Fight through the opening and hit them from behind! Now!"

Then, the Red Dragon formation changed in response to three rapid beats of the drum. Every other man spun around to face the opposite direction. The shields squeezed together, creating a two-sided wall that was smaller, but completely protected from front and back. Somehow, Master Bin had prepared them to face Black Shadow.

Black Shadow planted another kick into a shield and sent the warrior flying back. In the same momentum, he leaped through the crack of the wall and slashed a Red Dragon across the throat.

But the men were trained to face him: the most feared man in the Martial Society, the one man who could single-handedly disrupt the flawless formation. The Red Dragons withdrew under a single beat of the drum, and the shields closed, leaving a narrow crack. Then, the chains were swung in unison, not at him, but in front of him. Huge clouds of dirt swept into the air, swirling in a dense cloud that seemed to never die. More steel globes pounded the ground, and Black Shadow could do nothing but retreat. He couldn't see the weapons coming at him.

Li Kung looked on from far away, puzzled. He had noticed it for some time. Black Shadow never deflected, nor attacked with his left arm. It seemed like he didn't have one.

Li Kung held up his hand and readied his men. The bandits of Pigeons Head, all forty-four of them, grabbed their weapons and waited. Black Shadow was in the northeastern end of the formation—far enough away and too heavily engaged to be a threat. It was time to bring the battle to a new level.

Li Kung flung his hand forward and the bandits ran onto the plateau.

. . .

Master Bin's face darkened at the first sight of Black Shadow. His formation began to cave. Although his men could protect themselves by turning to face both fronts at once, the new openings created by Black Shadow would present his brother with an opportunity of escape.

Master Bin's fists clenched. His brother was fighting through his flawless formation. How did the immortal fail to foresee this? How could his brother escape so easily? Black Shadow was hammering the edge of the walls with little mercy, and soon, he would reach Wei Xu. The hated twin would be safe.

"Man the drums," Master Bin shouted. He leaped onto the chestnut stallion by his side and rode into the plateau, drawing his sword as he approached the slaughter. "Red Dragons!" he shouted. "Open for me!"

His men heard and responded. Four shields quickly shifted over, creating an opening in the east wall, and Master Bin charged through. The walls immediately closed behind him.

His horse trampled on the bodies strewn across the land, forcing it into panic. Master Bin dismounted with disgust. Lord Xu's thin figure was not far away.

Meanwhile, Black Shadow completely destroyed the entire left flank of the northern wall, but the Red Dragons regrouped instantly. They closed the shields to maintain the impenetrable formation, and systematically bombarded the sand with enough speed and frequency to keep him at bay. Black Shadow's sword was long lost; it was embedded in one of the shields, and he was only able to kill with his deadly kicks. Despite his speed, despite his inhuman fighting ability, Black Shadow was unable to crack the Octagonal Cage.

Master Bin slashed his way through the thick of the battle. Moments later, he stood face to face with his twin.

There was a smile on Master Bin's face, an expression of triumph, of victory, of a man preparing to slaughter a sheep. Then, without warning, Master Bin launched himself on his brother. He knew Black Shadow was far away, and he knew his brother was exhausted from enduring the long massacre.

Master Bin attacked his twin like a lion pouncing on its prey. Their swords crossed, just for a single collision, then, with an intentional twist, Master Bin forced both weapons to fly from their hands. He struck Lord Xu's armpit powerfully, twice, three times, before dislocating his brother's left shoulder and dragging him to the ground. Lord Xu fought back with a chain of short-range kicks.

Meanwhile, Dong watched nervously from the hilltop. His father had entered the very thick of slaughter, and Black Shadow was breaking down the Octagonal Cage formation. The walls were no longer complete. The men of the coalition were no longer trapped, though they still had to fight for their lives. The broken walls, now double sided, shifted back and forth on the plateau, murdering any man it could reach with its iron globes in full swing.

A group of men approached the battle, out of nowhere, and stopped a short distance away. They were carrying straw baskets. Dong squinted to focus his eyes. "Bandits?"

The bandits, numbering no more than fifty, formed a crooked line on the open space. Each man drew a bundle of hay from his basket and ignited it, then pulled out a small hunting bow and a quiver of arrows.

Dong became alarmed, and then checked himself. He heard one of his henchmen laughing.

"What's funny?" Dong asked.

The Red Dragon bowed his head. "The little criminals are trying to join the battle."

"Trying to join the battle?"

"Looks like it," the warrior said with a small laugh. "But they're standing so far away with hunting bows. Not even war bows. And the row of flames in front of them. Must be their wall of defense. It's so small even a child could leap across. The arrows will be completely spent before reaching the battle lines."

Dong forced a smile. Then he noticed the arrows, wrapped in cloth, conveniently lit in the fire before them.

The bandits pointed deep into the sky and released a volley of flaming missiles. The arrows were so poorly aimed that all of them landed short, and the Red Dragon warrior laughed out loud again. The bandits drew another round of arrows from their quivers, and after dipping the tip in the flames, fired into the air again.

This time, many of the missiles landed near the battle. One flaming arrow, completely spent, dropped onto a shield in the northern wall.

The shield exploded into a burst of flames so massive, so intense, that the men around it instantly caught fire. Fresh screams reached the heavens then, and murder and devastation on the plateau took on a new dimension. The blast hurled the adjacent shields of the northern wall flying into the air. As they landed, they too caught fire in an earsplitting explosion. The inferno reached out like so many groping arms, indiscriminately striking every man, igniting him.

Then, another volley shrieked into the air.

Dong screamed. The impenetrable shields, created by an immortal, caught fire faster than anything he could imagine. The flames were immense, unnatural, intentional

. . . He had never seen anything like it. "Red Headbands!" he shouted. "Attack! Attack! Save Master Bin!"

The sixty remaining Red Headbands responded with a shout, charging down the slope and into the battle. Out of nowhere, six masked figures leaped forward and attacked the Red Headbands head-on. The Six Guardians had been waiting. Dong panicked. He charged down the hill on a horse, only to be forced into retreat.

Meanwhile, a third volley of blazing arrows ripped into the battlefield, and the entire western line ignited. The fire reached out and consumed every man in its path, leaving behind screams of suffering and devastation.

Master Bin was locked in an empty-hand battle against his twin when a streak of flames crossed in front of him, so close to his eyes that he was almost blinded. The entire Martial Society was under attack. He knew then that the Immortal of Phoenix Eye Peak was behind the destruction. Only he, who devised the formula for the impenetrable shields, could possibly know that the treated wood was explosively flammable. Only the immortal, who had created a formation where every warrior stood so close together, could cause such devastation with a small fire on a spent arrow. Wei Bin had always been suspicious of the self-styled immortal. But in the face of overwhelming enemies controlled by Wei Xu, he never revealed his doubts. At that moment, when a fourth layer of flames rained upon his men, he began to understand who his true enemy was.

But he was too late. A sharp pain pierced his left side. In panic, he surged forward and slammed his forehead into Lord Xu's nose. He looked down and gasped in shock. The gold dagger that his brother always wore in his topknot was planted deep in his abdomen. Blood had not yet begun to flow, but he knew that the wound was grave. With a roar, he tore the blade from his body and swung at Lord Xu's stomach.

His twin parried, but the blow was a feint. Master Bin slammed his head into his brother's nose a second time, and with the same momentum, planted the gold dagger deep into Lord Xu's thigh. Master Bin didn't pull out the blade. He gripped both of his twin's armpits in a stifling lock, slammed a sharp kick into Lord Xu's knee, broke his balance, and shoved forward. The blow paralyzed Lord Xu's left leg; the right leg was completely disabled by the dagger. He could do nothing but stumble back. He was pushed directly into the southern wall of the Octagonal Cage.

The thunder of the steel globes amplified behind him. Master Bin drove his brother forward. The fires hadn't touched the southern wall, and the Red Dragons, trained to obey only the drums, were not given the order to withdraw. Slowly, consistently, the Red Dragons treaded on the dead bodies.

Master Bin pushed his twin into the jaws of the Octagonal Cage. There was a smile on his face. It was a smile of pain and humiliation long gone, finally replaced with triumph—a smile of victory, beyond years of hate and jealousy, beyond mutual contempt and fear of each other. Master Bin smiled, not because of his pending victory, but because finally, the one man, his twin, who dared to declare himself equal to the great leader of Redwood Cliff, was about to die.

The southern wall inched toward them. The steel globes approached the back of Lord Xu's head.

Once again they were young, running across the surface of Redwood Cliff together as twins, immersed in the childish games they played. Once again, they were laughing at silly pranks, chasing each other to the edge of the cliff in friendly pursuit. Almost like yesterday, when the great leader

Fei Long handed them their very first wooden swords; they were so proud of themselves, and of each other.

Master Bin closed his eyes.

Lord Xu's head exploded. The steel globe that struck him was perfect in precision, blasting through his skull like it was a paper lantern.

Master Bin opened his eyes and released his twin's body.

A powerful gust of flaming wind swept across the air and grazed the southern wall. Wei Bin stood dazed, as the entire line of shields in front of him began to explode. Fire shrieked into the sky and rained upon him. He stared at the deformed body of his twin, a tear in his eye. Men all around him caught fire and trampled each other.

Still, no one could break out of the Octagonal Cage. The openings that Black Shadow created were completely blocked by new walls of fire. As the deadly inferno began to spread across the plateau, the blankets of black smoke clouding the heavens now began to descend. The struggling warriors could not see nor breathe. Choking, fighting to escape the stinging fumes and blinding heat, the Red Dragons, Green Dragons, and every man of the United Martial Society Coalition began to cut each other down, each hoping to clear a path for himself.

"Father!" someone called. Dong's voice. Master Bin tried to stare through the smoke, but couldn't see his son.

"Father!"

It was a different voice this time, much closer to him. It was a voice he didn't recognize.

Then, from behind him, the same voice, now louder than ever, shouted, "Father! I will avenge you!"

Master Bin spun around. A heavy spearhead shot past his eyes, barely missing him. He didn't recognize the blackened face charging at him. Master Bin, despite his wounds, stepped aside and took the spear from his attacker. He turned the weapon around as a blast of flames scorched the back of his neck, and without so much as a second glance, stabbed his assailant in the belly. He turned to walk away.

Death was everywhere. Master Bin clambered across the sea of corpses, unable to plant his foot on bare sand, blinded by thick smoke.

The man he just stabbed emitted a high-pitched scream. Wei Bin turned and finally recognized him: Liu Yun, the son of Iron Palm Liu, whose entire family was exterminated by the Flute Demon, lay twisting on the ground. With another shout, Liu Yun yanked the spear from his body.

A huge explosion swept across the remains of the southern wall. The fire reached dangerously close. Pieces of burning wood shrieked across the air, ripping through clusters of frightened warriors with nowhere to run. Liu Yun somehow climbed to his feet. His hand clutched his belly, and with a laugh that hardly sounded human, jumped into the fire.

His flailing figure instantly ignited. But, still alive and screaming with unbearable pain, Liu Yun charged at Wei Bin.

The Red Dragon leader stood weak, stunned, for the first time in his life completely petrified. He could do nothing—could not even scream—while the burning figure leaped forward and wrapped itself around his rigid body.

Suddenly, a blast of incredible heat enclosed Wei Bin. A leather pouch on Liu Yun, packed with Li Kung's green powder, ignited with a dreadful roar. Wei Bin's clothing immediately caught fire. He tried to grab Liu Yun to fling him away, but his fingers couldn't close upon the flaming body. He struggled, twisted, screaming in agony. The heat seared his face. He was blinded and snarled in confusion, unable to breathe, unable to shake the flames that rapidly consumed him. He writhed, desperate, as Liu Yun's arms locked around him in a deadly embrace, as both flaming bodies wracked with unspeakable pain.

Wei Bin screamed until the last second. His own hands, already on fire, clawed against Liu Yun's charred flesh. But he could not break the embrace. Moments later, as both bodies fell lifeless to the ground, the final movement was a subtle squeeze from Liu Yun. With his last breath, he clenched his enemy tighter.

Li Kung watched from afar with fists clenched and mouth open. He had withdrawn his bandits to the far edge of the plateau. Black Shadow had disappeared when Lord Xu fell, and no more than a thousand men remained trapped in the growing flames. The encircling walls of fire were so deep and tall that none of the men could approach them. Each struggled to stand on the little island of bare sand where the air was still breathable.

Then, out of nowhere, shouts emerged from the edge of the plateau. Almost twenty men, all mounted on massive chargers, were approaching the fire. The riders had two wooden barrels under each arm, perfectly balanced on their mounts even without the use of their hands.

The rider in the front was exceptionally tall and muscular. As he closed in on the outer ring of flames, he leaped onto his saddle and stood vertically on the running horse. With a shout, he threw both barrels into the screaming fire. A splash of water exploded against the ground. He pulled his horse away. The men behind him, one after another, threw their barrels of water. The flaming walls were quickly broken apart.

Li Kung's eyes flashed. It couldn't be, he told himself. It was impossible. He leaped onto the sandy surface and ran toward the horsemen. The tall rider saw him from a distance and began to approach.

It couldn't be, Li Kung said to himself again. He charged across the plateau. He needed a closer look.

The tall horseman halted when he drew close. He lifted his hand. "Li Kung!" he shouted.

Li Kung stopped when he recognized the face. He felt weak, sick, suddenly unsure of where he was or why he was there. "Suthachai . . ."

PROPHECY EIGHT

With courage, there is silence
The concealed knife unforeseen
In futile defiance of destiny
Retribution continues, unexpected

Suthachai began to approach him. Li Kung stared, his mind swirling, his eyes moving in and out of focus. The Mongolian's face no longer held the bluish tint. The customary streaks of blood on his clothing were no longer there, and the foggy eyes of a dying man had completely changed. In front of him was a man so magnificent in appearance, of such towering presence, that Li Kung suddenly felt small and vulnerable.

"Li Kung," Suthachai said again, his tall charger striding forward.

A ghost! It had to be a ghost. Li Kung shook his head, hoping to break the illusion, wishing that if he closed his eyes then opened them again, the Mongolian would disappear.

Inside the ring of fire, a horseman who spoke Chinese shouted to the warriors of the coalition. "This way! An opening this way! Follow us to safety!" He spoke with a thick Mongolian accent.

The flames continued to roar on the plateau, but rising from behind were men shouting with hope and joy. "An opening! An opening!"

Li Kung listened, his eyes closed. For a brief moment, a smile emerged on his face. He was happy for them . . .

The sound of horse hooves—from a single horse— seemed to move closer and closer. His heart skipped a beat. Suthachai was still there. He threw open his eyes and stared at the carnage, just for a glimpse, before shifting his gaze to the approaching Mongolian.

His poorly trained men of Pigeon's Head were far away. But even if they were beside him, a meager fifty bandits could do nothing against the greatest warrior of the Mongolian plains. He needed a plan—a quick one that would dismount Suthachai. Without his enormous horse, the Mongolian would be too slow to chase him.

He reached into his pocket and grasped a handful of green powder. Just enough. He narrowed his eyes. Suthachai moved closer.

"Li Kung, I need to talk to you."

Out of the corner of his eye, Li Kung observed the twenty horsemen. They were not all equal in size and strength. He identified the weakest one—a young man who followed the rear—and he bolted into the wall of fire.

"Li Kung!" he heard Suthachai call from behind. There was no time to look back. He vaulted over the licking flames and charged toward the thin warrior.

Suthachai followed, but his horse couldn't jump the wall of flames. He turned to circle the plateau, charging toward the one opening in the inferno. Screaming survivors, fleeing the heat in absolute chaos, cluttered his only entrance.

Li Kung reached the smaller warrior in a flash. He doused the young Mongolian's legs with green powder, then kicked a flaming splinter into him. The young man screamed. His legs were on fire. He fell off his mount and rolled across the sand in panic.

Li Kung tore across the fiery encirclement, leaped over the wall of flames and onto the open plateau. He glanced back once. Suthachai had dismounted and was helping the young man.

It was all downhill from there. Like a blind rabbit fleeing the jaws of a crippled wolf, Li Kung ran as hard as he could and left Yellow Sand plateau far behind him. But he continued to see the hundreds of mutilated bodies, the charred faces, the screaming souls. The heat of the afternoon sun seemed to pierce his skin like thousands of bent nails, scraping and burning his flesh as if alive inside of him.

A lake loomed before him. He was at the foot of Phoenix Eye Peak. Somehow, the thought of Snow Wolf's tomb high above him brought a dancing excitement into his blood. He plunged headfirst into the lake.

He stayed under for as long as he could, his eyes closed, the coolness of the water sinking into his veins. Victory! He leaped off the shallow floor of the lake, emerging with a roar, and raised his face to the heavens to holler his triumph.

Then there was silence. Li Kung slowly wiped the beads of water from his forehead. Months of meticulous planning, of enticing the evil of the land to exterminate each other, was all meant for this moment. He had done the impossible. He had taken on the entire Martial Society and won. In one afternoon, he had eliminated every threat the Dragon Houses were capable of. Now, completely crippled, the remaining men of the Red and Green Dragons would only have enough energy to hate each other and kill each other until both sides perished. They no longer had the ability to hurt the innocent. Li Kung smiled. Evil had been vanquished in a single, massive fire.

For a second, Li Kung stared into the water. The deformed face of a man, his skull crushed, was staring at him from within the lake. In panic, Li Kung swiped his hand through the water, scattering the image and sending wave after wave of ripples across the newly disturbed surface. He turned, and another face stared at him. This one was screaming. Li Kung uttered a cry, slapped his palm into the water, and scattered the tortured face once more.

Everywhere, all around him, the sounds of dying men seemed to echo from the waters. He heard them—unmistakably heard their helpless cries for help, for hope. Flashing in and out of the water were reflections of their agony, brief glimpses of their hideous deformities, enlarged and animated, as if ready to spring from the lake in vengeance.

Li Kung spun around in a frantic wave of confusion. Their ghosts had followed him. Their evil souls didn't perish in the flames of hell, but followed, as if he were to blame. With a hollow scream of rage, the cords of his neck protruding, Li Kung smashed his palms into the lake again and again, sending water high into the air. "How dare you come after me! How dare you seek vengeance for the punishment of your crimes! You've threatened to ruin the lives of millions. You would've committed unspeakable crimes if I hadn't stopped you! Wei Bin! Wei Xu! What right have you to live?"

The tortured faces began to rear and buck in the water, diving in and out of the surface, their gaping mouths and bulging eyes shimmering with every ripple. Li Kung screamed, clawing at his own face before tearing at the water in wild, frantic swings. "What right do any of you animals have to question me? What right do any of you have to live?"

The faces began to disappear, one by one fading into the depths of the water, all except for one. Li Kung stared. He

234

had seen this face before. The face of a thin man, in his forties, wearing the black hat of a high-ranking government official. The face was not gruesome, but it was staring at him, and smiling.

Li Kung's lips began to tremble, his hands began to shake, and a deep chill began to enclose him. The face in the water began to come nearer. His smile was twisted with contempt. Eventually, a hand emerged from the depths of the lake, clutching a decapitated head by the hair. He turned the head so Li Kung could see it.

"Auntie Ma," Li Kung whispered. Then, screaming, "No! Leave her alone, father! Leave her alone!"

Li Kung leaped at the face, his arms outstretched, scattering the image with one stroke of his arm. It appeared again, this time deeper in the water. Li Kung took a deep breath, so deep he thought his lungs would burst, and dived into the water.

The lake was shallow. He rushed so hard into his dive that the floor of the lake loomed before him, faster than he thought possible. He couldn't reach around to shield his head, didn't have time to jerk his body around so he could strike the floor of the lake with his shoulder. He slammed into a rock, a flash of pain coursing through his head, then his face and his body felt numb, useless, and darkness settled around him.

• • •

Li Kung was standing in front of the metal door again, but this time, the woman inside screamed with every last bit of strength she had left.

"My baby!" she shouted. "Kung! My baby!"

"Mother!" Li Kung shouted. "Let me in! Let me in!"

"Is that really you?" the woman's voice was softer then, as if ashamed of her screams a moment ago.

"Mother! It's me. What are you doing in there?"

"Kung!" his mother's voice was suddenly strong and firm, exerting the authority that he was so familiar with. "Kung, listen to me! Get out of here. Get out of the province. Go away with the Three Saints of Yunnan. Tell them you want to be their student, and that you will be killed if they don't take you—"

"What do you mean, mother?

"Just do as I say, Kung!"

"Father will protect me—"

"Silence!" Li Kung's mother, with barely any strength left in her voice, whispered her command. The young Li Kung froze.

"Your father is not the same anymore. Leave now. Don't turn back. And most importantly, don't tell your father."

"I don't understand," Li Kung whimpered, holding back his tears. His little hands began to pound the metal door again. "Let me in, Mother. Let me in."

"Kung, my baby. Listen to me. Obey your mother this one last time . . . "

"Last time?" Li Kung started to panic. "Why is this the last time?"

There was silence behind the door. Li Kung started hammering the door with both hands. "Mother, just wait here. I'll go to the governor. He'll let you out."

"The governor is dead!" his mother said, her voice suddenly strong again. "Your father is governor now."

Li Kung paused. "Then I'll go to Auntie Ma. She's the governor's wife. She can help."

"Your father executed Auntie Ma last week," his mother said, her voice trembling. "She's dead."

Li Kung froze, his little hands clutching the massive door handles, his entire body bent back as if he could pull open the door with his weight. "Mother, I'm scared. Come out of there. I'm sorry. I'm sorry for whatever I did. Please, just come out. I'm scared . . . "

"My baby. Leave now. Go to the Three Saints of Yunnan. Leave now."

Li Kung's eyes opened and his arms thrashed around him, frantic; he was unable to scream, and his lungs felt as if they would burst. Somehow, he regained footing and he launched himself upwards. With a splash, he protruded through the surface of the lake.

A mist of raining water drizzled around him. The screams were gone. Li Kung looked behind him, then to both sides, and saw a world so calm, so quiet, that for a moment, he didn't recognize where he was.

He gasped for air, drawing in each breath in excruciating torment. His body shook in uneven pulses; his lips and chin quivered in shock. For a long time, he couldn't regain control of his body or his thoughts.

He remembered! He remembered!

Li Kung groped with his hands in front of him, as if thick walls of stone stood in his way, and waded toward shore. The heat, the cold, and the fatigue all struck him at once. The life force had drained from him, and the inner strength that he depended on over the months had begun to fade. His eyes wanted to close, if not from weariness, then at least to shut out the dreadful images forever.

With a crash, he collapsed onto the shore of the lake. He lay quiet with his eyes closed and face down, breathing heavily, indifferent to anything around him.

• • •

Li Kung's eyes flew open. How long he had slept, he couldn't tell. But it was already dark. The haze of smoke floating in from the plateau blurred the cold light of the moon. He remained motionless, quietly counting the stars, his body stiff and unresponsive. What was he doing there?

He closed his eyes. Was he alive, watching a pitch-black sky sprinkled with stars? Or was he dead, watching a bright sky completely covered in darkness, with tiny openings for light to shine through?

Somewhere in the distance, the sound of soft footsteps approached.

They were the footsteps of a woman. His heart skipped a beat. The ghost of a woman . . . Pun? His mother? How?

A set of round eyes gazed at him with such love and concern that he felt weak in all four limbs . . . He recognized her, even if he couldn't see her clearly.

"Ying . . . " he whispered. "I remember. Auntie Ma was the governor's wife. She was so kind to me. But my father killed the governor and he became governor. He executed Auntie Ma in the town square. And my mother learned about what he did, and he probably killed her too."

Ying rushed to his side, her large eyes welling with tears. She reached under his neck to help him sit. Li Kung, still shaking, wrapped his arms around her and buried his face in her bosom. In a moment, he relaxed.

"How did you find me, Ying?"

Ying drew a small handkerchief from her pocket and began to wipe the sweat from his forehead.

Li Kung grabbed her wrist and she froze. "How did you find me?" he asked again.

Ying sat back, pulling away from him. She picked up a twig and wrote the word "Mongolian" on the ground.

Li Kung's face darkened. He had completely forgotten.

Suthachai was alive and in the Middle Kingdom with twenty horsemen. The question of how the Mongolian survived the Soaring Dragon poison haunted him. He no longer knew what to feel.

Ying grabbed him and threw her arms around him, falling deep into his embrace. A tear trailed down Li Kung's cheek. He shook it off and gently pushed her away.

"Where is he?" he asked. "How did he find me?"

Ying shook her head. Li Kung took a deep breath, certain that somewhere in the darkness, Suthachai was waiting on his gigantic mount, watching him with weapon poised. "Why is he looking for me?"

Ying scratched two more words on the soft earth, in front of the character for "Mongolian." It read, "Speak to Mongolian." She pointed to her sentence, then at Li Kung.

"Are you carrying the green powder I gave you?"

Ying nodded.

"Let me have it. Mine dissolved in the lake just now."

She hesitated, but handed him the pouch. Li Kung patted her hand, reassuring her. "Where is he? Let me talk to him."

Ying ignited a small brand of fire, climbed to her feet and waved the light three times over her head. In a moment, the sound of horse hooves emerged from the darkness.

Li Kung shot forward, and a cloud of green powder flew from his hands. In a flash, he was behind Ying again. His hand gripped hers, gently, taking the brand of fire.

Suthachai emerged under the moonlight. His horse was dripping wet.

Li Kung stepped forward with the flame pointed at him.

Suthachai smiled. "I am covered with the green powder. If you want to burn me, then do it. But my horse is innocent. I drenched him with the water that your mentor gave me. It neutralizes your green powder."

Li Kung felt a wave of cold run up his back. He could smell the herbs in the liquid that Suthachai had poured on his horse—ingredients that only Shifu Two would know about. He took a deep breath, watching Suthachai's every movement. If he couldn't eliminate the horse, he would have no physical advantage over the Mongolian. Slowly, he lowered the flame.

"I am your old friend," Suthachai said. "You saved my life at least twice. Why would you want to burn me?"

Li Kung didn't respond. He motioned for Suthachai to dismount.

The Mongolian leaped off his horse, slung his heavy saber across the saddle and approached him unarmed. "I know you have many questions for me. Ask me. I will tell you."

Li Kung eyed him, keenly aware that Suthachai gave up the crucial advantage of speed by leaving his horse. He felt better.

"I think the first thing you will ask me," Suthachai said, "is why your mentor gave me the ingredients to neutralize your green powder."

Li Kung's expression remained unchanged. Suthachai continued, "I came here to look for you. The first place I visited was your three mentors' house. Old One was waiting by the door. He said he was expecting me."

"Expecting you?" Li Kung asked with disbelief.

"Expecting someone," Suthachai said. "He said it is not time for the Martial Society to disappear. Someone would come and change what seemed inevitable."

Li Kung fell silent. Suthachai continued, "I told him where my friends and I were staying, and I left. This morning, Ying arrived at the inn where I stayed. She gave me a piece of bark with two lines written on it. It said, 'Li Kung in trouble.'"

"Why would I be in trouble?"

"The second line read, 'Li Kung about to kill thousands.'"

Li Kung slowly turned to Ying. She took a step back.

"Ying went to the Three Saints of Yunnan for help this morning," Suthachai said. "She was worried about you."

"And so," Li Kung asked Ying, "my mentors pointed you to Suthachai?"

Ying nodded.

"I followed her to the Three Saints of Yunnan," Suthachai said. "This time, they had barrels of water prepared, which they gave to my friends. Old One told me that the fire element is in your blood, and you could not resist using fire. He said that even though Yellow Sand Plateau is covered with bare sand, you would find a way to burn your enemies. Old Two then said you had created a special oil that would cause tremendous fires and explosions. That is why he mixed something into the barrels of water. It can dissolve your oil."

A frown knitted across Li Kung's eyebrows. He didn't understand; he almost felt betrayed. Why would his three wise masters stop him from fighting evil?

"So I took the wooden barrels and left right away," Suthachai continued. "You ran away from me, but I knew you would look for water. This is the fifth lake we searched since leaving the plateau."

Li Kung remained silent, trying his best to absorb everything said to him. Suthachai was alive, and he was with mounted warriors from Mongolia. His mentors were trying to stop him. He didn't know what to believe next.

"Why are you still alive?" Li Kung finally asked.

"I wonder myself," Suthachai replied. "Somehow, I did not die. It was strange. I threw myself over the side of a mountain that night, and I survived the fall. The snow was soft. Of course I survived the fall. But the poison did not kill me. When I woke up, my entire body was swollen. I felt like I would explode. All around me were scorpions like I have never seen before; there were so many of them I thought I was truly in hell. They stung me, almost every one of them stung me, as if my blood attracted them. Much later, I counted over a hundred scorpion stings on my body."

"Where did they come from?" Li Kung asked.

"This morning," Suthachai said, "Old Two came to me from behind and asked me if a hundred scorpion stings were more painful than a single sting. He told me that he raised some massive scorpions to be extra venomous, and he thought it would be fun if they all stung me."

Li Kung's eyes widened. "I see! He told me he released the scorpions. So he released them west of Lake Infinite because he knew they could cure you."

"He presented the chance. It was up to fate to decide whether the scorpions actually found me. This morning, he joked that since scorpions had stung me, I lived. But a scorpion also stung you, and now everyone is going to die. He thought it was funny."

Suthachai folded his hands. "Every night these past months, I pondered what had happened to me. I thought of Fei Fei, and what could have happened to her body. Did her father at least bury her properly? Was her grave on Redwood Cliff? I never thought that I would be alive and she would be dead. Every night, I thought to myself that I had no reason to live. But I had to. She died so that I would have a chance to live."

Suthachai froze for a second, his eyes blank, as if lost in deep thought. Finally, he said, "And over the months, I thought about you many times. After we lost each other on Redwood Cliff, I do not remember seeing you again. At least not until the night Fei Fei and I were pursued by the Butcher and the Gentle Swordsmen." His voice trembled slightly.

"That night, when we left you on Lake Infinite, Fei Fei brought me to the mouth of a cave, and she ran off to find wood splints to bind my leg. I remembered crawling out of the cave to look for her. I saw you, and I saw what you did on the lake. I was impressed—shocked actually. But I was also worried about you. To help me, you offended the Red Dragons. You humiliated them, even. I was worried that one day, you would fall victim to their skilled fighters and overwhelming numbers."

Li Kung sneered and looked away. Suthachai continued. "But that night, I was in no condition to even help the woman I love. I knew she would die, and I knew that she was not afraid. But I didn't want her to kneel and beg the arrogant fools who hunted us. So I threw myself over the side of the mountain and she could be free to fight her battle."

There was a long moment of silence before Suthachai continued. "It was almost dawn. I thought Fei Fei would come down to die with me. The sounds of battle above me were long gone, and I knew she had won. It was in her blood to slay all of them. I tried to crawl uphill again, but my fingers were too swollen to grab anything. I hid somewhere—I no longer remember where—and waited for nightfall again. No one came looking for me. All day, there were voices on the top of the hill where Fei Fei fought her own people. By night, I felt better, and I crawled through the forest and found a small village nearby. An old couple who lived with their grandson took me in and gave me food. The village doctor was called, and my leg was set and bandaged. In a month, I was strong enough to ride, and since I still had plenty of gold on me, I bought a horse and returned to Mongolia. I wanted to look for you, Li Kung, but I could barely walk with crutches. At home, the Elder would be able to help me heal.

"Sometime last month, I recovered to my normal self again. I haven't felt this normal for almost a year now. I even participated in a wrestling match, and I beat Jocholai by the second beat of the drum." Suthachai smiled. "Jocholai is my best friend. He is here, in the Middle Kingdom right now."

Li Kung remained silent.

"But I thought of how you offended the Red Dragons," Suthachai said. "I thought of how they would hunt you down, like how they hunted Fei Fei, with large groups of skilled fighters all hidden in ambush. I learned, at the marketplace by the border, that there would be a duel between Fei Fei's father and uncle. I heard that an immortal had surfaced in the region, that he had lived for five hundred years, yet resembled a boy just past his teens. I heard that the immortal knew how to fly. That is what it looked like that night, on Lake Infinite, did it not? It looked like you were flying across the ice."

"And that's why you came back?" Li Kung asked. "Because you learned of who I've become? Or are you here to stop me so millions of innocents can suffer?"

Ying knelt behind him and placed a hand on his shoulder.

Li Kung pushed her hand off, still glaring. "Or are you here for revenge? I know about revenge."

Suthachai shook his head. "I came back to kneel in front of Fei Fei's grave. But more importantly, I came back to help an old friend."

"Help me?" Li Kung threw his head back and laughed. "Help me! Why do I need your help? Haven't you seen with your own eyes? Why do I need you to help me vanquish my enemies?"

244

"Who are your enemies, Li Kung?"

Li Kung started, as if a needle pricked into his spine. My enemies are clear, Li Kung answered to himself. Snow Wolf told me who they are.

"I don't have any enemies," he said. "They're all dead."

"You have acquired superhuman abilities from somewhere," Suthachai said, still seated on the soft grass. "You have grown up, and you became a great warrior. How could I not be happy for you? But only for a brief moment. Now, thinking back, I am ashamed that you came across terrible times and I could do nothing to help."

"Ashamed?" Li Kung asked, his voice hollow. "Terrible times? Do you feel pity for me?"

"Pity? No." Suthachai said. "I am just worried for you. Now that the world knows you for taking down the Dragon Houses, can you live a normal life again? Can you still have tea by the road without fear of poison, or sleep in an inn without fear of ambush?"

Enraged, Li Kung spun around and stormed away. A few steps later, he turned and came back, his glaring eyes wide with fire. "Who are you to question my actions? Who are you to question the ways of a goddess? The future has been foretold! Our civilization will come to an end if the black paste spreads across the land! I've prevented the greatest catastrophe of past and future generations!"

A look of hopelessness grew in Suthachai's eyes. In a moment, he took a deep breath, and said, "The Elder told me before I came here that one's true enemy would always linger around the battleground. Especially in a battle you have been part of. I believe your true enemy will be back, and he will be waiting on Yellow Sand Plateau by sunrise. Will you come with me?"

Li Kung laughed. "Why would I go anywhere with you?"

"You have destroyed your enemies, but I am telling you, there are more," Suthachai said. "These are the truly powerful ones. I am telling you that they will come back and wait for you on Yellow Sand Plateau. Don't you want to meet them?"

"Are you referring to the ones who escaped, or the ones who'll come back for vengeance? I've prepared for either of those. There's no escape."

"Neither of those," Suthachai interrupted. "The Elder is wise and difficult to fathom. You will need to see for yourself."

. . .

It was almost dawn before they arrived at the foot of Yellow Sand Plateau. Ying rode with Suthachai, and Li Kung walked ahead, his eyes barely focused, his mind lost in deep thought. The sun was high in the sky when the three reached the edge of the plateau. The thick stench of death continued to hover. Ying covered her face with both hands.

In front of them was a sea of corpses that stretched infinitely across the plateau. Li Kung stared. There were people in front of him, quietly plowing their way across the carnage. They were ordinary peasants, slow, lifeless, like puppets with broken strings being dragged across an uneven surface.

Two old men with bamboo canes, though trembling, hobbled around swinging their flimsy weapons in the air. Li Kung watched, his eyes out of focus. After a long time, he realized that they were fighting off the vultures. A group of young boys, their faces ashen white, were hauling the bodies into large piles. Perhaps the bodies would be loaded into wheel barrels and eventually taken away.

An old woman, her back hunched over a short walking

stick, fumbled through the mountain of bodies. She carefully gazed into each face, her own eyes blank and lifeless. Often, when the faces were too mangled to recognize, she would inspect the hands of the corpse. Li Kung watched her for a while, then focused on the other villagers combing through the dead. Old couples, young women with crying babies strapped to their backs, little boys with short sticks; each and every one of them seemed to be searching through the remains for someone they knew, someone they loved.

"Young man!" the old woman walked up to him, her dull eyes full of hope. "Ah Fu's about your age. Have you seen him? Have you seen my grandson?" She reached over and clutched his hand. Li Kung tried to break free, but felt weak and vulnerable. She drew an arc on the back of his hand. "He has a scar like this on his hand. A dog bit him when he was six, and the scar looks like a half moon. Will you help me find him, young man?"

Li Kung's mouth opened, but he couldn't utter a word. The old woman trembled, and she grabbed his forearm in agitation. "Will you help me find him? My eyes are not so good anymore. He has a scar on his hand. Will you help me find him?"

Ying stepped forward and took the old woman's hand.

"Oh, young lady. You will help me instead?"

Ying nodded, a tear in her eye.

"Oh, thank you. Ah Fu's parents died a few years ago, so I don't have anyone else in my family to help me. Thank you."

Li Kung stared. The hollow wail of a young child could be heard in the distance. Between his cries, Li Kung thought he heard him say, "Father! Father! Wake up, father! I made breakfast. Wake up and come home!"

Elsewhere, a young widow opened her mouth to shriek.

She clasped a headless body to her bosom. Her screams were so muffled she sounded like she was choking, and in a moment, she dropped the body to climb across the other corpses. She grabbed onto an arm, hauled away the ribcage of another victim, and slowly, her gaping mouth trembling, she reached into the soil and lifted a decapitated head from the ground. She closed her eyes, a sigh of relief escaping her lips. She held the head against her cheeks.

Li Kung turned away. A wave of nausea struck him. He could barely stand. He spun around and gazed at an old couple turning over every body, inch by inch, in search of the familiar face. The man could barely walk, while his wife, whose eyes were so swollen they appeared closed, uttered a haunting moan every time she came across a face too disfigured to be identified.

"Are you from the magistrate's office?" a woman's voice asked. Li Kung turned and looked into a pair of worried eyes. The woman carried a sleeping infant in her arms.

"Are you here to help us find our loved ones?" she asked, her voice bitter but strong.

"I—"

"You let this happen," she said, her voice becoming louder. "Why didn't anyone stop this?"

Li Kung couldn't respond.

"I don't care if you arrest me," she said. "I'm going to say it even if I spend the rest of my life in jail. The governor is weak and useless. The magistrate's office is equally worthless. Instead of providing leadership and protection for the people, you permit the Martial Society to make its own laws and settle its own disputes."

Li Kung looked at the infant, and the woman instantly drew back. "Arrest us, then!" she said, spitting at him. "My husband's probably in there! We'll starve to death anyway.

Why don't I sit in jail with my son for your crimes and maybe we won't starve!"

She spun around and ran off.

In the distance, the voice of a little girl called, "Father, father!" She was kneeling beside his body, shaking it while she called him. "Father! Father!"

"Are you really from the magistrate's office, young master?" another old woman asked. Li Kung couldn't bring himself to turn.

The old woman clutched his sleeve and tried to pull at him. "Sir, I don't mean disrespect. I just want to find my son."

"Please be patient." It was Suthachai speaking from behind her. "We are not the authorities here, but someone will be here soon, and your son will be found."

"Really?"

"Many survived," Suthachai said. "They may still find your son among the survivors. Please be patient."

Li Kung closed his eyes to prevent a tear from falling. The old woman began to weep.

"He wanted glory and respect," she said, between sobs. "Joining the Green Dragons made him feel so strong and so important. He told me last month when he came home with a pouch of coins that we will never be bullied again, and there will always be food on the table, and even meat. We could even eat meat! No one could say we're worthless anymore. I was so happy for him. It was better than farming. I was so happy for him . . . "

The old woman completely broke down. Li Kung lowered his head, felt blackness before his eyes. He suddenly collapsed to his knees, hot tears flowing, and he whispered to himself, "What am I doing here? What went wrong?"

In the distance, a group of men approached the plateau. Suthachai reached for his saber, then relaxed. They were battered Red Dragons, but they were numerous, walking with an air of vengeance. "Fei Fei's brother . . . " Suthachai whispered under his breath. Dong came with a large group of men, perhaps to collect the dead, but more likely to find someone to blame.

Li Kung, on his knees, lowered his head. He wrung his hands together. "What went wrong?" he asked himself again. "Did Snow Wolf mean for this to happen? Surely Snow Wolf didn't mean this."

The world began to spin and tilt, and he felt nauseous, hazy. It was impossible. How could he be responsible for so much loss and suffering? He killed evil men—he was certain—the goddess Snow Wolf had told him so. They were about to commit evil deeds against the world, and he had stopped them. What did he do wrong?

A warm hand took his. He opened his eyes to a wrinkled face and a soft smile of an old woman. Her eyes were swollen and faint, yet hopeful; her smile was drained and morose, but full of compassion.

"Don't cry," she said. "I too, came here for a loved one. Don't cry. We're all together, and we'll get through it together. We're here for you, my boy."

Li Kung suddenly flew to his feet. Without a glance at Suthachai, or Ying, or the group of Red Dragons approaching him, he bolted for the far end of the plateau. Suthachai reacted. He whispered an apology to Ying while dashing for his horse, and in a moment, began chasing after Li Kung on his gigantic mount.

Li Kung maintained a steady pace and Suthachai followed a short distance away. Much later, Li Kung slowed to a walk at the foot of Phoenix Eye Peak.

"Why are you following me?" Li Kung asked without turning around.

"You need me."

"I don't need anyone."

Li Kung heard the horse behind him stop, heard Suthachai dismount and continue to follow on foot. So the Mongolian knew that he was about to ascend the mountain. He didn't care. He reached into his pockets and pulled out a crumbling book. He flipped to the back. "The journals," he whispered. "Unearth the journals if I become lost, and I will find my way."

A map fell from the inner sleeve of the book and into his hand. He picked up his pace, disregarding the sound of increasing footsteps behind him, and began to ascend Phoenix Eye Peak. Just moments ago, the world was shattered in front of his eyes, and he couldn't take a step without questioning why. But with the thought of Snow Wolf's journals waiting for him in the caverns, there was a sense of renewed hope. She would help him, without doubt.

Finally, the footsteps of many men began to irritate him. He spun around, gazed past the Mongolian and noted the group of Red Dragons following him. Dong marched in front, his hand on his sword, his teeth bared. They had been following him for some time.

"You!" Dong shouted, moving faster to close the distance. "I've been watching you! You were the one who ambushed us with fire! I recognize you!"

Li Kung slipped forward, passed Suthachai, and stood before Dong before he had time to draw his weapon.

"What you don't understand," Li Kung said, "is that even your father couldn't defeat my Mongolian bodyguard. That's why he burned to death squealing like a little girl, because the Mongolians were too tough for him."

It made no sense at all, but Dong's face instantly darkened, then turned red. Li Kung withdrew, and without another glance, resumed his rapid walk toward the peak. Dong drew his weapon. Every man behind him followed.

Suthachai shook his head. "Li Kung, do not do this. I came to help you . . . "

There was a flash of steel. Suthachai lifted his sheathed saber and casually blocked. Dong stumbled back, his fingers numb and trembling, as if he had just swung blindly into a wall.

The Red Dragons swarmed forward. Suthachai moved like a cat, slipping and sliding around the frightened men, locking their joints and hurling them into one another. He never needed to draw his saber.

Li Kung stood at the edge of a steep cliff where the wind soared and the howling of ghosts floated forever through the atmosphere. He could almost see the rabbit population, far below, scurrying through the wild flowers, living and breeding for generations without a single threat to their existence. This was where he trained in the Flame Cutter. It seemed so long ago . . .

He heard heavy footsteps behind him and realized that Suthachai had caught up with him. But he could only think of one thing—the idea that Snow Wolf had left behind a solution for what had happened—and all else didn't seem to matter anymore. He closed his eyes, leaned off the edge of the cliff and began to run down the barren rocks he knew so well.

Suthachai reached the ledge and stopped. He drew his saber, stabbed it heavily into a crack between the rocks, and began to climb his way down.

Li Kung dropped onto the valley floor. The map in his hands pointed to the forbidden caverns behind the tombstone. He headed for the secret entrance, aware that Suthachai was watching. Somehow, it didn't matter anymore.

Snow Wolf's cavern was as bright and majestic as he left it. Li Kung stared at the tombstone, the running stream deep in the rocks and the layer upon layer of soft, floating light. Tears flowed down his cheeks. Was he a failure? Had he disappointed her?

He fell to his knees in front of Snow Wolf's tombstone and thought of Pun and how she had trusted him, yet he was unable to do anything to help her. Now, Snow Wolf trusted him. Fifty years after her death, she passed on her critical skills to transform him. But again, he didn't deserve the trust. He had failed her.

He bowed three times and rose to his feet. With his head down, as if too ashamed to look at her tombstone, Li Kung walked toward the forbidden caverns. It was dark. He doused a nearby stick of wood with green powder, created a small torch, and watched the flame grow. He wondered how many more things he would need to burn in his lifetime.

The tunnel was short. It led to a small room—the forbidden chamber—as outlined on the map. There was nothing in the room. He took two steps forward, located the exact center of the room, and dropped to his knees to dig.

He thought of the Octagonal Cage formation—a purely destructive instrument of war—that Snow Wolf had created and passed onto him. The formation would normally evolve into seamless walls, so dense and unpredictable that even a fly couldn't escape. Was it wrong for him to use fire? Did he misinterpret her instructions?

He wiped the sweat from his forehead, whisked off a tear from his eye, and continued to dig. He did modify the formula used to soak the shields. He added ingredients from the green powder to ensure a hellish inferno. She was clear in her instructions: he needed to be flexible and adaptable in battle. She gave him the task of eliminating the Dragon

Houses, alongside the lawless trash who threatened the common people. He had accomplished that. He had to protect the women and children. Yet . . .

He lifted his sleeve and wiped away another tear. Yet the lawless trash were ordinary people themselves. How many widows and orphans had he created on Yellow Sand Plateau?

His fingers closed around something, and his heart skipped a beat. The journals! The answers—inside the little book that he was pulling out of the earth—would break the cloud around him and award him with the precious lessons from *her* life. He shook slightly and dug harder, clawing away the soil. In a moment, he lifted a book, still caked in dirt, and held it close to his body. The answers lay within. The world was not so dismal after all.

A strange sound of grinding stone appeared out of nowhere, but he barely noticed. Carefully, with a hopeful smile on his face, Li Kung opened the little book that he unearthed. He held the flame closer. The first page was blank, then the second, the third. He tore through the pages, fluttering past the entire volume until the very last page. His heart stopped. Dark black characters filled the entire sheet. One sentence, the only sentence, covered the last page.

"The chosen warrior must die."

Li Kung stared, as all sense of life drained from his veins. It must have been a mistake. Perhaps he didn't locate the center of the cavern floor and the wrong book was unearthed.

The chosen warrior must die.

It was in her handwriting. He wanted to read it out loud, to convince himself that he didn't misinterpret the words. The rumbling sounds around him became louder, gathering momentum, but he didn't care. He could barely see anymore.

"What happened?" he asked out loud. "What did I do wrong?"

A massive boulder dropped from the roof of the cavern. Li Kung instinctively slipped away, but from his kneeling position, could not move in time. The boulder grazed his back. He felt a dull pain ricochet across his body, and with a short cry, crumbled onto the floor. His body shook, but he struggled. Snow Wolf was killing him—it finally dawned on him—and there was no mistake about it. But why?

Then, everything seemed to be falling around him. He scrambled to his haunches and dove away just in time as another heavy rock fell from above. Sand, pebbles, little stones, and heavy boulders all caved in at once. It rained upon him in heavy sputters, endless, pitiless. He stared at the narrow tunnel from which he had entered, intending to escape the same way he came. A gigantic rock the size of his torso began to drop into the entrance. He bolted for the opening. But he was weak, useless, in such agony and confusion that he had no chance of slipping through before the boulder landed, blocking the way. Another rock struck him then, this time across his right shoulder, and he gasped for air. The pain was unbearable. She had designed the cavern to fall faster than any man using the Flame Cutter could run. He would never survive.

Li Kung uttered a sharp cry when a second boulder tumbled into the entrance.

A tall figure leaped through the tunnel and intercepted the falling boulder.

Suthachai! Li Kung struggled to his feet. The Mongolian, who received the entire weight of the falling boulder against his back, fell to his knees and screamed in pain.

"Hurry!" Suthachai shouted.

Li Kung scrambled, avoided another stone threatening to crush his head, and rushed toward the tunnel.

Suthachai screamed again when another rock struck him. With a roar, he forced himself to his feet. "Hurry! Under me!"

Li Kung dove across the cavern floor, slipped underneath Suthachai and into the tunnel. The room behind him collapsed with an earth-shattering explosion.

• • •

Perhaps he was unconscious for only a short moment. The blood that dripped from his mouth, now in a puddle next to him, was still warm. He recognized the tunnel he lay in.

Every memory came back to him at once then, and a wave of dread clenched his heart. He thought of Suthachai, and, growling in pain, crawled back to the entrance of the forbidden chamber.

Li Kung found Suthachai crushed under a rock, twitching, but clearly alive. There was too much blood. The Mongolian's injuries were internal and severe, though his own wounds weren't any lighter. He struggled to his feet. Somehow, he would have to move the boulder.

"Li Kung . . . You made it."

Li Kung dropped to his knees again and reached for Suthachai's pulse. "You're alive? How?"

Suthachai couldn't answer.

"The rock was almost half your height. Are you human?"

Suthachai tried to laugh but choked on his blood. Li Kung wrapped his arms around the boulder, took a deep breath, his own injuries firing jets of pain through his body, and with a shout, lifted with all the power he could muster. The boulder would not budge. Li Kung dropped to his elbows and wheezed for air.

"Listen," Suthachai said, his voice weak and fading. "I

withstood the force of the falling boulder. When you throw a much heavier man, you must first decide the center of his rotation. Lifting his dead weight would be a waste of strength. But if you could flip him like you spin a ball, you would be able to send him great distances with little effort. I withstood the falling boulder, because I reached up and made it spin while it was falling. It rolled across my shoulders, and I moved with it.

"Like skipping a stone across the surface of the water?" Li Kung asked. "While the stone is spinning, it won't sink. It can fly across the water."

"Yes," Suthachai replied. "You learn quickly."

Li Kung climbed to his feet and stumbled down the tunnel. He was gone for what seemed to be forever. Much later, he dragged himself back with two sticks of wood, one of them only the length of his arm.

"You can't see behind you, so let me position your hand. We'll get this rock off your back."

Suthachai gripped one end of the wood and extended it behind him while Li Kung placed the other end against the upper part of the rock. "It's shaped like an egg," Li Kung said. "Fortunately, not the entire weight of the rock is on you, or you would certainly be dead."

He hauled the thicker stick of wood toward the other side of the Mongolian's body. "I'll place this under your backbone, and it'll serve as a ramp for the rock to roll onto."

Suthachai nodded.

"How did you spin a rock this size when it was falling?" Li Kung asked.

"Sometimes, you need real physical strength too." He could barely speak, struggling to support the log while Li Kung positioned himself.

"Why did you come back here, Suthachai?"

The Mongolian looked up.

"Why did you come back to China? Don't tell me you came back to save my life. You could never have predicted this."

"Not to save your life, Li Kung. Your existence was never in danger until now. Not your life."

Li Kung took a deep, painful breath, crouched low and planted himself against the rock. "We'll count to three. I'll push the boulder into topspin, and you'll push it into a horizontal spin. We'll spin it onto the log, and it'll roll off of you."

Suthachai nodded and closed his eyes to gather energy. "I'm ready."

Li Kung shifted his weight and prepared to push, then suddenly stopped. "I have one more question for you," he said, his voice lowered.

Suthachai waited.

"What did Pun ever do to you?"

"Pun?"

Li Kung's fingers began to turn white. He gripped the rock like he meant to crush it.

"Pun," Suthachai said. "Your mentors told me she died. How did it happen?"

Li Kung's hands shook with tension. "How did it happen?" he repeated.

Suthachai turned his head with great difficulty.

"Why did you kill her?" Li Kung's voice echoed in the enclosed tunnel.

"Why did you kill her?" he suddenly shouted, his voice hollow, cold. It resembled the cry of a dying animal, cornered and desperate.

"Kill her?" Suthachai asked. "I didn't . . . I never . . . "

"You," Li Kung growled under his breath. "I saw with

258

my own eyes. I held her while she bled to death. Do you think I'll ever forget?" He was shaking in spasms, twisting from his own pain. "All she ever wanted was to help you! Why?"

He leaned his body against the boulder. A slow trickle of blood dripped from his snarling lips. "Answer me! Why did you kill her? Answer me!"

He roared and shoved the boulder off of Suthachai's back with impossible strength. Suthachai was unconscious. The rock was jerked into a sudden topspin. "Why!" he shrieked. Choking, he shoved the rock into a horizontal spin and onto the log.

Li Kung collapsed, the unbearable pain tormenting every possible part of his body. The world blackened before him. The last thing he saw was the boulder slowly rolling into the cavern.

• • •

"Pun, will you forgive me? Will you?"

Perhaps it was the voice of his own ghost. The world was dark, and he was in a dream world . . . Or, perhaps he had died and become a wandering spirit, floating through the seven realms. "Pun? I didn't kill the man who murdered you. Instead, I killed so many others. I'm a friend to the man who murdered you. I don't know why. I don't know why. But he came back to save me from killing them all . . . "

Li Kung's eyes opened. Cold sweat dripped from his face and neck. "I'm not dead . . . "

He reached for a small, porcelain bottle in his pocket. "I should be dead. But those who deserve to die usually don't."

"Snow Wolf . . . " he heard himself calling out loud. He swallowed two pills from his bottle. He found Suthachai, checked his pulse and confirmed that the Mongolian was still alive, though barely.

His acupuncture needles . . . He couldn't recall the last time he carried them—but magically, the needles were there. He quickly located the vital points on the Mongolian's neck, and fumbling, almost no longer able to control his own fingers, he managed to insert the needles.

Suthachai opened his eyes. Li Kung shook three pills from his little bottle and held it in front of him. "Do you remember these?"

Suthachai coughed up blood. He supported himself on one elbow and reached across the tunnel floor for the pills.

"Pun," he whispered.

"Forget it," Li Kung said. "You don't owe me anymore. After you swallow these pills, I don't owe you either."

The pain was unbearable. Li Kung climbed to his feet, holding onto the stone walls with both hands. Without a glance behind him, he began to scramble out of the tunnel.

The damp air in the tunnel smelled of decay. Li Kung trudged forward, alone, with only the bare wall to lean against. It was cold, silent, and slippery with wet moss. But fresh air and water were only steps away.

Suthachai would never be able to make it out of the tunnel alone.

With a deep sigh, Li Kung turned around to walk back, his feet dragging behind him, so sure of what he had to do but no longer understanding his own decisions. A year ago, he would have told himself that he was going back because that was who he was. Now, he wondered whether he was going back because that was who he failed to be.

· · ·

The sun had begun to set. Along a rugged path winding down from Phoenix Eye Peak, a trail of thick blood, still red, lined the center of the road. Dong and his warriors followed, their weapons already drawn in excitement and anticipation. They saw it with their own eyes. Li Kung and the Mongolian, both severely injured, had dragged each other out of a distant valley and onto a narrow road. They were slow, limping, in obvious pain. Dong was certain that he would catch them.

After being defeated by a Mongolian who never even drew his weapon, Dong's men combed the roads of Phoenix Eye Peak with renewed courage, hoping for another chance to overwhelm him with their sheer numbers. Then, Dong saw both his enemies injured, and was instantly convinced. Vengeance was inevitably his.

He noticed the trail of fresh blood and his heart leaped for joy. With that much blood lost, there was no chance they could defend themselves against his seasoned warriors.

Elated, Dong spun around to face his men. He held up his hand. "We're closing in on the animals responsible for Master Bin's murder. We'll approach them quietly, in case they're aware of the trail of blood they left behind."

He pointed to the men in the back. "The senior students are to cut through the foliage and circle around them, and you are to move quickly. I want you at the bottom of the mountain and preparing an ambush on both sides of the road before they arrive. They are headed for the base of the mountain—there are spots of blood everywhere. I will chase them and push them, and I'll attack when I see you attack."

The designated group drew their swords and began to cut their way through the forest. Dong motioned for his remaining men to continue down the road.

• • •

At a distance, Li Kung and Suthachai watched them leave. A spasm of pain struck the Mongolian and fresh blood poured from his mouth. Li Kung reached over to catch the blood in a wooden bowl. "Save the blood," he said. "I may need another trail for Dong to follow." Suthachai held his chest, his face ashen white, and vomited again into the bowl.

"We'll go down from this side," Li Kung said.

Suthachai nodded and climbed to his feet. They both seemed to have recovered some strength, but if Dong found them, there was no chance of survival. They needed to hurry.

"How do you know?" Suthachai asked between gasps for air. "How do you know they won't follow this way?"

"I dripped the blood along the northern road," Li Kung said, "down the other side of the mountain. Did you catch every drop of blood in the bowl?"

"I hope so."

They heaved forward in silence. Li Kung's mind spun in aimless circles. He thought of the journals, which he had been instructed to unearth. But when he went for the journals, the cavern collapsed, and it was meant to bury him alive. She had meant for him to die. The chosen warrior must die . . .

His mind wandered back to his immediate predicament. Dong would eventually find new spots of blood, and he would realize that he had followed a ruse. Traces of their whereabouts would be found. They needed a new plan to stop the Red Dragons for good.

The golden streaks of sunset covered the land with a warm radiance. They lumbered downhill, carrying each other forward, their injuries numb.

"Why didn't you kill them?" Li Kung asked. They were

262

the first words he said since losing sight of Dong at the top of the mountain.

Suthachai caught his breath. "Kill them?"

"Dong. The Red Dragons."

"They posed no threat to us then."

Li Kung snickered but said nothing. He reached out to help Suthachai regain balance, then proceeded. Two steps, and he paused. Suthachai didn't follow.

Li Kung turned around. "We need to hurry."

"Did I really kill her?"

They stared at each other, the air tense, until finally, Li Kung responded, "Yes. You did. And you nearly killed me too."

"When?"

"A few days after the battle on Redwood Cliff. Near the Blue Lantern Inn."

Suthachai looked down, and for a long time, couldn't find words. Slowly, he shook his head. "I don't remember."

Li Kung turned around to walk away.

"Li Kung," Suthachai called from behind.

Li Kung stared straight ahead. He couldn't meet the Mongolian's gaze. All he ever wanted was a moment to confront Suthachai on Pun's murder. For almost a year, every day, this thought had consumed him. Night after night, he had repeated what he should have said six months ago when Suthachai was at his mercy. He knew he was fantasizing because Suthachai was supposed to be dead, but as if the gods answered his cries, Suthachai came back to confront his crimes. Now, finally, when both men faced the incident on equal terms, Li Kung couldn't even bring himself to turn around.

"If you need to take revenge for her," Suthachai said, "do so now. I will not fight back."

Li Kung trembled. He felt his strength gathering in his veins, once again empowered by the leisure of mercy, by the notion that he had the right to kill.

"I will ask you once again," Li Kung said. "Why did you come back?"

There was a long silence, as Li Kung waited, motionless. Somehow, he knew Suthachai would have a true answer for him this time. What really would bring a stranger back to this land?

"It was not yet winter when I was poisoned by the candles," Suthachai began, after a long time, "and we knew it would be a harsh winter. But there was a hunt going on. A massive hunt of such scale as never before seen on the steppe. We were to exterminate the predators of the land to protect our animals. The Elder did not approve of the hunt, but none of us listened to him. Eighteen major tribes and over thirty minor tribes participated, and it lasted for almost six months. By the time I left my home last year, we had already slain more wolves and leopards than we could ever count.

"It was almost spring when I returned to Mongolia. I was only partially recovered from the poison and from my injuries. I did not leave my tent for months. When I could finally move around, the dry season was already upon us. I expected our animals to have multiplied by then. I expected hundreds of young horses waiting to be trained, and herds of sheep and cattle so numerous that they would cover the land and stretch into the sunset. But strangely, we had less. The Elder explained. After we had slain the predators, we traveled deeper west to the winter grazing grounds. By late spring, our clan returned, and found a most unusual situation. Rabbits, gazelle, reindeer, all had become so numerous in one year that the grazing grounds were depleted well before the second rain season. They came from across the lands, and there were no predators to stop them. There was not enough food left for our own herds. Our animals could not reproduce.

"By the time I fully recovered, the tribes were planning another grand hunt. This time, we would kill the gazelles to make room for our herds. The leaders decided that if the number of gazelles were not controlled, our sheep would begin to disappear in three seasons. Then, without sheepskin, how would we trade for salt at the border?

"But the Elder spoke to the leaders before the hunt. He told them that to exterminate the gazelle and reindeer would be as foolish as wiping out the predators. If our herds were allowed to expand freely, there would be so many sheep and cattle that the land would also be depleted. There would not be enough food in a few years, and the tribes would begin to fight each other for land. There would be war. Humans would die. There would be no one left to tend to the animals, so the herds would shrink. After the wars, the people would rebuild their tribes, raise more animals, and some years later, the size of our herds would be the same again. But didn't we already have the same number of animals now—without war?

"I came back to China to tell you about this. The wolves were our enemies. We killed them. Then, the harmless deer became our enemies. We are going to kill them too. Soon, other tribes will become our enemies. I guess we can kill them too. By then, a new population of wolves will come along. We can start killing all over again. Yesterday, you killed the wolves, Li Kung. What now?"

• • •

Much later, at the foot of Phoenix Eye Peak, Li Kung suddenly broke the silence. "Forget it," he said. "You were blind, you killed Pun. I was blind, and I killed so many more. Who am I to ask why? It's over."

Silence resumed. They trudged forward, heads down, their minds roaming through so many memories, so many thoughts. Eventually, Li Kung said, his voice weak, "The battle between good and evil. Yesterday, I knew which side I was on. This morning, I had doubts. I thought I was evil. Now, I understand neither. Perhaps I'm just so insignificant in the grand scheme of things."

Darkness settled. Deep in the distance, almost halfway up Phoenix Eye Peak, the unmistakable light of multiple torches began to appear. They were moving rapidly toward the southern side of the mountain. Dong had finally discovered the ploy. It would be a matter of time before they combed the roads behind them.

A faint smell of fresh herbs floated in the air. Li Kung thought he was dreaming. Only Shifu Two grew herbs like that.

Suthachai inhaled.

"You smell it too?" Li Kung asked. Suthachai nodded. Li Kung lifted his face, closed his eyes and took long breaths. "Someone's growing rare herbs over there—for internal injuries. Let's go. He may have the medicine we need."

Suthachai agreed. They left the little road and pushed their way through dense foliage, following the scent while straining to see. The smell became thicker, and in a moment, they stood in front of a small cement house. It seemed newly built, with thick tiled roofs and heavy steel doors.

"I saw you from far away," a voice said, from within. "It's destiny. Come inside."

Li Kung and Suthachai looked at each other, unsure of how to respond. The voice sounded familiar.

"The Flame Cutter," the man inside the house said.

Li Kung's eyes widened. He stumbled forward, leaned against the metal doors and pushed them open. "Old Snake!" he called.

Old Snake seemed older, more tired, and slower than before. But he was there, at the door, his arms opened to catch Li Kung. Suthachai hesitated, recognizing the man he had threatened to kill on Redwood Cliff.

"The Mongolian . . ." Old Snake said with a smile. "You survived the Soaring Dragon Poison. But I have seen greater miracles since then. Come, this is perfect. Come inside. I too, have a miracle to show you."

He dragged Li Kung to the left wall and rested him on a chair. Many shelves lined the walls, each full of jars and boxes. "Not only do I remember you, I know you. You're the young doctor we invited to treat the Old Grandmother. You're a talented young doctor. These herbs on my shelves— you should know how to use them."

Li Kung took deep breaths and calmed. He nodded with a smile of gratitude. Old Snake reached over and took Suthachai's hand. "Similar injuries. I won't ask how you both got hurt the exact same way, but . . . come this way, I have something to show you." He pulled eagerly on Suthachai's hand. The Mongolian glanced once at Li Kung before following the old man. They walked into a separate room.

A piercing shout brought Li Kung immediately to his feet. It came from Suthachai. Bearing the agony and fighting the weakness, Li Kung threw a mixing bowl into the room as a diversion, then ran in.

No one attacked him. He saw Suthachai kneeling against the side of a bed, his fingers clasped together, his entire body shaking in spasms. A woman lay lifelessly in front of him.

"Fei Fei," Li Kung whispered.

PROPHECY NINE

Ten thousand myriad beings
Bleed to retain control
Yet birth among the living
Death inevitably precedes

• • •

Fei Fei was evidently breathing. Li Kung reached for her hand, placed his fingers on her pulse, then, almost in shock, drew his hand away. "Her pulse is strong! How can she still be unconscious?"

"She's never awoken since that night," Old Snake said, trembling with excitement. "But she's alive, and yes, her strength has recovered. All her wounds have healed. Any day now. Any day, she'll wake up."

Li Kung looked at him in wonder. "All those herbs grown around the house. They were meant for her. You never gave up."

Old Snake nodded with a smile. "How could I? I love her like my own daughter. How could I let her die?" He glanced at Suthachai, who, trembling by her bedside, still couldn't find words. Tears welled into the old man's eyes, and he placed a hand on Suthachai's shoulder. "I'm so glad you're here. I've dreamed so many times that she would see your face when she woke up one day. How impossible it was, and how real it is now. The joy of seeing you will cure her for good."

Suthachai turned and gripped Old Snake's hands. "How? Am I dreaming?"

"You're not dreaming! I couldn't help her that night when she fought the Gentle Swordsmen. She was so entangled in battle that any poison I used would've killed her too. But I was there, and I was prepared. As soon as she killed the last swordsman, I reached her, and I closed her wounds before she bled to death. I brought powerful medicine with me that night, anticipating the worst, and I poured it down her throat before she stopped breathing. And I took her body away, which the young master here saw me do."

Li Kung nodded. Old Snake turned to Suthachai again. "And she said one thing when I lifted her body."

"What did she say?"

"She called for you, Suthachai. She called for you."

Li Kung climbed to his feet, wide-eyed, the shock of the moment still etched on his face. Nagging in the back of his mind was the image of Dong and forty armed men, all searching for him and eager to slit his throat. Suthachai was in a daze, his large hands covering Fei Fei's lifeless fingers. Li Kung knew that asking him to run now would be impossible. He hadn't covered their tracks well. Dong would find them.

"The herbs," he suddenly said. He stumbled out of the room. Old Snake followed.

"Leave them alone," Li Kung whispered without turning around.

"Yes."

Once out in the main room, Li Kung grabbed another mixing bowl and dragged himself to the shelves. There were so many herbs, each carefully dried and properly sorted. He didn't have time to prepare them. Through the thick metal doors, still partially opened, Li Kung could see the torches descending Phoenix Eye Peak. They were all approaching his direction. There was no time to boil the herbs, and even less time to grind the ingredients into powder.

"Dong," he said.

Old Snake spun around to face the opened door and stared into the distance. The lights resembled the glossy eyes of wolves prowling the night.

"We can't thank you enough," Li Kung began. "But right now, we must go. Dong's been following us all day, and we're in no condition to fight him. He'll find us soon." He dragged the jars from each shelf, pulling the ingredients he needed, and began to stuff them into a sack.

Old Snake inched back, then abruptly grabbed the doors and slammed them shut. "What are you doing to me?" he suddenly shouted. "They'll find me here! They'll find Fei Fei!"

Li Kung was silent. He wanted to apologize, and explain that he didn't mean to cause the old man any harm, but he couldn't find the words. It seemed that everyone who trusted him eventually became disappointed.

Old Snake flattened his back against the doors, his anxious eyes stunned and frightened. "You don't understand," he said.

Li Kung stopped, slowly lowering the sack, and looked into the wrinkled face. Decades of fear and worry revealed itself all at once on that face. "I . . . " he stammered. "I didn't know you were here. We were being chased and we smelled the herbs outside. We came for medicine. Now we'll leave."

Old Snake shook his head. "You don't understand. The Flute Demon was a world-class leader in the Martial Society. The Red Dragon House respected her and the Martial

Society feared her. Finally, she died, making room for Dong to flex his muscles. Finally he can be a leader and have his words taken seriously. Would he ever give that up?"

Li Kung lowered his eyes. It was Fei Fei the old man worried about. If Dong killed her, no one would ever know. She was supposed to be dead. "Would he kill his own sister?"

"She's already dead! No one knows she's this close to waking up. This close!"

Li Kung looked away, feeling faint, wishing he were dead. He backed into the wall and slid downward until he felt himself seated on the wooden floor. He leaned his head back and stared at the ceiling.

"Where can I take her?" Old Snake began. "Wei Bin took away everything I ever had, to make sure I could never produce poison again. I don't know how to wield a sword. I can't fight so many Red Dragons." The old man sighed. "Perhaps she was meant to die early in life and anything I do to save her only defied the will of the gods. Who would believe, after all my careful planning, that you would stumble here, and the one person who would benefit most from her death would be following you. I left my life to fate long ago. Perhaps I should leave Fei Fei's life to fate as well."

Li Kung closed his eyes. There was nothing left for him to say.

"You needed to run," Old Snake continued. "You should leave now."

"Suthachai will never leave his beloved. He'll stay and die with her."

"I know," Old Snake said, his voice more gentle now. "At least I hope so. And what about you?"

Li Kung shook his head. "I have nowhere to run. I might as well stay. I deserve it anyway."

Old Snake broke into a slow chuckle. He seated himself

on the floor. "We'll wait here and die then? Shall we even pray for a miracle?"

"Pray to whom? I used to pray to Snow Wolf. Many people around here do."

"You did?" Old Snake laughed. "Do you really believe she became a goddess?"

"I don't know. If a goddess wanted to kill someone, would there be any chance that person can live?"

"Of course not."

There was a long silence. "Snow Wolf's not a goddess," Li Kung finally said.

There was another long pause, as each man pondered his own thoughts, his own dreams. Old Snake finally broke the silence. "She was an incredible woman."

"Who?"

"Snow Wolf. I was a young boy then, but I remember her. Her mere presence struck awe."

"Really?"

"Certainly." Old Snake leaned comfortably against the door. "But after I tell you about her, you have to tell me how you inherited her Flame Cutter."

Li Kung smiled. "We're waiting to die anyway. There's plenty of time for stories. Sure, I'll tell you about the Flame Cutter."

Old Snake chuckled. "I'm not afraid to die. I've never been, since I was fourteen."

"Fourteen?'

"And since then, I experimented with life and death every day. You know I grew up on Redwood Cliff. My mentor was the greatest poison user in the world—a man so capable in his art—he claimed there was not an element in this world he couldn't poison. And with the creation of the Soaring Dragon candles, he became famous for poisoning the air at will. I was his apprentice—for some reason his only apprentice—and I inherited most of his art."

Li Kung glanced out the window and noticed the approaching torches moving quicker than before, then, abandoning any new desire to escape alone, he smiled and gazed stiffly at the old poison user. Old Snake smiled back, once again reliving his boyhood. "That's how I became the greatest poison user alive after my master's death. Until the day I left Redwood Cliff, there was nothing in the world I couldn't poison." He sighed. "Who would have thought? The only poison I have left are the ones used to kill rodents outside—little poison nuggets—to keep them away from my herb garden."

Li Kung laughed. "Can you still kill a man with that?"

"Of course!" Old Snake became excited again. "Old Snake's poison can always kill. It's just that you need to get the nugget into the man's mouth. If you can stuff something that size into an enemy's mouth, you might as well slit his throat."

They both laughed. Old Snake wiped a warm tear from his eye. "Anyway, I promised to tell you something about Snow Wolf—since you used to pray to her spirit."

Li Kung closed his eyes. "We have time to exchange some stories. I'm listening."

"I was fourteen," Old Snake began. "Snow Wolf was a true hero. She won the respect of every person in Northern China. From age one when a boy could barely speak, to age eighty, while lying in their deathbeds, the population here couldn't stop praising her. Her fame even overshadowed her husband's, and many considered her the true leader of the Dragon House. Certainly, she was the true leader of the Martial Society.

"I looked up to her, and sometimes, she would ask me to

sit down to have tea, and she would teach me. One night, she asked me why people believed in so many gods. I said it was because people are afraid of death. That's why religions were created. She said that perhaps people aren't afraid of death, but of dying. The pain and suffering that we all must go through, right up to the point of death, is more horrible than death itself. No one knows what death is like, but we can only imagine—from the pain we experience—we can only imagine the worst. If a man could be made to believe that the moment after death is enjoyable and sensational, like flying in the clouds, then would they still be afraid of death? Wouldn't those old, sick, and about to die—wouldn't they appreciate this emotional relief? She was working on something—a tea that could be given to the old and dying. This tea would help them. Days, even weeks before death, they would be lost in a world where they would envision themselves flying through the clouds and floating into the heavens. They would believe in heaven, and they would look forward to it every day."

Li Kung slowly opened his eyes and stared.

Old Snake continued. "She trusted me, and asked me to help her find crucial ingredients to experiment with. For two years I helped her, until she died when I was sixteen. That was over fifty years ago."

Old Snake sighed. Li Kung glanced out the window, noted the approaching men, his mind in turmoil. "I was there—" he thought he heard Old Snake say. He shook his head clear to listen.

"I was the one who killed her daughter," Old Snake said, his hands wrung together in shame. "My master ordered me to do so. I don't know why I did it, perhaps out of fear. But that night, I heard it was uncovered that Snow Wolf had evil plans to overthrow the Wei family for absolute control of the Dragon House. The official word was that Lin Cha had fought her and stabbed her, but she had escaped. My master ordered me to bring the Soaring Dragon Candles to Pan Tong Village. I knew Snow Wolf's daughter was there. That was my mission. I had no choice.

"Lin Cha told the world that the Dragon leader Fei Long was killed by the Scholar, the Sun Cult leader, in a sword duel. Yet, that night I saw him with stab wounds all over his body. I saw him find his way to Pan Tong Village. I watched him go into the house where Su Ling was staying. There was another man inside the house, and I was afraid, so I remained outside. Much later I heard her crying for her father, and I knew then that the great Dragon leader Fei Long was dead. But Fei Long was still bleeding from fresh stab wounds when he walked in, so how could he have been killed in a duel three days ago?

"That night, I disobeyed my master and I didn't personally light the candles even though I was ordered to. Su Ling was the sweetest girl anyone could've ever met, and she was Snow Wolf's daughter. I couldn't bring myself to do it. I sneaked into the house from behind and replaced the candles in her kitchen with the poison ones. She would light incense and candles for her father's spirit—I knew that would be the first thing she would do—and she would die, moments after she lit the Soaring Dragon Candles. If she didn't die, I would be killed when I returned to Redwood Cliff. That is the crime I have been carrying all these years.

"Yes, Su Ling died of poison. I hid far away, on top of a hill, and I watched to make sure it happened. Then I saw her. Snow Wolf. She was stabbed and rapidly losing blood. I saw her stumbling forward as fast as she could. But she was too late. I watched her, and I saw her face when she realized that her daughter was dying. There was nothing she could do about it. I will never forget that face."

Old Snake sighed and slowly shook his head while staring at the ceiling. "The other man inside the house was long gone by the time I went back inside. I searched Fei Long's body but there was no jade. It was not on Su Ling."

There was silence for a moment. Then he continued, his voice trembling. "Fei Fei looked so much like Su Ling, except Fei Fei is stronger, and even more beautiful. She's a true warrior." Old Snake held his face in his hands. "Sometimes, I wonder if I looked after Fei Fei because she was so much like Snow Wolf's daughter. Fei Fei's voice. She sounds exactly like Su Ling. I murdered Snow Wolf's daughter. I wonder . . . But Fei Fei is like my own daughter. I would gladly shatter these old bones for her, if only I could do something to save her . . ."

Li Kung climbed to his feet. "May I ask you something?"

Old Snake looked up. "Of course."

"The tea Snow Wolf was experimenting with—what was in it?"

Old Snake shook his head. "I don't know. I was asked to look for only one ingredient."

"What were you asked to look for?"

"Lotus Crystals."

Li Kung started. His injuries began to agonize him again, and he swallowed hard. "Old Snake, listen to me. I know that I've brought nothing but trouble to you, but I ask that you trust me one more time. For the sake of Fei Fei, please trust me one more time."

Old Snake's face became more solemn. "Tell me."

"I've resolved to live, and I'll bring Fei Fei and Suthachai with me. We'll run out the back door," Li Kung paused, grimacing at the thought, "and you'll stay behind and kill Dong, and his followers. But . . . you'll die doing it."

Old Snake climbed to his feet, his eyes calm, free, impassive. "I'm listening. I'm ready to die, if Fei Fei may have a chance to live. I'm listening."

Li Kung stumbled forward and took the old man's hands. "I'm the one who deserves to die," he said, tears welling up in his eyes. "If there's anything I've learned lately, it's that I must live out my role in life, and it's not really my choice when I live or when I die. For me to die now would be too easy for me." He paused, realizing that he wasn't making any sense. "I'm sorry. I'm sorry you have to sacrifice. I've set matters off balance and now I must stay behind to clean my mess."

"Can you—" Old Snake looked into his eyes and searched. "Can you really escape? With Fei Fei? And you'll care for her, and help her recover?"

"I will," Li Kung said, more intensely now. There was little time left. "But there's no reason to trust me. So at least trust the Mongolian. He would give his life to protect her. At least trust him."

Old Snake smiled, like an old grandfather to his grandson. "I can't hope for more. You're a great doctor—far superior to me in medicine—and there's nothing better for Fei Fei than to have you treat her, and to have the man she loves caring for her. I'm old, and my time will come sooner or later. Just tell me what to do."

• • •

Moments later, Li Kung and Suthachai descended the hill behind Old Snake's home, pushing a wheelbarrow in front of them. Fei Fei lay within, completely wrapped in silk blankets, a thin veil covering her face to protect her from insects. Li Kung guided the wheelbarrow and glanced behind him to see if Dong had entered the house or not. They would inevitably arrive soon because the trail of blood and footprints led there. It was useless to look back. Old Snake would die.

"Slow your pace, Suthachai. I can't keep up."

"We need to bring her to a safe place," was all he said.

"Suthachai!" Li Kung said in a harsh whisper. "We need to conserve our strength in case Old Snake fails."

Suthachai paused. For the first time he took his eyes away from Fei Fei.

"We have every reason to live," Li Kung said. "I have Old Snake's formula, and she's getting stronger every day. She'll wake up soon. Our injuries are not life threatening. We'll recover, we just need to buy time. There's too much to do, Suthachai. Work with me, so we can live. There's too much to do."

Suthachai nodded. Li Kung pointed to a small fork in the road. "The soil is soft and dusty on that road. Take her, but drag her along the road. There's a thick blanket under her so she'll be fine. Drag her behind you so your footprints will be covered. I'll push this wheelbarrow in the other direction. I just saw a turtle go that way—there's water nearby. I'll lose the wheel tracks in the water before pulling it out on a rocky surface. It'll hide the tracks, and I'll come and meet you."

Suthachai nodded again. With some difficulty, he lifted Fei Fei off the wheelbarrow and rested her face-up on the ground. "Stay alive, Li Kung," Suthachai suddenly said. "You promised to cure her."

He nodded, turned, and pushed the empty wheelbarrow away. The Flute Demon and the Mongolian. They were together again. This was what Pun would have wanted.

· · ·

Dong stood outside the strange house with the metal doors. The dreaded smell of herbs was everywhere. He was eager to leave. But the footprints and the spots of blood were apparent—they all led into the house. His men were tired, fidgety, anxious to capture and slay the two they had been hunting all day. There was no turning back.

Dong lifted his hand and signaled for his men to follow. In three bold steps, he smashed through the heavy doors, and, with weapon drawn, stormed his way in.

He found himself in the center of a poorly lit room, large but hardly furnished. A short whimper came from a tall closet in the corner. Then a rustling sound.

Dong leaped forward, and with all his strength, stabbed through the closet until the hilt of his sword struck the wood. He withdrew his weapon. There were streaks of blood on his blade. He smiled.

The closet door slowly opened, and an old man fell out. He twitched once, his mouth gaping open. Something fell out of his mouth. In a moment, he lay still.

Dong turned the body over. "Old Snake!" he whispered.

In panic, he spun around, barged through his men, and broke into the small bedroom in the rear. There, on the table, was a single red candle. Dong stared. The flame on the candle licked the air above it.

Dong stumbled back, covered his face with his sleeve, then threw down his sword and hurried back to the main room. "Don't die!" he shouted. "Damn you, Old Snake! Don't die!"

He reached Old Snake's body, grabbed him and shook as hard as he could. His men watched in shock. One warrior peered into the back room and screamed. "Soaring Dragon Candle!"

There was absolute chaos. The men screamed, tried to

run and stumbled against each other. Dong lifted his face. "It's too late!"

The men slowed, each trembling in fear. "We're going to die here," one of them whimpered.

"There's no antidote," another said, his voice weak. "We're done for."

The men began to quiet, each pondering his own survival. None of them knew what to do.

"Why?" one warrior asked. "Old Snake himself was hiding in there, and he would be poisoned too! If he didn't make any noise, we never would've killed him. Why would he poison himself?"

Dong's eyes glowed. Then he noticed it. Something had fallen out of Old Snake's mouth earlier—a small brown nugget.

"Antidote!" someone shouted. A commotion resumed. Every man scrambled for the nugget on the floor.

"Quiet!" Dong roared. "If it was in his mouth, it has to be the antidote. It's a brown nugget, it melts slowly in your mouth! There should be more! There!" He pointed at the shelves. "Search the jars!"

Every man responded. The porcelain jars were yanked from the shelves and frantically opened, their contents spilling onto the floor. Moments later, a cry of triumph. "I found it!" someone shouted.

"Give me one! Give me one!"

The men desperately fought each other for the antidote. Dong was the first to snatch his share, and soon, every one of them managed to stuff at least one brown nugget into their mouths. Some of them laughed, a few sighed in relief.

Moments later, the entire room was littered with dying men. Their mouths were foaming, their bodies writhing in agony. Each died in bewilderment and fear. "I thought that was the antidote . . . " one of them said, his eyes closing, his body lying still forever. Dong was sprawled by the door, trying desperately to crawl. He knew he was dying, but he couldn't understand why. His father had stripped Old Snake of every possible means to create the Soaring Dragon poison. His father even told him once, in a rare moment of humor, that the most Old Snake could manage now were concoctions that killed rodents.

· · ·

The rain pelted, angrily at first, then washing them in slow torment. Li Kung and Suthachai glanced once at each other, for the first time with a new understanding between them. They must survive—together.

Dull silence. With heads bowed and eyes barely open against the rain, the two men made their way through the woods. They hoped to find the Three Saints of Yunnan by sunset. At the earliest sign of dusk, the rain stopped, and appearing in front of them, almost magically, was the house of the Three Saints.

Li Kung peered through blurred eyes. Something strange caught his sight. The sign on the front door read "The Two Freaks of Yunnan."

Two old men with long walking sticks, also soaking wet, hustled through the gray light. They approached the front entrance. The wooden doors opened, and Shifu Three emerged with a big smile on his face. "Welcome!" he said, his voice ringing across the surrounding forest. "Welcome to Old One's funeral. Come in, it's getting cold out here. Come in and have a warm drink."

Li Kung panicked, stumbling forward with a shout. "Shifu One!" he called, gasping for air. "Shifu One!"

"Li Kung!" a voice responded. It was Shifu Two, already waiting for him by the door. "You're just in time," Old Two said. "I knew you would come back to help us bury Old One. All our friends are too old. We need you. Come, have something to drink first."

The house was decorated for festivities. Yet a small coffin, its cover closed, was placed in the front of the room. An ink painting of Shifu One was draped over the coffin. Two old men seated in a corner were playing the harp. Numerous guests sat around eating and drinking, laughing with each other and immersed in conversation. Fresh fruits, small dim sums, and bottles of sorghum wine were scattered across many tables.

Old Two gave Li Kung a bottle of warm wine and a cup, then turned to attend to his guests. Laughter was everywhere. But Li Kung moved forward, dazed, in shock, unaware of the party around him. No one noticed him. Old One had asked him to come home for a surprise in six months. He had completely forgotten. He had thought that any surprise could wait. He never imagined that the surprise was his old mentor's passing.

Li Kung collapsed to his knees in front of the coffin. He hadn't come back in time, as promised, and so he had failed Shifu One as well. Hot tears welled in his eyes. He could not look at Old One's portrait any longer. He lowered his head and poured wine into the cup.

"I'm sorry . . . I did everything wrong . . . " He poured the wine on the floor as a customary offering to the dead, then filled the cup again.

A bony hand closed around his wrist and took the cup away. "Stop pouring it on the floor. You're wasting good wine." Li Kung lifted his eyes, and watched Old Huang swallow the contents of the cup. A bright smile lit up the wrinkled face. "Ah, that's good wine. Young man, are you really as stupid as you look? How can a dead man drink wine? The way you scattered it on the floor, even a live man can't drink it." He took the bottle away from Li Kung and turned around to leave, then halted and said, "When you've finished crying, I have a good book for you to read. Come find me."

Old Huang trotted off to chat with his friends. Shifu Three walked over. "You're weeping?" Old Three asked. "Why? Is it because you were soaked in the rain?"

"Stop!" Li Kung suddenly shouted. Everyone fell silent and turned to him. "How? How could you all be celebrating?" He spun around and turned to Old Three. "This is your brother!"

"Why shouldn't we celebrate? He died on schedule."

Li Kung's eyes widened. "On schedule?"

"Yes!" Old Two said from across the room. "He came, he enjoyed himself immensely, and then he left. I don't understand why you're unhappy." The room full of guests laughed and returned to what they were doing.

Old Three stood in front of Li Kung, so close to his face that he had to lean back. The beady eyes carefully studied him. "I remember. You were never happy when you had to start a big task, but you were always overjoyed when you had finished it. Correct?"

Li Kung started, angry, at the same time crumbling in despair. "What does that have to do with—"

Old Three held a crooked finger to his face to silence him. "You agree. So why are you weeping when Old One has finished his task with such glory? Hypocrite! Come. Celebrate with us."

"Li Kung!" someone shouted. "Is that your friend you left out in the rain?"

"That's . . . " Old Two peered outside, then jumped with

284

excitement. "That's the Mongolian who was bitten by a hundred scorpions!" He turned to an old man next to him and said, on the side, "I raised those scorpions. They were extra large."

Several men walked out to help the Mongolian.

Old Two turned to Li Kung. "Why is it that every time you're with this Mongolian, he's vomiting blood?"

A few other men carried Fei Fei into the room. Old Two reached out to read her pulse.

"The formula," Li Kung said, pulling out an old piece of cloth. "These are the ingredients that she's been treated with. We can—"

Old Two took one glance at the cloth and threw it aside. "Fool! How can she help herself heal if no one wakes her up first? Come!" He turned to Suthachai. "Come! Let's wake her up. Treating a sleeping girl is boring anyway."

•   •   •

Tao Hing stood on the edge of Redwood Cliff, his fists clenched, his eyes blurry and tearing. From a high vantage point, he could see the cloud of dark smoke hovering in the air, blown in from Yellow Sand Plateau. It stung with a toxic smell. The messengers loyal to him had been searching for him on horseback, and well before he arrived that morning, he had heard.

But Wei Bin had never informed him of the duel, and there was no chance for him to return in time. He couldn't prevent the battle.

Cricket had returned from an empty trip to the Mongolian steppes, but promptly left for Yellow Sand Plateau in search of his father's body. Master Bin was last seen burned alive in the middle of the encirclement, and there was a chance that his body had remained intact. The Red Dragons who formed the Octagonal Cage had virtually disappeared in the inferno. They were cremated before drifting away with the wind.

A messenger ran up from behind.

"Tell me!" Tao Hing said, without turning around.

"The Green Dragons just killed forty of our men. They're seeking blood. But Master Cricket couldn't stop our brothers from retaliating. They're descending Redwood Cliff right now, and they're going to attack the Green Dragon outpost on Northern Pass."

"Did you tell them that they are not to instigate any more conflicts?"

"I did, master. But they said . . . they said . . . "

"Go on!"

The messenger bowed his head. "They said that you could do nothing to stop them, and that they would follow your orders only if you show the courage to be their leader. They want you to help them kill the Green Dragons, sir."

Tao Hing trembled, his face twitching in fury. "They can't do that!" he shouted. "So many have already been killed, and we don't even know why yet. We must stop them!"

"But I also heard," the messenger said, "that Wei Jian has vowed vengeance. Thousands of men coming from every school in the Martial Society have sworn to help him. Somehow, the coalition has become even bigger. They're gathering in He Ku, and they are united. There are rumors that they intend to storm Redwood Cliff and punish us for the atrocities on Yellow Sand Plateau."

Tao Hing couldn't utter a word. He stared into the distance, a cold sweat covering his forehead. "They all hate us now," he whispered. "Master Bin, what have you done in my absence?"

"And one more thing," the messenger said.

"Speak."

"We found Master Dong's body in a little house by Phoenix Eye Peak. The men with him are all dead."

"What!"

"And . . . we also found Old Snake's body. The blood on Master Dong's sword . . . It seems that Dong killed him. And Master Dong and all his men died of poison."

Tao Hing covered his face with his hands and crumbled to his knees.

• • •

Fei Fei was flying, or floating, like an eagle soaring into the heavens with no worries and no fears. Sometimes she was on the ground where the land was bright, where peach trees blossomed in sweet-smelling gardens, and she would pick the fruits while a cool wind floated across her face. Often, she would find herself lying face up on a soft bed of clouds, and she would be in a bubble; from time to time she could roll off the clouds, look down at the world underneath her, and still rise freely to the heavens.

"Black paste," she whispered. All of a sudden, she understood, and the ground loomed before her. She dived into the mundane world. She didn't want to return, but she had to. She had promised him. She had promised to be strong.

"Black paste," she said again, opening her eyes. He was there, waiting for her, protecting her. She smiled and snuggled against him. "Suthachai," she said. "It lasted so much longer this time."

A tear dripped from his eye.

She was on a bed, inside a small room built of wood and stone. The weather was warm; there was no snow outside.

"Suthachai?"

He was silent, stunned, tears now flowing. She tried to lift her hand to his face and wipe the teardrops, but her arm was too weak to obey her. She tried again, but barely raised her elbow before dropping in exhaustion.

"Do not move, my love," Suthachai was suddenly able to speak. "Do not move. You will get well soon. Lie still and rest."

Her eyes widened. She remembered, and she smiled. "We're dead," she whispered. "We've come to the afterlife together. I knew we would find each other, Suthachai. I knew we would find each other . . . "

He took her hand. "We are alive, Fei Fei. I did not die. And Old Snake, and then Li Kung and his mentors healed you. We are alive! Now, keep quiet and rest. I am here. I will never leave you. Keep quiet and rest . . . "

• • •

A week passed, and Fei Fei recovered her basic mobility. She was able to eat normal quantities between long hours of sleep. Suthachai remained by her side every hour of the day, as promised.

"I've come to tell you a story," Li Kung said, seated in front of his two friends, a dimly lit candle between them. He looked into Fei Fei's eyes, then at Suthachai, and sensed the deep trust and respect they had for him. He breathed a heavy sigh. No one, besides Ying, would trust him so much.

Over the weeks, he had finally come to understand why his two friends were there, and why he stayed with them each day. It was because of his mistakes.

"I came to tell you a story," he repeated. Then, with a deep breath, he began his tale.

He told of how he first found samples of the black paste

288

in Wei Bin's underground laboratory, and how he was so determined to prevent this poison from spreading. He told of how Pun died and how he stumbled into Phoenix Eye Peak. Suthachai was dazed, unable to respond, but Li Kung spoke gently. He was no longer accusing, and for the first time, he told his story without blaming the Mongolian. He described how he fell into Snow Wolf's tomb, how he was tested and ultimately chosen to receive her gifts, how he later formulated the schemes to destroy the Dragon Houses. He told of how Wei Bin and Wei Xu died, and how Dong was deceived and killed by Old Snake. Fei Fei showed little reaction to the news of her father's death, and when she finally spoke, she asked about her younger brother Cricket.

Li Kung sighed. "Cricket is fine," he said. "I tricked him with a forged letter and he went to Mongolia to look for your body. He's back now. Eventually, he'll win the trust of his people."

· · ·

"What are you still doing here?" Li Kung asked, staring at the forty-four bandits in front of him. They stood in front of the Two Saint's old farmhouse, scattered and restless, but with heads held high and arms crossed in front of them. Li Kung stepped out from the doorway.

"We're not leaving, Master Li," one of them said.

"Something went wrong. You said so yourself, Master Li. And we're going to stand by you."

"Don't you have someone to rob or steal from?"

There was a sudden commotion among the bandits as they turned to each other, and then they were quiet. One Eyed Shu stepped forward. "We can't do that anymore or you would burn us alive, remember?"

Li Kung shook his head and looked away. "I can't burn any more people. Why don't you just go home?"

"We're not going anywhere. We're staying to help you. Whatever we did wrong, we're staying to help make it right."

"You didn't do anything wrong."

"Then whatever you did wrong, Master Li. Whatever it is, we're going to stay and help you make it right."

"And we're not accepting any money either!" someone in the back yelled.

"That's right!" Fat Shu shouted. "We've already been paid. Now we stay to finish the job!"

Li Kung sighed. "Skinny Lin, what about your dumpling shop?"

Skinny Lin laughed. "I changed my mind. I'm going to find a wife first and then open the shop. That way, I won't have to work so hard."

The bandits laughed, just briefly, before falling silent in front of Li Kung's solemn stare.

"Horseface Mi," Li Kung called, scanning the faces in front of him. A tall man with a very long face stepped forward.

"Yes, Master Li."

"Aren't you supposed to be a judge somewhere?"

"No, sir. Master Ying convinced me that I need to learn how to read first. I'll save my money, and I'll buy my government post after I learn to read."

They broke into laughter again, and then subsided just as quickly. The bandits fell quiet, some clearing their throats, staring at Li Kung, some of them shifting their weight from one leg to another, others folding their hands in front with fingers tapping their knuckles in taut anticipation.

Li Kung gazed at the good men in front of him, for the first time realizing that these men were indeed loyal to him, and that he had never once thought of them as good men. They were bandits, scum of the earth, criminals that he needed to use, and at best, dispose of with money and threats. But was he any different from these lowlifes?

I'm different, he said to himself, finally. I'm not in their league. They're simple people who made mistakes, and they're looking to redeem themselves. In their own crude way, they're looking to stay behind and make things right. I haven't even tried.

"Stay with me," Li Kung said, suddenly. "I need your help! Help me make this right!"

The bandits cheered.

. . .

Ying clambered up the rocky side of the hill, her ax leveled comfortably on her shoulder. She saw Li Kung at the top of the hill, staring into the sunset. She waved to him, a smile on her face. Her heart was thumping fast. She had wandered He Ku for two days like he had told her, and she looked forward to seeing him every moment of every day, though she didn't understand why. She wanted so badly to tell him that she had accomplished her task, and that she was worth his praise.

A bright smile filled Li Kung's face when he saw her.

She felt weak when he looked at her, suddenly uncertain of whether she would be able to walk anymore.

In a flash, Li Kung reached her and took the ax from her.

"This is heavy," he said. "You don't need to carry it anymore. The bandits around here will never hurt you—they answer to me."

She nodded, her large eyes peering into his face.

He took her hand and brought her to the rock he was

sitting on. "How's Suthachai and Fei Fei?" he asked. "Are they fully recovered yet?"

Ying flipped her palm, indicating "partially."

"It'll be soon. They're drinking the formula that I drank when training for the Flame Cutter. Shifu Two is also giving them something special. They'll be as strong as they used to be." Then, holding out his palm, he gently asked, "What did you find?"

Ying handed him a small piece of cloth with her own handwriting scribbled on it. Li Kung read out loud, "Killing continues. Wei Xu's son gathered all coalition and Green Dragon branches. Preparing for major assault. Red Dragons also sent for their branches."

Li Kung stared, a frown on his face. "And all across the land, the Red and Green Dragons are still killing each other? Even though the twins are dead?"

Ying lowered her eyes and nodded, suddenly unhappy that Li Kung seemed worried.

"I'm fine," Li Kung said, looking away. After a long time, he released a deep, painful sigh. "I don't know what went wrong. Maybe Snow Wolf never became a goddess after all." He stood up and walked away. "I need to go to Redwood Cliff."

• • •

"We need to go back. The great hunt is under way."

The Mongolian horsemen, all twenty of them mounted on their horses, waited for Suthachai to respond. It was early in the evening. They were on a small hill where the new sign reading "The Two Freaks of Yunnan" could still be seen in the distance.

Suthachai and Fei Fei were on new horses, which they

had purchased as soon as they could walk without pain. Fei Fei's complexion was glowing. The horsemen couldn't avoid staring at her, yet they knew better than to arouse the jealousy of the number one warrior on the steppe. They did their best to look straight ahead.

Suthachai glanced at Fei Fei, then back at his people. He slowly shook his head.

"They need us back home," one of the men said. "And they need you. You are the number one warrior. You belong on the steppe."

"I need to stay," Suthachai said, after a long time. "When I am finished here, I will go home."

"Why?" a lean warrior asked, bringing his horse forward. It was Jocholai. "You say that the people of China need you. But our people also need you. You are Mongolian."

"I am," Suthachai said. "But when we passed the market at the border, did you notice there were very few merchants on the street? If the Chinese salt makers are at war, the clans on the steppe will not have anyone to trade with. Then how can we have a constant supply of salt and tea?"

"Can you help them?" Jocholai asked. "Can one Mongolian stop the Chinese Martial Society from killing each other? I think you overestimate your abilities, my brother."

"I will not be alone," Suthachai said. "If you must leave, then please do so. I thank you all for coming here with me."

"We are pleased to have saved so many from being burned alive," a smaller warrior said. "Even if they are Chinese."

They bade him farewell, and without another word, turned around to ride away. One rider remained behind.

"Jocholai . . . "

Jocholai smiled. "One Mongolian can do nothing to help. Maybe two Mongolians can get something done." He turned his horse around. "You know where to find me. Blue Lantern Inn." He squeezed his horse's belly, sent it into a rapid gallop and disappeared.

Suthachai grinned. He was relieved that his best friend would remain by his side in this strange land. He took Fei Fei's hand. It would be a short battle. "Then we will go home," he whispered to her.

The sound of shuffling feet could be heard. Suthachai reached for his saber. Fei Fei's hand also closed around her weapon, a double-edged sword, but when she recognized the people approaching, she relaxed. "Li Kung's bandits," she said. "They're here. I need to go."

"Fei Fei." Suthachai stared at a plain-looking carriage emerging from the woods. "I do not understand. Why did Li Kung ask you to do this?"

"Because Old Snake said my voice sounds exactly like my aunt's, remember?"

"Your aunt?"

"My aunt Su Ling," she said. She squeezed his hand, and leaped off her horse. "Li Kung has a strange theory of why the Dragon Houses are at war. An extraordinary theory. He believes that one person is behind all the slaughter. And he needs my help."

"Who?" Suthachai asked. "We can kill this person, and the nightmare will be over!"

"How do you kill someone who's been dead for fifty years?"

Fei Fei drew away, turned, and hurried off.

Two rough-looking men pulled a little brown carriage up the hill, stopping at the mouth of a cave. Li Kung was behind them. He greeted Suthachai with a smile, then pointed into the cave entrance. "Bring her into the back and leave her on the pile of stones."

He threw a small pouch of coins into their hands.

"Thank you, Master Li! Thank you!" the men said in chorus. They quickly drew the curtain and lifted an old woman from the carriage. She was unconscious. Suthachai noticed that she had no legs. She was filthy, dressed in tatters, and her body emitted such a stench that even the Mongolian noticed.

"Li Kung."

"Her name is Little Butterfly," Li Kung said. "She has a story to tell us."

"A story?"

"Remember? The story she told me about how Snow Wolf died?"

"Yes," Suthachai said. "Fei Fei's grandmother poisoned her and stabbed her."

"That was a lie."

"How do you know?"

"I'm Snow Wolf's student. I know." Li Kung walked into the cave. "Let's go. The scent powder will only last a little while longer and then she'll wake up. We need to be ready."

· · ·

Inside the cave, the stinging smell of fresh blood filled the air. Li Kung lifted a handkerchief to cover his face. "Pig's blood," he said, aware that Suthachai was staring at him. "The smell of blood makes hell all the more convincing."

The Mongolian nodded. They seated themselves on two chairs in the back, behind a row of crackling bonfires, and waited.

The fire was steady, emitting a strong heat that drew sweat on their foreheads. They seemed to sit forever. Finally, Little Butterfly moaned, then coughed before turning over. Her hands clawed against the bed of stones that she rested on. Li Kung looked at Suthachai, held up his finger to indicate silence, then nodded in the direction of the cave entrance.

"Little Butterfly! Little Butterfly!"

Fei Fei's voice was distant, but strong. Li Kung smiled to himself. The delicate woman warrior would come through with her role.

Little Butterfly sat up, scattering the sharp gravel underneath. She grabbed a large pebble, raised her arm to throw, then, with a gasp, dropped to one elbow. Her bony joints jabbed into the stones as she struggled to sit.

"Your favorite missiles are all around you, infinite in number, but you'll never be able to throw them—"

"Who? Who are you? Where am I?" Little Butterfly tilted her head to listen, but the sound of crackling flames echoed through the cavern. "Who are you?"

"Little Butterfly!" Fei Fei said. "Who killed my mother?"

"Your—your mother? I don't know who you are. I don't know who you are!"

"Yes you do!" Fei Fei shouted. She took three bold steps and suddenly stood before the old woman. Little Butterfly could not react. Fei Fei placed a straw basket in front of her and shouted, "Eat!"

Little Butterfly shivered, sniffed the basket, and her face lit up. She reached inside, yanked a chicken leg, and began to eat. More food and fine wine were placed in front of her. She lifted her face and laughed, tearing at the meat, stuffing her face faster than she could swallow. More than once, she choked on her food, only to wash everything down with wine.

"Who killed my mother?" Fei Fei shouted.

"Who?" the old woman asked with her mouth full. Fei

Fei suddenly swept the meal away, scattering the basket and plates into the distance. Little Butterfly screamed, a look of horror on her face.

"Who killed my mother?"

Little Butterfly was motionless, as if possessed. "Su Ling . . . " she whispered. Her entire body began to shake. She twisted around, groping the ground, but everywhere she touched was covered with sharp gravel. "What do you want from me?" she screamed. "Su Ling, what do you want from me?"

"Who?" Fei Fei roared. "Who killed my mother?"

"Lin Cha! The old witch Lin Cha killed her. It had nothing to do with me!"

Fei Fei swung a flaming torch into the pebbles and a blast of fire ignited around the old woman. The flames were massive, roaring, the heat completely enveloping her. She twisted and writhed against the gravel in panic.

Fei Fei lifted a casket of water, threw it on the flames, and extinguished it before Little Butterfly could be burned.

"Where we are," Fei Fei said, moving closer, "is a land of pain, of endless torture, a place where you'll be burned alive for your crimes. This is where you'll suffer for eternity. You're here because I summoned you! You will stay forever!"

The old woman tried to crawl away. After groping around with charred fingers, she collapsed with a whimper.

"It wasn't my fault," she wept. "Let me go . . . It wasn't my fault . . . "

"Tell me now, and I will bring you back your meal. Tell me now, and I will let you leave here!"

"It wasn't my fault!" the old woman repeated. "It wasn't my fault. Why don't you ask your father Fei Long? He was the supreme leader. Why me?"

Fei Fei swept a burst of gravel into her face. She brought

her torch around, so close this time that the flame almost touched the old woman.

"Leave me alone!" Little Butterfly shrieked. "She deserved it! Snow Wolf deserved to die!"

"She was like a mother to you!"

"I hated her!"

"You stabbed her from behind!"

"Your father stabbed her!"

Fei Fei suddenly froze, her eyes wide. She looked to Li Kung for help.

Li Kung stalled, dumbfounded, but managed to signal for her to continue.

The old woman wept in long, dreary sobs.

Fei Fei crouched low and took the old woman's hand. "Little Butterfly," she said, "tell me the truth, and I'll let you leave here. You'll be forgiven for anything you did in the past, as long as you tell the truth."

Little Butterfly took deep breaths. "Really?"

"Definitely."

"I . . . I didn't mean to. But I loved him. I loved him with all my heart."

"Who?"

"Your father. The magnificent leader of the Dragon House! You will forgive me, Su Ling?"

"I will," Fei Fei said. "You're forgiven. Tell me what happened."

"But she—" Little Butterfly seethed, her teeth bared. "She was always there! I was younger! I was more beautiful! I gave him infinite pleasures!" She breathed hard, then gradually began to calm. "But that was not why. I would never have dared—"

"Dared what?"

"Plan Snow Wolf's murder."

"Then who planned it?"

"Fei Long did!"

Fei Fei clenched her teeth but said nothing.

"It was time," Little Butterfly said with a laugh. "Finally, after years of tolerance, he was resolved. He had to be rid of her! Who was she to overshadow the great leader of the Dragon House? How dare she? She was just a woman, no more than I was, but she commanded more respect than the man she served! How could a great leader like Fei Long tolerate that?"

Little Butterfly sneered, lost in thought. "So I helped him kill her," she said, with a short laugh. "Snow Wolf trusted me. I slept with her man for over a year, and she trusted me. That night, when she returned to Redwood Cliff, I followed her to Fei Long's chambers. He appeared weak, but in good spirits. He told her the truth. He was not wounded, but he released rumors to generate confusion until she returned. He invited her to drink with him by the silver pine forest. I went to prepare the wine, which I heavily poisoned, and she drank it. She trusted me and drank the wine . . . "

Little Butterfly began to laugh. "And yes, Fei Long stabbed her before she realized she was poisoned. He stabbed her from under the table. But she escaped. There was no way she could have survived the poison, but she couldn't be killed before the poison took full effect. She escaped because she was Snow Wolf.

"Don't blame me, Su Ling. It was your father's plan. I could only obey the lord. I could only obey the man I loved. But then, he broke my heart, so I killed him."

"What?" Fei Fei jumped. The old woman flinched. Fei Fei collected herself, realizing the role she was supposed to play. "Tell me. Tell me the truth and you will not be blamed."

"I . . . " Little Butterfly seemed lost.

"He broke your heart."

"Yes," she said, her voice dreary. "He broke my heart. I returned to the pavilion that night, and he was drinking alone. I was going to go to him, and return to his bed with him. But Lin Cha was there. The evil witch! I overheard. I heard everything. They had planned the murder together and merely used me as a tool. And her children, the evil twins—Wei Bin, Wei Xu—they were Fei Long's children! He slept with Lin Cha and she bore his children!"

Fei Fei flinched, disturbed, but Little Butterfly didn't notice.

"So, when Lin Cha left him, I stabbed him from behind," the old woman continued. "I stabbed him so many times, I couldn't even count. Even though he sliced off both my legs struggling to get away from me, I kept stabbing him. He was the great warrior Fei Long. His fighting skills were unmatched—even Snow Wolf couldn't touch him in a fair duel. But I, a mere servant girl, killed him. Yes! I stabbed him with a dagger that Snow Wolf gave me, because I hated him! I loved him so much. He kicked me into a cavern in the confusion, but I knew he was dead. I stabbed him so many times!"

She broke into a roaring laughter, her fists clenched, her body wracked with excitement. Li Kung closed his eyes. He lifted his hand and gave Fei Fei the signal. She doused a white powder over the old woman's face and rendered her unconscious.

. . .

Moments later, Li Kung stood staring at the moon outside. He would wait for his bandits to carry Little Butterfly to a well-furnished room. She would be fed and bathed. He sighed. After tonight, she couldn't possibly enjoy her remaining years as he had planned for her. She was reminded of how she had murdered both the man she loved and the woman she called mother.

Suthachai and Fei Fei stood next to him.

"Fear of hell is an interesting concept," Li Kung said, still staring at the moon. "We can use this strategy again."

They smiled.

"How did you know?" Fei Fei asked.

"Snow Wolf created me to kill Lin Cha's descendants. The question has always been why Snow Wolf would want so many people killed. Today, we found out why."

"But that doesn't prove anything," Fei Fei said. "She's been dead for fifty years. How is it possible that she caused the Red and Green Dragons to kill each other today? Did she want so many people killed?"

"That was her mission for me," Li Kung said. "To destroy the Dragon Houses so that the evil black paste would never be used to harm the world."

"Snow Wolf wanted to fight the evil," Suthachai said. "That is humane and noble."

"Not if she created the black paste." Li Kung reached into his pockets and pulled out the sheepskin. "Remember this?"

Fei Fei took the sheepskin and stared at the secret formula. "I don't understand."

"The lotus crystals," Li Kung said, pointing to a line on the sheepskin. "She asked Old Snake to find that one rare ingredient for her. He was still a young man then. She told him that it was for a special medicine, used to help old people face death. While in their death beds, the people who take her medicine would believe they were floating in heaven."

Fei Fei's mouth dropped, and her hands began to shake. Li Kung took the sheepskin back from her.

"You're right, it doesn't prove anything," Li Kung admitted. "It's not even in her handwriting. But I believe that she kept a journal. It's somewhere, and we'll find our answers in there."

"There was no journal," Suthachai said. "You have forgotten about the last time we went digging for that journal."

"There has to be," Li Kung insisted. "If she did cause today's turmoil, it has to be with a strategy too brilliant for us to comprehend. She would not want something so brilliant to die with her. She will preserve her legacy. There has to be a journal."

"Digging randomly in a network of caves and tunnels would be foolish," Suthachai said. "If she really has something she wants passed onto future generations, she would have left it in the care of someone. Like the war bows used in our clan. They are passed on from father to son for hundreds of years, and each son is taught to hand the bow down to the next generation. That is how things are made to last forever."

"Snow Wolf doesn't have children," Fei Fei said. "My aunt was the only one, and she died."

"I am her only heir," Li Kung whispered. "Unless she left it in the care of an old friend." He seated himself on the grass, tucked his chin into his knees, and stared into the distance. "An old friend . . . Fifty years ago . . . who would still be alive today."

There was silence. Long silence. Then out of nowhere, Li Kung jumped to his feet. "How could I have forgotten? He's expecting me!"

. . .

"Why did Northern Pass flood?" Li Kung asked the old farmer. "There are no major rivers within six days from here."

302

"Who knows?" the farmer shook his head, trying to move on. Li Kung ran up to him again.

"Has Northern Pass ever flooded before?"

"Not for the past sixty-four years. But now we can't even walk to town. We have to bring our water buffaloes with us when we trade at the market."

Li Kung opened his hand and showed the old farmer a gold nugget. "This is to help your family."

The farmer stared and his jaw dropped.

"Tell me," Li Kung asked again, "does anyone know where all this water came from?"

"Up there," the farmer finally said. He pointed up to Phoenix Eye Peak. "Some say that there is water running inside the mountain, and that's why there's a waterfall on the other side. But strangely, that waterfall has stopped and all the water is coming here."

"Something must have dammed the water?"

"Maybe," the farmer shook his head. He pocketed the gold nugget and waited for Li Kung to finish.

"Maybe a cavern collapsed in there and dammed the water?"

"Maybe," the farmer said again. He didn't have the answers.

• • •

The last time he had ascended the pavilion, Li Kung was certain that Old One would be there, playing Wei Chi with his friend. But this time, he ran so quickly that his feet barely touched the steps. Like a rush of wind, Li Kung sprang over the top step and into the pavilion.

Old Huang was playing a game of Wei Chi by himself. He looked up, into Li Kung's eyes, and smiled. "The Flame

Cutter. There can be no mistake. And I heard about the Octagonal Cage formation last month. You've truly inherited her most precious skills."

Li Kung drew forward, seated himself in front of the old man, and glanced at the black and white pieces scattered across the board. "You're playing by yourself?"

"That's the problem. I live too long. All my friends who can play this game are dead. First, I played with Old Wu, but she died early. Then, I played with Old One, but now he's gone. Strange. Aren't you a student of every person I ever get to play this game with?"

Li Kung didn't respond. He reached for a pot, respectfully filled Old Huang's cup with tea, and waited. Old Huang stared into the distance, as if lost in melancholy thoughts, then smiled, once again his usual self. "The land in this area is dry and rocky. But look at those flowers."

Li Kung's eyes followed his, swept to the bottom of the hill and noticed a pasture of wild flowers, mainly deep yellow, in tight clusters that painted the land in both dense and scattered colors. Many butterflies fluttered about in a haven of nectar.

"Beautiful flowers."

"Every year, the wild flowers bloom," Old Huang continued. "That's because the soil underneath is so fertile."

"Why?"

"There was a major battle here, many, many years ago. So many were killed. No one came to retrieve the bodies. The dead bodies made the land fertile."

Li Kung nodded, waiting, unsure of what Old Huang's intentions were.

"Soon, the flowers will fade and perish in the winter," Old Huang said. "But you know it's a good thing, because if they don't die, new life will never emerge. Next year's flowers will depend on their timely deaths. That's the cycle of heaven. After death and destruction, something will be born. That something will grow, flourish, fade, and die. Then another will be born."

He reached into his coat and pulled out a thick, cloth-bound book, heavily wrapped in canvas and sealed with a fine layer of wax. One side of the canvas was torn. "I know, I know. I invited you here. This book is for you." Old Huang laughed and slid the book across the little stone table in front of Li Kung. "My old friend asked me to keep this for her until the right time and not to read it. But I opened it and read it a few weeks ago." He chuckled, and said with a wink, "It was the right time."

Li Kung took the book in his hands and felt a warm tingle of hope.

"You're her inheritor," Old Huang said. "I was supposed to give this book to someone, anyone, so it might as well be you."

"Give it to someone," Li Kung repeated. "When? When Northern Pass gets flooded?"

"Yes!" Old Huang responded, suddenly excited. "Truly a genius, no wonder Old Wu chose you! When she told me she would choose a successor, I didn't think she could make wise decisions after her death. I'm so fortunate. I've lived long enough to place this book in your hands. Otherwise, I would have to instruct some other poor lad to do it for me, and I never would've seen the Flame Cutter again."

"Northern Pass flooded because the cavern caved in and rerouted the river inside the mountain," Li Kung almost whispered to himself. "I was supposed to die when the cavern collapsed. Which means this book is not for me."

There was a long pause. Old Huang studied him with interest. "I know," he said, leaning over. He reached out with a bony hand and grabbed Li Kung's wrist. "Listen to me carefully. The Martial Society has been hollowed out. Out of this destruction, new life will emerge. It's inevitable, like the wild flowers. After full bloom, the flowers must fade, and there will be destruction. When destruction has reached a limit, there will be silence and there will be nothing. From nothing, something will grow again. There is no reason to alter this cycle. It will be here forever. Tomorrow, a new generation of warriors will slowly grow into the role of brigands, knights errant, heroes and outlaws, con men and leaders, all of them armed, and all of them competitive. These roles must be filled, and will be filled. Do you understand?"

Li Kung sighed. "I understand what I need to do."

"But you must understand what you don't need to do!" Old Huang shouted.

Li Kung took a deep breath and sighed. He looked into the distance. "I'll try to bring balance back to the Martial Society, without getting any more people killed." Slowly, he picked himself up, tucked the book into his robes, and turned around to leave. Old Huang shook his head with disappointment.

At the edge of the steps, Li Kung paused and turned around. "Why me?" he asked.

Old Huang was focused on his chess game again. "Wild flowers are beautiful," he said, without looking up. "But I prefer to see them fertilized by manure."

• • •

Li Kung leaned back against his chair, his hands trembling. He was opening the journals for the first time. Suthachai bolted the door, and Fei Fei added oil to the lamp in front of them. Ying sat by herself in a corner.

With a nervous sigh, Li Kung began to read out loud:

*Fifth day of the twelfth month. I recognize the poison
in my body—the only powerful poison Little Butterfly
is familiar with. I took the pill of the Eighteen Saints
today so that the poison would be trapped deeper in
my organs, and I would have no chance to live. But in
exchange, I will be strong and alert for forty-nine days.
Afterwards, death is certain. I have gathered my men
in the caverns of Phoenix Eye Peak. I can still remember hiding in those tunnels and sleeping by the little
waterfall when I was a girl. I still remember that the
first time Fei Long placed a flower in my hair was in
that cavern. This is where I wish to be buried. This
is where I've ordered my men to make preparations.
I heard he has died. I heard he was stabbed multiple
times, and yet he was still unstoppable. He was able to
walk to Pan Tong Village by himself. What thoughts
would exist in a man who had just murdered his wife,
and, just before dying, seeks out his daughter for his
last words? I do not know. How did a great hero like
Fei Long transform into an animal? How many beautiful women did it take to destroy his soul?*

Fei Fei uttered a sigh, a frown on her face. Li Kung
glanced at her, then continued:

*Sixth day of the twelfth month. All day I thought of the
young Mongolian I saw running away from Su Ling's
body. If the poison user's apprentice returned empty-
handed after searching their bodies, then the young
Mongolian must have taken the jade.*

"Is she referring to my grandfather?" Suthachai asked. "The young Mongolian running out of her daughter's house?"

"I believe so."

"And the poison user's apprentice must be Old Snake," Fei Fei said.

"Old Snake told me that he was sent to retrieve the jade," Li Kung replied. "Lin Cha sent him . . . " He paused, waited for Fei Fei to jump up and dispute him. She said nothing. Li Kung glanced once at Ying, who had not moved from her corner, and with a nervous sigh, continued reading:

My daughter must have given it to him, for a barbarian would not know its value. A conference was held on Redwood Cliff. Every man, whether once loyal to me or to Fei Long, was required to attend. There was an official count of my crimes. The men were urged, in front of an audience, to reveal the atrocities that I had committed. They were also quick to praise Lin Cha for fighting famine and leading the common people out of disaster. I heard that the most outrageous stories were told about me. Every coward that I personally nurtured now tried to outdo each other with accounts of my crimes. One man that I found as an orphan and raised myself told a most hideous tale of how I kidnapped babies in the south for money, and how I would always kill the infants after pocketing the ransom. Another elaborated on the same tale, and told of how I drank the babies' blood after slicing them open.

"Maybe she's lying," Fei Fei finally couldn't contain herself.

"People wouldn't lie in their journals," Suthachai said. "My grandfather's . . . "

"This journal was meant to be read. She could be lying," Fei Fei said, more agitated now. She gripped Suthachai's hand. "The people of the Dragon House were never such cowards. Each stood behind their leader."

Li Kung ignored her and turned back to the journals.

By the end of the conference, the men I used to lead convinced each other that I castrated virgin boys, I killed for recreation, and that I killed my own father and drank his blood. If I could only contact my father now—but he has been in seclusion in Mount Hua for almost twenty years.

Seventh day of the twelfth month. A massive hunt for the jade dragon has begun. Men by the thousands have descended Redwood Cliff to comb the land for clues. Lin Cha has somehow gained control of everyone on Redwood Cliff—perhaps because Fei Xing, her husband, is the immediate heir to the throne. But there is not a moment that Fei Xing is sober. His face is gray and his eyes are red. His liver will soon fail. With his death, Lin Cha will control the Dragon House, and hence, control the entire Martial Society. This is certain. Yet, at such an unstable time, why would Lin Cha mobilize every man to find the jade? Clearly, Lin Cha is not secure of her own ability to lead. She needs the jade to prove that she is the leader.

"But the jade was with my grandfather by then," Suthachai said.

"But no one knew that," Li Kung said, looking up. "At

least not until the underwater stone tablet told the world to search in Mongolia."

"I ordered the search," Fei Fei said, weakly. "Because my grandmother wanted the jade so badly. Every day that she was sick, even when she looked like she was going to die, she hung on. She wanted to see the jade in her hands."

"Is that when she died?" Li Kung asked. "When she finally had the jade in her hand?"

Fei Fei nodded, swallowing hard. Li Kung shook his head. "I knew she was clinging onto something in life. So it was her jade."

"My grandfather's jade."

"I have released numerous rumors to entice Lin Cha," Li Kung began reading again.

But her whereabouts are unknown. She is determined not to surface, and even more determined not to react to any move I make. She is smart. This time, there is really nothing I can do to her. She knows that she will outlive me, and she is patient.

Eighth day of the twelfth month. Men loyal to me from across the land have continued to assemble, and now I have over eighty men. I've noticed Lin Cha's increased obsession with the jade. Perhaps this has gone beyond an insecurity of her leadership. This jade, clearly, has been something she wanted for years— something she wanted with such passion that even I am shocked. Lin Cha is confused. The jade represents power, but she already has power. She cannot stop until she has the jade.

"How could she have predicted . . . " Fei Fei couldn't finish her words.

"Your grandmother was obsessive," Suthachai said. "That's why she wanted the jade at all costs. That's why the Red and Green Dragons found it justified to invade my clan and kill my people."

Despite the loyal men who amassed around me, I could do nothing to draw Lin Cha out into the open. She is afraid of me—all of Redwood Cliff is afraid of me. Hundreds of armed men patrol the Grand Stairway day and night. They know they will outlive me, and they only need to wait. But I cannot possibly fade into the night without exacting the vengeance I deserve.

Ninth day of the twelfth month. I continue to think of the young Mongolian who witnessed the trauma of Su Ling's death. My poor daughter must have loved him; she at least trusted him. She gave him the jade. He could not have been an evil man. Fei Long carried the jade at all times, and clearly, he came to Pan Tong Village to secure the jade by putting it into his daughter's hands. I know my daughter. She must have given the little Mongolian the jade, so that it could be hidden in a foreign land. She intended to retrieve it from him when the situation was safer.

"My grandfather did write that in his diary," Suthachai said. "How could Snow Wolf have known?"

"She said she knew her daughter," Fei Fei said. "Maybe good strategy ran in the family, and giving the jade to your grandfather was the only safe thing to do at the time."

"So Snow Wolf was outside when Su Ling died," Suthachai said. "But my grandfather was keeping watch on the roof. He was a great archer, with a good eye—"

"If someone could detect her so easily," Li Kung interrupted, "she wouldn't be Snow Wolf." He looked down at the journals again. "Here, she wrote something else about your grandfather."

The young Mongolian could not possibly find the courage to return to the mainland and sell the one thing that reminded him of the Soaring Dragon poison's horrors. Only upon his death would the jade be found and taken to the market at the northern border. If this proves true, then Lin Cha must outlive the Mongolian. How could she bear to die without ever clasping the jade in her hands? Yet this Mongolian seems very young, likely to live many more decades. What if he dies young, like many nomadic people? Where would the jade be when that happens?

Tenth day of the twelfth month. Every night I toss and turn in rage. I am running out of time. Yet I cannot find Lin Cha. Because of my own neglect, I lost my husband to other women. Because of my own cowardice, I hid for half a day and lost my dear daughter. Because of my own stupidity, I permitted every person in the Dragon House to betray me. How will I ever redeem myself for my mistakes? But tonight, I woke up with a new desire. Suddenly, I understand. Killing Lin Cha is not meant to be. Snow Wolf is meant for something more, a vengeance of greater depth and magnitude. How can I face Su Ling in the afterlife unless I destroy the offspring of my enemies, much like how they destroyed mine? I am resolved. Lin Cha is to have no descendants.

Eleventh day of the twelfth month. All day, I prepared the architecture of my plans. The world outside continues in chaos. Lin Cha has appeared, but I learned of it too late. It seems that she came to feast with the common villagers of the region. She needs them for something. Perhaps she too, is losing patience, and she wants confirmation of my death. Yet she must hide if she wants to outlive me.

Twelfth day of the twelfth month. I am forced to postpone my plans for revenge another forty years. The seeds of conflict are just not there—there would be no one I could manipulate into challenging Lin Cha after my death. It's unfortunate that I could not kill her; she is likely to die naturally by then. But the vengeance would fall upon her children, and the children of those who betrayed me. The forces of conflict will rise again. Her children are both talented, yet competitive and suspicious of each other. Months ago, I observed this.

"Observed what?" Fei Fei asked, leaning forward. Li Kung stared at the words in front of him.

"I'm ready for what she wrote," Fei Fei said, louder this time. "Anything she wrote."

Wei Bin and Wei Xu could not bear to lose to one another as children. Thus, they will only destroy each other as adults. This was born in their nature, and enhanced by Lin Cha's upbringing.

"I know," Fei Fei said. Tears welled in her eyes. "Snow Wolf was right. I don't know how she knew, but she was right. My father and my uncle would never have stopped trying to kill each other. Until the very end . . . "

"Remember the story Little Butterfly told me?" Li Kung said. "About Wei Bin and Wei Xu's childhood?"

"I remember," Suthachai said. "One twin beat the other

in a sword fight, and the other tricked him and pushed him off a hill."

Fei Fei lowered her face into her hands.

"Yes," Li Kung said. "Snow Wolf was supervising their training, remember? That was why she believed they would grow up fighting each other. It was in their blood. It was in their upbringing. Their mother, Lin Cha, reprimanded them for not being more cautious of each other."

Fei Fei uttered a deep sigh. Suthachai wrapped his arm around her and whispered into her ear, "It's over, Fei Fei."

She nodded. Li Kung continued to read:

Fifteenth day of the twelfth month. The idea of pitting Lin Cha's twins against each other fifty years from now has brought me three consecutive nights of burning excitement.

Li Kung paused and glanced at Fei Fei but felt that she was calm. He continued:

I have not slept. I can only plan. I foresee the Dragon House splitting into two. The twins are both equal in talent and cruelty. It is not likely that one will be able to kill the other while Lin Cha lives. It is more probable that they will kill each other after her death. Somehow, I must initiate a war between them.

Sixteenth day of the twelfth month. I sent a handful of trusted men onto Redwood Cliff this morning. The back of the cliff, by the ancestral burial grounds, remains unguarded. Slightly below Fei Long's tombstone is the designated plot of land for Fei Xing to be buried. He is the younger brother and the next generation's leader. According to family tra-

dition, he will be buried there—it is inevitable. Lin
Cha will be buried next to Fei Xing, on his right.
I instructed my men to plant a copper cauldron in
Lin Cha's plot of land. They will insert an ancestral
decree inside the cauldron . . .

Li Kung's mouth dropped in shock. He could read no further.

"I remember that," Suthachai whispered, turning to Fei Fei.

"I was there," Fei Fei said. "I watched my stupid brother Dong read the ancestral decree, even when I tried again and again to stop him. My father was glaring at him but couldn't prevent him from—"

"But what if he didn't read it?" Suthachai asked. "What if someone was wise enough to quietly make the decree go away? Wouldn't Snow Wolf's plot then be a failure?"

"No," Li Kung said, shaking his head. "It was unearthed in front of thousands, as Snow Wolf expected. If someone took away the decree without reading it, the two Dragon Houses would blame each other for hiding important secrets. They would suspect that the scroll was a treasure map, or a secret martial arts manual left behind by ancestors. They would kill each other for it. Regardless, Snow Wolf's scroll would lead to war." He sighed, and continued to read:

And the decree will appoint all power and wealth to the
younger brother Wei Bin. The decree, made of cloth,
was woven together with poison so that anyone tear-
ing it apart would be harmed. This alone will elevate
the tension and suspicion between the twins.

"Stump's hands!" Fei Fei interrupted again. "I never figured out who poisoned him. So Snow Wolf left poison dust in the scroll."

"I saw powder scattering from the scroll when it was torn," Li Kung said. "Both Pun and I saw it . . . " He paused and noticed a strange, defensive look on Ying's face. Maybe she didn't want him to mention Pun anymore. "The poison powder," he said quickly. "The ancestral decree was so outrageous that it was guaranteed someone would try to tear it up. War was imminent at Lin Cha's funeral." He turned back to the journals.

> By the time Lin Cha dies, the copper will be brittle, and it will be apparent that the decree had been buried for decades, which, when unearthed at her funeral in the presence of both twins, will push them into the brink of war.
>
> Seventeenth day of the twelfth month. The little round lake outside of He Ku remains a popular source of fish for locals. But years ago, Old Huang and I noticed that the lake was drying. In about forty years, the fishermen will see the bottom of the lake. Here is the ideal location for me to embed my message.

"The lake!" Suthachai jumped to his feet. "She planted the poem at the bottom of the lake! She knew when it would dry, so—"

Fei Fei pulled him back to his chair. "Wait, let him finish."

> Lin Cha's obsessive desire to acquire the jade has not escaped my mind. If she does not live to see the jade, she will instruct her favorite son to search for it. The one

who holds the jade is to be leader of the Dragon House. How could the twins resist fighting for it? I will leave behind my instructions at the bottom of the lake. The locals will believe that it came from the gods because they will find it forty years from now. I will carve a poem on a stone tablet, plant it at the bottom of the lake, and I will tell the world the whereabouts of the jade. The struggles will begin.

"I recognized her handwriting," Li Kung suddenly said. "Not the handwriting in these journals, but near the wind tunnels by Phoenix Eye Peak. She wrote a poem behind the wooden instruments, the ones that created the ghostly wails. I recognized her handwriting, because the poem was carved, and the poem under the lake was carved. But I . . . I had no idea that she could be responsible for both."

"So, by knowing when the lake would dry," Fei Fei said, "she directed us toward the jade at a specific time. Forty years after her death. Almost fifty, to be exact. When the jade surfaced, the Red and Green Dragons would fight for it. That was inevitable. And, the poem . . . " Fei Fei's eyes widened, and she couldn't continue.

"What about the poem?" Suthachai asked.

"The poem . . . " she whispered. Li Kung lowered the book and stared.

"The poem," Fei Fei repeated, "described the exact location of the sheepskin. The formula for the black paste. It was hidden in a training room on Redwood Cliff. But my father told me that his aunt, Lady Wu, first brought him to that training hall. She brought my uncle too . . ."

Li Kung gasped. "So both twins knew the hiding place in the training halls. It was just that she didn't know who would inhabit Redwood Cliff fifty years after her death. That's why, with the poem at the bottom of a lake, she was able to remind both of them." He looked down and read:

Eighteenth day of the twelfth month. The ongoing preparations are already in their critical stages. I have decided that the crucial link to my redemption will lie in a chosen warrior. There is too much unknown fifty years from now, and only a live human can execute this revenge for me. I will search for a man who is naïve yet brave, kindhearted but decisive, determined yet easy to manipulate. I need a warrior of tremendous intelligence, who will not fall to greed, nor succumb to hopelessness. I need a man who wants to save the world. Thus, I have begun preparations.

"She tested me for all that," Li Kung muttered. "Naïve yet brave. I am naïve, but how was I brave?"

"You are," Fei Fei said. "It took the spirit of a great warrior to survive those caverns."

"She wanted someone kindhearted," Li Kung said with a smile. "Didn't I bury all those skeletons? I thought they were real villagers. There's a fine line between kindhearted and naïve. She needed someone who wants to save the world, someone determined but easy to manipulate. I guess I was perfect for her." He shook his head and read on:

My men are planting the devices I created so I can carefully select the soldier who will carry out my vengeance. Mechanical elements will be installed in the tunnels, beginning today. My own burial spot, the cavern in the heart of Phoenix Eye Peak, will be his testing ground.

Twenty-first day of the twelfth month. I must immediately prepare the skills that my chosen warrior will need. I need to attract people to these grounds, or how will I be able to choose the hero? Rumors of a treasure will generate a continuous inflow of explorers. I must also take measures to prevent too many people from entering. All this, I need to ponder.

"When did these rumors begin?" Li Kung asked suddenly.

"Rumors?"

"Rumors of a treasure in her cavern. She used that rumor to attract explorers."

"I don't know," Fei Fei replied. "But I've heard of those treasures before. Ever since I was a child. But no one could find it, and often, people who set out to search for it never came back."

"I know where they are now," Li Kung said.

"Can a rumor last fifty years?" Suthachai asked.

"It can if a treasure is involved." Li Kung looked down at the journals and continued:

Twenty-third day of the twelfth month. I have resolved to spread rumors that Phoenix Eye Peak is haunted. The northwest wind on this mountain is strong and consistent. Large wooden instruments will be constructed and placed in a wind tunnel I found last night. The steady wind should be reliable forever. These instruments will emit haunting cries every time the wind rushes through. The presence of ghosts on the mountain will discourage the ordinary man, as well as the cowardly treasure seekers. Yet I cannot permit a man of greed, despite his courage, to inherit my skills.

Li Kung paused. "I remember the wind tunnel. The instruments generated ghostly wails only when the wind entered from the north or the west. But sometimes, wind would not come from those directions for months."

"Then how did she maintain the ghostly cries all year long?" Suthachai asked.

"Maybe she didn't," Li Kung replied. "Maybe that's why there were so many skeletons in the first cavern. People went up there when they didn't hear the ghosts. And she knew that. I'm sure she knew that. She couldn't keep all the cowards away from her caverns. That's why she had to kill them. Here," Li Kung pointed to the words before him.

The treasures must be covered with the deadliest of poisons, so men of greed will be eliminated. If the common man avoids Phoenix Eye Peak out of fear, and those seeking fortune are promptly killed, then who will become my chosen warrior? That will leave only a man driven by something else, who did not come in search of anything, who will not leave in fear of anything. Perhaps a man pushed to the edge, at his most vulnerable, and under distress.

His voice was trembling, as he thought of Pun, of burying her at the foot of Phoenix Eye Peak. He had not returned to her grave site since.

"It was destiny," he mumbled. "A man pushed to the edge, at his most vulnerable, under distress. It was destiny."

Swallowing hard, he continued:

Timing is crucial here. In forty years, the lake will dry, and the issue of legitimate leadership and the jade dragon will once again surface. The twins will begin

fighting for the jade. Upon Lin Cha's death, the ances-
tral decree buried in her grave will ensure that the wars
begin. The ensuing chaos will drive many heroes into
despair. The opportunity to create my chosen successor
will thus be enhanced. Forty to fifty years from now,
Su Ling's death will be avenged.

Twenty-fourth day of the twelfth month. I have
pondered carefully over the collapsed village in the sec-
ond cavern. How should I portray the landslide trag-
edy to him? The skeletons of dead children awaiting
burial? Time is running out for me. The men have
already gathered a significant rat population. They've
begun to treat the canvas clothing so the chosen war-
rior will have ample smoke when chasing the rats.

"The smoke!" Li Kung shouted out loud. "So she planted that too."

"You mean, the smoke that pushed the rats out of the
tunnels?" Suthachai asked. "That was ingenious."

"There was so much smoke I could barely breathe. I
merely burned shreds of canvas, and they were obviously
treated to emit clouds of smoke. But only some of the skeletons were dressed in canvas clothing. Others were not. Does
that mean—"

"There were others who entered the tunnels," Fei Fei
said. "Others who were not poisoned, who were kindhearted
enough to start burying the dead villagers, but were not smart
enough to escape the tunnels. They were eaten by the rats."

Ying's face turned ashen white. Li Kung thought of the
half-eaten body dressed in fine silk robes, and he grimaced.
He was fortunate. It was destiny. Either way, it was not his
choice. Staring down at the journals, a cold sweat over his
brows, he read on:

321

Yet I feel that something is missing. How do I convince my chosen warrior that the Dragon House is responsible for atrocious crimes? First, there must be a crime. Then, to drive him to action, he must understand that the Dragon House could pose an urgent threat. He must eliminate this threat in order to save the world. Therefore, there must be a threat.

Twenty-eighth day of the twelfth month. The local villagers in the six regions have begun a campaign. I believe they are looking for me, on behalf of Lin Cha.

Ying clapped a hand over her mouth. They turned to her. Suthachai and Fei Fei had already forgotten the mute girl sitting behind Li Kung.

"Old Gu was among those villagers," Li Kung said, looking back. "Snow Wolf knew about what happened."

Ying shook her head, cringing. Fei Fei walked over to her and took her hand. "Ying," she said gently, pulling the younger woman to her feet. "Come sit with us."

Li Kung also reached out and took her hand. "Your grandfather was a good man, Ying. Maybe he was fooled back then, but he truly believed he was acting in the name of . . . " Li Kung paused, "justice," he finished with a whisper. He took a deep breath. "Justice," Li Kung repeated softly. "How I've wondered about that word."

He noticed that Ying had calmed a little. He returned to the journals.

Who would have thought? I've always believed that karmic retribution means there is justice in the heavens. My life's work, from fighting off foreign pirates to reining in local bandits; from leading the common people out of famine to rebuilding the lives of thou-

322

sands—all mean nothing now. The same villagers I've slaved each day to protect have finally turned against me. Perhaps justice really does not exist. Perhaps only human intervention and retaliation holds true. It is now clear what I need to do. Every person who betrays me, including the villagers who dare to hunt me, will watch their children crumble to dust in front of them! Retribution will be complete!

Thirtieth day of the twelfth month. I have decided to use the Dreamer's Potion. I will perfect it. At its highest stage of potency, the elixir thickens into a black paste, and it will no longer be used for the old and the dying.

"The black paste!" Fei Fei said. "The black paste!"

"You were right, Li Kung," Suthachai said, breathing with weariness. "Snow Wolf created this evil to destroy the world, and . . . "

Li Kung, his lips trembling, stared at the words in front of him. For a long time, he could not read, nor could he lift his eyes from the journals. Finally, Fei Fei reached over and took the book from his hands. She continued to read:

The enhanced Dreamer's Potion will bring its user to the heavens, only to return to consciousness and to harsh reality. Why would anyone live the boredom of daily life if they can sleep in the clouds and fly among the rainbows? The user will seek to return to the dreamy state. More of the enhanced Dreamer's Potion will be needed, and absolute power will fall to those who supply it. I will arrange for the twin who occupies Redwood Cliff to inherit this treasure, and to use his greed and ambitions for instant profit. He will be

323

the urgent threat that my warrior must look for. Unfortunately, there is little time left for me to study the strange reactions that have appeared. The human body quickly shrivels and becomes very thin. The user may even die.

"She didn't know," Li Kung interrupted. "She didn't know what evil her elixir would cause. She didn't have time to research the strange reactions."

"Are you saying she wouldn't have used it if she knew?"

Li Kung shook his head. "I don't know. It doesn't matter now. Shifu Two is a few days away from creating an antidote—a counteragent. The black paste will never be a significant threat again." He sighed, and took the journals back from Fei Fei's hands. He continued to read:

Fourth day of the first month. It is to my benefit if the users die. Across the foot of Phoenix Eye Peak, thousands of villagers charged through the narrow trails, banging on gongs and shouting their slogans. "Slay the evil wolf!" they screamed in unison. I watched from afar; I even recognized some of the faces. One man I did recognize—did I not save the life of his mother just two years ago? Why am I concerned with the well-being of their children? If they shrivel and die from using the Dreamer's Potion, wouldn't it requite the sins committed by their ancestors? Justice will be served.

Fifth day of the first month. I personally traveled to Redwood Cliff today under disguise, and in a secret compartment of the training hall I placed the formula of the Dreamer's Potion. Lin Cha remains in hiding; she is certainly not on Redwood Cliff. Neither are her sons. But now, I no longer wish to kill them. The vengeance of tomorrow will be far more elaborate and satisfying.

Ninth day of the first month. The strategies, the battle formations, even the Flame Cutter, will be left behind for my heir. I have completed the writings. My men have finished the mechanics of the rat tunnels. I have thought carefully about my future heir. What if he fails? What if he abandons the mission? Time and time again, the ungrateful and cowardly endure. The chosen warrior will be no exception. If he fails, if he defies me, then he too, must face retribution. And why would I permit a stranger to inherit my skills, only to use them for his personal fame? Years from now, my strategies, my skills, will only be associated with his name, and not mine. The chosen warrior must die! Only then can the legacy of Snow Wolf remain untarnished.

Eleventh day of the first month. The chosen warrior must die. The forbidden cavern in the back has been destroyed and reconstructed to collapse quickly. Even with the Flame Cutter, he will not be able to escape. One of my men pointed out that the trap is flawed. What if someone held the cavern together before it could totally collapse? That would buy him enough time to escape. But I laughed. The chosen warrior will have no friends nearby, just mercenaries. The weight of his mission will render him isolated and distrustful of others. His unique abilities will enhance his loneliness. No one will risk his own life for my warrior. Nevertheless, I listened to the advice of my men. Heavier boulders will be used by the cavern exit.

Li Kung released a deep sigh. He turned to Suthachai and didn't know what to say.

"You changed destiny," Fei Fei said, gripping the Mongolian's hand. "You were strong enough to intercept the boulders. She never would've dreamed that a Mongolian wrestler would stand by the cavern exit that day."

"Snow Wolf predicted everything," Li Kung said. "She was right. I trusted no one. But she didn't know about you. She couldn't foresee that I did have a friend by my side."

"Does that mean she is not a goddess?" Suthachai said in a low voice. "She is a mere human?"

No one said anything. After a long time, Li Kung resumed reading:

Fourteenth day of the first month. I am close to the end of my days. The Sun Cult remains in the back of my mind. They are strange, ruthless, immune to poison, indescribable in speed, and indestructible in combat. They alone will change the course of my plans. The fighting ability of the Sun Cult could destabilize the balance of the Martial Society. However unlikely, it is possible that the Dragon House will remain united in the face of a common enemy. It is also likely that the pathetic Martial Society will join hands against this threat, and fail to kill each other off as planned. I have pondered this. I have some days left, and with everything else in place, it will be my priority now to destroy the Sun Cult.

Eighteenth day of the first month. Tomorrow, I will hand these journals to Old Huang for eternal safekeeping. He will hand them to his heirs, and so on, until the time comes for the legacy of Snow Wolf to live again. My suicidal battle against the

Sun Cult will commence. Most of my men will die tomorrow when we execute our traps to ensnare the Sun Cult. I intend to slay all four hundred members but capture the five brothers alive. I've identified the youngest of the five brothers to be the one to survive. The boy is the least powerful among them. If I cripple him, he will never become an overwhelming threat to the Dragon House. Yet he will grow up to be a formidable force of balance. Some of their bodies will be laid to rest in the tunnels around my tomb. They will contribute to the rat population, and they will be dressed in the thick canvas clothing that I have perfected. Also, if I succeed in exterminating the Sun Cult, I will have access to their incredible wealth, which is rumored to be stored underneath their zhuang. More gold than a hundred men could carry, I heard. It would certainly be enough for my chosen warrior's mission. If all goes well, the five brothers will be eaten alive in front of the cowardly villagers, who continue to hunt me. It will serve as a warning and a final statement to all. Thus my redemption for losing Su Ling will begin.

. . .

Li Kung paced through the room, back and forth, his chin resting against his chest, his eyes staring at the floor. His breathing was quick, short, as if he couldn't draw enough air to support the rapid thoughts roaming his head. He had finished reading Snow Wolf's journals for some time, but Suthachai and Fei Fei remained frozen in their seats. Not a word had been exchanged among the three. Li Kung could not stop pacing the room.

The door creaked open and a bandit's face peered in. "Master Li?"

Li Kung halted in his tracks. "Come in."

One Eyed Shu entered and greeted Suthachai and Fei Fei with a smile. He turned to Li Kung. "Master Li, bad news."

"I'm expecting it."

"Thousands of people have gathered in He Ku. Every house that sent representatives to Yellow Sand Plateau is now screaming for revenge. Jian just summoned every House master in the country, and they're here, with specially picked warriors. I heard that the Green Dragons alone number over a thousand. They may storm Redwood Cliff together, with the rest of the Martial Society—at least three thousand men."

Fei Fei jumped to her feet, but Suthachai gripped her hand. "We will save Cricket in time," he said to her. "But the rest of them have their own destinies to face."

Fei Fei nodded, and seated herself.

"Have you found out how the Red Dragons are preparing?" Li Kung asked.

"I believe they also sent for their branches in the southern regions. They may have fewer men, but Redwood Cliff is easier to defend. I think . . . " The bandit paused, unsure of how Li Kung would react. "I think this battle will be so bloody that—"

"What else have you found?" Li Kung asked, controlling himself. "Is Cricket still able to control his men?"

One Eyed Shu shook his head. "I don't believe so. Even though he's the official leader now."

"Do you know when they intend to attack?"

The bandit shook his head again. "I don't know. But they say that it would be right after the rain season, because

328

it will be easier to bombard the Grand Stairway with fire. After the rain season—that's in three weeks!"

Li Kung sighed, stumbled back a step, and could barely remain on his feet. "Good. Thank you. You may go."

One Eyed Shu bowed once before leaving the room. The door slammed shut behind him.

Li Kung slumped into a chair against the wall. "She won. Snow Wolf won. The entire Martial Society will kill each other off."

Fei Fei stood up. "We can still beat her!"

"How do you beat someone who's been dead for fifty years?" Li Kung replied with a glare. "Would it help if we smash up her tomb?"

"We can still stop them," Suthachai said. "They are not dead yet."

"With the three of us?" Li Kung asked. "How? Thousands are preparing in He Ku for the showdown, and who knows how many are preparing on Redwood Cliff?"

Suthachai leaned forward. "You are the chosen warrior. You have the ability to undo what your teacher has done. Stay focused. To win, you just need a strategy superior to hers."

Li Kung shook his head. "How could I hope to outsmart Snow Wolf?"

"You have a distinct advantage, Li Kung. Snow Wolf cannot plot new strategies. She has been dead for fifty years."

• • •

Much later, after a long moment of silence, Li Kung slowly sat upright in his chair. "Snow Wolf's strategy is thorough and all encompassing. But almost everything was used to instigate war. There are only two elements that maintained the war."

"What is that?"

"First," Li Kung said, "the warrior she trained to do her work."

"You're no longer doing her work," Fei Fei said.

"So the second element is the source of balance. The common enemy."

"The Sun Cult?"

"She eliminated the single balancing agent," Li Kung said, leaning forward. "Once the Dragon House had no one to go to war with, they had no choice but to go to war with each other. There could have been a tripodal balance in the Martial Society, but she killed off the Sun Cult to destroy that. We need to create a new common enemy for them to unite against."

Each paused, silent, trying to stomach the idea. Finally, Fei Fei said, "Who would be powerful enough? There are thousands of men bent on killing each other. Who can cause them to suddenly unite together for survival?"

"The government?" Suthachai asked.

"That would mean more lives," Fei Fei said. "The emperor would view the Martial Society as a rebellion. He'd crush every single person involved."

"We may not need an army," Li Kung said. "The common enemy could be a concept."

"A concept?"

"Such as fear of death. Maybe even fear of what happens after death."

They looked at each other and waited for Li Kung to continue. Li Kung narrowed his eyes in deep thought. "We can formulate the plan," he whispered. "It's hard to say how much time we have, but, if they really wait for the rain season to pass, we have at least two weeks. We do have enough men—all the bandits on Pigeon's Head, then there are the Six Guardians. But like Snow Wolf's plot, we too, will have a third concern. We need to break the power balance before we can do this. It's too risky."

"The power balance?"

"Black Shadow. Black Shadow is completely unpredictable. This one man can foil our plans if he doesn't understand our intentions."

"No one can find Black Shadow," Fei Fei said. "He appears and disappears at will."

Li Kung spun around in his chair. "Do you remember the story Ying's grandfather told me? About the five brothers of the Sun Cult? The youngest brother, the only survivor, lost his arm while his brothers were eaten alive."

"Yes."

"Do you remember if he lost his sword arm?"

"It was his other arm," Fei Fei said. "You told me he stabbed his brother after the wolf tore off his arm."

"Strange," Li Kung mused. "I have a strange feeling about this. Black Shadow is also missing his other arm. Indescribable speed. That was how Snow Wolf portrayed the Sun Cult. Has there ever been anyone capable of such speed?"

"Uncle Tan," Fei Fei suddenly said. "He could be Uncle Tan!"

"Who is Uncle Tan?" Suthachai asked.

"The servant," Fei Fei responded. "He also has only one arm—the left arm. And he was like a brother to Wei Xu. Black Shadow only protects the Green Dragons, but he doesn't take orders from anyone because no one can ever find him. Yet, he always appears when he's needed. He has to be someone close to Wei Xu."

"There are plenty of people who lost one arm in battle," Li Kung said.

Fei Fei shook her head. "No, it has to be. I recognized the voice." She turned to Suthachai. "Do you remember that night Black Shadow gave us a sample of the Dreamer's Potion? The black paste?"

Suthachai nodded.

"He spoke to me like a kind uncle when I was a little girl," Fei Fei said. "I remember now. Like Uncle Tan."

"Assuming that Black Shadow really is Uncle Tan," Suthachai said, "even if we can get him to admit to his disguise, we can never convince him to help. Can we prevent him from interfering?"

"But we'll know where to find Black Shadow," Li Kung said, standing up. "That's the hardest part."

"What would it take to make him understand?" Fei Fei asked.

"Time," Suthachai said. "Plenty of time to explain everything. We need to keep Black Shadow seated in front of us for an entire day, so we can talk to him."

"We need to capture him and tie him down," Li Kung said. "Then we can explain why we need his help—why thousands will need his help."

"Capture Black Shadow?" Fei Fei asked in amazement.

"Snow Wolf did it before. She did it to his entire family," Li Kung said. "Why can't we do it now to the youngest brother with only one arm?" A bitter smile flashed across his face. "We can only assume that Black Shadow is Uncle Tan, and also the last brother of the Sun Cult. If we're wrong, we'll be in trouble."

"How much trouble?"

"We're about to challenge Black Shadow to a duel,"

he said. "We'll find out if we're wrong in the middle of the fight. That's how much trouble."

. . .

The letter to Uncle Tan read:

Uncle Tan, please assume your disguise at this time, and go to the giant fir tree on the south bank of Lake Eternal. I have left the official letter of challenge inside the tree hole, as agreed upon some months ago.

The official letter of challenge read:

We agreed, when we last spoke to each other, that a fair duel would take place after Wei Bin lost his ability to threaten the Martial Society. Wei Bin can no longer do any damage. I have already killed him, with his evil twin. They both died squealing like little girls. Unfortunately, I cannot grant you a fair duel at this time. I understand that you are deeply disturbed by the death of Wei Xu, and you are itching to face his murderer. Therefore, as a friendly gesture, I hereby challenge you to an unfair duel. You will come alone, as always, and I will bring some of my friends. Maybe you are not bent on revenge, but this formal challenge is your only chance to find out who murdered Wei Xu, and perhaps find out why.

. . .

The tall figure of Black Shadow firmly treaded through the

forest. His face was not masked, but he remained dressed in black, his long sword dangling by his side. It was early, and the thin forest was bright. A large clearing appeared in front of him, and he slowed. He noticed that all around him, dull brass plates were randomly strewn across the ground. He smiled. Was this supposed to be an ambush?

A lean, muscular man stood in the middle of the clearing. He was completely naked except for a loincloth, his bronze skin shining from a layer of oil covering his body. His hands were wrapped with coarse fabric.

Black Shadow stopped. "You're the one who challenged me?'

"I am Jocholai," the nude man said with a thick accent.

Black Shadow noticed that he was unarmed. He looked across the forest, detecting the movement of several more people. "Since you're already here, why not come out? I was expecting more."

"Uncle Tan?" A light, pleasant voice.

Black Shadow shuffled back. Even he couldn't maintain his composure. "Fei Fei?"

Fei Fei stepped out of the forest, a double-edged sword in her hand.

"You're still alive!" Black Shadow could barely speak.

"It's good to see you," Fei Fei said with a smile. "Though, the Flute Demon never liked Black Shadow. It's so much better this way, without the mask."

"You . . . You're the one who challenged me?"

"She's one of the friends I warned you about in this unfair fight," Li Kung said, appearing from the right side of the forest. "We've met before, Uncle Tan. But last time, I also had a mask on." He pointed across the clearing. "And that's Suthachai. The girl next to Suthachai is Ying. She will not be fighting."

Black Shadow bowed. "Pleased to meet you, sir. My pleasure, little lady." He looked at Fei Fei then, and slowly, his face changed. "Your father and uncle were killed. Why are you fighting on the side of their murderers?"

"You'll come to understand, Uncle Tan. After this battle, you'll understand."

Black Shadow grunted, then turned to Li Kung. "You're not a fighter. You don't hope to beat me with only the Flute Demon and two Mongolians, do you?" he asked.

"There are about twenty more," Li Kung said. "They'll be here soon."

Black Shadow nodded. "I'll wait for the rest of your friends."

"We can start now!" Li Kung shouted. He leaped forward, his body twisting into motion, and with a violent snap, he hurled a metal ball into the ground. It connected with one of the brass plates. An earth-shattering boom cracked the air.

"Is that all?" Black Shadow laughed. "You'll pester me with sound?'

Suthachai charged, saber at full swing, and Black Shadow heaved back to avoid his attack. His long sword whipped across the air with a shrill kiss, connecting with Suthachai's weapon in a shower of sparks, flashing left and right, cutting with varying speeds and irregular angles. Suthachai kept his heavy saber at close range, backing away from the assault, rapidly losing his footing. He was confronting a hurricane.

From the left side, Fei Fei slipped into the battle, her lighter sword quick and agile. But as soon as her swings connected with Black Shadow's weapon, she seemed to be sucked into an endless maelstrom where all she could do was block and evade. Steel collided in a flurry of rapid sparks.

In a moment, Suthachai blinked, and he was kicked heavily in the chest. The huge Mongolian flew back and crumbled in a heap. Fei Fei attacked, but with one blow was thrown back into the edge of the forest.

Li Kung continued to make the earth-shattering noise. Suthachai was already on his feet. He used his incredible strength to pound Black Shadow's sword with every collision, but to no avail. He struck empty air again and again. In a moment, he retreated alongside Li Kung. They were forced toward the back of the forest.

Fei Fei was next to Suthachai then, dodging in and out, ferociously battling to keep Black Shadow at bay. They were losing ground, retreating with full speed.

The forest began to thicken. Li Kung continued to pound the brass plates with his metal balls. Jocholai followed from behind but made no move to join the battle, and Ying stayed on the side. They fell deeper and deeper into the woods.

Suddenly, Suthachai and Fei Fei screamed a shrill cry of war, striking out together with an unusual burst of strength. Li Kung simultaneously threw himself back and shouted, "Now!"

Ying rushed into the foliage and sounds emerged from all around them. They heard cages opening, then the snarls, growls, barks . . . Black Shadow froze. Somewhere around him was the howling of the gray wolf.

Jocholai leaped at him then, the textured cloth that Li Kung had strapped on his hands clinging to the fabric on Black Shadow's leg.

Black Shadow drew back and swung his long sword at his new assailant, but the skinny Mongolian was slippery with oil and uniquely skilled in wrestling. He glided under Black Shadow's body, maintaining a secure hold on his leg despite the oil on his own body, and latched himself around the other knee. Black Shadow's sword was too long for such close-range combat. Suthachai and Fei Fei were closing in, and he couldn't move with Jocholai pinned against his ankles. The snarling of wolves intensified. Jocholai continued to slither around him, preventing him from running.

Then, a roar of flames swept across the forest in a massive circle, enclosing them in a fiery ring. The wolves howled. They ran from the flames, toward the inside of the circle, suddenly appearing in large numbers. They were small predators, frightened and desperate, yet every bit as formidable. Their lips were drawn back, their fangs bared.

Black Shadow weakened, but with a burst of energy, flung Jocholai into the distance to free his sword arm. He leaped away, just in time to avoid the heavy saber swiping down on his head. He released a high-pitched shout and attacked his assailants with full fury.

"Eat him alive!" Li Kung shouted to the wolves. "Like you ate his brothers fifty years ago! Eat him alive!"

Black Shadow froze. The howling of the wolves became louder. Suthachai struck him on the side of the head with his saber handle, sending him reeling.

Like his brothers were eaten alive . . .

Black Shadow shook his head clear and turned to fight.

"Bite him!" Li Kung shouted. "He'll stab his own brother! Bite his arm off!"

Black Shadow uttered a scream. The sword fell from his hand. Trembling, he stared as Suthachai pummeled him with the butt of his saber, as the slippery Mongolian came out of nowhere and locked down his left leg again.

Black Shadow swayed. His mouth dropped open. Jocholai barred both his knees with joint locks. Li Kung moved past him in a blur and pricked him with a little needle.

One gray wolf charged at him in the confusion. Black

Shadow couldn't move, vacantly staring at the dripping jaws approaching him. He closed his eyes.

Suthachai leaped forward, wrapped his arms around the predator's neck, and with a snap and a toss, flung the animal away.

In a moment, the ring of flames died. The wolves retreated into the forest.

Li Kung pierced Black Shadow in the back of the neck with another needle. Then all four of them retreated.

Black Shadow slowly opened his eyes. He looked around him, the expression of shock long gone, and pointed a weak finger at Li Kung. "How did you know?"

He collapsed. Fei Fei quickly stepped in to catch him. "Uncle Tan," she called. She lowered him onto the soft ground while Ying came forward with a sack of heavy ropes. Fei Fei pulled out a handkerchief and wiped the sweat from his forehead.

"We did the impossible," she whispered, looking up in awe. "We defeated Black Shadow."

PROPHECY TEN

In the face of death and the dread of dying
The heavens were forced to clear
The redemption brought a neutral calm
The legend of Snow Wolf brings eternal fear

"Why did you kill them?" Li Kung asked, his childish face brimming with tears, his little hands wringing in front of him. "Why did you kill Auntie Ma?"

Li Kung's father, now Governor Li, stood up from his chair to pace back and forth. He was dressed in a plain cotton robe, his sword dangling from his belt, the black headpiece of the government official left on the chair he had been seated in. Li Kung had come to speak to his father, despite his mother's warnings, despite witnessing the execution of hundreds in the town square. Before approaching the Three Saints of Yunnan, Li Kung wanted to bid his father farewell.

"Why did all those people have to die? Were they bad people? Was Auntie Ma a bad person?"

Governor Li shook his head. "You're too young to understand, Kung."

"I'm not too young."

"They weren't bad people."

"Then why did you kill them?"

"Because they were going to rebel against the emperor. Because if we let them rebel, there will be war for many years. People will die. Innocent people will suffer."

Tears streamed down Li Kung's face then. "Auntie Ma was not a bad person. How can you say that?"

"I know she wasn't," his father said, his voice softer then. "And I sacrificed her. And people will hate me for it for many years to come. But her husband was a rebel leader and the rebels were going to gather around her. I had to execute her. I'm sorry, Kung. I'm sorry . . . "

Li Kung gasped for air when he opened his eyes. Ying was sitting next to him, watching him, her muscles taut and her jaws clenched. He could have been screaming in his sleep.

"My father," he said.

Ying shook her head. She squeezed her eyes shut and a tear trickled down her cheek. Li Kung lifted a shaking hand and brushed the tear away. "I believe him. I remember his face. I believe him."

Ying lifted him into a seated position.

Li Kung looked into her frightened eyes. "I remember," he whispered. "That's why I went away with my three Shifus. I didn't agree with his version of justice. I didn't think those people should have died. But these past months, I did agree with Snow Wolf's version of justice. And I did believe the people in the Red and Green Dragon Houses should die. Who is the villain here, Ying? Who is the villain?"

• • •

Black Shadow opened his eyes and jumped into a sitting position. "Black paste!"

"Shifu Two never figured out how to turn this into a white paste."

340

Black Shadow stared at Li Kung, then at Fei Fei.

"Drink this, Uncle Tan." Fei Fei held a steaming bowl in front of her. "This is the antidote."

"It's called the Dreamer's Potion." Li Kung took a step back and seated himself on a cushioned armchair. He clasped his hands together. "Snow Wolf called it the Dreamer's Potion. But we have a counteragent now."

Black Shadow shook his head clear, then climbed to his feet. They were in a large room, with tall, airy windows on three sides.

"The Two Saints of Yunnan live here," Li Kung said, his voice quivering. "No longer the Three Saints—there are just two left."

"Uncle Tan. Drink the antidote. The Dreamer's Potion really does poison you."

Black Shadow looked at Fei Fei, at her lovely face, glared into her concerned eyes, and relaxed. He took the bowl from her and swallowed with one gulp. "Flute Demon . . . " he muttered.

Li Kung picked up Black Shadow's sword and held it in front of him. "Your sword."

Black Shadow snatched his sword with such speed that Li Kung hardly felt it leaving his hands. Fei Fei placed a thick, cloth-bound book on the table, and with a smile, turned around to go.

"Why give me my sword?"

Fei Fei shut the door behind her and left him alone with Li Kung.

"If you want to kill me, you won't need the sword," Li Kung said. "But if I wanted to kill you, I didn't need to wake you."

"What do you really want, Li Kung?"

"I don't know," Li Kung replied. "But it took extensive preparations to bring you here so we can talk. It took Suthachai an entire day to capture two wolf packs. It took Ying also an entire day to buy so many gongs for me to make noise and cover the sounds of wolves in captivity. We didn't do it to prove anything. It wasn't even a fair fight. What I want is a chance to speak truthfully, and honorably."

"Honorably . . . " Black Shadow repeated. "Am I to believe that? You ambushed Lord Xu with fire. Where's the honor?"

"That's true," Li Kung said. "But you're already here. Why not abandon the hate and vengeance and listen to what I have to say."

Black Shadow stared, his eyes piercing, his lips squeezed into a sneer. "Fine," he finally said. "Why don't I listen to what you have to say? After all, you did find a counteragent for this black paste. Dreamer's Potion, as you call it."

"As Snow Wolf called it."

The mention of the name Snow Wolf brought a flash of tension in Black Shadow's face, but he calmed and seated himself by the table. "Yes, as Snow Wolf called it. Before I listen to anything, I want to know exactly who you are, and how you know about my past."

"Who am I?" Li Kung asked. "No one, really. My father is a government official from the south. I lost my mother, and I became an apprentice to the Three Saints of Yunnan." A bitter smile stretched across his face. "Too bad. I didn't learn much from the Three Saints. I was training to be a doctor, but I ended up being a mass murderer instead. I also became the sole heir to Snow Wolf's strategies."

"And her Flame Cutter," Black Shadow said.

"Yes, and a few other tricks and schemes. There's not much I can tell you about myself. I'm an ordinary person, caught in extraordinary times. I was chosen to be a hero." Li

342

Kung laughed. "Heroes fight for justice. Every person has a different version of justice. I stood by the one version taught to me—justice according to Snow Wolf—and I killed plenty of people for it." He pointed to the cloth-bound book on the table. "I need you to read her journals. Afterwards, you'll understand."

Black Shadow leaned back, more comfortable now, and took the book in his hand.

• • •

Cricket, the young boy left with the burden of leading the Red Dragons, stared at his own reflection and could no longer recognize himself. So much had changed. One year ago, well before the first snowfall in early winter, he had accompanied Old Snake and Fei Fei to the ocean. They searched for wild herbs. He remembered standing at the edge of a cliff, overlooking wave after wave smash into the rocks underneath him, and he had joked with Fei Fei.

"I'll train so hard this winter," he recalled himself saying, "that next year, I'll be able to jump off this cliff and climb back up without being injured."

This year, at the first glimpse of autumn, he had already returned to the ocean. He stood on the same cliff, alone, staring at the foggy waves, wondering what would happen if he really did jump.

A puddle of water lay by his feet, offering a reflection of himself. His face was incredibly thin, his hair disheveled, and the dark bags under his eyes made him look twice his age. Both Fei Fei and Old Snake were dead. So was Dong. And so was his father. In less than a year, he was the only one left in the family, and the only one left to inherit the hate and burden of vengeance.

But he had no choice. The Red Dragons still numbered over a thousand members, and a few of the skilled warriors remained. There was room to rebuild. They were still wealthy—incredibly wealthy—and the core of their salt business was unscathed by recent events. If only there could be ten years of peace and quiet, he would put his mind to reconstructing the empire again. He would attract heroes from across the land to stand by his side, and together, he would regain the trust of the common people. Mothers would once again allow their sons to study martial arts on Redwood Cliff.

Ten years of peace. That was all he asked. But somehow, in the face of a massive invasion on Redwood Cliff, he didn't have ten days.

- - -

"How do they hope to invade a natural fortress like Redwood Cliff?" Li Kung asked Black Shadow. "Shoulder mounted catapults again? Are they assuming Tao Hing's not prepared for that?"

The sun had already set. A small candle, placed on the table between them, brought only enough light for them to see each other's faces. Yet, upon the realization that they shared the same urgent vision, hope emerged in a powerful sparkle from both sets of eyes. The wars had to be stopped. "Tao Hing is out of the picture," Black Shadow said, leaning forward. "He's been captured."

Li Kung fell silent. He eyed the mysterious warrior, unsure of whether to believe him or not.

"You don't believe me," Black Shadow said with a cold smile. "Someone from the White Tiger House captured him. He was trying to talk the leaders of the coalition into betraying us."

"When was this?"

"Only a few days ago," Black Shadow replied. "In He Ku."

"Tao Hing wanted to offer the coalition an excuse not to attack," Li Kung said. "There's no other reason for him to take such a risk. Where is he now?"

"Locked away. Even I don't know where he is at this point."

"They killed him."

"No," Black Shadow shook his head. "They need him to lure Cricket from Redwood Cliff. It's their secret weapon. Cricket never told his men—he's afraid they would desert him right away. And because Cricket is still lying to his men, Jian also hid this from the rest of the world. He's going to display Tao Hing as his prisoner, suddenly, with a sword held to his throat at the foot of Redwood Cliff. The Red Dragons will instantly fall apart. That's how it will end."

• • •

"Horses should never be ridden into the ground," Jocholai said in the Mongolian tongue.

"I understand," Suthachai replied, handing him the extended reins. Jocholai was returning to Mongolia for as many animal heads as he could carry. He was told that animal heads were crucial for manipulating a thousand men. It was all part of Li Kung's elaborate scheme to defend Redwood Cliff.

Jocholai pulled on the reins. Four fresh mounts, properly saddled and carrying bags of provisions, began to follow.

"But you need to be back here before the rain season is over," Suthachai said. "That leaves us very little time."

"Yes," Jocholai said with a nod. "The great hunt is over. The deer heads may be rotted."

"Rotted is fine," Suthachai replied.

"Your friend Li Kung knows black magic?"

"No, no."

"Then why use animal heads?"

"Because no one else knows black magic either," Suthachai said with a laugh.

Jocholai was silent for a moment. "Chinese are strange." He turned his horses and rode off.

"Tell our friends . . . " Suthachai called behind him. "Tell them I will be home soon."

Jocholai shouted, without turning around, "They are expecting you with your bride!"

. . .

"This is where I'll kill you," Li Kung said, pointing to a steep ravine to his left. Three walls of sheer cliffs enclosed the narrow gorge in a drop that seemed to go forever. Black Shadow nodded. "Hundreds of blunt arrows will be fired at you," Li Kung continued, "and no one will see the nets. Everyone will believe you fell into the rapids down there, and Black Shadow will be dead for good. Even you could not survive a fall like that."

They walked along the edge of the cliff. Black Shadow didn't speak, lost in deep thought. Perhaps the one-armed warrior didn't trust him. But he had no choice, Li Kung mused. The coalition had gathered again, and Wei Jian was under pressure to invade Redwood Cliff.

"Old Huang told me," Li Kung said, "that a new order of warriors would emerge in the Martial Society. The old ones have died and there are vacancies. It's inevitable. I believe the young men of the Dragon Houses can be heroes. At least Cricket will one day make a difference."

"Cricket is young," Black Shadow replied, "and Jian is completely useless. His days are still spent in brothels and gambling houses."

"Cricket is young," Li Kung repeated, avoiding the topic of Wei Jian. He remembered Black Shadow's obligation to Wei Xu's only son. "Eventually, Cricket will grow up. Many of the younger Green Dragons are honorable men. They may be idealistic, but perhaps we need that now. We need their dreams. We need them to bring new life back into the Martial Society."

Black Shadow smiled. "You sound like an old man. I believe you're only a few years older than Cricket."

There was a long silence. Li Kung stared into the distance and sighed. "Thank you, Uncle Tan."

"I haven't begun to help you yet."

"I know. Thank you for believing me."

"It's not you I believe. It's her journals. Her journals explained everything. Everything I can't find an answer for. There's no choice but to believe it."

There was another long pause. They walked quietly along the edge of the cliff. Li Kung stopped, turned to Black Shadow, and asked, "What really happened that night? That night when Snow Wolf captured your entire family, and . . . "

"When my arm was bitten off, and I stabbed my brother?"

Li Kung swallowed and nodded. Black Shadow thought for a moment, and said, "You know what happened that night. Snow Wolf exterminated my entire clan. My brothers were eaten alive by her wolves, but I was left behind. When I woke up that night, with what was left of my arm in a tourniquet, I was no longer a leader of the Sun Cult. I became a frightened, wandering boy. Everyone in my clan was dead. There was no more Sun Cult. I roamed the land, stealing food and running from everyone. Eventually, I became sick, and I lay under the rain, waiting to die. Wei Xu found me."

Li Kung's eyes widened. "I see now . . ."

"Yes, he saved me. And since then, I was his close friend and servant. And this is why I will look after his son for the rest of my life."

Li Kung opened his mouth to say something, but Black Shadow held up his palm to interrupt. "There's no need. I understand. Wei Xu was not a good man, but I have a loyalty to uphold. What passed has passed. I'll help save his children and the House he worked so hard to build."

Black Shadow continued to walk ahead.

"And the martial arts you use," Li Kung asked from behind. "They're the martial arts of the Sun Cult?"

Black Shadow nodded. There was silence. Li Kung stood in awe. Those in the Sun Cult were such deadly warriors that a boy, barely old enough to study martial arts, who grew up without a real teacher, became as invincible as Black Shadow. Yet, Snow Wolf exterminated their entire clan.

"The old values of virtue and valor are long gone," Black Shadow said, breaking the silence. "There's only greed. You can be the one bringing back these ancient qualities, Li Kung. But you became an old man overnight. I believe you'll become a hermit before you reach thirty. Soon, you'll be so insane, you'll see the world like the Three Saints of Yunnan."

"I can't lead the heroes of the land," Li Kung said. "I don't qualify."

"And you believe," Black Shadow answered, "that after all this effort to bring peace to the Martial Society, Cricket and Jian will qualify? Two young men, so naïve? Can they stop the hate?"

Black Shadow stopped walking and turned to face Li Kung. "Who can stop the hate?" he asked again.

"I don't believe the hate is that strong."

"They've been killing each other for years," Black Shadow said. "Each side believes the other killed their leader, plus countless members of their House. They hate, Li Kung. They're out for vengeance."

"But they may not be ready to die for vengeance," Li Kung said. "They may be trained warriors, but they're still afraid to die. And worse, they're afraid of what happens after death. I don't agree with Snow Wolf. Some men are not afraid of the moment before dying. They're afraid of death itself."

Black Shadow turned away.

"And somehow, I believe they don't even hate each other."

Black Shadow paused. "Is that what you believe?"

"Men join the Martial Society under a hierarchy of command," Li Kung said. "Like in the imperial army. Whatever the commander believes, they must agree. This is what's expected of them. To not hate and not scream for revenge would be suicidal at this point. But deep inside, would they truly hate so intensely that they would give up their own lives? They lost some brothers-at-arms, maybe even some close friends. But would they die for that?" Li Kung shook his head. "They've been insulted. Their courage was challenged, and now there's no way to back down. Even the commanders have lost control of their men, so now, it's the men who drive each other to be afraid."

"Afraid of what?"

"Afraid not to hate!" Li Kung said. "Afraid to be the first to show weakness, or show disloyalty to the dead leader by not seeking vengeance. What terrible fate awaits those who dare suggest truce with the enemy? What would happen to a man who dares to be different from everyone? Who, in the

Martial Society, would have the courage to admit coward-ice? Even Cricket, who's now the leader on Redwood Cliff, could not call for peace. His father was killed, he should be screaming the loudest. He would be labeled a wimp and a disrespectful son."

"And your plan can change that?"

"Yes! We can give them an excuse not to fight! All they need is an excuse. No one wants to die. Everyone is sick of killing. All they need is an excuse."

• • •

The sound of heavy rain pounding Li Kung's fishing boat resembled a hundred wasps captured in a drum. The straw raincoat did little to protect his slender body. The round bamboo hat, slightly tilted on his head, caused consistent, vertical streams of water to trickle around him, like the bars of a cage. Wind, rain, fog, all attacked him at once. He was alone on Lake Immortal.

The storm was so powerful that he could barely see the end of the fishing pole in front of him. Yet he could sense another boat approaching. Li Kung smiled. Cricket had found him in the fog.

He lifted his eyes. Cricket's tall figure stood in front of the oncoming boat, a fishing vessel, but a much larger one. The new Red Dragon master insisted on meeting in the cen-ter of a lake under pouring rain. Nothing could be burned in the rain, and Li Kung wouldn't have the use of his superior running speed on a little fishing boat. Tao Hing had taught the boy well.

The larger boat pulled up next to him. Li Kung tilted his hat back and smiled. "Do you remember me?"

"I know who you are," Cricket replied.

"I treated your grandmother last year. You saved me from a violent death, remember?"

"I regret that."

"And in return, I lured you away with a forged letter and saved you from a violent death."

Cricket sneered. "A man of your talent wouldn't come all the way out here for a mere exchange of words."

"I came here to help you."

The rain poured harder and the boats rocked. Cricket laughed. "And why would I need your help?"

"Because you no longer have Tao Hing by your side."

Cricket's face stiffened, and he couldn't answer.

Li Kung leaned forward, his drenched raincoat stuck to his back. "Aren't you going to ask me where he is?"

Cricket took a deep breath, and in a low voice, barely a whisper, asked, "Where is he?"

"The Green Dragons have him. He was secretly meeting with the leaders of the coalition, and someone turned him in."

Cricket shuddered but maintained his posture. He lowered himself into a squat and looked into Li Kung's face. "If it's true, they would've paraded their catch across the land already. Why would they keep silent about it?"

"Because you've kept silent about it. It'll be even more delicious if they display him in front of your men in the middle of an invasion. Your men's morale will die, and then you'll charge down from your fortress to rescue him. That's when they'll capture you in battle, and all of Redwood Cliff will surrender. It'll be sudden, unexpected. Your men will never have time to regroup and continue fighting."

Cricket listened, his eyes wide, his breathing rapid and painful. "It's possible," he said, shaking his head. "But you could be lying. Why should I trust you?"

"Because you're backed onto the edge of a cliff and your survival—and Tao Hing's survival—is at stake here." Li Kung reached into his pocket and pulled out a silk scroll. He tossed it to Cricket. "And because your sister wants you to."

Cricket shook his head, holding the scroll but not opening it. "Do you think I'm an idiot?"

"It's in her handwriting. And she wrote about your favorite hiding place when you were eight. No one else in the world knows this."

. . .

The messenger could barely speak. He was home, in the Garden of Eternal light, in front of the new lord Wei Jian. He came to deliver bad news, and never had he been in a more hostile situation. Trembling with anxiety, the messenger related the story of Black Shadow's death. He told of how a secret letter had summoned Black Shadow to a distant mountain gorge. Some locals were in the area, and they witnessed hundreds of flaming arrows trapping him and pressuring him to the edge of a ravine. Sadly, Black Shadow was forced over the edge and into the endless drop. The rocky rapids at the bottom swallowed him, then spat him back out in an unrecognizable form. He was later found, still covered in black clothing, but his face was completely mutilated.

"No!" Uncle Tan shouted in desperation. "How could this happen? How could anyone kill Black Shadow?"

Wei Jian stumbled back, his face equally distraught. He glanced at the leaders of the Martial Society assembled in front of him. They stared back in blank anticipation.

"How?" Jian roared at the messenger in front of him. "Who saw it? Who did it? Red Dragons?"

The messenger shook his head. "We don't know, sir. But . . ."

"But what?"

"But the men said there are ghosts in the area. Demons."

Jian's lips trembled, but he couldn't speak. He looked vacantly at Uncle Tan, then at the crowd of warriors in front of him. Slowly, he collapsed into his armchair. Murmurs flooded the room.

• • •

"Blood," Fei Fei said. She placed a handful of gold in the meat vendor's hand and watched his eyes widen. Saliva began to trickle.

"I brought the alcohol," Fei Fei said, pointing to six large caskets beside her. "Remember, save every drop of blood. I'll be back for it before the rain season's over."

The meat vendor couldn't move. His eyes remained fixed on the gold in his hands, more gold than he had ever seen in his life. And in return, he only needed to save the blood from the daily slaughter. Blood that he would otherwise wash away before closing shop each night.

"And don't forget," Fei Fei continued. "One-third alcohol, two-thirds blood. If the blood becomes too thick, I'll come back for compensation."

"Yes, yes," the meat vendor quickly said, finding his words. "I know. One-third alcohol, two-thirds blood. There'll be plenty of blood for you. Twenty more pigs coming in for slaughter tomorrow, plus two cows. There'll be plenty."

• • •

The Chen Performing Troop, exhausted from a long day of shows, began to dismantle their props on the little stage. Their audience had become smaller and smaller every time they returned to He Ku, and revenue continued to drop. Short of a quick miracle, the entire troop of actors would have to disband by the end of the year, each going their separate ways to make a living. Depressed and frustrated, all eight men, professional actors for decades, hung their heads and silently packed their belongings.

One member of the audience, exceptionally tall and muscular, stood in the middle of the open square and watched them pack. He had a bulging sack tucked underneath his arm.

"Chen Performing Troop," he called with a light Mongolian accent. "My name is Suthachai. I would like to hire you for a short but flawless performance. Here is enough gold to support your troop for a lifetime." He tossed the heavy sack onto the stage. The stage shook with the impact.

"A private banquet?" one of the actors asked, running to the sack. He opened it, peered inside, and almost fainted.

"A private banquet in hell," the Mongolian said.

• • •

"Old master," Fei Fei said, seating herself in front of the fortuneteller, "please, let me give you some money first. I just need to ask a few questions."

The fortuneteller looked down, and in front of him was a short stack of gold coins. "You don't need to pay so much to have your fortune read."

"Not my fortune, old master. I have other questions to ask."

354

"Ask me," the fortuneteller said, quickly pocketing the coins. "About a loved one? About an enemy?"

"About demons. Demons from hell."

The fortuneteller's mouth dropped. "D-demons? I don't summon demons. I read palms, and faces. I don't do anything evil—"

Fei Fei held up her hand. "I'm not asking for anything evil. I just want to know what they look like, what they say, how they act."

"How am I supposed to know?"

"You know from stories and legends," Fei Fei said, gently.

"Stories and legends are fiction. I don't know anyone who's actually seen a demon before."

"Then just tell me about them in fiction," Fei Fei pressed on. "I prefer that."

. . .

Fei Fei shook her head. The ghostly cries on Phoenix Eye Peak could be heard in the background. "The plan is too complicated," she said. "Anything can go wrong."

"Nothing will go wrong!" Li Kung said, clearly agitated. "We need to rehearse it some more. We need to understand the details."

The sun was about to set. Suthachai placed a hand on Li Kung's shoulder. "Maybe we should rest. You're not thinking clearly."

Li Kung brushed the big hand off his shoulder. "I *am* thinking clearly. The plan is simple, really. It just involves many people."

"It involves bandits and stage actors, fake blood and

intestines," Fei Fei continued to shake her head. "Anything can go wrong."

"Let's go over it again," Suthachai said. "We'll think about it together."

"But you know," Fei Fei said, looking directly into Li Kung's eyes, "you know that if anything goes wrong, I'll start killing them. I'll protect my brother at all costs."

"I'm aware of that," Li Kung said, swallowing hard. "Black Shadow said the same. He'll kill every Red Dragon who threatens Jian's safety."

"I—" Fei Fei looked at Suthachai, then clenched her teeth and said, "I *am* doing this for the sake of the Martial Society—to stop the killing—to give thousands of young warriors a chance. But there should be no delusion: I will kill those thousands myself if my brother's life is in danger."

"I understand!" Li Kung retorted.

"Let us look at the plan again," Suthachai said, quickly intervening. "We will wait for Cricket to come down with his elite warriors."

"Whatever is left of them," Fei Fei answered.

"And they will be in White Clay Village," Li Kung continued, his brows knit in visible agitation. "Our timing is essential, I know. But Black Shadow is on our side, so there's no one out there who can overpower Cricket. There's always time—there's some cushion in our timing. We expect Jian and the warriors of his coalition to come in with Tao Hing as prisoner. They may or may not kill him—"

Fei Fei screamed. "We need to strike before that! We can't let Tao Hing die!"

Li Kung took a deep breath. "We can only try."

She turned her face, frustrated, squeezing her eyes shut. "This is not going to work."

"It will work," said Li Kung, suddenly unsure of himself again. Then, summoning his courage, he continued. "Horse's face, with horns, with claws. That's the image the old fortuneteller told you, right? That's how demons are supposed to look?"

"Yes."

"The Six Guardians, Black Shadow, and all three of us. That's enough demons. We'll take our positions around them in the darkness. We'll have some bandits infiltrate both sides. When the Red and Green Dragons clash, we'll use Snow Wolf's wooden instruments and generate our ghost cries. They'll stop. I'll go first, I'll attack one of our bandits and drag him into the darkness. He'll scream. Bloody intestines will be thrown back into the open. They'll think he's been killed and mutilated. Then Black Shadow will go next. He'll show himself, but he's fast enough. No one will see him too clearly, and he'll take the next person."

"What if they scatter?" Suthachai asked.

"We can't let them scatter," Li Kung replied. "We have them in a circle. We'll jump out in front of them and haul the next man away. We'll frighten them, and force them to turn around."

Suthachai didn't seem convinced. Li Kung continued, "The leaders of the coalition will be in front with Jian. They want to prove their courage, so of course they'll be in front. There will be thousands following them and I'll cut them off with fire."

"More fire?"

"That's the only thing you seem to be good at," Fei Fei said.

"It is," Li Kung said. "But it's effective. We'll only use it to keep them at bay."

"Someone will recognize those walls of fire," Suthachai

357

said. "Your bandits told me that no one has ever used fire like that, except for you."

"That's a risk we'll have to take," Li Kung said. "We don't have other means to cut off thousands. Hopefully, the confusion will blur whatever they remember about me. Then we'll chase them northwest."

"Their first reaction," Fei Fei interrupted, "would be against each other. They'll think the demons are fake—merely surprise attacks from the enemy."

"I understand," Li Kung replied. "Which is why we need to strategically kill off men from both sides. We can't rush in to save Tao Hing because that would be taking sides. He'll be safe in the chaos."

They seemed unconvinced. Li Kung bit his lip and forced his mind to churn over his plans. "The actors. They must be prepared. We'll strike and disappear, strike and disappear, sometimes using fire, sometimes using sound, and we'll chase them far away, enough so their men can never catch up."

"How many men do we need to drug?" Suthachai asked.

"We'll try to single out less than a hundred from each side, and hopefully, these will be the leaders. Old Snake's sleeping powder—"

"It must be used at close range," Fei Fei said. "He taught me how to make it when I was a little girl. He assumed I would use it at close range."

"I studied the formula you gave me last night," Li Kung said. "We can modify it. We need to mix it in woman's blush powder and scatter it from a higher elevation. Blush powder is finer and will float for a longer time. And if any of them avoid breathing it in, I'll personally run up and throw the sleeping powder in his face."

"And the bandits can carry so many men up Phoenix Eye Peak?"

"They're used to carrying off unconscious victims. It shouldn't be a problem. And the actors should be prepared by then. Ying will scatter the blood in Snow Wolf's cavern, much like the same scene we created for Little Butterfly, and we'll place them in the darkness. They'll wake up confused, like Little Butterfly. They'll wake up in hell.

"You and Suthachai will quickly discard the horse's heads, and you'll paint your faces white. I'll dress up as Black Shadow. Uncle Tan will miraculously wake up with Jian. Then the Demon King will pass judgment on everyone in hell."

"The Chen Troop is prepared," Suthachai added. "The old one will play the Demon King."

"And the Demon King will permit vengeance by some dead people who turned into demons," Li Kung continued. "I'll come out as Black Shadow's ghost and attack Cricket. I'm fast enough to mimic him. Cricket will then lead his men out in retreat. You and Fei Fei will attack the Green Dragons in vengeance, and they'll have no choice but to run. You're both demons. They have to run."

"And if they don't run?"

Li Kung sighed. "You may have to kill a couple of them."

Suthachai looked away, but Fei Fei nodded. Li Kung felt a shiver run through his back. The Flute Demon still preferred to kill her enemies, despite everything she promised to do. Stay alert, he told himself. There's only so much one could control.

"This is the difficult part," Li Kung continued. "We'll need to chase them through Snow Wolf's tunnels, until we can shift Cricket and Jian into the same area close to each other. You'll attack Jian. Uncle Tan, for once, will do nothing about it. Suthachai, you'll drag Jian away, and wait for Cricket to save him—this is crucial—*in front of everyone*. This is the first formal announcement that they're facing a common enemy. This must be flawless."

"I will do my best."

"Uncle Tan will call for the two Houses to unite against the immediate threat. I will attack Cricket, masked and disguised as Black Shadow's ghost. Uncle Tan will interfere and save Cricket. Then both of you will continue attacking the Green Dragons. You'll chase them all the way out to the surface."

"And Cricket will bargain with Jian?' Fei Fei asked, shaking her head with disbelief. "Would any of this work?"

"Cricket agreed to trust us," Li Kung replied. "In return, we'll have to trust him. Yes, he'll bargain with Jian. He'll talk his sister's ghost into sparing the Green Dragons. In return, Uncle Tan will plead with Black Shadow's ghost to spare the Red Dragons. The Six Guardians dressed as demons will attack the rest. They'll be screaming for help."

"And if Jian refuses to bargain?"

"Then Uncle Tan will step forward and agree to the exchange. Somehow, we'll get a truce in front of two hundred witnesses."

"Somehow?"

Li Kung clenched his teeth. "Yes, somehow."

• • •

Deep in the caverns of Phoenix Eye Peak, Li Kung paced the intricate tunnels one last time. He had drawn subtle symbols at each tunnel fork, and twice, he had led Fei Fei and Suthachai through the designated path.

Now, while the two lovers rested in each other's arms somewhere above, Li Kung came down alone for one last look. He assured himself that ample torches were placed everywhere, that the minor tunnels, into which Fei Fei and Suthachai would disappear, were indeed dark. It would be dangerous. The leaders of the Martial Society were no simpletons, and all of them were skilled in battle. For him to rely on speed alone in these narrow tunnels would be suicide. He could only rely on fear and surprise. It could be unpredictable.

He approached Snow Wolf's tomb and suddenly felt the urge to smash the headstone, as if it would help him now. How easy it would be to kill the enemy and end the conflict. But he was up against a faceless enemy. Li Kung sighed. She was not faceless. She merely died fifty years ago.

He had half a mind to run then. Run away from this and travel to the south where his father was governor, and where his mother was imprisoned. With his current abilities, saving his mother would be simple. Suthachai and Fei Fei would return to Mongolia without risking their lives, and his two Shifus, with no further agenda now that the black paste had been neutralized, would be able to travel the land again. He would bring as much of Snow Wolf's gold as he could carry, take Ying, and leave that very night.

A smile grew on his face, briefly, before he shook his head and reminded himself that daytime fantasies were bad for him. There was no point in dreaming. There was nowhere to run to, and nowhere to hide.

Above the cavern, streaking down like sheets of velvet, the afternoon sun slowly, inevitably, began its descent. The shadow of Snow Wolf's giant tomb seemed to climb his body. Li Kung drew back, consciously avoiding her shadow. She had wiped out the Sun Cult to destroy the balance of power, forcing the Dragon Houses to have no enemy to unite against. But do people only unite because of a common threat?

A soft hand was placed on his shoulder, so quiet, so gentle, so familiar. Li Kung leaned against Ying's body and rested his head against her heart. He didn't know when she came, but somehow, whenever he needed someone to lean on, she was always next to him. "What if?" he asked. "What if fear is not the only thing that drives people?"

Ying placed a hand on his forehead to show that she was listening.

"What if people also unite out of love? I know, Ying. Some people say that love is really fear of loss. But what if we add another element to our battle plan?"

Ying kneeled down next to him, drew a little knife from her belt and started to scribble on the soft ground.

"Enemies won't love each other?" Li Kung smiled. "Of course they won't. So we'll give them something else to love and protect. We have two more days. We can try something."

$$\bullet \quad \bullet \quad \bullet$$

"Any news?" Li Kung asked the following day, on the surface of Phoenix Eye Peak. Suthachai and Fei Fei were waiting for him.

"This is it," Li Kung said. "Everything seems to be ready. Almost everything."

"The rain stopped," Fei Fei said. "Jian may attack tonight."

"I haven't heard from Cricket," Li Kung said, looking away. "He doesn't trust me. And why would he? The last time anyone trusted me, there was carnage on Yellow Sand Plateau. I brought the flames of hell to them and now I'm offering to do it again."

"Cricket has no choice," Fei Fei said. There was silence.

"Where will you go after all this is over?" Suthachai asked, finally.

"I don't know."

Fei Fei reached over and placed a hand on Li Kung's shoulder. "Why don't you come to Mongolia with us?"

Li Kung looked up, for a second moved to tears, but with a light smile, shook his head. "I can't."

"Why not?" Suthachai asked. "There are more stars at night."

"I can't go to Mongolia," Li Kung said with a smile. "I ride like a woman. You said so yourself."

They laughed. "I'm a woman," Fei Fei said. "If you ride like me, you'll survive."

Rapid footsteps approached them. One of their bandits emerged, running as hard as he could.

"Tell me," Li Kung said in a commanding tone.

"I have a note from Cricket, sir."

Li Kung extended his hand and snatched the letter.

"What is it?" Fei Fei leaned over to read.

"The branch masters never showed up," Li Kung said. "Cricket is alone on Redwood Cliff with a few hundred men."

A wave of cold passed over Fei Fei's face. She grabbed the letter and read it over and over again. "The cowards!" she screamed, throwing the note down. "How could they hope to survive if Cricket loses Redwood Cliff? Jian will exterminate the branches one by one. They'll all be killed!"

Li Kung sat back, his mind spinning. "Perhaps we should advise Cricket to flee."

"My little brother would never run," Fei Fei said, her voice trembling, "and Jian will never stop hunting him if he runs. Killing off the Red Dragons is a way to declare supreme power—why wouldn't he take it since it's so convenient?" She suddenly stood up. "I need to go. I have to fight by my brother's side."

"We can still follow our plan!" Li Kung intercepted. "Nothing has changed. We weren't going to permit the coalition to ascend Redwood Cliff anyway. Our show is in White Clay Village, at the foot of the cliff, and whether a thousand men came to protect the cliff or not has never been important."

"But if we fail, Cricket will not be able to hold them," Fei Fei said.

"If we fail," Li Kung replied, "Cricket wouldn't be able to hold them, with or without a thousand men. Why don't we try—at least try. If all fails, we take Cricket and run. Jian won't follow you to Mongolia."

"Redwood Cliff will fall."

"I know," Li Kung said. "The few hundred men will be slaughtered, and the branches exterminated one by one. And Snow Wolf will win."

•   •   •

Large groups of armed men, clustered into their respective Houses and moving quickly at the heels of their leaders, now began to flood the streets of He Ku. The coalition had been mobilized. Like swarms of hungry fireflies, their torches held high above them, the Houses of the Martial Society suddenly filled the quiet streets.

Ying watched from a safe distance, her mouth dropped in awe. Master Li was not prepared for this. There seemed to be thousands—more men than anyone predicted. One Eyed Shu told her just yesterday that the numbers were exaggerated to boost morale. But the Green Dragon coalition, though intimidating in numbers, was no longer a formidable enemy. Li Kung should be able to deal with them—whether they were hundreds or thousands—it shouldn't matter.

With that thought in mind, Ying allowed the wretched anxiety to ease from her heart. She would do as she was told and follow the progress of the marching invaders.

But what if Li Kung had made a mistake and never anticipated so many? It was the most outrageous and farfetched plan Li Kung had ever come up with. Ying often questioned if it was too elaborate or too complicated. But somehow, there was no better alternative.

Ying turned her horse around and started to climb the soft hill next to Middle Pass, and in a moment, she was on a high enough elevation to see. The lights were spreading apart instead of marching in unison. Large clusters of men were heading south, and a much smaller portion of the original crowd headed north, toward Middle Pass. Ying leaned into her horse's mane and covered her face with both hands in relief. So Li Kung was right after all. At least half the coalition didn't want bloodshed. How could she have doubted him?

The line of invaders began to cluster again as they approached Middle Pass and bottlenecked for a moment at the mouth of the road, before forming a long stream of bobbing torches, uneven and half hearted, into an endless trickle toward Redwood Cliff. Ying nudged her horse forward. She would maintain a safe distance in front of the invaders, and she would watch them at key points. Li Kung expected more deserters, despite the relative calm on the spacious road. It would happen at the key points.

It's because no one wants to fight anymore, she heard him say to himself every day. It's because they all just needed a respectable reason to go home.

The warriors at the front of the line stopped as expected. She too, brought her horse to a halt so she could watch. The wave of oncoming torches slowly piled together into one massive cluster of light, and she could almost hear them speak among themselves. They were talking about the dead frogs scattered across the road.

What about the dead frogs lying on the road? There were hundreds, maybe thousands. Over twenty bandits traveled deep into the south to buy these frogs from every market they could find. Would the Green Dragon coalition know that these frogs didn't just die on Middle Pass? Ying held her breath. Hundreds of dead frogs were a bad omen for sure. But Li Kung told her it didn't matter whether they believed in bad omens or not. All they needed was an excuse.

To her incredible relief, several clusters of men began moving away. They were turning back! Ying could barely contain her joy, but out of duty she began to push forward again. Not that many retreated after all. She could not count the numbers beneath her, and, since only a select few in each group carried a torch, she had no means of seeing the warriors themselves in the dark. There could still be a thousand men. That was twice the number waiting on Redwood Cliff. If Li Kung could extract a hundred men, fifty from each side, what would the remaining warriors do to each other? Would they really stand by because their leaders were missing?

Ying wrung her hands and moved on. Why wouldn't Master Li simply allow these scary people to kill each other off? They were all armed and ready to kill. Wouldn't the world be better off without them? Now, Suthachai and Fei Fei were also thrown into this unpredictable battle when all they wanted was to go back to the steppe together. And she looked forward to attending their wedding. Li Kung had promised to go.

She bit her lip. Promises were useless if any of them died in this dreadful battle.

The train of warriors stopped again. This time, she knew, they would not proceed for some time. Li Kung had told her so. They would argue with each other, they would procrastinate, and hopefully, many would turn tail and leave. Dangling just over Middle Pass were numerous heads of rotted animals, collected from the Great Hunt on the steppe, which Jocholai had brought to China on eight Mongolian warhorses. Some of the heads were displayed on spikes, some dangled from tree branches overhead, but all of them faced the invading warriors.

Black magic, Li Kung said to her just two days ago. She remembered writing the words, "Some don't believe in black magic." And Li Kung laughed. "Why do they need to believe? All they have to do is pretend to believe, and they won't have to fight anymore."

Ying remained motionless on her horse, squeezing the reins in her hands, her eyes locked on the distant lights. Many torches began to turn away, as predicted. But not that many. Not nearly as many as Li Kung had hoped.

The remaining men in the scattered coalition began to mobilize again, and Ying took a deep, painful breath. Four people, dressed as demons, would fool a thousand men. Why couldn't Li Kung just go home?

In the near distance, Ying thought she saw lights at the end of Middle Pass. She turned to observe the coalition moving more rapidly now, their bobbing torches almost dancing with excitement. These were the diehards, the resilient hordes eager for war. Then, a strange thought flashed through her head. She jumped in her saddle. Lights at the end of Middle Pass? Lights at the foot of Redwood Cliff?

She squeezed her horse's belly and ordered it forward.

Li Kung wanted absolute stealth. Could the Red Dragons have descended Redwood Cliff to confront their enemies? Shouldn't they have remained hidden in their natural fortress and fight the invaders from their superior elevation?

Then she saw them. Positioned at the foot of Redwood Cliff, standing in a semicircular arc, completely enclosing the Grand Stairway, was a tremendous crowd of civilians. Elderly ladies who could barely walk, old men hunched over crooked canes, mothers with suckling babies in their arms, small children carrying large torches, all standing at least twenty rows deep in front of the only entrance to Redwood Cliff. There must have been thousands of them.

Ying could not believe her eyes. What did this mean?

· · ·

When the civilians began trickling into the mouth of the Grand Stairway, Suthachai nearly lost his position on the roof of the compactor mill. He was supposed to remain hidden until Li Kung intercepted the invaders with a wall of fire. He was sitting in the shadows with his heavy saber in front of him when he first noticed a small group of elderly couples hobbling toward the Grand Stairway. Suthachai leaned forward for a closer look. Villagers returning to White Clay? But White Clay Village had been deserted for days in anticipation of the invasion. Why would the villagers return now?

Then, emerging from the woods in scattered clusters were more villagers. Women with young children, teenage boys holding torches, older farmers carrying pitchforks. They came wave after wave, their movements slow but steady in a firm march toward Redwood Cliff. Suthachai squinted, shook his head clear and stood up for a closer look. Each villager stopped at the foot of the Grand Stairway. Before his eyes, hundreds of civilians packed themselves into the mouth of the only entrance to Redwood Cliff, piling their feeble bodies into layer upon layer of human walls so thick that they seemed impenetrable.

Suthachai panicked. More people would become victims in this ridiculous war. Women and children, unarmed and clueless, would make quick casualties. He had to warn them. He had to chase them away.

He slipped out of the protective shadows, about to lower himself to the ground, when Fei Fei moved out of her own position to grab him. "Wait!" she whispered.

Suthachai spun around and shook her hand off. "The villagers!"

"Where did they come from? Why are they here?"

Suthachai stared. He noticed torches high up on Redwood Cliff, trickling down the Grand Stairway. The Red Dragons had noticed, and their scouts were coming down to assess the situation. Why were they here? Who had organized them?

"They're here to intercept the invasion," Suthachai finally said. "The Red Dragons cannot come down. The Green Dragons cannot go up. Unless they kill the villagers."

"The villagers are not armed," Fei Fei whispered.

"They will be caught in the middle of this war!" Suthachai surged forward. Fei Fei grabbed his sleeve, spun him around, and clamped her palm over his mouth. "Wait! We'll discuss with Li Kung—maybe he knows what's going on. Wait for me here. I'll go and find him."

Suthachai reluctantly nodded. He scaled the cement wall and slipped back into position. More women and children gathered in front of the cliff. How many more were arriving? They're organized, Suthachai said to himself. Organized and determined.

In a moment, Fei Fei reappeared. "I can't find Li Kung."

"Look," Suthachai said. "Many more villagers now. They are taking up positions in perfect lines." He gazed into the distance. "Do you see Black Shadow?"

"He's not here yet."

The inflow of civilians seemed to never end. Who could have organized them?

Then, he noticed something, and he waved Fei Fei over. "Do you see?" he pointed.

"Where?"

"The old man in front! He just arrived."

Fei Fei leaned forward. "The one with the cloth hat?"

"Yes! That is Old Chen!"

"Old Chen?" Fei Fei asked in wonder. "The old man from the Chen Performing Troop? He's on the mountain disguised as the demon king."

"That is him," Suthachai said, "and I recognize two others. And there are two bandits dressed like villagers on the left. Do you see them?"

Fei Fei squeezed his hand, drew his attention away from the cliff. "The invasion!"

Suthachai reached for his saber, his eyes glaring at the hundreds pouring through the village of White Clay. Their torches held high, shoulder mounted catapults in front, while warriors with long spears and double-edged swords followed closely behind.

"Where's Li Kung? Where's Black Shadow?" he thought he heard Fei Fei ask.

Suthachai stared at Li Kung's position again. The young doctor was nowhere in sight. Perhaps he retreated at the last minute? The Mongolian shook his head with a snarl. Impossible. Li Kung could not be a coward. But why wasn't he here?

Then, there were three short blasts of the horn, and Suthachai spun around in alarm. A new wave of men descended Redwood Cliff, this time armed warriors. They weren't supposed to come down yet. Had Cricket lost control of his men?

The invading vanguard, originally charging down Middle Pass like madmen, suddenly slowed to a walk. Some turned to look for direction, others merely stopped in their tracks and stared.

"Let's go!"

Both Suthachai and Fei Fei spun around to the familiar voice. Li Kung was standing behind them, his demon mask tucked under his arm.

"Let's go," Li Kung repeated. "We'll start by killing their mothers."

•   •   •

Well before nightfall, when reddish streaks were still in the horizon, Li Kung had already seen them. He was on Phoenix Eye Peak, going over the plan with the Chen Performing Troop one last time, when out of nowhere, he noticed clusters of light approaching Redwood Cliff. He panicked for a moment, just long enough to gaze in the direction of He Ku where the coalition had already mobilized, before breathing a sigh of relief. The scattered lights heading for Redwood Cliff were much slower than those in He Ku, and whoever was traveling to White Clay Village did not move like warriors. Perhaps a few villagers were going home, or a few messengers, their letters already delivered, were loitering around to watch the invasion. He knew, from paid informants in He Ku, that the coalition was set to mobilize immediately after sunset.

He turned back to the Chen Performing Troop, about to review the plan one more time in detail, when something else caught his eye. The lights approaching Redwood Cliff were slow and scattered, but they were streaming in from all directions.

Li Kung waited for a moment, speechless, then suddenly shouted, "The common friend!"

"Who?" one of the actors asked.

"Who needs common enemies to kill when you can have common loved ones to protect?" Li Kung launched forward, running as fast as he could down Phoenix Eye Peak. He saw them clearly then. Villagers from across the region—the old and the crippled, pregnant women, scampering children—they were all there.

Two days ago, Ying, with One Eyed Shu and twenty bandits, had spread the word in every village they could possibly travel to. The Martial Society was at war again. There would be renewed bloodshed of a magnitude that might dwarf the slaughter on Yellow Sand Plateau. Many would die. Didn't they all have a neighbor's son who had joined the Martial Society?

And the civilians responded. Li Kung never anticipated so many, so determined, so well organized. Halfway down the side of Phoenix Eye Peak, he realized it was time to change plans.

He spun around and charged up the mountain again. There was little time to lose. He needed the actors, and he needed the few bandits that were nearby if he was to take full advantage of the situation.

Quickly, he gave new instructions to his actors. He ordered them to strip their demon costumes, resume their normal attire, clean the ashen white makeup from their faces and tie down their scattered hair like respectable villagers.

The entire time, Li Kung's eyes never left the approaching lights on Middle Pass. Not enough warriors were abandoning the invasion, and, despite the new turn of events, a thousand armed men would be difficult to neutralize.

Li Kung charged down the mountain. The actors were right behind him, but he needed to get to his bandits and prepare them. He needed the pig intestines and the caskets of fresh blood. And more importantly, he needed to dress his younger actors as coalition warriors.

Li Kung veered sharply to the east, tore across the northern hills as fast as he could, and approached the bandits who would infiltrate the invasion. They were already waiting for him.

"Take off your clothes," Li Kung said, for the first time completely out of breath. "I need those clothes." He pointed to their coalition uniforms.

The bandits looked at each other. Li Kung pointed down the hill, at the streams of villagers still gathering at the foot of the cliff. "Ambush the villagers and take their clothes. You're good at it."

The bandits stared, speechless.

"I'll explain later!" Li Kung shouted. "Right now, just do as I say. You'll still be hauled away by demons, but just dressed as villagers."

"Yes, Master Li," they said in unison, quickly discarding their clothing.

"Fat Shu, notify the Six Guardians and tell them to stay back. We don't need them right now." Li Kung grabbed two uniforms and turned to run away. "And don't let me catch you harming the villagers. Use my sleeping powder."

"Yes, Master Li," was all he heard behind him.

• • •

Suthachai once told him that every day the animals of the steppe must outrun the fastest predator. And every day, the predators must outrun the slowest prey. How fast you ran really didn't matter, as long as your prey was slower. How strong you were didn't matter, as long as your enemies were weaker. And don't we all move much too slow, Li Kung asked himself. Compared to the eagles in the sky, the horses on the steppe, aren't we but pathetic humans with two legs?

Yet when the coalition of armed men, all trained fighters of the Martial Society, arrived at the foot of Redwood Cliff, they froze in their tracks. In front of them were defenseless civilians, frightened, old, sick, widowed. They were but elderly couples and women and children. But at that moment, clustered at the mouth of the Grand Stairway, Li Kung could not help but notice. The civilians were stronger and more determined, with more reason to die than the coalition had to kill.

Li Kung lifted the demon mask from his face. In front of him was a stunned army of invaders, each frozen behind one another, as if none of them dared to stand before the villagers. Behind the cluster of civilians, the endless trail of Red Dragons was scattered along the Grand Stairway. Each warrior had stopped well before the base of the cliff, and almost all of them were avoiding eye contact with the women and children.

Li Kung had already notified Suthachai and Fei Fei, his bandits were prepared, and his actors had infiltrated the scene. Only one thing pricked at him. Where was Black Shadow? How could he remain behind, whether out of cowardice or not, after so much mutual planning, and so many days of preparation? Li Kung had yet to spot Wei Jian. Perhaps Black Shadow took flight with Wei Xu's son, leaving behind members of the coalition to invade by themselves.

Li Kung recognized a familiar face standing quietly among his men. One of the few important leaders of the Martial Society to have survived Yellow Sand Plateau, Master Liang of the White Tiger House, was not as vocal as he used to be. A year ago, Master Liang would be in front barking orders and taunting his opponents. Now, he stood hidden behind his men, his eyes on the ground, his weapon limp by his side.

Harsh words were already being exchanged at the mouth of the Grand Stairway and Li Kung could not resist. The sun had set, and the darkness exerted heavy pressure on the torches clustered at the foot of the cliff. There was little time to waste. Li Kung's movements were quick and clean, and in a flash, he stood behind the coalition warriors. It was dark enough. They would not recognize him.

"What are all of you doing here?" one warrior screamed, loud enough for all to hear. "Move out of the way!"

The woman standing in front of him took a hesitant step back. Another old lady, leaning over a cane, stepped forward, lifted a trembling finger and shook it in front of his eyes. "Would you tell your mother to move out of the way?"

"You're not my mother!"

"If your mother isn't here, then shame on her. But I'm here! My son was a warrior of this Martial Society, and he died on Yellow Sand Plateau."

"The Red Dragons killed him!" someone shouted. "That's why you should get out of our way so we can take revenge for you."

The villagers roared. Some raised their torches and repeated, "You're not getting past us! You're not getting past us!"

Li Kung waited. The warriors of the coalition froze, looking at each other, and then at the civilians in front of them. Some turned to Master Liang, others simply stared.

"What do you want?" a Green Dragon shouted. He pointed the butt handle of his sword at Redwood Cliff. "Are you here to stop us from killing them?"

"No more killing!" an old woman shouted. Suddenly, every civilian behind her began to chant. "No more killing! No more killing!"

"Master Liang," one warrior shouted. "The cowards paid off these civilians so they can hide behind them!"

"Cowards!" the coalition men shouted in unison. "Cowards!"

Another uproar, this time from the Grand Stairway: the Red Dragons were screaming at the top of their lungs. "Let us through! Let us through!" They tried to charge down, their torches waving, but the villagers huddled by the stairs drew closer and planted themselves. The first wave of Red Dragons slammed into the front row of villagers and stumbled back. The elderly couples, their arms wrapped around each other, were gathered so densely that they didn't budge.

Li Kung slipped away. It was time. Warriors from both sides were screaming into a maelstrom of indistinguishable sounds. But they would not attack the civilians. At least not yet. Perhaps, if the Green Dragons could work themselves into believing that the civilians were there to protect Redwood Cliff, there would be bloodshed. But not yet.

Li Kung stood behind the mud houses of White Clay, in full view of his hidden bandits, and flashed quick hand signals. The bandits responded. Suthachai was on a distant rooftop, also watching for his signal. Fei Fei was hidden at the far end of the village, but he was certain that she too, was waiting for him to initiate.

Li Kung spun around, lowered the demon mask over his face, and began to circle the chaos. They were waiting for him. He could not stall any further.

The shouting at the mouth of Redwood Cliff began to subside. Some drew their weapons and tried to threaten the villagers, but to no avail. Others continued to taunt the Red Dragons who stood a meager twenty steps from them. But no one made a move to break through the human barrier.

Then, ever so quietly, the wailing cry of the haunted mountain emanated from the forests. The ghostly moans came in long dreary waves, projected by many bandits blowing through the same instruments. It grew louder and more intense, but no one seemed to notice.

Li Kung fidgeted. Perhaps the wooden instruments, smaller replicas of those on Phoenix Eye Peak, were not powerful enough. Even when no one was shouting, the sound of a thousand people shuffling their feet would overwhelm his meager ghost cries. There was no time. He had to move his instruments closer.

Li Kung headed for his bandits again when he heard new shouting. He paused, listened for familiar words, and finally breathed a sigh of relief. The Chen performers had found each other in the chaos. The gods were watching after all.

Old Chen, wearing a gray cloth hat, was trying to beat an armed warrior with his cane.

"I don't have a son like you! You're a disgrace to my name! You're a disgrace to your ancestors!"

The younger Chen performer cringed and took the weak beating on his shoulder. Old Chen's cane struck again and again, while shouting in his feeble voice. "How dare you call me a Red Dragon! I'm here to take you home. I wouldn't stoop so low and join one of you!"

All eyes were on them, but only for a moment. The Green Dragons began to back away, their weapons sheathed, their faces intentionally turned, as if the disgraced young man was not one of theirs.

"How am I a disgrace?" the younger Chen performer shouted. "You told me to be strong! You told me to be a real man! Now you're standing in my way!" He drew his sword and waved it in front of him. "Leave me alone!"

The old man froze, his cane held above his head.

Next line! Li Kung almost screamed to himself. His heart was pounding. Old Chen had little time to remember his words. Almost a thousand warriors, standing on opposing sides, were staring at the actors.

Old Chen slowly lowered his cane, a convincing look of anguish on his face. "You idiot! Real men take care of their families. Real men never forget their vows to the family name! Are you going to kill me? Then I deserve it! I raised a fool! I deserve to die!"

The younger Chen actor was silent, while old Chen, panting in heaving spasms, lifted his cane again. Li Kung held his breath and waited. The show was awkward, poorly rehearsed, but no one seemed to notice. Many in the coalition couldn't help but stare, and some of the men began to move in for a closer look. Their focus had turned.

Li Kung hurried. The ghost cries had to join the battle before the demons. Moving the bandits and their instruments into White Clay would be dangerous. They would be exposed, and, if discovered, there would be no time for them to run. But no one would have time to search for the weeping ghosts, Li Kung told himself. Especially if demons were chasing them.

Behind him, Li Kung heard Master Liang for the first time.

"Shut up, old man!" Master Liang shouted. "All of you!

I don't know where you came from and I don't care. But you're interfering with the United Martial Society Coalition, and you will all die here tonight if you don't go home this instant!"

A woman stepped forward and spat in his face. Master Liang stumbled back to wipe the saliva from his eye.

"Then kill us!" an old man shouted. "Kill a defenseless old man!"

Master Liang drew his sword.

"I don't care," the old man said. "I just buried my son on Yellow Sand Plateau. Why not kill me? I don't care."

"I'm not going to cut down my father to kill Red Dragons!" the younger Chen performer shouted.

Li Kung smiled. The young actor delivered it well. Behind him, a few more voices echoed, "I'm not killing women and children for Red Dragons!"

"I'm not going to cut down my father to kill Red Dragons!" the younger Chen performer repeated his line.

"Master Liang!" The strong voice of a young man. "Lord Xu would never hurt an unarmed villager! We're a coalition of honor!"

"Coalition of honor!" someone shouted. A few repeated, and in a moment, hundreds of warriors were chanting, "Coalition of honor! Coalition of honor!" Master Liang stared and slowly withdrew his sword.

Meanwhile, Li Kung reached the edge of the forest behind White Clay Village and motioned for the bandits to come forward. He directed them to move along the shadows, staying close to the mud houses that formed the perimeter of the village. He watched them shuffle into the open, the wooden instruments carried on their shoulders like coffins, a big smile on their faces. Li Kung motioned for them to hide, then moved away.

Li Kung slipped through White Clay and noticed that it was relatively quiet in front of Redwood Cliff. No one knew what to do next. The moment was weary, awkward, as if suspended in time and frozen in space.

Li Kung stood behind the coalition again, and waited.

The wails of the weeping ghosts emerged quietly at first, with a single instrument playing while other groups of bandits secured themselves into position. But as soon as all instruments joined in with their hideous cries, every warrior, elderly couple, woman, and child jolted into motion.

"Who goes?" Master Liang shouted at the top of his voice. The warriors around him spun in random directions, their eyes flashing to every little movement. Torches were held higher, fingers wrapped around weapons, warriors moving closer to each other.

"Who's there?" A few men carrying torches stepped off the road for a closer look, but before truly entering the darkness, they quickly returned.

"Ghosts!" someone shouted. "The ghosts on Phoenix Eye Peak!"

"Then let the ghosts come!" an old woman shouted. Everyone turned back to her. "I'm ready to die tonight. Let them kill us so you can get to your enemies! Don't you want that?"

The wails lifted to a deafening shriek, and the coalition spun around to stare into the dark.

Li Kung secured his mask, took a deep breath, and leaped out of the shadows. He reached the cluster of villagers in three massive steps, grabbed Old Chen by the collar and hauled him away.

Old Chen shrieked. "Help! Help me, my son! Help me!"

The younger Chen actor charged. "No! Father! No!"

"Demon!" someone shouted. "Did you see that? A demon!"

Out of nowhere, a line of Green Dragon warriors lifted their weapons and chased.

"Help him!" someone on the Grand Stairway shouted. Several Red Dragon guards tried to push their way through the army of civilians. But the villagers, once resolved to stand their ground, suddenly didn't know how to respond. Some tried to step aside, but there was no room for them to clear a path. Others simply stared with mouths gaping open.

Li Kung dragged Old Chen by the collar and ran as hard as he could. The frail old man was heavy, he grumbled. The younger Chen actor was close behind him, and not far away, at least six Green Dragons were chasing with weapons drawn. There was a hideous shriek, a high-pitched scream that resembled the laughter of a hyena. The Green Dragons froze, shouted something to young Chen, and retreated back to their group.

Li Kung swerved into the shadows. At least the Flute Demon sounded like a real demon. He reached under a bush, grabbed a mixing bowl full of blood and intestines, and emptied it on Old Chen. "Lie still," Li Kung whispered. The younger Chen arrived. Li Kung lifted a finger. "He's dead. Start weeping." He spun around and disappeared.

A dark, thundering laughter broke out into the night. The coalition turned. A black horse, its enormous rider standing vertically on its bare back, was storming into them. The rider had the face of an ox and was dressed completely in black with bull horns protruding from his head. His arms were spread like a soaring vulture.

Every warrior drew his weapon.

The enormous demon suddenly dropped from his

horse, his entire body dangling horizontally along the side of the animal, and, as his horse charged down the side of the road, he reached out and grabbed a warrior by the belt.

The coalition stumbled away. The demon was instantly on his feet, standing tall on the speeding horse, the man he snatched like a rag doll held high above his head. With a cold laugh, the demon threw the man into the coalition. Entire lines of men collapsed under the impact.

"No! No!" Some turned to the screams of the younger Chen actor. He was stumbling back into the open, his clothing stained with blood, his arms around a lifeless old man. Dark fluids and intestinal matter was everywhere. His leg was injured, his neck coated with fresh blood, and he was shaking the old man's body. "No! Father, no!"

The demon that stood on the charging horse disappeared into the night.

"Where did that come from? Who's out there?"

"Demons!" someone shouted. "The same demons that killed Black Shadow!"

The men began to panic, but they stood their ground. Behind them, the women, children, and elderly couples reached for each other's hands, locked their fingers together and braced themselves.

"Help us!" an old man shouted. "You call yourselves warriors? Help us!"

Another scream, this time more dreadful than the first. An old woman was being dragged away. The demon was lean and quick, with the face of a horse and the agility of a woman. Her laughter was shrill and hollow, and tucked behind her dark robes was a metal flute.

"The cry of the Flute Demon!" someone shouted. "The Flute Demon's ghost!"

The old woman shrieked. Another cluster of Green

Dragons broke out of position to chase, screaming, "Help her! Help her!"

A deep laugh. The tall demon standing on the massive charger appeared out of nowhere and brushed past them. The Green Dragons swung their weapons but he had already disappeared. The old woman, hauled away by the fast demon, was gone. Lay strewn across the earth were ripped body parts and puddles of blood.

Li Kung launched from the other side, reached one of his bandits holding a pitchfork, and grabbed his coarse clothing. The bandit screamed in agony. Blood flew through the air. Li Kung dragged the bandit into the shadows.

"Men!" one of the coalition leaders shouted. "Formations! Face the enemy!"

The massive demon with the ox's face charged in and stomped a warrior in the chest, sending him flying into a line of men behind him. A path was cleared. The demon reached in, grabbed an old man in front and carried him away. The old man screamed all the way into the darkness.

"Face the enemy! Face the enemy!"

The warriors finally came to, lifted their weapons, spun around, their backs to the villagers then, and moved into position. They were not trained to fight alongside each other—their fighting styles and their weapons were all different. But somehow, each warrior in the coalition, in the face of a common enemy, found his place in the defense.

"Let us through! Let us through!"

Li Kung peered from his hiding place and his mouth dropped. The Red Dragons were pushing their way off the Grand Stairway, through the dense lines of villagers and into the front. Their weapons were also drawn, but they were not focused on the invading coalition. Each man was staring into the dark, waiting for the demons to emerge.

Li Kung darted away then, deep into the darkness, and circled the scene. He reached Fei Fei in a flash, held up his hand to signal a stop to the assault, then took off again. In a moment, he was in front of Suthachai. The Mongolian had already lifted his mask, and he nodded in understanding. He pointed his saber at the thousands gathered in front of Redwood Cliff and leaned back to laugh.

Li Kung stood frozen and stared. In a matter of seconds, hundreds of Red Dragons poured through from the Grand Stairway and into the front lines. Their eyes were glaring into the unknown, their mouths clenched and firm, their weapons poised and ready. They stood beside their Green Dragon cousins and the flimsy coalition, whose battle lines were already formed.

Li Kung could hardly believe his eyes. At the mouth of the Grand Stairway, standing side by side, were a thousand Red and Green Dragons, each with their weapons drawn, all facing the same direction. Their unified numbers effectively shielded every villager behind them.

There was a glow on their faces, Li Kung thought. Maybe it was the torches suddenly condensed into a small space. But their faces glowed with a powerful energy. A human energy. Their eyes no longer displayed the souls of lost men who waited for the warrior beside him to attack in order to follow. Their arms, their weapons, locked in a readied stance, no longer displayed the flimsy intent to fight only if no one else retreated. Suddenly, a thousand armed warriors, magnificent in every way, collectively stared down their faceless enemy.

Li Kung smiled. Their lines were so dense that even Black Shadow could not have assaulted a single civilian.

"Black Shadow!" Li Kung whispered. Just a moment ago, from a higher vantage point, he noticed a small light approaching on Middle Pass. A strange feeling had welled in his heart then, a feeling of comfort, as if finally, everything was going to be all right.

He leaped onto the horse behind Suthachai and whispered into his friend's ear. "Notify the Six Guardians for me."

In a flash, Li Kung was gone. He crossed White Clay, tore through Middle Pass, and approached the single light as fast as he could. Someone with a lantern was rapidly approaching Redwood Cliff. He moved closer. There were sounds of running horses—more than one horse. Li Kung rode harder. Maybe a couple of messengers bearing news from Black Shadow.

Then he saw them, and his mouth opened in shock. How could it be, Li Kung thought, his head pounding. A wave of joy and skepticism struck him all at once. How could it be?

Tao Hing and Uncle Tan, each on a fresh mount, were speeding toward Redwood Cliff.

Li Kung slipped into the center of the road, held up his hand, and shouted, "Uncle Tan! Tao Hing!"

"Li Kung!" Uncle Tan responded. He jerked his horse's reins and came to a full stop. "Li Kung! Are we too late?"

"We have a truce," Tao Hing said. "Where's Cricket? Are we too late?"

Li Kung laughed. "You're early. Much too early."

• • •

The following morning at sunrise, Li Kung sat on the coast and gazed stiffly into the ocean. Uncle Tan was beside him, munching casually on bean cakes and drinking rice wine.

"So what was the official excuse last night," Li Kung asked, "for Jian to come up with a truce?"

Uncle Tan smiled. "He called for a time of peace to honor our parents and ancestors."

"Really?"

"Our scouts were quick. They watched the villagers mobilize, and they reported back to the Garden of Eternal Light, just when I was preparing my demon mask. Then other scouts started pouring in. They reported that almost half the invasion went home. That sealed the decision. We had no choice but to call a truce."

Li Kung laughed. "It wasn't a unified coalition. It wasn't even a unified Green Dragon House."

"Thanks to Tao Hing," Uncle Tan said. "He already planted the seeds of peace some weeks ago before he asked to be captured. As you said, all they needed was a reason not to fight."

Li Kung smiled. "Asked to be captured. So Tao Hing found a crazy way to infiltrate the Green Dragons."

"Yes, some weeks ago. He knew there would be uncertainty and some division in this flimsy coalition. Asking to be captured so that he could whisper among us was either very bold or very foolish. Pick one."

"History has already chosen," Li Kung said. "He succeeded, so it's a supreme act of courage and wit."

"Did you stay behind to watch last night?" Uncle Tan asked.

"Of course I did."

"How long did they hold their positions?"

"Not very long at all," Li Kung said. "They agreed to divide themselves into small groups and escort the villagers home. Not a single warrior came back to fight. I'm sure everyone went home after that."

The waves struck the rocks gently, for once, as the full heat of the sun began to shine against their faces.

"Do you believe," Li Kung began, "that Jian would have ever accepted the truce if the coalition didn't abandon him?"

Uncle Tan smiled. "Do you believe Cricket would have ever accepted a peace agreement if his branch masters showed up?"

"Men of skill and power have too much pride," Li Kung said. "But the reality is, the coalition retreated, and Cricket's own branches deserted him. Everyone is tired of death and slaughter. Destruction has reached a pinnacle and must decline, then enter a stage of quiet. I see that now. It was inevitable."

A long silence. Uncle Tan tossed the empty wine gourd into the ocean. "You were right. No one hated each other enough to die for revenge."

"Do human beings really become gods?' Li Kung asked. "Or goddesses?"

"I believe so," Uncle Tan said. "When they've reached a certain level of greatness or enlightenment." He paused for a moment, sipping his wine. "But not Snow Wolf. She was evil."

"She was merely a victim."

"You believe so?"

Li Kung closed his eyes. The full force of the morning sun illuminated his face. He listened to the gentle rocking of the ocean, felt the cool breeze against his skin, and for the first time, believed he was completely at ease.

"I believe so," Li Kung began, opening his eyes. "Snow Wolf was a true heroine of her time. She achieved what everyone could only dream of. Physically, intellectually, socially, she rose to heights that the world coveted. Because of that, greed and jealousy surrounded her, and her tragic end was inevitable. The Dragon House also reached a pinnacle of power and wealth. Someone, somewhere, would want possession of that power. That's why the Dragon House splitting into two was also inevitable." Li Kung took a deep breath. "I think I understand now. Shifu One, Old Huang, they all tried to teach me, but I wouldn't learn. The Red and Green Dragons dominated the land, and with the black paste, their power also reached a pinnacle. They fought each other for possession of this new dominance. But if they didn't, someone else would, because it was there. That's why these wars were inevitable. I merely accelerated the cycle and the violence. But it would've happened anyway. Who am I to believe that I could make a difference? As for the legendary Snow Wolf, her brilliant strategy could only exist as part of the life cycle. She didn't really influence what was destined to happen."

A bitter smile emerged on Li Kung's face. "The violence between Wei Bin and Wei Xu reached a peak and was due for a stage of calm. The two Dragon Houses lost so many men and so much power in the process, that they too, had no choice but to live through a stage of calm. There was nothing left to fight over. It's time to rebuild."

"Are you saying," Uncle Tan interrupted, "that eventually, the Red and Green Dragons will grow and flourish again, and soon afterwards, they'll be at war again?'

"Someone will grow and flourish, and yes, they'll be at war. How could they not?" Li Kung asked. "If they already have wealth and power, wouldn't they want more? From somewhere? If they don't act as aggressor, someone will devour them. The taller trees are more vulnerable to violent winds." Li Kung laughed. "Like a wild flower, Old Huang would say. At full bloom, it can only fade. As a sprout, it can only grow."

• • •

388

Though the coalition refrained from invading Redwood Cliff, the deep hatred between the Red and Green Dragons never subsided. Yet, with the drastic loss of so many on Yellow Sand Plateau, both sides agreed to live on separately, but peacefully, for fear of losing the few men they had left.

Tao Hing took drastic measures to rebuild the Red Dragon House. The few senior students on Redwood Cliff were sent to scattered branches across the country, one after another, and former branch masters were brought in. With so many newcomers, the men no longer united into their own separate gangs, and very quickly, loyalty and obedience was restored.

Under Uncle Tan's advice, Jian officially removed the assembly of the short-lived coalition. The pressure, the power, the responsibilities that he never wanted finally vanished. He returned to his original state, where, heavily intoxicated, he would spend most of his existence in brothels and gambling houses. Uncle Tan took on the task of single-handedly rebuilding the Green Dragon House.

Fei Fei visited Tao Hing and Cricket only once. She sat speechless at the edge of the cliff, her eyes staring into the endless distance. Her little brother sat beside her.

"Is this really the last time you'll set foot on Redwood Cliff?"

Fei Fei turned away and nodded.

"Why?" Cricket asked. "The Mongolian is welcome here. We can all be together again. Why live as a nomad?"

"Black Shadow is no more," Tao Hing said, standing behind them, "and the Green Dragons have few good fighters left. The entire Martial Society is empty. If Fei Fei returns, the balance of power will be disrupted. People will focus on making weapons instead of farm tools. Money will be spent on mercenaries instead of businesses. This state of calm will be over."

. . .

Jocholai, Suthachai, and Fei Fei stood at the edge of the Mongolian desert, with six fresh horses shifting impatiently beside them. They stood in front of Li Kung and Ying.

Suthachai placed a hand on Li Kung's shoulder. "When will you come and visit me, my friend?"

"Soon," Li Kung replied with a smile. "I'm going south to visit my father, but I'll be there for your wedding. I promise."

"Then farewell for now," Suthachai said with a bow. He turned around and mounted his horse.

"Farewell, Li Kung," Fei Fei said. "We'll see you soon?'

"Certainly."

She jumped onto her horse. "I'm sorry we couldn't thank the Two Saints of Yunnan before we left. But can you tell them that we're eternally grateful? They took care of me and they cured Suthachai."

"They've wandered off to the west," Li Kung said. "If I do see them again, I'll be sure to tell them."

"Thank you." She pulled on her horse. They began to ride off, leaving behind a cloud of dry dust. Then, Fei Fei turned around and shouted, "You're destined to do something great, Li Kung!"

Li Kung bowed, and waited for them to disappear. "I hope not."

Made in the USA
Lexington, KY
27 October 2013